THE
SILVER THIEF

ALSO BY EDWARD W. ROBERTSON

THE CYCLE OF ARAWN

The White Tree
The Great Rift
The Black Star

THE CYCLE OF GALAND

The Red Sea
The Silver Thief

THE BREAKERS SERIES

Breakers
Melt Down
Knifepoint
Reapers
Cut Off
Captives
Relapse
Blackout

REBEL STARS

Rebel
Outlaw
Traitor

THE
SILVER THIEF

THE CYCLE OF GALAND, BOOK 2

EDWARD W. ROBERTSON

Copyright © 2015 Edward W. Robertson

All rights reserved.

Cover illustration by Miguel Coimbra.
Additional work by Stephanie Mooney.
Maps by Jared Blando.

ISBN: 1519783515
ISBN-13:978-1519783516

To Robert Asprin.

Mallon and Gask.

The Collen Basin and other lands.

1

The ship bore the assassins across the sea.

A storm mustered to the north, black clouds that promised reckless winds. Captain Naran stood on the prow. Swaying with the roll of the ship, he faced the coming darkness.

Dante clutched the rail. "Is that as bad as it looks?"

The corner of Naran's mouth twitched. "Are you worried we won't make it? Or that we will?"

"Gladdic doesn't worry me."

"You're that sure you'll be able to kill him?"

"He's extremely dangerous," Dante said. "But everyone has to sleep sometime."

The waves were larger by the minute, heaving the carrack up and down like children bouncing a ball on a taut sheet. Behind Dante, sailors called to each other from the rigging, trimming the sails to the shifting and strengthening winds. The air smelled of sea spray and rain.

"How long do you think it will take?" Naran said.

"A few days to locate him, then a few more to remove him. But there's more to this than Gladdic. Killing him sets things square for the murder of Captain Twill, but we still don't know why Mallon is so interested in the shaden. They've gathered hundreds if not thousands of shells. I don't like to think what they intend to do with them."

"What do you suspect them of?"

"Too often," Dante said, "when they've had that kind of power, they've used it to kill people like me."

The captain nodded. He hadn't wanted his position—it had been thrust upon him when Gladdic executed Twill—but Naran had always borne a sober authority, and he wore his new office well.

"My crew and I may be able to help you find the shaden," Naran said.

"Think so?"

"Over our years in Bressel, we've developed a number of resourceful contacts." He smiled thinly. "After all, we're nefarious pirates."

As the clouds neared, Dante retreated to the cabin he shared with Blays. Blays was installed in his bunk with a stoppered jug of rum and one of the books from the ship's surprisingly large library of picaroon novels.

"I've got to tell you," Blays said, swinging his bare feet to the boards and waving about the book. "It's a lot more relaxing to read about these things than to live them."

"Good news and bad," Dante said. "Storm's on the way."

"Tell me that's the good news because it's one of those storms that drops live fish on the deck. If I have to eat hard tack and salt cod for one more day, then I'll eat it. I'm not going to starve, after all. But I *will* complain about it."

"By all indications, it's a non-fish-bearing storm. But it shouldn't delay us more than a few hours. The good news is that while we're locating Gladdic, Naran's offered to drop some feelers on the black market and try to track down the shaden."

"That could save us some time." With a hollow plunk, Blays unstoppered his rum and took a swill. The smell of spices mingled with that of the coming rain. "He's not concerned about being spotted? Last time he and his crew were seen in Bressel, they were stealing a piece of the royal navy."

"We're landing down the coast at Averoy. We'll sneak in overland. Naran has plenty of friends in the city who'll help him keep a low profile."

"So we slit a throat and then go catch up with some shells. Which should be relatively easy, given that they're snails. Think any of this will blow back on Narashtovik?"

A sudden swell sent Dante reeling toward the wall. He caught himself on a line running along the ceiling and used it to guide himself to his bunk. "We'll be as careful as we can. But you know as well as anyone that there's nothing harder to clean up than spilled blood."

The ship plummeted down another swell. Outside, rain began to batter the deck.

The storm abated by morning, leaving them with calm seas and a cool, steady wind. Two days later, a sailor cried out that he'd spotted land.

They made port that evening. Averoy was a prototypical fishing town. Weatherbeaten seaside cottages, outnumbered by scores of small docks. Boats heading in and out of the bay, anchored around the small, rocky islands. Gulls everywhere. Squadrons of pelicans glided over the low waves. Sometimes, one would break rank, tuck its wings, and plunge straight into the sea, bobbing to the surface a moment later.

Dante had visited the town a few times as a boy and had always been charmed by its houses. Some stood on short stilts while others had screened slits below the roof and at the base. His dad had told him these features allowed the sea breeze to keep the interiors cool, but Dante had imagined better uses. The slits were there for the passing of secret notes. Meanwhile, when their neighbors annoyed them, the stilted houses stood up and walked away.

That day, they had no time to take in Averoy's sights. As soon as the *Sword of the South* made berth, they located a tailor, paying her well to start immediate work on sets of simple trousers and the short-sleeved jerseys favored by rural Mallish folk. With this arranged, Dante and Blays returned to help unload the ship, which had picked up a great deal of goods during its voyages to the Plagued Islands and the lands further south.

The garments were ready by morning. Five sets in all, enough to accommodate Dante, Blays, Naran, and the two sailors accompanying them to Bressel.

Blays dressed in his trousers and jersey, then turned in a slow circle, holding one arm slanted up, the other down. "I make a pretty striking peasant!"

"Good thing," Dante said. "If you screw this up, I'm demoting you to chief potato tiller."

With funds in short supply, the five of them struck out on foot toward Bressel, which lay over twenty miles up the coast. The remainder of the crew stayed in Averoy, tasked with smuggling some of their goods into Bressel, которые shouldn't be any more complicated than hiring another boat. One that *wasn't* wanted by the Mallish crown.

The rutted dirt road stretched through a forest. Stumps and clearings indicated the woods were harvested regularly for lumber. So did the thunk of axes. Naran told them to keep an eye out for the baron's men. The trees were far too short for use as masts in the royal navy, and the king had hence ceded the land to the baron of Averoy, who'd found it more profitable (or less work, anyway) to sell his trees to shipwrights and those in need of firewood. That meant a steady presence of baron's men collecting payments and ensuring no one took more than had been agreed. Most likely, these men wouldn't be on the lookout for Naran, Dante, or the *Sword of the South*, but you could never be too careful.

Less than half a mile west of the road, the ocean beat against the shore. It was high summer. Cool enough beneath the shade of the trees, but sticky and humid. Which meant Bressel was going to be murder.

They met a trickle of traffic on the road. Dressed as peasants, but armed like soldiers, Dante and the others drew a number of looks, stirring Dante's paranoia. Yet by late afternoon, no trouble had come to them. Instead, they came to the deforested plains around Bressel.

Naran left one of his men in the woods, along with all of their swords, which were illegal in Bressel without the proper writs. Dante and Blays strolled into the grassy field surrounding the great city. They were accompanied by Naran and Jona, a sailor with a black and red beard who'd proven more than capable of keeping his head in a tight situation.

A trait that was about to be put to the test. The outskirts of the city were a haphazard mash of slums, homestead farmers, and transient markets, all of which ebbed and eddied like the tides and currents where the Chanset flowed into the Aster Sea. Yet the city's interior was blocked by a contiguous and quite permanent wall. Barring more advanced sneakery, the only way inside was to pass through one of the gates, all of which were watched over by Bressel's finest.

"Remember our story," Dante said, angling through the grass to the dirt road leading to the city. "If questioned, we're sharecroppers from Averoy. We've been saving our money for months in preparation for a trip to Bressel. Now that we're here, we intend to spend every last penny."

Blays bit his lip, peering at the sprawl of cheap buildings and the walls and spires beyond. "This is a bit slapdash even by our standards, isn't it?"

"The ship's barber cut our hair short. Got rid of the beards. We're dressed like commoners. What more can we do to disguise ourselves? Beseech Lia to grow us each a pair of breasts?"

"Does she do that?" Blays motioned to the wall. "The last time we were here, it was to escape from prison and steal a royal vessel. On top of that, you're essentially the king of Narashtovik, Mallon's most ancient of enemies. What are the chances they'll let us through without impaling twenty of their guards on our blades?"

"It's been weeks since the last time we were here. These guards see thousands of people every day. What's more likely to cause trouble? Walking through the gates like normal people? Or climbing over them like wretched crooks?"

"All right," Blays said. "But if they spot us, I say we do the honorable thing and run away."

The stink of leather tanneries wafted nearby. Goats brayed to each other from the yards of single-room homes. A steady flow of pedestrians and the occasional rider passed up and down the dung-thick street. The rich brown hue of Naran's face drew the occasional glance, but none lingered. Bressel was the biggest city for a thousand miles in all directions and home to people of all stripes.

The sun sat low in the west, pouring yellow light across the ramshackle buildings. The day was cooling and the smell wasn't so bad. Within blocks, the houses stood shoulder to shoulder, newer wooden structures grafted onto the slanted bones of older ones. The wall loomed ahead. The gate was a two-door iron grille, currently open, but occupied by two men in the dark blue of Mallish military. On their shoulders, an embroidered silver ring indicated they were city watch.

People massed around the entry, waiting to be assessed and let through. Others departed without issue, business in the city done for the day. Dante exchanged looks with Naran and the four of them joined the crowds. With the sun setting, they came before the guards.

"Business in the city?" asked a man with a thick pale scar that started halfway up his forehead and continued well beyond his hairline.

"We're from Averoy," Dante said. "Here for a bit of fun. We've been saving for—"

"Yes, yes." The guard's eyes traveled to Blays' waist and the long knife sheathed on his belt. "That a sword, son?"

"Why, no," Blays said, the portrait of innocence. "Swords are illegal in Bressel."

"Then I hope you're not attempting to commit a crime. Give it here."

Blays unsheathed the dagger, handing it hilt-first to the watchman. "Careful. I hear these things are sharp."

The man took it, squinting at its point. Dante reached for the nether lurking in the stone walls around him. Shadows winged to his hands. Not enough that anyone untrained would notice, but enough to be ready.

The guard laid the blade along his forearm, crossbar resting on the inside of his elbow. The tip almost but didn't quite reach his wrist. He tossed it back to Blays, who snagged the hilt mid-air.

"An inch longer, and it'd be mine," the guard said. "Don't let me see it out of its sheath again."

Blays smiled brightly. "Frankly, the damn thing frightens me. I only wear one so nobody else will use one on me."

The guard beckoned them past without looking at them, already losing interest in favor of the next batch of travelers waiting to be let through. Without obvious hurry, the four of them walked west in the general direction of the river splitting the city in two.

"Close call," Blays said. "For a minute there, I thought he was going to confiscate Matilda."

Jona glanced away from a young woman at a fruit cart. "You name your knives?"

"You don't? Then do you call every woman you know 'girl'?"

Behind the safety of the walls, the buildings leaped to three and four stories in height. Towers and temples dwarfed these. Further west, the spire of the Odeleon seemed to climb halfway to the clouds. It was said that Bressel was home to half a million citizens. That sounded impossible, but after more than a month spent in the sparseness of the Plagued Islands, two more weeks on the featureless sea, and a day in sleepy Averoy, the crush of people made Dante believe it just might be true.

As it had been in Averoy, however, they weren't there to gawk. Naran led them straight to the wharfs.

Dante gestured ahead of them. "You said you're friends with an innkeep?"

"He was fast friends with Captain Twill," Naran said. "After what Gladdic did to her, he'd no sooner turn us in than he'd swallow his own arm."

The inn was set on a small hill overlooking the river, whose waters were deep gray in the twilight. Lanterns burned from the prows of barges and skiffs. The inn's common room was boisterous and crowded, smelling foully of tallow and sweetly of rosemary. Despite the clamor, the innkeep came over to Naran at once. After a quick talk, the man showed them up to their room.

He closed their door firmly behind him, pressing his broad back against it. "Tell me you're here to answer what they done."

"Indeed." Naran nodded to Dante and Blays. "With the aid of my new friends, our answer will thunder like Gashen's axe."

The innkeep smiled, mustaches bunching. "Any help I can give is yours to take."

He returned downstairs. Blays clapped his hands to his knees. "So. Shall I remedy our appalling lack of fighting steel?"

"We should be back before midnight," Dante told Naran. "If you haven't seen us by morning, change lodgings."

Naran furrowed his brow. "You don't trust my man?"

"If we're not here, it means we've been taken. And it won't be long before they've tortured us into confessing everything we know."

"Then might I advise not getting caught?"

Dante headed downstairs, Blays beside him. They exited the inn, the common room's laughter fading quickly. The wharfs drew drunks aplenty, time-beaten men who tossed dice in the warm night air and argued over whose turn it was to buy the next bottle. The city's soldiers had better things to do than police rowdy laborers who largely only hurt each other. Dante and Blays didn't see their first watchman until they were halfway back to the gate.

The gate's interior was surrounded by a sprawling plaza of pubs and shops which remained lively despite the fall of night. Blays hooked into a crooked alley that terminated against the twelve-foot wall, leaving the two of them surrounded by blank stone on all sides.

"Good, right?" Blays tipped back his head to take in the surrounding buildings. "No one's going to be able to see me unless they're standing in my pocket."

Dante nodded. "See you in an hour."

Blays departed the alley and Dante headed out after him. As Blays strolled toward the gates, Dante installed himself on the patio of a tavern with a view of both the gate and the alley. He ordered a wheat beer, sipping without hurry. When it was empty, he ordered a second.

By then, the city lay in full darkness. Shouts and cackles rebounded through the streets. It was strange to sit in Bressel as a common traveler. Mallon's capital was separated from Narashtovik by many hundreds of miles, and the two regions had warred on multiple occasions — most recently, little more than a decade ago, in the conflict that had relocated Dante to the north — yet if you plunked the two cities side by side, the main difference would be the architecture. Beyond that, they could very well be different neighborhoods of the same settlement.

An hour after Blays had left the city, guards called out from the wall. Iron squealed. The grilled doors swung shut. A heavy bolt clunked into place.

Dante stirred, wandering toward the alley. It was presently empty, but it smelled more strongly of urine than the hour before. He summoned the shadows to his hands. The air was thick, humid, hot. With the breeze blocked by the walls, sweat popped out along his brow.

Shadows stirred. Dante straightened, tightening his grasp on the nether. A figure materialized from nowhere, resolving into Blays. He carried a long bundle of thin sticks of kindling. It was a bulky load. Enough to conceal several swords within it.

"Any problems?" Dante said.

Blays shook his head. "Naran's men are on their way. Told them to meet us at the inn. Anything on your end?"

"Nope. I drank beer the whole time you were gone."

"How come you get to sit around drinking beer while I'm lugging pounds of metal through a dark forest?"

"Because you're the one who can walk through walls."

"Fair enough." Blays narrowed his eyes. He sniffed at the air. "Are you sure drinking beer was the *only* thing you did?"

They left the alley and made their way back toward the inn. Between the darkness of the night and the crowds during daylight, it felt as though they would be able to come and go without fear of being recognized, but Dante knew they couldn't grow too bold. If the wrong set of eyes drifted their way, it could botch everything.

And the closer they got to Gladdic, the sharper the eyes would be.

Blays shifted his grasp on the clacking bundle of sticks. "Maybe we should forgo all this sneaking around and forge ourselves a writ of arms. Or buy one from the armsman's guilds. I still know some people there."

"The swords are only for emergencies. I'd rather not carry them at all. It would only draw attention."

"Yeah, I suppose writs would cost money. After the last few weeks, we're a bit short on the currency of the realm. Or the currency of anywhere else."

"Then after we kill Gladdic, let's not forget to rob him."

They returned to the inn, where all had been quiet in their absence. Naran's other crewman arrived within half an hour. Dante was glad for his haste. It had been a long day of travel. Although he wished to spend as little time in Bressel as possible—he'd now been away from Narashtovik for more than two months—at that moment, what he most needed was sleep. Before going to bed, he used needles of nether to kill two moths flapping around the candles, then set the bodies next to his bed.

He woke early, disturbed by the stirrings of the sailors as they headed downstairs to eat breakfast and start running down leads on the shaden. After a meal of bacon and hash, Dante got to work, too.

The city was enormous, even larger than Setteven, the Gaskan capital. Under other circumstances, finding one man within its sprawl would have been a daunting assignment. Gladdic, however, was an ordon, a highly-ranked priest of Taim with public responsibilities. On top of that, Dante already knew two of the places the man often spent time: a small temple grounds in the middle of the city, and the Chenney, the giant prison tower where Dante and Blays had been held captive during their last visit to Bressel.

Back in the privacy of their room, Dante called to the shadows, pulling them from the crevices in the planks of the floor. He sent them into the corpses of the two moths he'd slain the night before. The small, brittle bodies soaked up the nether like rain-hungry sand.

The moths' wings stirred. They lifted, beating clumsily.

Across the room, Naran raised an eyebrow. "What's this? Remorse for killing them?"

"I'm putting them to work," Dante said. "They'll be able to see into places I can't."

The captain, normally stoic, watched in wonder as the two bugs swirled across the room. "Are they...alive?"

"Reanimated. As soon as my connection to them is severed, they'll be as dead as before."

"That's remarkable."

"That's one word for it," Blays said. "Another might be 'a

crime against man and gods.'"

"That's six words." Dante sent the moths winging to the window. "Anyway, it's only a crime if it doesn't work."

The two insects passed through the half-opened shutters and ascended into the sky. Dante sat on his bed and sent his vision into the moths. Early morning light glimmered on the wide river running down the middle of the city. The panorama below—houses, temples, shops, stables, spires—was so dizzying Dante had to cling to the bed for support.

He sent one moth west across the river and the other to circle the city. He could have located the Chenney by description alone. It was one of the largest buildings on the west side, a brute block of stone eighty feet high, many of its windows blocked by iron bars. Dante stationed the west-bound moth above the double doors of the front entrance where it had a view of the street.

Finding the temple took considerably longer. This was a small central building on a grounds of raked pebbles and manicured plants. Compared to the offices of other priests of Gladdic's stature, such a simple edifice was almost but not quite an ostentatious display of humility. An iron gate enwrapped the grounds. Dante posted the second moth on its highest spike.

Then, he waited.

Soldiers in blue uniforms came and went from the Chenney. Sometimes they bore miserable-looking men and women, blasphemers and scofflaws bound for the cells, their faces cut and bruised. At the temple, monks strolled between the hedges, chatting or admiring the small slice of nature within the city.

Morning turned to afternoon. Afternoon drew on, sweltering and lazy. As the sun came to its rest on the horizon, Dante withdrew his sight from the moths, rubbing his aching temples.

"I haven't seen him all day." He stood, legs stiff and sore. "I need a break."

Blays reclined on his bed, spinning a small knife between his fingers. "We're in no rush, are we?"

"He didn't gather all those shaden to decorate his beach house. He has plans for them. I'd rather not give him time to fulfill them."

"You're assuming he was in charge of gathering the shells. Those orders might be coming from above."

"In any event, he could have gone anywhere while we were in the islands," Dante said. "We might have to expand our search soon."

He gave himself a few minutes to stretch his legs, then returned his sight to the moths'. After nightfall, there was very little traffic at either the temple or the Chenney. Dante watched listlessly.

As midnight neared, Naran returned from the streets. He had a bounce in his step. "Have you found Gladdic?"

"Nothing all day," Dante said. "Don't tell me *you* did."

"I did not. But I do have a lead on the shaden."

Dante pulled his attention from the moths. "Where are they being held?"

"I said I had a lead, not the answer. I'm friendly with a woman named Frey, quartermaster on the *Hound's Tooth*. She informed me that a Mallish vessel called the *Sunfinder* arrived from the Plagued Islands earlier this morning."

"Can you put eyes on it?" Blays said.

"It's being watched as we speak."

"See if you can learn its schedule," Dante said. "If it heads upriver, or to another port, it could take us straight to the shaden."

With the prison and the temple both so quiet, he grabbed a few hours of sleep. The next morning was more of the same. After two fruitless hours of Dante spying through the moths' eyes, Blays popped to his feet.

"I'm not doing us any good in here." Blays planted his hands on the small of his back and stretched his spine. "I'm going to take a peek around the streets."

"What if you're caught?"

"Then those who catch me will regret having shown up to work today." He glanced yearningly at the bundle of sticks concealing their swords, then exited into the hall.

As the hours wore on, Dante found himself drowsing off. The room was stuffy and hot. He opened the windows wide and stood beside them, out of sight of the noisy street.

Blays came back shortly after the four o'clock bells of the

Odeleon. Sweat sheened his face. "I found Gladdic."

Dante heaved himself to his feet. "How'd you do that?"

"By possessing functional eyes and ears. He was riding in a carriage surrounded by dour men ringing bells and yelling to draw crowds. They were leading a wagon full of prisoners. Word on the street is that Gladdic intends to execute them."

"Executions? When?"

"By the look of things? Any minute."

Dante went for his shoes. "If the crowd wants an execution, then we'd better go give them one."

EDWARD W. ROBERTSON

2

Bells rang around the carriage. A wagon rumbled behind it. Criers exhorted the crowds at the sides of the street, the members of which replied with a hailstorm of questions. Hooves clacked on the cobbles. It added up to a racket so tremendous that the man sitting beside Gladdic on the carriage bench had his palms clamped to his ears, scowling. Gladdic soaked up each and every note. Only the untrained ear heard cacophony.

The trained ear heard the most beautiful music known to the gods: that of heresy being corrected.

The carriage took its time coming to the Plaza of the Hour. Gladdic didn't mind; the vehicle's roof kept off the sun, while the walls were open to allow a breeze. In time, they rolled around a corner and into the square. Four hundred people were there already, jockeying for portions of the shade cast by the three-story buildings overlooking the cobbled grounds. Vendors scurried into the square hauling hand-drawn carts laden with pastries and smoked fish.

Followed by the wagon, the carriage came to the stage, a chest-high wooden platform at the north end of the square. The stage was often used for plays, fiddling, foolery, and other entertainments and diversions. Hence it was no mystery that it also shared its space with public punishments.

The vehicle rocked to a stop. A footman set a small staircase beside the carriage and backed away, bowing low. Gladdic stood and descended.

Rowen approached from the stoop of the temple at the corner of the square. His gray robes were unable to disguise his unseemly bulk. Golden bracelets jangled on his wrists. The three blue stripes on his collar announced him as an ordon. Officially, that was Gladdic's rank as well.

Like a barge towed upstream against the current, Rowen drifted beside Gladdic and smiled at the prisoners as a farmer might regard a crop of swollen melons. "Where from?"

"Where do you think?"

"Collen again?"

Gladdic nodded once. "In Collen, heretics grow better than any plant. As if there's a flaw in the soil itself."

Rowen dabbed his perspiring brow with a crisp white cloth. "Why persist in open worship of Arawn? They know exactly what will come of it."

"These people weren't arrested for worshipping Arawn. They're here for worshipping Carvahal."

"*Carvahal?* But *our* people worship Carvahal. He's a member of the Celeset!"

Blue-shirted guards arrived, unlatching the wagon's gate. The chained prisoners plodded down the ramp and into the plaza. Eight men and four women. Twelve total, aligning with the twelve houses of the Celeset. Its significance would be lost on no one.

"Don't be troubled, Rowen," Gladdic said. "I have no intention of persecuting those who bend their knee to Carvahal, Lia, Simm, or whoever they so choose."

"Then why do so in Collen? Won't that only spark further unrest?"

"If it exposes further heresy, then so be it. Here in Bressel—indeed, across Mallon—all acknowledge that Father Taim stands first and foremost in the Celeset. The other gods have their role, and may speak more loudly to you than the Father, if that is how your ear is attuned. But there is no questioning who stands at the head of the heavens."

Rowen grunted. "Except in Collen."

Gladdic nodded, ignoring Rowen's obvious commentary

about Collen in favor of watching the prisoners being led to the stage. Gladdic never tired of the sight. They knew what was coming, yet they were all so docile. It was as though, in the end, they admitted their guilt. And wished to be relieved of it.

"Correct," Gladdic replied once the guilty had disappeared behind the platform. "If one understands Arawn's place, then there is no danger in worshipping Carvahal. But if one *venerates* Arawn, as the Colleners do, then one's vision of Carvahal will be warped as well. For Carvahal is Arawn's brother, yes? And while he stole the fire of the gods and delivered it to humanity, this wasn't a *good* act. It led to the corruption of our souls. The defiling of ether with nether. I fear that, in Collen, they fail to understand this. Until such a time as they do, those who worship Carvahal must be corrected."

Rowen frowned. "Does the Eldor know of this?"

"Does he know of it?" Gladdic glanced over his shoulder, as if expecting the Eldor any moment. "Why, it was his idea."

For the day's event, a scaffold had been built across the stage. From it dangled twelve nooses. Guards brought up twelve stools, placing one beneath each noose. The crowds ventured away from the shelter of the buildings and their awnings, braving the summer sun for a better view.

Heavy footsteps trundled up the steps of the stage. A shaved head rose into view, supported by a broad-shouldered body wearing the gray robes of Taim—and the red trim of Gashen. Seeing the haldac, the crowd murmured.

The large man was followed by a much shorter male. The haldac directed the heretic to the stool on the far left of the stage. The man climbed it. The haldac secured the noose around the offender's neck. The executioner left the stage and returned with a young woman, securing her in the noose beside the first heretic.

The haldac repeated this process until all twelve stools were filled. This took several minutes and was not particularly exciting. That, however, was the message: justice was implacable. It played out without haste because it was inevitable. Watching the haldac lead the guilty to their places one by one, it was hard not to imagine yourself being led up to the stage, placed atop a stool, and fitted for the rope.

When all were in place, Gladdic straightened, ensuring that his robes, collars, and sleeves were tidy and straight. Guards maintained an open path through the middle of the crowd. Gladdic nodded to Rowen and walked along this path toward the stage. The crowd smelled overwhelmingly of sweat, along with the perfumes of jasmine and florine they used in an attempt to mask the odor.

He was sweating as well, but he never minded that. Sweat was the body purging itself of ill humors. Its role was the same he played for the city.

A small platform stood across from the stage. Some preferred to take the stage itself, the better to speak directly to the crowd, but Gladdic felt it was necessary to create space between the condemned and he who passed judgment. He took the platform, eyes moving from one prisoner to the next.

"As mortals, our existence relies on the order of the heavens." Gladdic gave a short pause between each sentence. Enough time for them to begin to absorb his words, but not enough time to dissect them. "Disorder above rains chaos on those below. Hence, the violation of celestial order is a threat to all those who are capable of death."

Again, he gazed at each of the condemned in turn. Only three were angry or prideful enough to meet his eyes.

"But perhaps that is the goal?" Gladdic took a step toward the edge of the small platform, turning his back on the heretics and facing the crowds. "These people *worship* death. Arawn. I have, in my investigations, heard some go so far as to say that it is their duty to kill their fellow men. Because that reunites them with Arawn all the faster."

The jeers of the masses obliged him to pause again. Bits of fetid cucumber flew toward the stage.

Gladdic turned back to the condemned, stiffening his spine. "Regardless of their goals, it is our goal—our sacred charge—to oppose them. To stop them from breaking the heavens and the earth along with it. When so much hangs in the balance, if we show mercy, we only hurt ourselves."

He pointed across the dozen noosed men and women. "They who stand before you are heretics. Threats to the order of the skies and our lives on earth. For this, there is only one fate."

He fell silent. The haldac thumped back up to the stage. This time, he carried a long red crook. He walked to the far left side of the platform, hooked his staff around the leg of the small man's stool, and yanked. The man dropped a foot. Not nearly far enough to snap his neck. The crowd bayed, hands lifted above their heads.

The hanged man swung in a slow circle, legs kicking. The haldac moved onto the young woman. He hooked her stool and removed it from beneath her feet.

He turned off each prisoner with the same patient inevitability he'd displayed in leading them to the stage. By the time he saw to the twelfth heretic, the first had quit moving. The hanged man was quite likely still alive, however. Gladdic had seen a man hang for thirty minutes, get cut down and tossed in a pile with the other corpses, only to gasp for breath and sit upright. The peasants had thought it a miracle. Faced with the possibility of a hostile mob, the attending priest had had no choice but to agree that Taim himself had pardoned the criminal, and thus so must the city.

Since then, Gladdic ensured that, in any hangings he oversaw, the offenders would be left to swing for no less than sixty minutes.

"These ones were lucky," he mused, projecting his voice. He held up his palm, lightly cupped, elbow bent as he gestured across the row of heretics. Each one of their faces had gone red and purple, the eyes bulging grotesquely. Those on the right end of the stage continued to kick and jerk. "There is great pain in strangulation. Yet compared to some deaths, it's a mercy."

From his robes, he produced an oversized book and held it aloft. Its binding was black. Its front cover bore an image of a white tree.

"*The Cycle of Arawn*," he said, turning in a circle, book held aloft for all to see. "The words with which they poison your souls, turning you away from the face of the truth. Some poisons are so vile there is only one way to be rid of them."

He drew the ether from the air around him and the sky above. Shards of light glinted on his upstretched hand. The shards grew brighter and brighter until flames leaped from the pages of the book. Smoke billowed away, pages crackling, yet Gladdic didn't drop the book. Instead, he summoned more ether to the base of the book, letting it absorb and disperse the heat of the fire.

Ash swirled around his head. "From this day forward, just as this book burns, so will all who follow its lies!"

His eyes shifted across the field of sweating faces. He prayed for a riot. An uprising. Anything that would allow him to crack down on the city as he had done in the Collen Basin. Some of the crowd looked leery or fearful of his announcement, but none appeared angry or outraged. He shouldn't have hanged the latest apostates. He should have burned them. Should have—

He went still. Someone was...*watching* him. In fact, many were—some members of the audience had returned their attention to the swaying bodies, but others continued to observe him for further pronouncements—but this person was watching him with something more than physical eyes. Gladdic reached into the ether, feeling for any signs of its use. Nothing. He withdrew.

With terrible caution, fearful of being caught even though it would also be heresy on the part of the observer, he extended his focus into the nether.

Nothing there, either. No secret awareness or hidden spies.

Yet he had learned to trust his instincts. They had been honed by years of use, allowing him to look into a man's eyes and see the innocence there—or the treachery. As opposed to the instincts, the mind couldn't be trusted. It was too eager to explain things to itself in the manner it wished to hear them. In this case, his mind wished to tell him that his feeling was no more than paranoia, or a false expression of his senses, like when lights dazzled the eyes from within.

The soul, however, had finer instruments of detection. And rather than yearning to delude itself, it hungered always for truth.

He cast down the smoking remnants of the *Cycle*, tattered pages fluttering. The book struck the ground with a thud.

"Remember what you've seen today," he said. "And remember it again if ever you hear their lies."

He had intended to say more, but he stepped down from the platform, the feeling of the *presence* hurrying him back to his carriage. It had spooked him, yes, which in turn angered him. Anger clouded most minds. For Gladdic, it made him as sharp as a razor.

He climbed the steps to the open-walled carriage. Most people in his situation would have opted to go to the Chenney. Much safer there, with its guards and host of monks. He, however, opted for the temple — and its much greater privacy.

He gave orders to the driver. The carriage rattled away through the summer streets, making any number of turns. Yet whichever way it turned, the presence followed.

He had been away in the Collen Basin for more than a week. The number of letters awaiting him at his office in the temple was enough to make a lesser man beseech the Celeset for help. Yet correspondence was influence. Influence was policy. Gladdic stretched his fingers and wrists, got his ink pot and blotting sand, and began to answer his letters in the order in which they'd been received.

With the afternoon wearing on, and the heat finally beginning to abate, a knock sounded at the door.

Gladdic's head jerked up. With a lurch of light, he summoned the ether to his hands. "Who is it?"

"Pryer, sir," a man called. "From the Eldor."

Gladdic exhaled through his nose. "Enter."

Pryer opened the door and stepped into the chamber, coming to a stop fifteen feet from Gladdic at his desk. The man was so thin it looked like he'd been crushed in the hand of a giant. Though he was one of the Eldor's favored assistants, he had a nervous, twitchy cast to him that called to mind a small, long-legged shorebird.

Pryer placed one foot forward, bending at the knee in the appropriate bow. "My lord. I have stunning news from the Plagued Islands."

Gladdic waited. His cheek twitched. "Has this news stunned you into silence?"

"No, my lord."

"Then speak."

"The *Sunfinder* arrived in port yesterday morning. According to Captain Krieg, the Tauren have…been defeated."

"Defeated?" Gladdic's throat tightened. "And the *Sunfinder* arrived yesterday?"

"Yes."

"Then why am I being told of this today?"

Pryer swallowed. "Captain Krieg had fallen ill. It was decided that he must be treated and healed lest he spread that illness to his questioners."

"Surely one of the monks could have questioned him while the others were tending to him."

"But my lord, if his sickness were contagious…"

"Then we would quarantine and treat any who fell ill." Gladdic's hand gripped the padded back of his chair. "This information concerns the fate of the kingdom. Before that, one life is nothing. Do you understand?"

Pryer lowered his head. "I'll make note of this policy at once."

Gladdic clenched his teeth, waiting for his anger to retreat. "The Tauren had subjugated nearly the entire island. How were they *defeated*?"

"An alliance united against them. Spearheaded by the Kandeans."

"What is the extent of the Tauren losses?"

"Vordon is dead. Deladi's army lost at least five hundred men, with reports of as many as a thousand. The Deladi tolaka have splintered. Most have already made peace with the other regions."

"And the shaden?"

"There are none available. Some were spent in the war, but there seems to be a great deal of hoarding. Even if supplies are restored, the Tauren won't be able to provide a tenth of what they were giving us before."

Gladdic closed his eyes. Years of work dashed apart overnight. And through no fault of his own. In fact, he had asked to send Mallish soldiers to the island to buttress the Tauren. He had been denied on the grounds that the soldiers would suffer the island's plague, and would hence be stuck there for the rest of their lives.

Yet now that their Tauren allies had fallen, it exposed how short-sighted such thinking had been. How many lives would it have cost to garrison the island? Three hundred? Five? What a paltry sum to pay for the permanent security of the Mallish nation.

Gladdic spoke slowly, keeping his emotions in check. "We made very certain the Tauren had all they needed to claim the island. I want a full investigation of how they could have lost the war."

"That may not be necessary." Pryer shifted his gaze past Gladdic's right ear. "The reason the Kandeans won is because they had the aid of Dante Galand."

The name hit Gladdic's head like a maul. "Dante Galand?"

"Yes, my lord. He used his skills with the dark art to lay waste to the Tauren army. There are rumors that he's the one who stirred up the war between the islanders in the first place."

"How reliable is this?"

"Any number of Kandeans will swear to it. Descriptions from the Tauren soldiers support their claim."

"Deeply troubling. If Galand is..." His mouth clicked shut. The loss of the shaden's power was a disaster. Yet if Galand was behind it, it was also an opportunity. One that could finally convince the king to move on Narashtovik.

Unlike others he knew, Gladdic had never spoken directly to the gods. Sometimes, however, he was granted flashes of insight so deep and pure that they could only have come from the divine. In an instant, he understood whose eyes had so disturbed him at the executions. And that Galand was here to kill him. He wasn't sure why—either the man had some personal tie to the Plagued Islands, or he'd discerned Gladdic's involvement—but Gladdic knew in his soul that it was so. His skin crawled with simultaneous dread and thrill.

"I require time to digest this information." He gestured toward the door. "Let Horstad know that no one is to disturb me tonight under any circumstances. Do you understand?"

"Not even the Eldor?"

"If the Eldor wishes to see me, he will summon me to him.

Now leave me."

Pryer bent at the knee, backed up two steps, and turned for the door. Once he was gone, Gladdic bolted the door, climbed the stairs to the crow's nest in the temple's modest spire, and gazed across the raked pebbles and trimmed hedges of the yard. Again, he touched both ether and nether, and again, he felt no foreign spiders scrambling across the strands of the celestial web.

Yet they had returned to the city. And their first act had been to come watch *him*. To underestimate them, to downplay their intentions, would be to risk his life.

He remained in the spire until twilight. When at last he descended, he checked each room of the temple. All were empty. He barred the front doors, moved to his inner sanctum, and bolted the entry.

The bones were already in place, concealed beneath the floorboards, arranged in their hexagon. He walked to his desk, removed a knife from the drawer, and lifted his robe, exposing his stomach. He pressed the knife against his skin until blood welled forth. He held his arms out to the shadows. They rushed from all corners of the room. His outstretched hands shook. The ritual was wrong. Foul. A corruption of life and sky. He could feel its wrongness in the heat of his blood and the cool of the shadows. Yet experiencing its allure—the rush of it, the power—allowed him to understand the minds of those he stood against.

"Come forth," he whispered.

A silhouette emerged from the heart of the shadows.

3

One by one, the condemned were marched up the stage. Dante watched from the rear of the plaza, shaded by the overhang of a pub. Blays stood beneath the awning of the bakery next door. Close enough to support each other if they were spotted, but far enough away that they wouldn't be recognized together.

Across a sea of hundreds of citizens, Gladdic ascended his platform and spoke.

Dante listened to his rhetoric and condemnations with a growing sense of disquiet. Mallon had always persecuted Arawn's followers. That's what had driven Dante to Narashtovik in the first place. Back then, though, you heard very little talk of heresy and blasphemy, largely because every Arawnite with a lick of sense left Mallon at the first opportunity.

So what was the increased fuss about? Had an Arawnite underground blossomed in Bressel? Or had Gladdic and his ilk decided that, after witnessing the revival of Narashtovik, Arawn's ancient homeland, Mallon would be the next to fall—unless they put a stop to it here and now?

Whatever the case, Gladdic was a believer. Dante could see it in his gestures. Hear it in his voice. Dante was too, of course, but there was a frenzy within Gladdic's eyes that marked him as something more: the breed of fanatic for whom there can be no coexistence.

Gladdic made a final pronouncement. The red-trimmed haldac mounted the stage.

Dante moved to the neighboring awning and stood beside Blays. "Let's get out of here."

Blays kept his eyes on the stage. "Why?"

"We're not going to do this *here*, are we?"

"Not unless you want to be added to the main event. But I'd like to see what they're about to do."

"I'll give you a clue," Dante said. "It's going to involve a lot of dangling."

"Right. And seeing that will cement my resolve to see this through."

Dante fell silent. Once upon a time, Blays had held no qualms about putting the blade to anyone who needed it. But times had changed and so had Blays. If he needed to witness the executions to hone his motivation, Dante wasn't going to complain about having to see another twelve dead bodies.

The next few minutes unfolded exactly as expected. They kicked. Bulged their eyes. Spun in erratic circles. Dante thought, for a moment, about killing them from afar to put them out of their misery, but he couldn't risk drawing Gladdic's attention. Eventually, the stage went still.

"Well," Dante said. "Looks like justice has been served."

Blays turned down the corners of his mouth. "Justice is a bit like baking macaroons, isn't it? One misstep, and you've ruined everything."

"Not everything can be compared to cookies."

In front of the stage, Gladdic was banging on about heresy some more. As Dante and Blays withdrew from the plaza, Dante sent his two dead moths soaring high above the square, circling erratically. He might well have been able to kill Gladdic on the spot, but the assassination had to be clean. If the act exposed him, it could mean war between Mallon and Narashtovik. The city had had a few years to recover since the wars with Gask and then Spiren, but it could only bring to bear a fraction of the resources Mallon had at its command.

They returned to the inn without any trouble. Before leaving to see the execution, they'd left a note asking Naran to stay put if he returned in their absence. He awaited them now, along with Jona.

"We've located Gladdic," Dante said. "Wherever he goes, I'll follow him. We may be able to move on him this same night."

Naran smiled grimly. "I was hoping this news would bring me more joy. The most that can be said is that it feels like catching your breath after a deep dive."

"Considering the alternative is drowning, that sounds pretty great."

"Is there anything I can do to help?"

"As a matter of fact, there is. Some weeks ago, you told me a group of norren had set up trade in the city?"

"Indeed. They came to sell their craftwork for local silver."

"That's excellent," Dante said. "Because, before we risk our lives and nation going after Gladdic, I'd better alert my people as to what we're doing."

"There are any number of courier services in Bressel. Why the norren?"

"They're the only people I trust to deliver a letter. After all, Blays and I have been made official members of a clan."

"Hang on," Blays said. "You want to send a *letter*?"

Dante eyed him. "That's the idea. Or do you think we should yell really, really loud?"

"I think this is like Lyle's parable of the man who withheld a carrot from the starving family and showed them how to grow a garden instead."

"Rude and obtuse?"

"Send Narashtovik a letter, if you want to tell them something once. But if you want to *talk* with them, you should send them a loon."

"The loons were broken when we traveled to the Plagued Islands." Dante's cheeks went hot. "But I can make more."

"Allowing us to talk to them as much as we want. Though for the sake of your reputation, you might want to leave out the part where you thought it was a better idea to send them a letter."

"Captain Naran, please arrange a meet. Now if you'll excuse me, I have to give some rats a very bad day."

Jona and the other crewman gave him a quizzical look. Naran

stood to go. Dante followed him outside and down the stairs. While Naran trotted off into the depths of the city, Dante located the nearest alley.

It smelled like most of the city's alleys did, which was to say like shit. For once, though, this was to the advantage. The very rot that repelled humans drew numerous rats. After a glance to all sides, Dante summoned the shadows, killed two rodents with lances of black force, and pocketed the bodies. He returned upstairs.

"Fair warning," he told Jona and the other sailor as he removed the corpses from his pockets and set them on the table. "This is about to get messy."

Without being asked, Blays provided him with three knives of varying length and thickness. With practiced quickness, Dante chopped off the rats' heads, peeled away the skin, and scooped out the pink-gray mush inside. After a thorough rinse in a bucket of water, he was left with two relatively clean skulls.

Blays scooped the shavings and remnants into an empty bucket. The two crewmen watched in fascination and disgust. Using the butt of his heftiest knife, Dante cracked the skulls, separating a portion of the ear canal and jaw from each, then pairing a piece of ear bone from one rat with the jaw from the other.

He got out his own knife—thin-bladed, with a handle carved from a deer's antler by a norren craftsman—and cut the back of his well-scarred left arm. At the first whiff of blood, nether flocked as thickly as migrating swallows. Dante poured the dark blots into the pieces of skull while at the same time drawing forth the shadows that lurked inside the bone itself. As carefully as he could, he linked the nether within each ear to the opposite rat's jaw.

He eased his touch back from the components. The links held true, the shadows within them moving as slackly as the currents of a broad and level stream. This was the most delicate part of the construction: if the links were faulty, the nether would bleed away, leaving the bones inert. Yet after a full minute, they remained strong.

Dante picked up a set of paired bones and handed them to Blays. "Excuse the blood."

Blays took the pieces. "If I had a penny for every time I've heard you say that, then I would have a few hundred pennies."

As the two smugglers watched in consternation, Blays headed into the hall, closing the door behind him. Dante held the other two pieces of rat to his ear. Muffled footsteps receded down the hall.

"Testing," Blays' disembodied voice said into his ear. "Ahem: the recipient of this message owes its sender a sum of no less than one thousand silver chucks."

"Denied," Dante said. "Now get back here."

"Er," Jona said. "Last time I checked, we *are* here."

Dante waved a hand. "I'm talking to Blays."

"No, you're not?"

The door swung open. Blays walked in, juggling the two pieces of skull in one hand. "Worked like a charm. Which I suppose it is."

Jona rose halfway from his seat. "Hold on. You mean to say that you—" he pointed at Dante— "were in here, and he was out there. And you *heard* each other?"

Dante eyed the two men. "What you're seeing is a military secret. If this fell into the hands of King Charles, or King Moddegan of Gask, it could cause the loss of thousands of innocent lives."

"What're you suggesting? That we'd sell them the secret?"

"Don't tell me it wasn't your first thought."

"My first thought?" Jona folded his arms. "Sure was. Luckily, I'm so rich with thoughts I had a second one. And this time, I thought about how Charles is the bastard in charge of the people who killed Captain Twill. As for Gask, they've been beheading pirates and smugglers since the days of Lyle. I've lost a dozen friends to their axes. To hell with all of them."

Dante turned to the other sailor, an older man named Fenk who grew profuse gray whiskers. "What about you?"

Fenk snorted, shoulders hopping. "I look like I give a shit and a half about the lords of the land? I'm a seaman, through and through."

"Glad that's settled."

"And without any death threats," Blays said. "That's a first."

Dante ran his finger over the delicate portion of rat jaw. "They're a norren invention. Ingenious design. If they get us back in touch with Narashtovik, we'll be able to call for aid against anything that crops up here."

Jona scratched his multi-colored beard. "You talk like we're starting a war. Ain't we only killing Gladdic?"

"That's the plan. But wars have been started for far less."

The loons were almost but not quite finished. Between the pockets of Blays and the two smugglers, Dante turned up twine, shell, and even a bit of wire. He used these to tie the pieces of each bone together. When he finished, he had a pair of dangling objects that resembled norren earrings. Of rather poor quality, admittedly. If they'd been in Gask, that would be a clue that they weren't norren at all—the norren being fastidious craftsmen. But they weren't in Gask. They were in Bressel, where norren were virtually unheard of.

With the loons completed, there was nothing left to do but keep the moths' eyes on Gladdic's temple, and wait for Naran to return from arranging the meet with the norren. A few minutes later, a robed monk departed the temple. Wary of the disguise stunt Gladdic had pulled on them in their last encounter, Dante sent one of the moths after the monk as he traveled on foot through the city. The man arrived at a temple of Gashen—there were no signs out front, but the brutal architecture identified it at once—and entered.

Dante kept the moth right behind him as he found a cell, got a book from the shelf, and began to read. Ten minutes later, Dante was reasonably sure the man was exactly what he appeared to be, yet he left the moth with the monk anyway.

There was no other activity until Naran came back at sunset, sweaty from travel. "The norren were disinclined to act as letter-carriers."

"What?" Dante lurched to his feet. "But they must be sending people back and forth to the Norren Territories all the time. It wouldn't cost them anything to bring something back with them."

"Which I argued to no avail. However, after I let slip that the interested party was from Narashtovik, they became rather more accommodating. They await you on the north end of the city."

Blays squinted at the captain. "You couldn't have *opened* with that part?"

They waited until the fall of twilight to head downstairs and trot north toward the meet. The trek took them through a number of piers, then around an enclave of white stone buildings, and at last to the northern fringe just outside the gates, which remained open despite the coming night. There, lively bunches of merchants haggled under the gleam of pungent oil lanterns. Shoppers and pedestrians circulated between the stalls and shacks.

The norren had staked out a small field between a stable and an inn whose frame leaned as off-kilter as the drunks supporting themselves against it. The norren had put up half a dozen of their characteristic round yurts. Typically, their walls were thickly insulated to deal with the harsh winters of the hills of the Norren Territories. To deal with the heat of high summer in Bressel, the yurt walls had been replaced with single-layered deer hides, most of which were currently rolled up to let breezes blow in and out.

Eight norren sat on the trampled grass outside their tents, gathered loosely around a small cook fire. Though they were seated, their size was as imposing as a bear. The shortest of them would top six feet, with most of the men closer to seven. Their bodies were as stout as barrels, their limbs as thick as the branches of a mature oak. The men grew beards that grew from the base of their throats to the heights of their cheeks. The only small thing about them was their ears. These were round and petite, almost lost in the tangle of hair and beard.

Dante came to a stop fifteen feet away. The norren looked up from their work on various wood carvings, paintings, and fletching that represented their nulla, the life-craft the norren dedicated themselves to perfecting.

"Pardon me for not introducing myself properly," Dante said. "But I believe my friend Captain Naran has already done so."

Two men and a woman rose from their seats around the fire. The woman took two steps toward Dante. She towered over him, hair collected in a single rope as thick as any they had on the *Sword of the South*.

"That depends," she said, "on whether you believe it's possible to introduce someone from afar."

Dante's mouth twitched. It had been a while since he'd dealt with norren pedantry. "If not, I'm here in person to complete that introduction."

"In that case, my name is Lenna. And yours isn't necessary."

"This is my friend." He gestured to Blays. "I don't think you need his name, either."

"I don't. I must say it's surprising to see you here in Bressel. Unless you have business here. In that case, the surprise would be if you *weren't* here."

A pause ensued. One of the seated norren resumed whittling, a steady scrape of iron on wood. Dante said, "What clan are you from?"

"Wandering Bear," Lenna said. She kept her gaze steady on him. "The ancestral enemy of the Broken Herons."

Dante nodded, touching his chin. Years ago, to earn the support of the norren during the Chainbreakers' War, he and Blays had become official members of the Herons. The norren penchant for inter-clan squabbles had decreased since winning their independence from Gask, but as the war had receded on the seas of time, some of the old grudges had been re-exposed.

"Well," Blays said. "Then it sounds like we're in a unique position to begin to mend that rift."

Lenna laughed, but it didn't necessarily sound like she was amused. "What do you want from me?"

Dante nodded to the north. "Do your people come and go from the Norren Territories?"

"I'm not currently in the Territories, so I can't be sure. If you're asking whether the Wandering Bears in Bressel sometimes return to the Territories, the answer is yes."

"I need something delivered to Narashtovik. The object in question is quite small." He produced one of the loons from his pocket, holding it up to the moonlight. "It's a long way to deliver an earring, I know. But it would be a great comfort to know Olivander had this in hand."

This time, Lenna's laughter was more jovial. "We could try to find room in our luggage. What do you offer for this service?"

"I thought you'd undertake it free of charge. In recognition of our shared interests."

"You mean I should do you this favor because you helped us win the Chainbreakers' War."

Blays chuckled. "Norren precision is as bracing as parting your hair with a bowshot."

"That's right," Dante said to Lenna. "You *should* help me for winning the Chainbreakers' War."

She eyed him. "I would say that war was won by many thousands of norren, including hundreds and hundreds of dead ones."

"I would never imply otherwise."

"You just did." She waved a thick hand, cutting off his objections. "This argument isn't worth its words. You may think you're famous for winning the Chainbreakers' War. You're right to think that. But that's not where *I* first heard of you."

"Really? Then how do you know me?"

"From Dollendun. Where you were the first human player to master Nulladoon."

At the very sound of the word, Dante's heart lifted. Nulladoon was without doubt the most engrossing game he'd ever played. It resembled a pitched battle in miniature form, complete with tiny landscapes for your toy-sized soldiers to maneuver through. However, these soldiers weren't mere men and women. They included sorcerers, giants, dragons, and countless other creatures of legend. Combined with the fiendishly complicated strategies involved in deploying, moving, and engaging them, Nulladoon made chess look as complicated as a coin flip. Since its play exposed so much about the two opponents' mindsets, norren sometimes used it as a measuring stick for the people playing it.

"I love the game," Dante said. "It's been way too long since I played. But what about it?"

"The 'about it' is simple." Lenna gestured to a yurt. "Play me. And I'll do you your favor."

"I don't have time."

"Then I don't have time to deliver your loon."

"I'm not exaggerating," Dante said. "I have critical business that must be taken care of tonight."

She folded her arms, rocking on her feet. Fearing she'd topple and crush him, Dante had to restrain himself from stepping back.

"We're here to sell our nulla," she said. "This makes the Wandering Bears grow stronger. In asking me to send one of my people away, you ask me to weaken my clan."

"But it's for the good of Narashtovik. If my city stays strong, we'll be stronger together."

"The clans don't need your city. When great trouble comes, a city has to stand and face it. But a clan can walk away."

This argument had the flaw of implying that her clan was already strong enough to withstand whatever ills came its way, but Dante didn't think that would sway her. He gritted his teeth, casting about for answers. He could offer money, but he had no real cash on hand, and anyway, the norren didn't always care about silver. He could offer to play her on a later date, but if he killed Gladdic, he needed to get out of Bressel before the body went cold. The relationship between Narashtovik and norren had been his trump card, yet Lenna had brushed it aside like a cobweb.

"You don't really want to play Nulladoon here in Bressel," Blays said.

"Yes," Lenna said. "I do."

"The Nulladoon *we* learned wasn't a game between two players. It was a sport with an audience. If you want a *real* match, you can't play it here, where the nearest norren are five hundred miles away on the wrong side of the mountains. You two should play in Dollendun."

"That sounds like a good deal for you. Largely because the game will take place so far in the future it may never happen at all."

Blays laughed heartily. "Trust me, if we weren't in the middle of some very nasty business, Dante would be setting up the playing field as we speak. I'm surprised he hasn't decreed it a part of Narashtovik's weekly church services."

She thrust out her jaw, mouth pursed. "Promise me we'll play by year's end."

"I swear it," Dante said. "So start thinking what your wager's going to be."

Lenna smiled, fox-like. "I'll have your loon in Narashtovik within one month."

He handed over one of the two loons. She inspected it, then wrapped it in a piece of soft leather. After a quick goodbye, Dante and company were back on their way to the inn.

"I've sailed two thousand miles in all directions," Naran said with a glance over his shoulder. "And the norren are easily the strangest people I've ever met."

"Lenna's one of the more reasonable ones." Blays stepped over the jutting legs of a man sleeping in the middle of the road. "I've met norren who wouldn't even talk for fear of saying something untrue."

The nine o'clock bells rang minutes later. By the time they got back to the inn, it was nearly ten.

Naran cleared his throat. "So. Is tonight the night?"

Dante paced across the room. "I'm going to confirm he's still inside. If so, I see no reason to wait."

"What do we do after?"

"Run as fast as we can," Blays said. "When the powers that be find a body, they tend to pin it on whoever's closest."

"And what about the shaden?"

Dante peered out the window at the blackened streets. "From what I can tell, Gladdic's in charge of the shells. We're not talking about a crop of potatoes here. The shaden are extremely valuable. If Gladdic dies, the scramble to secure them will be so obvious we could see it from the Collen Basin."

Blays thumbed his nose. "I say we light out to the woods for a few days. Leave Jona and Fenk here to keep their ear to the street while you watch with your scouts."

"That works for me. The question for Naran is this: does your involvement end with Gladdic? Or will you continue to help us hunt down the shaden once he's dead?"

Naran moved beside Dante at the unshuttered window. "My gut tells me I should sail away. For the good of my crew."

"But?"

"But the *Sword of the South* has profited so much from the Plagued Islands. Twill might not have had the ship without them. They lost hundreds of lives defending themselves against Mallon. I feel like I owe them a debt."

"You're a good man," Blays said. "That makes it harder. If you don't find a way to shuck off the weight, it'll crush you forever."

Hands planted on the windowsill, Naran bowed his head. "We'll help you find the shaden. And destroy them."

Dante said nothing. Command, be it of a ship or a city, came with many burdens. Heaviest of all was the choice to do what your heart commanded, at risk to your people, or to walk away and keep those people safe. Those who never had to make that choice were always fastest to judge.

For himself, he had come to believe that, in the end, every choice was wrong.

He seated himself. "I'm going in."

He delved into the mind of the moth that remained in flight above the temple. The insect landed on the outside wall and crawled toward the window. This was glass, but it had been left open to let the night breeze do its best to cool the structure. Dante stopped the moth on the sill. Inside, a tall, sepulchral man sat at a desk reading a thick tome, his back bent like a fishing pole with a whopper on the line. There was little light, but there was no mistaking Gladdic.

"He's still there," Dante said. "He's alone in a small temple. You'll be able to walk right through the walls. I say we move now. Before he has the chance to relocate somewhere more secure."

"Sounds like a plan." Blays raised a hopeful eyebrow. "Swords?"

"Too risky. Besides, I don't intend for you to come in contact with him."

"Then how exactly do you mean for me to kill him? Pray for a spate of indoor lightning?"

"You're there to get me inside. And watch my back while I take care of him."

"In that case, I hope he's got a stuffed chair I can kick back in."

"You're not insulted?" Dante said. "That I want to handle this myself?"

"He's an ethermancer, right?"

"Right."

"*And* some sort of covert nethermancer?"

"Also right."

Blays held up a palm. "So he has not one, but two eerie powers capable of tearing me to shreds. If you want to take that on yourself, be my guest."

Dante turned to Naran. "It shouldn't take us more than three hours. If we're not back by the three o'clock bells, you should leave the city."

Naran tensed his jaw. "My vendetta against Gladdic doesn't end if you die."

"Yes, but it *will* end after he tortures us into revealing your location, then burns you on a pyre. If we fail, you can return in a few months after things have quieted down."

Dante killed a third moth and sent it three hundred feet above the rooftops for a clear view of the streets between their inn and Gladdic's temple. With assistance from Naran, who knew the city fairly well, he worked out a route and committed it to memory.

This done, Dante and Blays descended to the street. The night was warm, smelling of the river and its muddy banks. They walked to the bridge, a stone structure whose middle was raised high enough for sailing vessels to pass through its arches. Its center sported a cluster of homes and shops. Dante skirted around these, laughter and the clank of pottery drifting on the air.

Out in the open streets with the goal of murdering one of the capital's highest-ranked priests, it felt as though a sign was hanging over their heads. Yet to the observer, there would be no clue as to the dark intent of their hearts. How many others were walking about at that very moment with malicious plans of their own? The thought was enough to make Dante want to retire to the highest and remotest tower he could find.

Past the other side of the bridge, a pair of watchmen glanced their way, but paid them no special mind. Dante played out the possibilities in his head. Blays would shadowalk through the wall and unlatch the door. With the moth watching over Gladdic, Dante would know if the man became aware of their entrance. If Gladdic remained oblivious, Dante would sneak up behind him and put a bolt of shadows through his brain. If he got up to check on the disturbance, Dante would ambush him from the darkness.

Whatever course the killing took, it would have to be as swift as a flood. While Dante had finally learned to touch the ether in the Plagued Islands, he remained a rank amateur. Gladdic, meanwhile, would be as skilled with the light as Dante's Council members were with the shadows. And the priest knew the nether as well. If it came to a toe-to-toe fight, Dante's money wouldn't be on himself.

A brisk walk took them through the quiet neighborhood around the temple. Soon enough, they stood outside its grounds. A wrought iron fence surrounded swaths of raked gravel and small topiary gardens. In the center, a modest edifice looked over the neat surroundings. Its walls were round and stone, its main building three stories high, topped by a short spire just large enough to contain a stairwell.

"So," Dante said softly. "Got an idea on the fence?"

"I was thinking we might climb it."

"Any ideas where we're not witnessed by everyone who glances in our general direction?"

Blays peered up at the row houses around the temple. "Most of them appear to be asleep. I say we find the darkest spot, climb on up, and get inside before anyone has the chance to raise an alarm."

Dante had been considering conjuring a shadowsphere to cover their entry, but the patch of pure darkness would be more conspicuous than two silhouettes. When you had powers that reflected those of the gods, it was always tempting to use them. But often, the down and dirty route was more effective than any magic.

They retreated from the pavement around the temple, circling through the back streets to approach from the north, where few lights shined in the row house windows. After a minute of silent observation, they crossed to the fence. Blays grabbed hold of two pickets and hauled himself up, latching onto the upper rail. He hooked an elbow around it and reached down. Dante grabbed his hand and pulled himself up, catching the rail. The pickets were topped by spikes, but with some careful maneuvering, the two of them dropped to the other side of the fence without injury.

Dante moved behind a square of shrubs trimmed to resemble hourglasses, then stopped and shifted his vision into the moth just inside the window of the temple's third floor. There, Gladdic remained hunched over his desk, eyes scanning the pages of his book.

"We're looking good," Dante murmured. "Care to step inside?"

A plain wooden door sat in the building's north face. Dante checked to see if it was unlocked, but it held fast. The two of them retreated to another growth of shrubs.

"What happens if something goes wrong up there?" Blays whispered. "Are you expecting me to run away?"

Dante eyed him. "How long have we known each other?"

"Just checking. In that case, if he starts to wallop you, try to stay clear of his neck, belly, and groin."

"Why?"

"Because that's where I'm going to be stabbing him."

Nether rushed to Blays' form. Fast as a blink, he vanished. As he moved toward the temple, he left a ripple in the shadows that Dante was able to follow as long as he concentrated. He watched closely, hoping that this would be the time he witnessed the key to teaching himself to shadowalk, but by the time Blays passed through the stone wall of the ground floor, Dante knew no more than ever.

A minute later, the wooden door opened soundlessly; either they were very lucky, or Gladdic didn't brook disturbances from squeaky hinges. A silhouette moved into the opening and lifted its right hand.

Dante emerged from the shrubbery and met Blays inside. Blays motioned to the ground floor, gesturing that it was all clear. Dante pointed to Blays, then the ground floor, then himself and the upper floors. Blays nodded and pointed out the stairwell.

Dante stepped into it, letting his eyes adjust to the near-total darkness. The steps were stone. No chance of creaking. He got out his antler-handled knife and nicked his arm, feeding the blood to the thirsty shadows. He ascended slowly, nether held tight in his hands. He'd been in such situations countless times, but as always, his heart raced in his ears. Though he'd found that you could learn to ignore your body's fears, he no longer believed he'd ever be rid of them.

Gladdic was on the third floor. Dante paused at the second floor landing to listen, but the chambers beyond were silent and dark. He continued to the third story. Two candles flickered at the far side of the chamber, light and shadow battling for control of the walls. At his desk, back to the stairwell, Gladdic turned a page, reached for a quill, and jotted a note on the parchment beside him.

Something rustled below, the sound so faint that, a second later, Dante wasn't sure it had been real. Gladdic showed no sign of having heard it.

The man was as quick as a snake with both nether and ether. Dante would have to hit him before he knew the shadows were upon him. Inhaling through his nose, Dante called the nether in a rush so thick it threatened to blot out the air around him. The instant it was in his grasp, he launched it forward in two bursts: one aimed for Gladdic's head, the other for the center of his back.

Both blows struck true. And both dissolved like a pinch of sand cast into a breaking wave.

Dante yanked the nether from its holds in the crannies in the stone. Gladdic stood stiffly, spinning on his heel to face Dante. Dante launched another volley of black bolts at the priest. Gladdic didn't so much as raise his hand. He summoned no ether or nether in defense. As before, the assault vanished into his body, the shadows swirling into him as if he was drinking them.

Acting on instinct, Dante drew on what little ether he could command. It coalesced into a pearly ball the size of a marble. He shaped it into a point and jabbed it toward Gladdic.

The priest jerked backwards, twisting his shoulders. Rather than taking him in the throat, the ether struck him in the right collarbone. With this, all the color faded from him. Not that he went pale—rather, from head to toe, he turned pitch black. Including the glossy claws that now curled from his fingers.

His eyes, though—these gleamed silver, twinkling with the coldness of the stars. Dante's blood ran even colder.

4

Raxa trudged up the stairs behind Gaits. He was always lively, but that night, he had an extra bounce in his step. Under normal circumstances, she would have resented this.

But tonight was different. Tonight was payday.

He emerged onto the rooftop. Six stories high, the top of the Marrigan—in a touch of irony, their den was still named after the blue-blood who'd built it—held a commanding view of Narashtovik. To the north, the bay glimmered under the stars. To the west and south, the city spread before them. And to the east, the spire of Ivars and the blunt body of the Sealed Citadel stood as monuments to history.

Blackeyed Gaits strolled to the iron railing enclosing the rooftop. He leaned his forearms over it, smiling at the distant bay. The early summer night was already cooling, the breeze tousling his ear-length black hair.

"Quite a view, isn't it?" he said.

"Marvelous." The sea breeze was stirring less pleasant scents as well, but after so many years living in the slums, Raxa took them as a natural part of life. "Is this a ploy?"

"For what?"

"To put me in a good mood so you can negotiate me down."

Gaits had a flair for the dramatic: as he swiveled his head to regard her, he ducked his chin, only to swing it up at the last moment. "You think I'd try to lowball you? For the Torc of

Dalder?"

"I think you'd try to lowball me for the soul of your own mother."

"Yes, but in this case, I care about the torc." He turned back to the night, twisting one of his many rings. "We're not up here to soften your brain."

"Then why?"

"We'll get to that." With a movement so graceful it bordered on magic, he produced a leather bag, its bottom sagging with weight. "Payment in full. In exchange for one priceless torc."

"Do you even understand what the word 'priceless' means?"

"Don't get technical. If it has no price, then I owe you no money."

Raxa grabbed the sack. She jogged it up and down, clinking the silver coins inside it. "Feels light. Do I need to bite it?"

Gaits shrugged one shoulder. He was wearing a new shirt. Looked like silk. "Fedder died on the job. This wasn't some street rat with no family or people. He was a scion of Dallagor. Do you have any idea what it takes to cover up something like that?"

"Shouldn't cost a thing. A foolish boy went missing. Happens all the time."

"In our circles? Sure. But people like the Dallagors, they're going to call in trackers. Bounty hunters. It's in our best interests if they're fed certain crumbs. Led in certain directions. Doing *that*, without it coming back on us, gets expensive."

After a moment, she pocketed the bag. "You said you had something else for me."

Gaits wandered toward the east side of the roof, giving Raxa no choice but to follow. He folded his arms, holding his right elbow in his left hand as he regarded the towering silhouettes of the Sealed Citadel and the Cathedral of Ivars.

"Those two structures hang above us like a pair of proud gods," he said. "Wherever you are in the city, they're watching over you."

Raxa moved to the railing. "Can't be that powerful. Or else they wouldn't need those walls around them."

"Indeed. Know what else? The Celeset has *twelve* gods, not two. I think there's room for far more deities in Narashtovik."

"Let me know when you're done being abstract."

He snorted. "Do I need to spell it out for you? This city's been resurrected. It's got money spilling from every pocket. Nobody's going to notice if we help ourselves. By the time they *do* start to figure out what's happening, we'll be rich enough to buy an army of our own." He gestured grandly to the dark buildings beneath them. "We're up here for perspective. To find the vision to restore the Order of the Alley to its former glory."

"Very inspiring. Now what about the job?"

"Can't you allow yourself *one* moment to dream?"

"Every moment spent dreaming is one you could have spent working to make that dream real."

Gaits sighed, but he was smirking. He pointed toward the Citadel. "Galand's gone. He's been gone for weeks. No one knows when he'll be back—or even if he's alive. I think it's high time we redistribute some of the Citadel's treasures."

"To ourselves?"

"That counts as redistribution."

Raxa smiled. "What's the target?"

"The Jerrelec Collection. Your standard baubles and jewelry, though more ancient than most. It's rumored there's even some gold in there."

She couldn't help raising an eyebrow. She'd only seen gold twice in her life. "This is in the Sealed Citadel?"

"Correct."

"You know that's not just a name, right? Got an entrance for me?"

"We have someone inside who'll be working with you."

"And how do I *get* inside?"

"This is the heart of the city's government," Gaits said. "It's home to priests. Monks. Soldiers. Staff. There are hundreds of people inside those walls. Now, you may never have been inside the Citadel, but you've passed by it, right? How big do you suppose its garden is?"

"Not nearly enough for hundreds of people." She tipped back her head. "You want to sneak me in with their food delivery."

He nodded, grinning toothily. "The wagons come every fortnight. Only this time, they'll be carrying an extra..." He looked her up and down. "130 pounds of human surprise."

"What about extraction? I can't stay there two weeks until the next delivery."

"These hundreds of people produce more than their share of garbage and waste, too. That cart goes out three days after the food comes in. And when it does, it'll be carrying an extra 130 pounds of human ex—"

"Save it," Raxa said. "That's the best you've got? Cramming me into a mound of shit?"

He did his one-shouldered shrug. "It's a little trash, that's all. Just pretend it's that apartment of yours and you'll feel right at home."

She stared at him. "It's not about the trash. It's the risk. Three days inside?"

"What would you prefer? That we load you into a trebuchet and fling you onto the roof of the keep?"

"Sounds less likely to get me killed."

"You're the best sneak we've got. I say you're up to the risks. If you've got a better idea, I'm all ears."

"I don't."

As she spoke the words, though, an idea came to her with spooky clarity. Goosebumps touched her arms. This was a habit of hers, if you could call it that—sometimes, when she expressed a firm belief, it was disproven in the next instant. By and large, she wasn't superstitious. People said all kinds of things about the gods, but the gods never said anything back. When it came to her jinx, though...there were times she was afraid to express her beliefs out of fear they'd be turned on their head as soon as she expressed them.

"Hold up," she said. "I heard rumors that during the war, they were bringing people in and out of the Citadel—while it was under siege."

"Those aren't rumors." Gaits motioned to the hill north of the Citadel. "You're talking about the tunnel from the carneterium."

"The body locker?"

"You got it. The place where they take the dead to be poked and prodded until they reveal what killed them."

"Or the investigators find what they want to believe. These

newcomers are strange."

"That's probably why they built the tunnel—so no one can see what they're inflicting on the bodies." He clasped his left fist in his right hand, drumming his fingers over its back. "Won't work, though. The tunnel into the Citadel was closed as soon as the war ended. Unless you can muffle a sledgehammer, there's no way in."

"Or so they want you to think. I'm going to see for myself."

"Do not get made. If they catch you sniffing around, and the next day the crown jewels go missing, they may be able to add two with two."

"I'm the only one you trust to get inside, right? So trust me to investigate my own route in."

"This is about much more than you." He swung away from the railing, bringing his face within a foot of her own. His expression, normally wry, was now as hard as the slopes of the Wodun Mountains, his eyes as bright as their glaciers. "This is the first wave in a sea change for the Order. Do us proud, or step back and let someone else turn the tide."

In other circumstances—down in the bar, say—she would have deflected his earnestness with a quip. "You know I can do this, Gaits. If you didn't, we wouldn't be here."

"Yeah," he said. "I know."

He finished with the details. She headed downstairs and straight toward the Strongbox. There, Trunk checked her for picks and prybars, his meaty hands deft through years of practice. Done, he stepped back with a nod. Inside the vault, she located her box and opened its door with the key around her neck, releasing the crisp smell of metal coinage and the musty smell of papers.

It was rumored that some members of the Order kept enough in their box to keep them fed for a decade. Raxa had enough for two or three months. She put her payment for the torc inside, fishing out a few bits of silver and iron for walking around money, then locked the box and replaced it in the wall.

Downstairs in the bar, she stopped to write a note, folding it into her pocket. She hit the streets, angling northeast toward the high hill facing the Citadel. Within blocks, the neighborhood toughed. The blades on her hip—a knife, and a longer weapon with pretensions of swordhood—dissuaded anything stronger than glances. It was early summer and there was still a bit of chill to the night's marine air.

After a long walk, the buildings faded behind her, replaced by ragged grass grown high during the spring rains. A dirt trail led toward the base of the hill.

It was easy to be accepted in places you had no business being. The first trick, which even the civilians knew, was to avoid notice. Act like you belonged there. Stride around like you owned the place. Absolutely no gawking or shifty eyes allowed.

If you couldn't escape notice, you discouraged interruption. A man and a woman posing as a feuding couple could dissuade even armed guards from approaching. Under the right circumstances, applying makeup or lightly poisoning yourself to appear diseased could ensure nobody got close enough to ask you any questions.

Lastly, if you failed to avoid notice or discourage interruption, you had to convince the man who'd marked you to disengage and move along. Easiest way to do that was to tell them the story of why you were there. Any story had to be plausible on its face, but the absolute best ones had something beyond that: details that would make anyone questioning you too uncomfortable to ask more. Hints of sex stuff shut down some people fast.

Another way was to convince them you were there as part of a fun, harmless conspiracy—say a servant stopped you in the baron's halls and you told him you were an old friend there to surprise him. Did it work every time? Not even close. But it succeeded often enough that a good story could be a better defense than any sword.

So she would walk into the carneterium like it was her second home. Traversing the halls, she'd unfold the note she'd written to herself and appear to be inspecting it. And if anyone stopped her to ask why she was there, she'd explain that her husband, who'd been unfaithful to her, had been killed in a duel. His body was here and she needed to see it—alone.

Thieving could be a lot of work sometimes.

She came to the cave set in the base of the hill. A lantern flickered weakly in the entrance. Damp air oozed from the cavern. It was heavy with incense, but that couldn't mask the smell of bloating flesh. Seeing no one, she picked up the lantern and walked into a tunnel.

She'd only gone a few feet before the passage forked. The way ahead smelled foul. The fork, though, smelled more like your run of the mill cave. She took it.

The stone walls were eerily smooth. The hallway descended, stretching on for hundreds of feet without any doors or side passages. Bit of grit on the floor, but nothing else of notice. As best as she could tell—and she was definitely fuzzy on this—she was heading south or southeast.

The tunnel continued for what felt like a mile, then ended so suddenly she almost walked into the blank wall of dark basalt.

She reached out and touched it. It was as perfectly smooth as the walls. She lifted the lantern. No gaps or seams where the wall met the ceiling. She felt it from top to bottom. All rock. Solid.

She went back to Gaits and told him she had her way in.

With no need to coordinate around the Citadel's incoming wagon schedules, Raxa wasn't slated to hit the job for another four days. Even so, the morning after visiting the carneterium, she got up early and returned to the Marrigan. There, she removed nearly her entire payment for the torc from her locker and divided it equally into six small burlap pouches.

Cash in her pocket and blades on her hips, she headed to the first home. Communal building on Flinders Street. Not a great neighborhood, but there were much worse. Including hers. Inside the building, she climbed the musty stairwell to the fourth floor, found the door with the two dogs' heads carved on it, and knocked.

A woman answered, a little old to be a mother, but a little young to be a grandma. Seeing Raxa, her face crinkled with a smile. "Back so soon?"

"I had a good month," Raxa said. "How was yours?"

The woman—her name was Parrie—rolled her eyes. "Busy, no thanks to you."

"I warned you."

"You did. And I didn't listen."

"If at any time you're not happy—"

Parrie slashed her hand through the air. "None of that. I've never been happier. The busyness is the main reason why."

Raxa smiled. "How's Avie?"

"Running wild with a pack of others. She makes friends like a cobbler makes shoes."

Raxa laughed. When she'd found Avie, the girl had been living alone, hiding in one of the abandoned ruins on the town's outskirts. So alone and wary of strangers that Raxa had had to coax her out by leaving almond pastries on a stone and retreating far enough that the girl felt safe to come out and get them. A year later, she had more friends than she had fingers and toes. A lot of that was Parrie's doing. The woman acted like a curmudgeon, but Raxa knew that, behind the bluster and the scowls, she was as soft as warm wax.

"Be sure to buy her something nice. She's got a sweet tooth." Raxa handed over one of the smaller sacks.

Parrie accepted it, blinking at its weight. "This is way too much."

"Then save it for the tough times."

"*I* never had this much growing up."

"I don't know how long I'll be around," Raxa said. "Could be a year, could be twenty. Or anything in between. It's my job to make sure they'll be fine long after I'm gone."

Parrie snorted. "I'll take your money, if that's what you want. But I've heard the stories about you. I've got a feeling you'll outlive us all."

Raxa spent a few more minutes catching up, spending as much time asking about Parrie, who had recently been taken on as a clerk for a justice of the peace, as she did about Avie. After twenty minutes and a cup of tea, Raxa extricated herself and went on her way, walking downhill to the home near the bay where Georj Fenner lived with Ven.

Georj answered the door with a grin. Before he could finish saying hello, Ven sped from the depths of the house, crashing into Raxa's legs and hugging her waist tight. She laughed and hugged him back.

During the thirty minutes she spent catching up with them, sipping from a cool glass of wintrel-spiced tea, she forgot all about the scheme against the Citadel. But as soon as she hugged Ven goodbye and stepped outside, there it was, a stone block in the sky, a monument to itself, paired with the great spike of the Cathedral. Just as Gaits had said, everywhere she went, they followed.

At her next visit, Mr. and Mrs. Kinnel were out, but Bina was there, along with the Kinnels' older daughter Yenna. Everything seemed fine. Next was Svin, who already looked an inch taller than the last time Raxa had seen him.

Fifth on the list was Fedd and his foster father Herrick. They lived right outside the Pridegate in a two-room house standing on a time-worn foundation of black rock. The yard was littered with bits of wood and pieces of furniture salvaged from the thousands of homes that had been abandoned in the outskirts of Narashtovik prior to the coming of Dante Galand. Nearly every piece showed pale green mold or lichen, and was apparently so valueless it could be left out in the open without being stolen.

Raxa knocked on the door. After getting no response, she gave it a good pounding with her fist. She went around back, but the yard was empty. She knocked a third time, waited, then walked away. On the street, she glanced over her shoulder. A shadow moved behind a cracked shutter that had been closed tight a minute before.

She finished her rounds with Tera, dropping off the fifth of her six coin purses, then returned to the Marrigan. Gaits was asleep, so she killed time down in the bar, returning a sliver of her payment to the Order in exchange for a light afternoon buzz.

Once Gaits was up and about, he summoned her to his room. The view had nothing on the roof, but the space was meticulously tidy.

"Got my maps?" she said.

He hoisted a mug of tea. "They're coming tonight."

"Tonight? The more time I have to study, the better the chances I pull this off."

"You know, most sneaks don't even *get* maps of the hit."

"Sure," Raxa said. "And most sneaks aren't trying to break into the most well-guarded structure between here and Setteven."

"You're the one who thinks the guards won't be a problem."

"Getting *in* is no problem. Staying alive once I'm inside is another matter. Will I have the Authority of the Knife?"

Gaits tipped back his head and set down his tea. "This is the Sealed Citadel. We want a zero-casualty mission—and that includes you."

"But if push comes to shove?"

"Then yes, you're authorized to do whatever it takes to protect your life. But Raxa, for your sake and mine—don't let it come to that."

She nodded and returned to the bar for another ale. The afternoon was growing hot, a sluggish breeze meandering through the open shutters. Judging enough time had passed, she got up and headed past the Ingate, sticking to the northern faces of the buildings to shield her from the sun. Half an hour later, she exited the Pridegate, returning to Herrick's trash-strewn yard.

He was out in the yard tossing around sticks and debris. Seeing Raxa, he straightened. He'd cut his black whiskers short for the summer.

"Raxa." He smiled, dirt griming the creases of his face. "Didn't expect you for another two weeks."

"Surprised? Where's Fedd?"

"Sent him over to the market. With a few pennies of his own to spend, too. Don't expect him back until nightfall."

"Too bad." She jingled the pouch in her pocket. "Maybe next time."

Herrick's brown eyes lingered on her pocket. "You keep that safe until then, yeah?"

"Yeah." Keeping her eyes on Herrick, she stuck her fingers in her mouth and whistled.

It had been one of the first things she'd taught them. The front door swung open. Hesitantly, a young boy emerged into the sunlight. He was as tan as a Bresselian, his hair black and shaggy.

"You get back inside!" Herrick hollered. Teeth gritted, he

glanced back at Raxa.

The boy was already reaching for the door handle and retreating inside. But it was too late to cover the puffy black ring around his right eye.

Raxa grabbed the collar of Herrick's thin gray blouse, yanking him close. "Is that your work?"

"Get your hands off me." He grabbed for her wrist, but she snatched his thumb, levering it back until he stopped resisting. "I said let go!"

She released his thumb, swept her hand to her belt, and drew a knife. She put its edge against his throat.

"I'm going to ask you some questions," Raxa said. "You're going to answer."

He tried to pull his neck back from the knife, but she kept it tight. He grimaced. "It's broad daylight!"

"Then everyone will be able to see how black your blood runs."

"All right. All right!"

"Why?"

Herrick grimaced; a bead of blood ran down his neck. "He's more trouble than he's worth."

"That's one of the reasons I pay you," Raxa said. "So you can make the effort to help him lead a civilian life."

"What do you think I'm trying to do? How else am I supposed to get him to listen?"

"You don't hit them. No matter what, you don't hit them. That's the first rule."

"I know it is."

"Then why?"

"He doesn't *listen*. I give him chores. Nothing more than I had as a kid, mind. Enough to earn his keep and build some discipline. And eight times out of ten, when I come home, he hasn't lifted a finger."

"And you think if you hurt him bad enough, he'll become a perfect gentleman. Happy to do your bidding without a trace of resentment."

Herrick's jaw hardened. "So maybe it don't make sense, do it? But you tell me what else to try when you already tried everything else."

"Try again," she said.

"All right."

"I'm going to ask you one more question. It's very simple. It's not a trick. Do you want him or not?"

A tear slipped into Herrick's whiskers. "I do, Raxa. I wouldn't have taken him if I didn't."

"Then act like it," she said. "Because if you don't, I can find him another home. But if you *do*, then you'll never lay hands on him again."

She withdrew the knife, wiped the veneer of blood on the leg of her charcoal trousers—which were dark for reasons exactly like that—and sheathed the weapon. As Herrick rubbed his neck, inspecting the smear of blood on his fingers, Raxa stalked to the shack and opened the door. Fedd stood inside the dark room, staring up at her.

"He hit you?" she said. The boy nodded. She moved closer, touching his shoulder. "If he does it again, you tell me. You understand?"

The boy nodded again.

She walked outside. Herrick stood in the yard, squinting, although his back was to the sun. Raxa got out the sixth sack of coins and underhanded it hard at his chest. He turned away from it, shielding his head. The sack struck him in the ribs and fell in the grass. He grunted, stooping to pick it up.

"Buy him something nice," Raxa said. "Like some shoes."

Herrick reddened beneath his summer tan. Raxa turned on her heel and walked back toward the gate. During their conversation, she'd kept her cool, but now she steamed like a kettle. Before she could turn back and do something stupid—despite everything, she believed Herrick when he said he wanted to keep the boy—she broke into a run, drawing looks from a pair of guardsmen in the black and silver of the Citadel.

But maybe she *should* hurt Herrick. These were her kids. She'd pulled them off the street—often, places far worse than the street. She'd found them parents she trusted to do right by them.

It had started two winters back. Dead dog in an alley. Covered with snow. And two tiny cloth-bound feet poking from beneath it. She'd pulled away the dog; its legs were stiff, but it hadn't yet frozen through. And underneath it was a toddler. The boy sat up to look at her, back pressed to the wall, but he didn't look afraid.

"Are you here to hurt me?"

His voice was a young child's, but his tone was a veteran soldier's. As if he didn't even care, in the end, but just wanted to know how the rest of his day was going to turn out.

"No," Raxa said. "No. I'm here to get you out of here."

The boy stared, then reached up. His hand was as cold as the snows. One of his fingers was already discolored. Days later, however, it would turn out to be the only digit he'd have to have amputated.

That had been Ven. She'd found Bina two months later, and Avie a few months after that. Now, she was up to six. She wasn't sure how many more she could handle. Costs added up. The people she chose were the good ones. Honest. Wanting to help. Too often, that meant they were nearly as poor as their former street urchin fosterlings had been. Raxa's purse was only so deep.

But if six was as many as she saved from a life like hers, then she would have done far better than most.

She went home. The apartment was small, stuffy, hot. Inside, bugs crawled on the moldy walls. Outside, human vermin stalked through the mucky streets. Raxa stretched out in bed, hands behind her head, and smiled.

"Well," Gaits said. "Don't you think you should tell me how you intend to make entry?"

Raxa wagged a finger. "Trade secret. Why would you need to know?"

"So that if anything happens to you, I'll know where to recover your body."

"Anything happens to me, you won't want to get within a mile of the Citadel. The less you know, the better."

"On the one hand, this is completely true." He regarded her with a look that almost but wasn't quite a glare. "On the other, it's damned annoying to have no idea how you intend to do this."

"If I told you, it would only frustrate you more."

"Great. Now you've made it even worse." Gaits sighed testily, turning toward the distant Citadel. Night lay on the city, but lights gleamed in the windows of the keep. "I believe we're done here."

She was making entry that night. She'd had the map for two days. It was crude, but like Gaits had said, most times you had no map at all. Maybe it was better that way. A map made you think you'd know your way around. Gave you false confidence. But it didn't show you where the guards were patrolling. Where the servants would pass by at the exact wrong moment to land you in the dungeon — or at the end of a noose.

"No sense sitting around." Raxa pushed off from the railing around the roof. "Keep a bottle handy. I'll be back before morning."

She already had everything she needed: map, knives, a doughty pack, her personal lockpicks, and some more specialized tools checked out from the supply room. She set out to the east. It was only nine o'clock and the streets were thick with pedestrians out for a night on the town. The Cathedral of Ivars grew taller and taller. Eventually, she stood beneath it, the Sealed Citadel across the plaza, its outer walls thirty feet high and the keep far higher.

Though the church doors were closed, a few pilgrims stood outside, laying down prayer boards: thin wooden squares carved with the position of the Celeset's stars during their birth. Otherwise, the plaza and the fortress across it were nice and quiet.

Raxa headed north without any hurry. On the fringe of town, she stopped at a tavern for a beer and a plate of beef hash. When the midnight bells pealed across the sky, she rose and continued to the hill with the cemetery on top of it and the body locker beneath it.

It was as quiet as her first visit. This time, though, she was carrying a small shop's worth of burglary equipment. She moved to the side of the cave, bit her lip until she tasted blood, took a deep breath, and stepped into the shadows.

The world became a place of shadow and silver. Mercury-colored light glowed from anywhere it pleased: the trees on the hillside, the flies on the air, from within the cavern itself. Even where there was no light, she was somehow still able to see through the darkness. The air tasted sharp and metallic and refreshing. Her body felt like an arrow in flight.

No time to waste enjoying herself. She jogged into the cave. A hooded figure sat inside the foyer, reading by the light of the lantern. To him, she was perfectly invisible. She still hadn't had to use the cover story she'd devised for coming here. It was a shame how much prep work went to waste on most jobs.

She made her way to the tunnel she'd investigated the other night. It and the hallway leading to it were deserted. She stepped out of the shadows and into a darkness so total she had to reach out to the cool stone wall for support.

Knowing the floor was smooth and unbroken, she walked forward blind, one hand trailing along the wall while the other reached out before her. After what felt like forever, her leading hand touched blank stone.

Raxa moved back into the shadows. Within them, walking through the rock was no trickier than walking through a gauzy curtain. She emerged into a prison cell, the bars on its small window swirling with silver motes. She returned to the humdrum world, opened her pack, and changed into a set of servant's clothes: a gray shin-length dress with ties at the end of the sleeves so they could be secured above the elbow if the weather warmed. A white tree embroidered on the breast marked her in the employ of the Citadel.

The disguise was as basic as basic got. But she couldn't move through the shadows for more than ten or fifteen minutes a day before her brain lost its hooks on the place and she tumbled back into reality. There was no way around it. Most of her time inside the Citadel would be spent out in plain sight.

She returned to the shadows long enough to slip through the wall and into the hallway beyond. This was empty. And totally dark. Recalling the map, the stairs were to her right. She shuffled that way. Rats—she thought—skittered through the darkness. The air smelled like mildew, old sweat, and gentle rot. Eventually, her toes banged into a stone step.

The stairwell took her up to a yawning hall with a lantern at the far end. A quick poke around revealed a score of large storerooms aching to be burgled, but that could come later. She continued to the ground floor.

She exited into a small foyer next to a high-ceilinged hall. Voices murmured somewhere ahead, carrying across the vast stone spaces. Without pausing, Raxa forged onward, following the wall until it came to the stairwell to the upper floors. This sported a lantern at each landing, providing enough light to climb by.

The Jerrelec Collection was supposed to be housed on the top floor. She ascended, stepping lightly. The air smelled dusty but otherwise clean. A door creaked above her. Heavy footsteps began their descent. Raxa carried on. At the next landing, a man in a thin black doublet with a white tree on the chest glanced her way. He was heavyset, mostly muscle, with a thick beard and an air of authority. Raxa lowered her eyes and stood to the side of the stairs.

He moved past her with the slightest of nods. She recognized him—Salamander? Ollimander? Something like that. The chief in Galand's absence. Raxa climbed upward, reaching the top floor without interruption.

The hallway was lit well enough to see it was empty. Her target was three doors down on the right. Door was locked. She bit the inside of her lip again, drawing enough blood to make the shadows happy, and walked into the realm of black and silver. She crossed through the stone wall. The room beyond was empty of people, but crowded with cabinets and display cases.

She smiled and departed the shadows.

The room was pitch black. She groped around her stuff until she found her flint and lit a candle. Jewels and silver shined from pegs and the dark cloths used to showcase them. One case held nothing but gold rings. Raxa gave herself a moment to enjoy them. After all, a good thief had to know what the best merch looked like.

Enough admiration. Time to start grabbing. She wrapped the larger necklaces and idols in cloth so they wouldn't clink and sorted various rings, bracelets, and earrings into a compartmented wooden box. Finished, she hefted her pack. By weight alone, she was carrying a fortune.

She crossed back into the hall. At the far end, a silvery figure entered a door, closing it behind themselves.

So far, everything had gone as smoothly as Raxa could have asked. Getting inside the Citadel was the hard part. Once you were there, and dressed as a servant, nobody was going to pay you any mind unless they caught you somewhere you weren't supposed to be. All she had to do was walk downstairs, hit the dungeon, and get the hell outside.

But something held her back. The man of the house was gone. And his room was just down the hall.

Sending a quick prayer to Carvahal, who looked over all thieves, she walked forward, counting down doors. At Galand's, she tried the knob. Locked. A quick jaunt through the shadows got her inside the room.

She relit her candle, revealing a space that was both orderly yet cluttered. Shelves along the walls were full of books, most of which looked older than the bones in a crumbling tomb. Benches and desks displayed a crazy amount of knives, scalpels, small skulls, bits of bone, a glass case full of pinned moths, assorted gewgaws, and tiny wooden statues so well-crafted they had to be norren craftsmanship. For the right person, there might be treasures here, but nothing hit her eye as worth carrying out.

The candlelight glinted from something hanging on the wall. A sheathed sword. The scabbard was black and curved, filigreed with silver, though not half so pompously as the blades of most nobility. A bright blue sapphire winked from the scabbard's tip.

Raxa set a chair beneath the sword, climbed up, and unhooked the scabbard's strap from its pegs. She began to draw the weapon, but stopped when she'd only exposed the first six inches. The blade was *white*.

She tapped her nail against its flat. Wasn't metal. Almost felt like wood. Or more like…bone.

Raxa unsheathed the rest. The entire sword was white, gently curved, edged on one side. It was lighter than expected, as if it was hollow. There wasn't a single nick on its cutting edge. Ceremonial? She set the edge against her thumbnail to test its dullness.

She cocked her head. And took a second look across the room. All those trinkets. Scalpels. Pieces of animals. Aside from the strangeness of the collections, some of which looked like active experiments, these were the personal quarters of Dante Galand. Nethermancer extraordinaire.

Raxa withdrew her thumbnail from the sword, walked over to the desk hosting most of the pieces of bone, and laid the edge against the wood. As soon as she pressed down, the sword sliced an inch into the table.

With a gasp, she dropped the hilt. The blade remained embedded in the wood. Effortlessly, she pulled it free, eyes traveling up its white length.

"Uh oh," Raxa murmured. "Looks like someone left their favorite toy behind."

5

Gladdic moved forward, silver eyes shining from the infinite darkness of his body. Dante reached for another bolt of the ether that had finally knocked Gladdic back a step, but he produced nothing but a handful of sparks in the air between them.

Even so, Gladdic halted in his tracks. Dante followed up the sparks with a lance of shadows. As before, Gladdic absorbed the nether without so much as a grunt. Dante lashed out wildly with enough nether to knock down a small house. Gladdic inhaled, chest swelling as the shadows sank harmlessly into his body, and stepped forward, lifting his claws.

Dante turned and ran for the stairs.

"Blays!" His feet thundered on the steps. "We have to get—!"

Blays spilled out onto the second-floor landing right beside him, clutching an armload of papers. "What's happening?"

Dante raced down the steps. "What are you doing up here?"

"Why are we running?" Blays fell in beside him, glancing back up the steps. "Did you ruin everything?"

"No time for talking."

"I'm taking that as a firm 'yes.'"

Dante came to the ground floor and raced toward the door he'd come in through. His leg banged into a table, spilling him onto a plush rug. Shin throbbing, he got to his feet. Blays had gone to open the door, sword in hand. As Dante reached him, his eyes went wide.

"Oh," Blays said. "Run!"

Gladdic's silhouette seemed to flow across the dim room. Dante sprinted outside. He and Blays dashed across the moonlit plaza. A dog barked nearby. Dante flung himself at the wrought iron fence, grabbing tight and hauling himself over its points. Blays dropped to the other side, landing in a crouch. Dante came down beside him, stumbling, his wounded leg threatening to give out beneath him. He sent a wave of shadows to his shin. Attracted by the blood leaking from the gash there, they soothed the wound at once.

"What in hell?" Blays said.

"Don't know," Dante panted.

"That thing looked like it was carved out of coal!"

"That *thing* was Gladdic."

Blays swerved south, putting them on a parallel course with the distant river. "You're sure about that? Because I have a distinct memory of Gladdic being human."

"I've been watching the temple all day. Gladdic never left. When I went into the room, he was sitting at his desk. I hit him with the nether, but it was like he absorbed it. He didn't even have to do anything. When I struck him with the ether, that's when he turned into…whatever that was."

"Maybe that's what he's always been. And the ether only revealed his true form."

They entered the tailors' district. With the shops shuttered for the night, the street was quiet, their footfalls echoing from the walls.

Blays glanced back, but they appeared to be alone. "Here's another thought. What if that wasn't him at all?"

"What else would it have been?"

"You're the wizard. You tell me."

"You know how to use the nether, too!"

"Yeah, but for me, it's only a hobby," Blays said. "For you, it's more like your wife."

They veered east, heading back toward the river. Dante slowed his pace. "I have no idea. But that felt like a trap."

"Not a very good one, given that we're currently running away rather than bleeding to death."

"If that thing wasn't Gladdic, that means Gladdic knew we were coming for him. Even if it was him, it felt like he was ready for us."

"So what do you want to do now?"

"Tell Naran what happened," Dante said. "And that we're going to have to back off."

Blays raised an eyebrow, but said nothing. As they came to the bridge, they slowed to a walk. The warm night was tranquil, but every scrape of feet or distant laughter felt like a sinister intrusion. The further they got from the temple, the more Dante questioned his quick decision to run. Could he have fought harder? Tried more subtler methods of attack? Called up Blays to help him?

But there was no denying what he'd seen Gladdic do. The nether had been useless against him. If Dante and Blays had stayed to fight, they'd be dead.

To Dante's relief, Naran, Jona, and Fenk were all in the inn awaiting their return.

Naran lurched from his chair, eyes darting between Dante and Blays. "Well?"

"The good news is we're alive," Blays said. "The bad news is that Gladdic is, too."

Dante explained exactly what had happened. Naran's expression went from shocked to nonplussed to his typical stoniness.

"Gladdic—or this thing pretending to be him—did it hurt you in any way?"

"I didn't give it the chance," Dante said. "But I think the claws and the inexorable advancement toward me were strong indicators of intent."

"Then we don't know how strong Gladdic is. You left before finding out if he has the power to hurt you."

"That sounds amazingly close to an accusation of cowardice."

Naran's brow creased. "It's a statement of fact."

"I *do* know that my weapon of choice didn't so much as scratch him. We need to back off and reassess."

"Your strategy for disposing of him? Or whether that's possible?"

"There's more at stake now than vengeance on Gladdic,"

Dante said. "I suspect this was a trap. If he gets proof that Blays and I were involved, he'll use it as fuel for his anti-Arawn propaganda. He may even use it to stoke war against Narashtovik."

The captain squeezed his eyes shut, sighing through his nose. He ran a hand down his face. "Then what do you suggest we do?"

"Get out of the city. For now. Let the situation cool down. In the meantime, we'll try to learn everything we can about what happened tonight—and, if that's really Gladdic, how we can kill him next time."

"If you're still committed to your vows, then we've got no quarrel. Where do you intend to take us?"

"I hadn't thought that far," Dante said. "Whetton, maybe. We know our way around and we could get back to Bressel within a few days."

"I think you should consider the Collen Basin."

"Collen? Why would we want to go there?"

"Because," Naran said. "That's where the most recent shipment of shaden have gone."

He went on to inform them that, while they'd been out dealing with the norren, Jona and Fenk had been keeping tabs on the *Sunfinder*, the Mallish vessel that had returned from the Plagued Islands. They'd been assuming that its cargo would either be offloaded in the city, or piled onto a barge to be taken further up the Chanset River. To their surprise, however, the crates had been piled into a wagon caravan—which had set off down the road to Collen.

"Makes sense," Blays said. "The Mallish have been clamping down on the Colleners lately. Bet you they're using the shells to power their oppression efforts."

Dante frowned. "The Mallish aren't supposed to be using nether at all. It's blasphemous to Taim."

"I'm sure the priests giving those orders never touch the stuff, then. Just like they never drink wine, eat to excess, grope youths, or curse."

"We might be able to net two fish with one swoop. Collen's never rejected Arawn and the nether the way the rest of Mallon has. As we're figuring out what the Mallish are doing with the shaden, I may be able to research what just happened with Gladdic."

"You think the Colleners will have any clue about that?"

"If there are any archives on the nether anywhere in greater Mallon, they'll be in Collen."

After consulting with them, Naran decided that Jona and Fenk would stay in Bressel to keep eyes and ears on local developments. Dante and Blays started packing, preparing to leave that same night. Fast as he could, Dante constructed a new loon, giving Jona one piece of it and keeping the other. By the time he'd finished, Blays had returned from downstairs with the staples of the road: sausage, cheese, crusty bread, dried apricots and figs.

The five of them left the inn together. Once they were out of sight of the building, and reasonably sure they weren't being followed, Fenk and Jona parted ways, meaning to find a new spot to hole up in on the off chance Gladdic knew where they were staying. Dante, Blays, and Naran continued to the Late Gate, so-called because it remained open all night.

Passing a rustling alley, Dante stopped to slay a pair of rats and then reanimate them, sending one ahead of them and the second trailing behind.

"I'm not seeing anything," he told the others. "But that doesn't mean they're not there."

Blays swerved around a malodorous puddle. "Now that we've had some time for our brains to settle, do you have any idea what went on back there?"

"If anything, I'm *more* confused. Hey, when I made my tactical retreat, were you stealing Gladdic's papers?"

"I thought I'd make myself useful. I didn't have anything else to do."

"Besides watch the front door."

"*I could* have done that. But then you'd be without these." Blays reached into the shirt of his peasant garb and retrieved a thick roll of papers.

Dante itched to read them, but it was the dead of night and he had a city to flee. He tucked the roll into the round leather case that carried his other papers. As he walked northeast, following

Naran's lead, he flicked through his internal archives of everything he'd read related to the use of the nether, casting about for anything similar to what he'd seen in Gladdic's temple.

There was one story from the *Cycle of Arawn* that rang a bell. Stathus the Wise, one of history's most venerated nethermancers, had taken many disciples under his wing. One of these, Kennen, was considered the favorite to take Stathus' seat—but when Stathus died, that honor passed to a different disciple named Vanya. Grossly slighted, Kennen had turned to darker and darker methods to undermine his new superior. Dante couldn't remember the precise phrasing, but one of those methods had involved a shadowy reflection who would tell you your enemies' secrets in exchange for an awful price of some kind.

He wished he could consult the book. At that moment, however, he didn't have a copy of the *Cycle*, both because it weighed five pounds and he was traveling, and because in Bressel, owning the book would get your hands chopped off—or, these days, get your entire body burned on a pyre. He didn't think the story had much more to say about the shadowy reflection, but once he had access to the *Cycle*, it couldn't hurt to check.

With some thinking, he was able to recall a few other stories of silhouettes, doppelgangers, and demons that were as black as caves. None mentioned silver eyes, though.

Two hours after leaving the inn, they came to the Late Gate. The blue-clad guards gave them a long look, then waved them through. The three of them headed southeast through various slums until they came to the Long Arm of the King, the nickname for the cobble and mortar road striking east toward Collen.

This led through a few miles of sharecroppers, then the stumps of harvested forest, and then into the forest itself. By that point, it was nearing five in the morning. Sunrise wasn't far off. At Blays' suggestion, they headed off the road and into the woods to clear a quick camp.

Dante laid out the blanket from his travel kit. The abruptness of their departure from the city still had him reeling. "We're sure this is the right move?"

"It was your idea," Blays said. "So absolutely not."

Naran rolled his spare shirt and trousers into a pillow. "I'm not happy to leave. But I understand the threat staying would pose to Narashtovik. There's the honor of the Kandeans to think about as well. Capturing the shaden will help disarm those who tried to conquer the Plagued Islands."

Dante stretched out on his blanket. "I just hate to step away from a task before it's complete."

"Maybe this *is* a part of that task," Blays said. "For all we know, Gladdic's using the shaden to do whatever it is he did back there at the temple." He kicked off his boots and wriggled around for comfort. "Besides, if we stayed, what was our next step? Cowering in our room until Gladdic gets so old and senile he forgets how to summon the ether? Better to move on. Like my dad used to say, fighting the current is the best way to drown."

Dante agreed, yet it still felt like defeat. He closed his eyes. That night, he dreamed of silver eyes, black claws, and nether that refused to come no matter how hard he called for it.

They woke a little before noon, ate, stretched, and got on their way. The forest wrapped them in welcome shade. Eighty miles lay between Bressel and the border of the Collen Basin, and another forty miles from the border to the city that gave the basin its name. The Long Arm of the King was in excellent maintenance, however. Dante thought they'd arrive within five days of hard walking.

He kept his rat scouts ahead and behind them. Traffic on the road was light. Once, when a group of mounted soldiers approached from the west, heading toward Collen, Dante and the others diverted into the trees and waited for them to pass. By the end of the first day, the land began to rise, the cobbled road spooling up and down the low hills.

Whenever they took a break from travel, Dante dived into Gladdic's papers. Most of the material was either administrative trivia or theological discussion of the glory of Taim. Dante was about as interested in these topics as he was in the mucus patterns of nightcrawlers. Even so, he read the works to the end, eyes sharp for anything that might help him understand Gladdic's plans, abilities, or mind.

Two other pieces held far greater potential. One was three

pages, front and back, devoted to the matter of a Bresselian monk who was able to use the nether and had requested Gladdic's permission to do so in service of fighting the enemy. Gladdic's response considered the matter fairly, but eventually found that no matter how noble an act of heresy might be, it was still heresy. The letter concluded with the idea that, if they stooped to the use of the nether, they would destroy one monster only to replace it with themselves.

The second piece filled less than half a page. It was highly cryptic, with multiple references to "those that once walked" and "Star-Eaters." The overall thrust involved deducing the location of a site in the northeast. One where "lives fell like rain" and "blood sloshed to the knees." It finished with this: "With the finding of this site, the Star-Eaters, in all their terrible purity, might be returned to scour that which—"

It broke off mid-sentence. Dante read it several times. Could "Star-Eaters" refer to whatever he'd encountered in the temple and its star-like eyes? If so, were they an outside force Gladdic wished to ally with? Or was he himself a Star-Eater? There would be no answers to be found in the forest. But perhaps he could find the truth in the libraries of Collen.

As night neared, they made camp in the lee of a hill. It was warm enough to go without a fire without any discomfort. There was no hint of rain on the air, either. They scraped the ground clean, stirring the too-sweet smell of rotting maple leaves, ate, and bedded down.

"So," Blays said. "Before we get to Collen, you want to tell me what the place is like?"

"You grew up in Bressel." Dante gazed up at the dark boughs and the stars beyond. "How do you not know about the Collen Basin?"

"Oh, I don't know. Because I *grew up in Bressel*? A city so big you could live in it for eighty years and find a different street to walk down every day? Where all the world comes to *us* for a taste of our overflowing wealth, culture, wisdom, and style? Where the people in the streets are as many as the stars in—"

"It's probably because you were illiterate. Are you at least aware that Collen's the most rebellious territory between here and Voss?"

"Everyone knows that."

"If there's anyone who didn't, it would be you. Collen is the only holding in all of Mallon that hasn't permanently renounced the worship of Arawn. And during the times they have renounced it, it's been due to Mallish military coercion."

"How have they gotten away with that?" Blays said. "Mallon's gone through three Scours dedicated to burning, smashing, and defenestrating everything Arawn and Arawn-adjacent. The last Scour was only a century ago."

"Because." Naran's deep voice contrasted with the chirp of the crickets. "They're the only ones who've always been willing to fight back."

"That's the gist of it," Dante said. "Collen's been trouble from the start. In the early days, the fighting was so bad Queen Ingrid considered giving up all claims to the land. She eventually settled on a policy that's endured, with exceptions, to the present day: that Collen be allowed to follow its own laws and customs so long as it pledges fealty, pays taxes, and contributes soldiers in time of war."

Blays shifted on his blanket. "Let me guess. That arrangement functions so well that, every few decades, a Mallish king will notice Collen's at perfect peace—and decide that means he can afford to squeeze them again."

"Exactly right. But it runs both ways. The Collen government is a democracy. They elect their leaders like a small-town guild."

Blays laughed. "They elect their *kings*?"

"Every few years. Typically, the first order of business of a new despot is to undo everything their predecessor did. Often through the use of bonfires and street mobs. Actions which have the unique property of attracting Mallish soldiers."

"This system sounds about as stable as an eight-year-old on his ninth pint."

"More than a few Colleners aren't too impressed with it, either. Meaning that, every few generations, a group of seditionists tries to abolish the electoral process and install a monarch. The smart ones bring the Mallish in on their side, promising that in exchange for the crown's help, the basin's new regent will pledge complete fealty. As a result of all this, some historians have compared the Collen Basin to a colony of dagger ants. I disagree. Dagger ants might never stop fighting, but they never fight with themselves."

"I see," Blays said. "And we're going there on *purpose*?"

The others went to bed. Before doing the same, Dante summoned as much ether as he could, condensing the light from the air itself. Ether was the only thing that had hurt Gladdic—or whatever had been pretending to be Gladdic. Dante had only just begun to use the lightness during their trip into the afterlife. Considering it had taken him over ten years to learn that much, he feared his skills would never be more than trivial. The only way to avert that fate was constant practice.

The next day took them higher into the hills, some of which might have qualified as small mountains. Pines replaced many of the leafy trees. Despite the increasing ruggedness of the terrain, the road remained cobbled, though portions were cracked or showed erosion of the mortar between the stones. Rare to find such a well-maintained road so far into the wilds. Dante supposed the armies of Mallon often needed to get to Collen in a hurry.

The hills crested and began to descend. The trees thinned to scattered stands, replaced by grass gone long and yellow in the summer. It was far warmer and drier than on the other side of the hills. With little shade, they sweated crazily. The road straightened, heading directly northeast. A sluggish stream oozed beside it. Dante would have suspected the road was built to parallel the stream, but both were so straight he began to think the road came first and someone dug the creek later.

Soon, the grass thinned, too, replaced by pale green sagebrush, swaths of yellow cheatgrass, and gigantic round balls of thorns. A few villages sprung up around the road and waterway, small farms mostly, but with the occasional outlet for provisions. Most of the locals were blond, with the washed-out blue eyes so common to the Basin, their skin tanned light brown from the constant sun.

"Captain Twill was from here," Naran murmured as one such village passed behind them.

Blays swiveled his head, taking in the broad brown vistas. "No wonder she wanted to get away."

Naran gave him a severe look, then laughed. "At least it's very difficult for anyone to sneak up on us here."

In one of the villages, a merchant sold canvas-covered wooden hoops you could hold above your head with a thin rod, keeping the sun off you as you traveled. If Dante had had any money, he might have bought one.

Miles ahead, buttes rose from the horizon. Years ago, Dante had read many books about Collen, including two or three that had been illustrated. Buttes featured prominently in all of them. Seeing them in person made him smile with recognition.

Green tongues of farmland ran between the buttes, sprouting in sharp contrast to the gray and yellow surroundings. The crops were wheat and asparagus irrigated by ditches just like the one that ran beside the road. Some of the buttes bore stone towers overlooking the farmland. More than one of these towers was a ruined shell.

As they neared the city of Collen, Dante's loon activated. Jona had a piece of news: while there had been no talk on the street of an attempt on Gladdic's life, Gladdic had left the city just hours after Dante. Jona had only caught wind of this after the fact, meaning he hadn't been able to follow Gladdic, but word was that the priest had been heading north. Making it unlikely he was following them to Collen.

Dante passed this along to the others. "If Gladdic's gone, is there any reason for Fenk and Jona to stay in Bressel?"

"Maybe not," Naran said. "But there's no reason for them to leave, either. Tell them to remain in place and try to learn whatever they can without exposing themselves to danger."

Dante relayed the orders, then continued along the road. A few miles later, the pavement quit abruptly, a rutted track extending from its end. Bits and pieces of river stones and mortar lay half-buried in the dust.

"What do you think caused this?" Blays nodded at the wreckage of the road. "The Great Mule Rebellion of 719?"

Dante toed a loose rock. "Does this look recent to you?"

Blays bent for a closer look. "Unfortunately, I let my membership in the Roadmasters' Guild lapse years ago. But the break still looks pretty jagged."

"I think it was intentional. And I doubt it was the Mallish who wrecked their own investment."

They moved along the rutted path. As the day drew on, what remained of the road led to a great butte.

Dante knew at a glance this was the city of Collen. The plateau climbed two hundred feet above the plains, its top stretching four miles across. At the base of its southern rim, a second town thrived. The smaller houses were wattle and daub, the roofs thatched, doors and windows enclosed by the hides of deer and sheep. The larger buildings were comprised of mud bricks. Most of these were pale gray, but the bricks of some structures had been dyed orange, yellow, or light blue. What little wood was in use was generally reserved for doors and shutters. A few homes and temples sported wooden stumps carved into elk, bears, the dragons of Jorus and Daris, or relief images of hunts and battles.

The lands surrounding the butte were criss-crossed with ditches and heavy with farming. A road switchbacked up from the town on the the southern side of the butte. Semi-circular holes had been carved from the rock along the switchbacks. People went in and out of the caves. Large basalt-hewn towers jutted from the top of the plateau, swarmed by the rooftops of hundreds of smaller buildings, most of them made of pale brick.

"I'm guessing most of the interesting places are up top," Dante said. "First we'll find a place to stay. While you two start after the shaden, I'm going to do a little research."

The closer they got to the bottom of the butte, the thicker traffic got. Farmers, mostly, wearing loose beige clothing, driving wagons drawn by a mule or two. The lower town smelled like dust and animal sweat and looked large enough to house a few thousand people.

On their way to the switchback path, Dante drew a great deal of looks. Far more than Naran, whose deep brown skin and elegant features were rare even in cosmopolitan Bressel. Blays, meanwhile, received almost no attention at all.

After a while of this, Dante glanced at Blays. "What are they looking at? Is there something on my face?"

"You mean besides your face?" Blays said.

Naran cocked an eyebrow. "Blays jokes, but he's correct. Your dark hair. That thin nose and sharp cheekbones. You look more Mallish than the king."

Dante blinked in sudden recognition. Blays was blond, with eyes blue enough to be a Collener. And while Naran certainly looked foreign, his appearance wasn't inherently threatening to the Colleners.

Dante, by contrast, looked as unwelcome as a rattlesnake.

Blays chuckled softly, reaching the same conclusion. "Looks like I'll want to do the talking."

"What else is new?" Dante said.

Naran gave them a sidelong look. "Exactly how long have you two known each other?"

"Since our youth. Which may explain why we seem to be stuck there."

The base of the road up to the butte was congested by a pair of mule teams who'd gotten snarled trying to pass each other. Rather than unhitching the animals to maneuver them free, their owners appeared to be attempting to untangle the mess by screaming at each other. Both men were red-faced, dust flying from their short sleeves as they gestured at each other. The larger man offered an insult of some kind. The smaller man lifted his fist and stepped forward.

A woman darted from the crowd. Her arms and legs looked carved out of ironwood. A golden ribbon fluttered from her right elbow. She intercepted the shorter man's wrist mid-punch, sweeping her leg behind his plant foot. The move should have sent him crashing down hard enough to break his arm, but the woman guided his fall so gently he barely winced.

"Good training," Blays murmured.

"Don't fight your brothers." The woman kneeled over the mule-driver, still holding his wrist. She grinned at him. "And if you have to fight, don't do it on the road."

He blinked, mouth hanging open. His expression swiftly darkened. "I'm an earther. How dare you touch me."

"You'll have to forgive me. But it was in service of protecting another earther."

The downed man scowled. The taller man, who remained standing, barked with laughter.

"Get your ass off the dirt before you spoil it." He extended a hand to the fallen man. "Come on and let's get this sorted out."

The short man gave the woman a burning look, then took the other man's hand and stood. The onlookers dispersed, hurried along by the woman with the golden ribbon and the arrival of three well-muscled men who wore different-colored ribbons of their own.

With the way cleared, Dante and the others continued upward. The switchback was steep, but carved twelve feet into the hillside, it didn't feel at all treacherous. They reached the first turn. Smoke rose from the heights above them, but there was no visible fire. On the next leg of the path, caverns had been holed into the rock along the trail. Baking bread and roasting meat wafted from the entries. People wandered in and out, munching pastries.

"New mission," Blays said. "Acquire pies."

Dante pointed up the butte. "The city's right up there."

"And it will still be there after we've had our first warm meal in a week. The sooner you bow to my demands, the sooner we'll be on our way."

Dante sighed through his nose. They backtracked to a bakery. The interior was warm from ovens, which were vented out the slopes above, explaining the smoke they'd seen earlier. In some ways, the soft flatbread and flaky pastries reminded him of Tantonnen, another wheat-rich farmland. In Collen, however, the meat was slow-roasted on long skewers, the air thick with cloves, bay leaf, gannon seed, and green pepper. Rather than beef and poultry, the meat appeared to be mostly goat, lamb, and venison.

"It pains me to admit it," Dante said, dealing with the last of something flaky and stuffed with crushed raspberries, "but this was an excellent idea."

They paid in Mallish coin, which the proprietor stared at. In the end, though, the man scooped it up, proving once again that money always trumped politics. Back outside, the sunlight was blinding. Once they trusted themselves to move, they carried on up the switchbacks, which seemed to comprise a town of their own, complete with residences dug into the cliffs. The levels below them spread out in slanted terraces.

A shout drifted from the top of the path. A second rang out a moment later. Dante frowned and continued up.

The shouting grew louder, angry and chaotic. At the top of the switchback, people surged into the path, running downhill in a roostertail of dust. Someone slipped, skidding down the slope and landing heavily on the trail below. A cloud of dust followed them down.

"Oh hell," Blays said. He reached for his sword and charged up the trail.

6

Dante swore, taking off after Blays. Naran followed, an alarmed look on his typically stoic face. They were already two-thirds of the way up the road and soon ran into the first of those who'd fled from the top.

"What's going on?" Dante called out. "Why are you running?"

Several people brushed past him. One woman glared at him, jaw held tight. "Your masters are killing our people."

"My masters?"

She turned to the southwest and spat over the cliff's edge. "The Mallish."

"*I'm* not Mallish. I mean, I was, but now I'm—"

Blays grabbed the shoulder of his shirt. "There will be plenty of time to renounce your bloodlines later. Now come on!"

They hurried upward, dodging the citizens streaming down from the plateau, until the trail ejected them into an open square on the top of the butte. Ahead, buildings stood thickly, towers rising above them. A welcome wind blew steadily from the southwest. Ahead, shouts turned to screams. Dante and Naran ran after Blays.

After passing through a few blocks of low brick buildings, they skidded to a stop at the edge of a plaza. There, a contingent of thirty Mallish soldiers in dusty blue finery faced off against a crowd three times their size.

Both groups hurled insults back and forth. Dante's eyes roved for the leader of the mob. Before he could identify one, a stone flew from the citizens and cracked into a soldier's forehead.

A Mallish sergeant brandished his sword. "Charge!"

The bluecoats rumbled forward, blades in hand. Blays unleashed a string of profanity salty enough to make Naran blink.

"Let me guess," Dante said. "You want to give them a hand."

"Like hell!" Blays sputtered. "The last time we got involved in a fight like this, it dragged us into the middle of a war."

The citizens broke, rushing toward the buildings behind them. Some flung stones back at the Mallish. A man tripped to the rectangular setts paving the square. Two soldiers fell upon him, kicking and bludgeoning him.

"Anyway," Blays went on. "I figured *you'd* want to help."

"Me? Why?"

"Because you hate the Mallish."

"I don't hate the Mallish. I hate their leaders who insist on perpetuating a centuries-long holy war they're completely wrong about."

"Which is what those fine fellows in blue are doing right now."

"Even so," Dante said. "We can't get involved. That would compromise our ability to track down the shells. In Gladdic's hands, those are way more dangerous than any soldiers."

As a contingent of citizens entered an alley, they turned to hold their ground, armed with clubs and knives. The eight soldiers pursuing them were outnumbered two to one, but they didn't so much as slow down, ripping into the Colleners with practiced discipline. Screams rang out. Bodies dropped on both sides. The citizens wavered, then scattered down the alley.

Forty feet from that brief battle, a second skirmish ended just as quickly. The Mallish troops ran after the retreating Colleners. In moments, the plaza was empty of everyone but the wounded.

Dante drew his knife and cut the back of his arm. Nether winged to him from all sides. "Let's get to work."

"Didn't we just agree to stay out of this?"

"The fighting, yes. But these people are hurt. They need help." Dante jogged forward. "This can only help us. If we hope to find anything here, it won't hurt to make friends with the locals."

Blays and Naran followed him across the black setts. Five bodies lay at the entrance of the alley, including one soldier. One of the four citizens looked thoroughly dead, so Dante headed for the next-worst, a man with a deep slash down his chest and gut. He clutched his wounds, gasping rapidly. Dante kneeled beside him, shadows swirling in erratic loops.

The man's eyes rolled in pain. "What are you doing?"

Dante positioned his hands over the man's body. "You have nothing to worry about. In a moment, you'll be better than ever."

He bolted upright, swiping a bloody hand at Dante. "Get away from me!"

"Do you see that red substance all over your hand?" Dante said. "That's blood. It happens to be yours. In another minute, more of it will have moved outside your body than remains in it."

"Don't you dare." The man collapsed on his side, waving feebly. "I...I forbid you..."

Muttering something unpleasant, Dante poured nether from his hands. It slipped into the man's wound like a dark knife. More blood welled forth, but the flow thinned to a trickle, then stopped altogether. The man's gasps slowed. He touched his stomach, gently at first, then roughly. He swabbed the blood away from his shirt, revealing light brown skin unmarred by any wound.

He swung up his head and glared at Dante. "What have you done to me?"

"I saved your life," Dante said. "No need to thank me."

"Don't tell me *they* have something against nether," Blays said. "I thought they were all filthy heretics."

The man got to his feet, brushing grit from his pants. During their brief encounter, a small crowd had emerged from the nearby buildings and alley.

The man pointed accusingly at Dante. "Did you see that? He *healed* me!"

Three witnesses nodded. A woman stepped forward. "I seen him."

Naran moved beside Dante. "Am I missing something? That man was about to breathe his last."

"Tell *them* that!" Dante said. He put himself in the aggrieved man's face. "What's the matter with you? If not for me, you'd be dead right now!"

"That's right." The man smiled hotly. "And you robbed me of my chance."

"Good news." Blays gestured south. "If you're that intent on dying, there's a very serviceable cliff right over there."

"I was supposed to die at the hands of the Mallish. To stain their hands with blood they'd carry with them until the day they died—and faced their judgment by the gods. To do such is a Collener's highest calling."

"Really? I think you guys should aim a little higher."

"You stole my honor." The man moved before Dante. He stooped, picked up a pinch of dust, and flicked it at Dante's feet. The crowd murmured. "I challenge you to a duel."

This provoked a flurry of chatter from the observers. Dante glanced around, searching for any sign of a joke. "Let me get this straight. I prevented you from suffering a gruesome death. And now you want to fight me?"

"I *want* to kill you. But a duel's legal, and while it won't restore my honor, it will salve it." The challenger motioned to Blays and Naran. "Are these men your Arms?"

"My Arms?"

"One who fights in your place, Mallisher."

Dante turned to Blays. "Would you say you're my Arm?"

Blays rubbed his chin. "More like your brain. But if there's really going to be a duel, I suppose I can mop the floor you've soiled."

The man smirked. "Excellent. I'll send for my Arm. In the meantime, we'll remain here."

He approached a young man, speaking quickly. The young man nodded and dashed off into the streets.

"Pardon my ignorance." Naran leaned toward Dante. "But we need access to Collen's resources. How is fighting a duel with a local going to curry any favor with these people?"

Dante held up his palms. "What's the alternative? Refuse, and be scorned by everyone? Blays is the best swordsman I've ever seen. We'll be done with this in a few minutes. With any luck,

Blays' prowess and honor will so impress someone they'll jump at the chance to help us find what we're here for."

"That seems optimistic."

Dante had no response ready, mostly because he was afraid Naran was right. The offended man was busy speaking to several people who were referring to him as Ked. Other Colleners were attending to those who'd been wounded in the skirmishes with the Mallish soldiers, but their ministrations largely took the form of holding the injured party's hand while murmuring to them about how their deaths would blacken the souls of the Mallish until the gods would have no choice but to smite Bressel into a smoking crater.

Dante watched with mounting frustration and irritation. He could salve every one of the wounded within minutes. To not do so felt not only cruel, but inefficient. He'd long admired the Colleners from afar for their ongoing resistance to Mallish rule, but perhaps they resisted not out of principle, but from madness.

The crowd stirred. A woman was entering the plaza, trailed by the young man Ked had sent out and a handful of other citizens. A golden ribbon winked from her right elbow—she was the woman they'd seen on the switchbacks breaking up the fight between the two mule drivers. She walked with the rolling gait of someone who had a lot of muscles to move. Her blond hair was pinned tightly at the back of her head.

"Cord!" Ked called. He jogged over to greet her. An act which, Dante noted, he would have been completely incapable of performing if he'd still been suffering from the giant gash down his torso.

"I hear you have a fight for me." She sounded happy at the prospect, her voice booming out like a street preacher's promises of salvation. "Where's my match?"

Ked nodded in Dante's direction. "That's them over there."

Cord strolled up to them. Her eyes traveled to Dante's black hair. "You must be the one who robbed Ked of his deathright." She turned to Blays. "Which makes you his Arm?"

"Begrudgingly," Blays said.

"Who would begrudge the chance to fight for honor?" She looked him up and down. "How can such a man be an Arm?

Where's the rest of you?"

"I'm like a fine whiskey. It doesn't take much to knock you on your ass."

Cord tipped back her head and laughed.

An older man made his way through the crowd, which now numbered at least sixty, and stopped before Dante. "You have been challenged to duel. Do you understand the rules of the contest?"

"We just got here," Dante said. "I don't understand *why* I've been challenged."

The man's face was lined with years of sun. His cheeks sprouted thick gray muttonchops. "You have offended Ked Kenzie, a respected earther of Collen. He has challenged and you have accepted. Since you chose to use Arms, Ked's Arm gets to choose which weapons shall be used."

Ked smirked at this. Cord flexed her hands. "We'll use the only weapon worth using. The wheel."

The crowd broke into applause. The old man turned to a man with a red ribbon knotted around his elbow. "Two wheels. Right away."

The other man nodded and ran out of the square. Blays raised his eyebrows at Dante, but Dante could only shrug. Across from them, Cord began to twist at the waist, swinging her arms back and forth. Once she wrapped up that exercise, she lifted her hands high above her head, bent down to touch her toes, then ran her hands up to her kidneys before stretching backward.

Watching her, Blays' amused expression grew thoughtful.

The runner came back with two seven-foot wooden poles. One end of each pole was carved into a point. The other end was weighted with a leather bag the size of a fist. This appeared to be stuffed with something small and lumpy, such as pebbles. The runner handed the poles to the old man, who passed one to Cord and one to Blays.

Blays hefted the pole. "This is the wheel?"

"That's right," the old man said.

"I hate to be the one to tell you this. But your wheels are missing their rims. And all the rest of them. If anything, these appear to be spokes."

Cord laughed. "You're lucky these are dueling wheels. The real ones are metal on both ends."

The whiskered man ushered the crowds back, clearing a circle. He came back to Blays and Cord. "This isn't a fight to submission nor to the death. Merely to first fall."

Blays tamped the sack end of the pole against the plaza stones. "If you get knocked down, you lose?"

Cord scoffed. "What kind of an Arm doesn't know how to duel?"

Blays cocked his head. "Enjoying this, are you?"

"We're standing in the sun. We're about to fight. What's not to enjoy?"

He hefted his weapon. "If you're in such a good mood, mind giving me a minute to get the feel of this thing?"

"Practice all you like. If you think it will help."

Blays gave her a look, motioned Dante and Naran back, then took a few exploratory jabs and swipes with the wheel. Dante had almost no firsthand experience with a spear, but he could tell by watching that the wheel, due to its weighted end, handled significantly different.

After a minute of practice, Blays brought his feet together, resting the ball of the wheel on the ground. "Thanks for your indulgence, Cord. Now are you ready for your drubbing?"

She frowned at him. "Are you sure you wouldn't like a lesson first?"

"Cord!" Ked shouted. "Will you get on with it?"

The woman twisted her head his way. "What joy is there in defeating an infant?"

"This isn't about joy. It's about honor."

"Honor *is* joy."

"I may not have a Collener's experience," Blays said. "But I've had a weapon in my hand since I had the strength to swing one. Let's do this."

She grinned at him. "Think your spirit will make up for your lack of skill?"

They faced off twelve feet away from each other, out of range of the wheels' reach. The crowd fell back several steps.

The old man overseeing the duel lifted his right hand. "In the witness of all, let the purity of combat guide us to truth."

He dropped his arm and backpedaled away. Cord stalked forward, smiling broadly, her wheel held in her hands like a staff. Blays edged to his right, holding his weapon closer to the ball, spear-like. Cord flicked the pointed end at Blays' legs. He deflected it with a deft gesture. She repeated the probe. Blays intercepted, letting the shaft of his weapon guide her spearpoint past him, and jabbed toward her midsection.

She swept her wheel sideways into Blays', knocking the point of his weapon wide. She shifted her grip toward the pointed end and whipped her wheel into a spin so fast it whistled through the air. The weighted end slammed into the back of Blays' ankles.

His feet swapped places with his head. He tucked his chin to his chest, twisting his body to land on his right shoulder. As he fell, he slapped his right hand against the setts, landing in a pile. His wheel clattered away. The audience lifted their arms and cheered.

Cord planted the ball of her wheel on the stones, leaning on the pole. She frowned down at Blays. "Why, you're not any good at this at all!"

Blays untangled himself and sat up, rubbing a skinned elbow. "Maybe you're *too* good at it. Ever thought about that?"

Naran nudged Dante's ribs. "What now?"

"I apologize or something and we get on our way," Dante said. "And I never try to help anyone ever again."

Blays stood and dusted himself off with a series of claps. He turned to Ked and bowed low. "The gods have spoken. You were right. My friend's a prick."

The old man moved to the middle of the ad hoc ring. "Cord, Arm of Ked, has won the duel to first fall. Ked, what boon do you choose from the defeated?"

Ked cleared his throat, chin held high. "I choose service."

"Service it is. As a duel of first to fall, the offender will serve the offended for a time of three months."

"Hold on," Dante said. "Boon? *Service?*"

"Of course," Ked said. "What did you think the duel was about?"

"Honor?"

Ked laughed. "Do you really think that knocking your Arm on his ass makes up for what you took from me? A duel judges guilt. Now that you've been found guilty, it's time to decide your sentence. You're a sorcerer, yes? Three months spent killing the Mallish for me should start to make up for stealing my deathright."

"You're lucky I bothered to play along with this farce until now. Walk away with your honor intact."

"You're in Collen now. Bound by Collen's laws. You—"

Shadows rushed from the pavement, whirling around Dante's hands. "I am bound by nothing."

"Sirs and madams." Blays stepped forward, barring an arm across Dante's chest. "I request a minute to confer with my colleague."

The old man's whiskers twitched. "This isn't how things are done."

"Highly unusual, I'm sure. But unless you'd prefer to see everyone in this square turned inside-out, you need to give me a damn minute with my friend."

The man swallowed and stepped back, speaking softly to Ked.

Blays pulled Dante aside, nodding Naran over as well. "Threats of violence are wonderful things. But if you want to get anything done in this city after this, we need to find a way to settle our differences without offending their basic sense of justice."

Dante gritted his teeth. "I'm not going to be this idiot's servant. Especially not if he means to use me as a weapon against Mallon. That's the last thing we need. This is so stupid!"

"Do you want to solve the problem? Or do you want to keep whining about it?"

"I don't see why those have to be mutually exclusive."

"We have two options." Blays began to pace. "First, you can deny their claims and get us kicked out of Collen. That won't stop us from coming back, but it will make it much harder to follow the shaden. And it will probably make it impossible to get answers about Gladdic's transformation."

"So my alternative is to knuckle under to their ridiculous demands in the hope it'll make it easier for us to find answers we don't know are here."

Naran tapped the tip of his nose. "If you're the only one who has to 'serve,' Blays and I could still move freely. As soon as we've found the shaden, you could leave with us."

"That's not the worst idea on earth," Dante said, relaxing marginally. "Though I was really hoping to get some research done."

Blays shrugged. "If they think it's going to help you fight the Mallish for them, maybe they'll let you do all the research you want."

"The only other idea I've got is to hunker down in the woods until the norren get my loon to Narashtovik." Dante went still. "Unless. What happens if I refuse to serve?"

"Oh, I'm sure they'll just let you walk away. Either that, or they'll attempt to lock you up in chains, at which point you'll attempt to irrigate their fields with their blood."

Dante raised his voice to Ked and the old man. "What happens if I tell you no?"

"You can't do that!" Ked said.

The old man folded his arms. "If service is refused, a second duel must be fought. But this time, to the death."

Cord clapped her hands together. "Excellent!"

"I refuse my service," Dante said. "And accept this new duel."

A frisson sparked through the crowd, most of which had remained present while Dante was conferring with Blays. The old man looked to Ked, who nodded.

"A second duel it is," the old man said. "Will you be using Arms?"

"Damn right," Ked said.

Dante held back a smile. "What happens if I decline my Arm?"

"Then you must fight for yourself." the old man said.

"And who chooses weapons?"

"Why, you would."

Dante nodded. "Then I decline my Arm."

"Very well. Choice of weapons?"

"The nether."

"What!" Ked squawked. "That's cheating!"

"They're your rules, asshole." Dante unbuckled his sword and cast it aside. "But since I'm such a good sport, I'll offer you an alternative: we drop the whole thing and walk away."

Several of the onlookers chuckled. A handful jeered Ked. His face reddened. "Maybe…"

The old man shook his head. "You've already accepted. By law, you must proceed."

"Don't worry, Ked," Cord said. "This is my duty. It must be done."

Ked flung his hands wide. "But you don't know how to use the nether!"

"I know that, you fool." She tossed aside her wheel. "I'll just do as the old ones did and use my bare hands."

Ked looked as though he might vomit. Cord rolled her neck, cracking it, and did some toe-touches.

"Er," Blays said. "Are you really planning to kill her?"

"It'll be fine," Dante said.

The spectators cleared a wide ring around them. The whiskered old man moved to its middle.

"This mortal duel will settle all matters between the two opponents. Understood?" He waited for Dante, Ked, and Cord to nod. "Then fight with the grace of the gods."

He scampered back. Cord bounced on the balls of her feet and sprinted toward Dante. Dante called the shadows to him. Before he had a plan, she was leaping for him. He dived to the side, landing on the setts and doing his best to remember Blays' lessons about how to fall without hurting yourself. He got to his feet and ran back, palms and knees stinging.

"Running isn't fighting!" Cord yelled. She popped to her feet and charged again.

Dante plunged his mind into the stones before her. He took hold of the nether within a rectangular swath and softened the material to mud. Cord plunged into it, falling to the knees. As she bellowed oaths of surprise, Dante hardened the mud back into rock, catching her fast.

"Hey!" She grabbed her right thigh and pulled. Her leg didn't budge. "What low-down treachery is this?"

"I win," Dante said. "I've killed you."

Cord formed an O with her mouth. Then began to laugh. "No you haven't! Could a dead woman do this?" She produced two fists and extended the middle finger of both.

"You can't get out, can you? So you have two choices. One, we call it a draw, I let you free, and we all go our separate ways. Or two...I leave you here until the sun kills you. And I win."

"What's the matter? Don't have the heart for killing?"

"Trust me, he's got the heart," Blays said. "Along with the liver, kidneys, lungs, spleen, and gonads. If you can believe it, this is him being *merciful*."

"Mercy." Cord spat in the dust. She strained her legs again, then relaxed, considering Dante. "You're Mallish, aren't you?"

"By birth," Dante said. "I haven't lived there in years."

"Then I choose to stay right here. I'll have been killed by one of the Mallish. The highest honor I can receive."

"You can't be serious!"

She wrinkled her brow. "This is what I've always wanted. It's the honorable thing to do."

Dante sighed heavily. "Fine then. Glad to have given you your fondest dream."

He turned and walked away.

"Wait!" Ked called. He jogged behind Dante, slowing to a halt, his face anguished. "You can't just leave her."

"Really? Because everyone here seems intent on forcing me to do just that."

"Let her go. Please."

Dante crossed his arms. "And it's settled between us?"

Ked bobbed his head. "I concede. Victory's yours."

"No it's not!" Cord grabbed her thigh, pulling mightily. "Come a little closer and I'll show you how much life I've got left in me."

The old man tugged the whiskers on one cheek. "He's conceded, Cord. Duel's over."

Hearing the official pronouncement, Dante returned to the nether in the stone holding Cord fast. To give them a bit of a show, he snapped his fingers, shifting the rock into mud. She fell forward with a grimy splash.

Gesturing to Naran and Blays, Dante walked toward the nearest road out of the square. He had no idea where he was going, but he knew quite firmly that he wanted to get away. Black stone buildings looked down on him.

"We got out of that without killing anyone," Blays said. "A modern miracle!"

Dante shook his head. "I've never had someone work so hard to make me kill them."

"Except Cassinder."

"Well yeah. But he deserved it."

"Despite the relatively happy turn of events, I think you should treat this as a lesson. When we're traveling someplace unfamiliar, it's probably not a great idea to dive into a situation knowing nothing of local culture."

"Ked was dying," Dante said. "How was I to know he'd take getting healed as a mortal insult?"

"If our travels have taught me nothing else, it's that the entire world is insane. There's probably somewhere out there where they'd sock you in the jaw for handing them a sack of pure gold."

"Ah," Naran said. "So you've been to the Belbring Islands?"

Dante swerved around a puddle of wet blood whose owner had probably been all too happy to shed it. "Play it careful from here on out. We're here to capture the shells and find out what we can about Gladdic. We can't afford to get dragged into local conflicts."

By universal agreement, their first order of business was to find an inn where they could wash off the grime of travel and catch up on local gossip. Though the city's blocky, flat-roofed brick and basalt structures looked unfriendly, they soon located a rollicking pub surrounded by stables with lodging upstairs.

After a quick bath each, the three of them returned downstairs to scare up information. At the moment, most of the building's activity was concentrated under the roofed-in patios, leaving the common room relatively quiet.

They ordered a meal of what turned out to be noodles jumbled with bits of goat and asparagus. After, Dante flagged down their server.

"I'm looking for your best library," he said. "Public or private."

The man stacked their sturdy earthenware plates. "What is it you're looking for?"

"History and theology."

"I'm not much for reading. But I'll ask Bree. She's got a nose for books." The man headed off with their plates. He came back five minutes later. "Bree says there's no doubt about it. You'll want the Reborn Shrine."

He provided directions. Dante tipped him from their dwindling supply of coins. The man trundled off.

Dante turned to the others. "No sense wasting time. I'm going to the shrine."

"We'll look into the shaden," Naran said. "What if we need to find you?"

"No worries on that front," Blays laughed. "He's got new lore to track down. He'll be in that shrine so long they'll have to start charging him rent."

Blays and Naran went to the bar to order drinks and circulate through the patios. Dante headed outside. It was malevolently hot, but the elevated butte had a good breeze going for it, blowing steadily out of the southwest. It was probably brutally windy in the fall and winter. Which explained why most of the windows were on the northeast sides of the buildings.

In the streets, the people were your average spectrum of city folk, with a large number of farmers mixed in—"earthers," they seemed to be called—as well as soldierly-looking people with ribbons tied around their elbows. Dante continued to draw stares, but most weren't overtly hostile.

He made the final turn to the shrine and stopped in his tracks. Ahead, open ground surrounded a complex of stone structures. Some were partially or wholly demolished, but there was no mistaking their religious nature.

As to *what* religion...Dante had no idea. In Mallon, the churches tended to be baroque, full of statues and buttresses that seemed to be less about buttressing and more about impressing. In Narashtovik, the cathedrals were angular and severe, though no less tall. By contrast, the central building of the Reborn Shrine was bell-shaped, its peak eighty feet high. Rather than being composed of a single type of stone—basalt would have been the natural choice, given its prevalence in the basin—it was patchwork, a harlequin blend of basalt, sandstone, limestone, and at least three different types of granite. Some pieces glittered in the sun while others drank in all light. Even the dome was split between gray, yellow, and a white rock shot through with bright flecks of silver.

As Dante stood gawking, a robed figure emerged from a small domed tower beside the main structure and strolled over to him. The monk was young, his blond hair cut so close to his scalp it glowed like a fuzzy halo.

"Are you a visitor to the Reborn Shrine?" As the monk spoke, his gaze flicked over Dante's black hair and gray eyes, but his voice was timid, clean of any hostility.

"I am," Dante said. "I came to use your library. But this building, it's...stunning."

The monk turned, glancing at the main temple as if just noticing it. "Ah, yes. It's the pride of the city."

"I've never seen anything like it. Why go to the trouble of using so many different kinds of stone?"

"Ah. The different stones. You see, in one sense, what you're looking at isn't a single shrine, but many. Each time the Mallish invade, they destroy the shrine. And each time we rebuild it, we use a different kind of stone. This way, Mallon's crimes are visible at a glance. After the twelfth cycle of destruction and rebirth, Arawn himself will step forth from the doors of the Reborn Shrine to lay waste to Mallon." The young monk looked at him from the corners of his eyes, blushing. "Or so it's said."

"So it's been destroyed ten times already?"

"Did you count the varieties of stone?"

Dante pointed to the shrine's entrance. Above the doors, a stylized sailing vessel was carved into a chunk of pure white stone.

"That's Phannon," he said. "The earthly waters. Eleventh sign of the Celeset. I assume the count started with Arawn?"

"A nice deduction. Ten times this place has been torn down. And ten times it's been rebuilt. The most recent reconstruction followed the Third Scour."

"It hasn't been harmed in the last century?"

The monk allowed himself a tentative smile. "Much longer than average. Maybe the Mallish are afraid to fulfill the prophecy." He beckoned toward the main building. "Would you like to see the inside?"

"Very much so." Dante fell in beside him.

The monk cleared his throat. "Ah. You said you were here for the library?"

"That's right. I'm a monk myself. Devotee of Carvahal. I've traveled from Gallador in search of certain knowledge. Have you ever heard of something called a Star-Eater?"

The monk shook his head.

Dante laughed modestly. "I know so little about my subject that I'm not sure if I'm even looking for information on Star-Eaters. More broadly, I'm looking for knowledge about... demons. Or perhaps people who can become demons."

The monk reached the massive doors and opened one with nary a squeak. "That sounds horrifying."

Dante loaded his voice with portent. "It's thought that these demons are heavily connected to the nether. Possibly to Arawn himself."

The other man closed the door. They stood in an airy entry. The floor was paved with black marble and green granite.

"I'm sorry," the monk said. "But we won't have anything about Arawn here. Nether, either."

Dante blinked. "I was told you have the best theological library in the Collen Basin."

"And, with all modesty, that is true."

"I thought Collen has held to the old ways. That you believed, as we do in Gallador, that Arawn remains one of the twelve gods of the Celeset."

"Ah," the young man said. "But the Mallish don't. And they like to hang those who do. Owning or writing a blasphemous book is written proof of your own heresy. You see?"

"Whereas it isn't so easy to convict someone who confines their beliefs to the space between their ears."

"Just so."

Dante flapped his shirt to dry the sweat he'd accumulated during his walk. The room smelled of stone, dust, and charred gannon seed. "In that case, what can *you* tell me of what I wish to know?"

"I know nothing about any of that."

"What about your brothers and sisters?"

"I can ask. Starting tomorrow morning. Would you like to return then?"

"No," Dante said slowly. He wasn't sure why he wanted to stay. Stubbornness played a role, certainly, but it probably had more to do with the fact he was within spitting distance of a library he'd never seen before. "If I could, I'd like to see your collection."

The young man nodded and led him deep through the building, stopping at last inside a yawning round room sixty feet high. The ceiling was painted with the twelve constellations of the Celeset. Beneath it, a ring of glass windows shed light on five floors of bookshelves. The air smelled like leather and parchment, slightly musty, but in better care than most libraries he'd been to.

"This is a hell of a place!" Dante's voice echoed more loudly than he'd intended.

The young monk suppressed a smile. "We believe truth must always be available for those ready to receive it. Our rules are simple: no damage may be done to the books, and none may leave this room. Otherwise, I'll help you find anything you want. My name is Hodd."

Hodd had claimed to know nothing about Star-Eaters or nether-bearing demons, so Dante asked for any books of local lore on monsters, the more outlandish the better—but restricted to the more respectable authors. Hodd nodded and disappeared into the stacks. He returned shortly with a dozen books.

All who lived had a vice of some kind. Some men became slaves to whiskey or wine. Others became bound to plants that blunted the sharp edges of the world. For Dante, his vice was knowledge. As he paged through the volumes, hunting for any hint of man-shaped monsters with starry eyes, he often found himself caught up in stories and history, as hooked as firmly as a halibut in the bay of Narashtovik.

He tore himself away as best he could, skimming along. He'd

brought his own writing materials, but found himself with precious few notes to make. The sun sank behind the western hills. A second monk passed through the stacks, lighting lanterns as she went. Most of the other patrons handed her a coin or two as she went by. Dante was tempted to act ignorant—he didn't like to spend money even when he wasn't on the brink of utter poverty—but, wishing to stay in their good graces, gave her one of his few pennies.

After hours of work, he still hadn't found anything close to what he'd seen in Gladdic's temple. Hodd brought him more books, then departed for dinner and evening devotions. Dante read on.

The ten o'clock bells rang. Squeezing his temples, Dante sat back. Most of the stories he'd been reading felt more like fiction than fact. Then again, he was specifically looking for the more far-out tales. Maybe he was approaching this from the wrong angle. What if he focused on books purporting to be practical histories? Any mentions of Star-Eater-like beings in those would carry far more weight. The chief problem with that idea was that such mentions would be far fewer, but at the very worst, it would teach him real history. If he built a foundation of knowledge, he might be better equipped to home in on the areas of history most likely to provide him with the answers he sought.

With Hodd warning him the library would close at midnight, Dante asked for a new batch of books focusing on the more tumultuous periods of Collen's history, especially accounts of its most renowned sorcerers. The young monk obliged. Dante dived in, flipping pages as quickly as he could glean the gist of their contents. An hour later, a stack of discarded books stood at the side of his desk.

But a venerable tome opened before him. *An Account of the First War of Mallon and Collen*, by the historian Flinders. Dante tried to skim through it, but soon found himself absorbed in its records.

According to the author, nine hundred years ago, a much smaller Mallon had been good friends with an equally modest Collen Basin. Collen had traded wheat from its fields, wine from its vineyards, and spices from the lands to its southeast in exchange for Mallish lumber, iron, dyes, and coffee brought in from its port. The two regions had been close enough that marriages were common between their merchants and aristocracy. To hear Flinders tell it, it felt inevitable that, in time, the two regions would become one.

For some time, Collen had been feuding with the then-kingdom of Almers, on the coast to their south. To put an end to the conflict, Collen secured a trade arrangement with Almers, sending grain and Mallish steel in exchange for Almerian pottery and dye.

That spring, the rains never came. As the wheat struggled to grow, blight struck the fields, worse than any locusts. In desperation, Collenese sorcerers turned to the nether to regrow their dying fields.

But the shadows only made the blight worse. Entire prairies turned brown, dust swirling through the sky. Within the year, the entire basin was on the brink of starvation.

As Mallish goods continued to flow into Collen, Collenese debt rose. They couldn't return the goods to Mallon without breaking their pact with Almers, which would almost certainly renew the war. Instead, they continued to trade with Almers, banking on the goodwill of their Mallish friends.

It might have worked. But Collen's merchants weren't the only ones in dire straits. Starving commoners trampled through Mallish lands, plundering the fields, robbing honest farmers. Collen's nobility tried to recall their outlaws, but it was no use.

By year's end, Mallon had declared war. Since then, the conflict had never truly ended.

Dante was in the middle of his notes on the subject when Hodd came through to inform him the shrine was closing for the night. With permission, Dante marked his spot in the *Account* and stood, limbs stiff.

"Thank you," he said. "What time does the library reopen?"

"Seven in the morning," Hodd said. "You, ah, are very enthused to learn."

The streets were much quieter on the way back. The temperature had dropped twenty degrees and the smell of dew hung on the air. Men and women argued behind shutters that were closed despite the chance for them to cool down their houses. A sense of uneasiness lay on the city. Worry about the Mallish? Or Dante's own anxiety over being in a strange city reflecting back on him?

He found his way to the inn. Blays and Naran were downstairs chatting with a table of weatherbeaten farmers. Blays gave Dante a small nod and shifted his eyes upstairs. Dante nodded back and headed up to their room. Blays and Naran showed up after an interval of time sufficient to have consumed another beer.

"Well?" Blays said. "What'd you find?"

Sitting on his straw mattress, Dante leaned his elbows on his knees. "Nothing."

"What do you mean, nothing? You've been gone for eight hours!"

"Not finding something takes much longer than finding it. I went to the library of the Reborn Shrine, but they claimed they don't have any books concerning Arawn or the nether."

Blays cocked a brow. "Claimed?"

"I think they suspect I'm a spy from the Mallish priesthood. Here to ferret out heresy."

"It's possible they think that," Naran said. "Or it may be that after hundreds of years of Mallish attacks, they've learned better than to make any of their beliefs available to the public."

Dante sighed. "Either way, I'm going back tomorrow. If they've spent this long hiding their beliefs from the Mallish, they may have found ways to express secrets in plain sight."

Blays unlaced his boots, tossing them aside. "Well, you have fun with that. Naran and I will continue to drink beer and chat up the locals. Grueling work, but we're dedicated to the cause."

"Actually, I did get one piece of info. Many many years ago, it seems that the Colleners were harvesting their fields."

Blays stared blankly. "As opposed to what? Declaring their vegetables had worked so hard to grow that it would be cruel to eat them?"

"Not harvesting. *Harvesting*. Growing them with the nether. Like they do in the Plagued Islands."

"And?"

"And," Dante said slowly, "it's very odd to find that same long-lost skill here. During roughly the same time period as the first Harvesters arrived in the islands. It could be related. Even if it isn't, it hints at the idea that, a thousand years ago, the world was far more sophisticated than we think. The more we travel, the more we hear the echoes of that time."

"Fascinating," Blays yawned. "We didn't make much more progress than you did, but the smart money is that if the shaden are still here, they'll be found in the company of Mallish soldiers. We'll start looking around for troops tomorrow."

"Sounds smart. Just be careful."

"Yes, that's the standard operating procedure when dealing with companies of soldiers. Speaking of, that riot in the plaza today? As far as we can gather, it wasn't caused by anything."

"Except by definition."

Naran went to the window to eye the streets. "What he means is there was no provocation. Nothing, at least, beyond the presence of Mallish soldiers in Collen."

"Right," Blays said. "It feels like this whole place could catch fire at any moment. For once, let's try not to be the ones who light the spark, eh?"

Dante collapsed into bed. It had been an extremely long day, but he forced himself to get up as early in the morning as he could bear. He trudged back to the shrine. Hodd wasn't in, but another monk brought around the books Dante requested. This time, rather than hewing to a single topic of study, he cast a wide net, hoping to dredge up something unexpected from the depths.

By noon, he'd accumulated nothing more than an empty stomach. Outside the shrine, the monks had a stall where they sold the excess food they made each day. Dante made use of it, eating dumplings stuffed with spiced potatoes and soft, sweet cheese. They were markedly similar to the ones people ate in Narashtovik. Then again, everywhere you went had a dumpling of *some* kind.

He got back to work in the library. There were times when his research was so numbing he flipped through entire works with no recollection of their subject. With the afternoon rambling on as endlessly as the stacks themselves, footsteps whispered down the strip of carpet running along the shelves of books. As they neared, Dante glanced up.

Blays stood over him, smiling widely. "Uncovering any ancient secrets of existence and the universe?"

Dante gestured helplessly at the tome in front of him. "I thought this one would have references to the Star-Eaters, but it's as useless as they all are."

"Good." Blays flipped the book shut with a musty whomp. "Because we've found the shaden. Let's move."

7

For most people in the Order, extraction was the worst part of any job. You'd gotten in safe. You had the loot in hand. But one wrong turn into the servant's quarters, or a stumble in the dark against a table, and it could all come crashing down on your head.

For Raxa, it was the easiest thing in the world.

She belted on the sword, blew out her candle, and slipped into the shadows. The room had been almost pure dark, lit only by the moonlight that managed to slip through the curtains. The shadowlands were far brighter — the room was utterly coated in nether, all of which glowed silver. Raxa used to find it spooky. Now, it was a comfort.

She walked through the wall into the hallway. Empty. So was the stairwell. She descended, forcing herself not to run. Near the bottom, a candle wavered; a servant was on his way up, dressed in a gray smock with a white tree on the chest. Raxa pressed herself to the wall and let him pass.

On the ground floor, the same voices that had been arguing on her way in were still at it. She strode to the basement door, which was closed, and passed through the stone wall around it. The basement was silent. Down in the dungeons, a man was moaning from his cell, but she didn't break stride.

She stopped halfway down the hall. Which cell had she come in through? Should have marked it somehow. The dungeons weren't on her map—their inside man hadn't expected her to be down here.

She was already growing short on time. Staying in the shadows was like standing on a roof and holding onto a rope slung over the side of the building. The longer you were there, the more people kept climbing up it. At first, it was easy to hang on tight, but the more climbers who piled onto the rope, the more you started to strain.

She had a few minutes left before she was going to have to let go. But her shoes were definitely starting to skid toward the lip of the roof.

She ducked into a cell, then tried its far wall, casting around for the tunnel back to the body locker. Nothing but solid rock. She returned to the passage and tried the next cell down. A man slept inside. She backed out and tried the next. This time, she popped through the wall and into a smooth, empty tunnel.

"About time," she muttered. Nerves fluttering, she returned to the disappointment that was reality.

The tunnel was as black as a whale's gut. Knowing the floor was empty, she walked forward blind, holding her stolen sword out before her. The smell of the dead grew stronger. Soon, the tunnel spilled her into the workings of the body locker.

She belted her sword. A lantern glowed to her left. The rustle of a turning page sounded from the entry. Raxa snuck up to the edge of the foyer, then popped into the shadows. She sprinted across the entry and into the night.

Halfway to the shelter of a towering elm, she lost her hold on the rope holding her to the nether. She was expelled with a jolt, her skin prickling painfully. She'd spent too long inside.

But her work wasn't quite done. By rule, anything you grabbed while on a job for the Order became the Order's property. If you picked up something beyond what the Order had been expecting—a second set of jewelry, say—you had the right to purchase it from them at fair price.

The sword, though? The sword was priceless. Even if they assigned a price to it, it'd cost more than she could steal in a thousand years.

She strode across the field and into the city. She was due at the Marrigan within a few hours, but she had to get home first. And she had to do it with no shadow-juice left and thirty pounds of the most valuable artifacts in the city on her back.

Good thing she was the best.

The outer neighborhoods were quiet. A few people on stoops enjoying the cool summer evening. This was a poor part of town, but a good one. Fishermen. Sailors. Honest workers. Her neighborhood and those around it were rats' nests. If she circled around to come in through the east, though, she'd only have to travel through a few blocks of deep trouble before she got home.

She cut to the southeast, walking briskly. After a detour around the heavily patrolled Heirs' District, she traveled through four miles of sleepy row houses. She drew a few calls from drunken men, but it was the dead wrong time for her to engage. None of them followed her further than half a block.

In time, she came to the border of her neighborhood, affectionately referred to as the Dumps. She entered on Hallivan Street, cutting quickly to Loggidan, a stretch of dirt road fronted on both sides by longshoremen. Rough customers, but generally not the type to be trawling for trouble.

Someone whistled behind her, the noise shrieking through the night. Raxa neither slowed nor sped up. The whistle repeated. Footsteps. At least three pairs.

"Hey, girl!" Someone laughed raspily. "Hey, *girl!*"

No point trying to threaten them. Men like that never took you seriously. Not even when the moon gleamed on the blade of your knife. Most times, she'd have run—she knew the Dumps as well as anyone—but burdened by her pack, there was no way she could outpace them.

And there was no way she was dumping it, either.

A rock clattered behind her. She spun, walking backwards. Three silhouettes followed her.

"Walk off," she said. "You don't want this."

"Come closer and let's find out," the raspy man called.

"You keep following me and people will die."

"Oh, only if you try to get cute."

Raxa swore silently. She couldn't run. Couldn't escape through the shadows—they were done with her for the day.

They were too close for her to hide. She was blocks away from her building. Even if she made it there before they caught up to —

A man emerged from the alley ahead of her. He was nearly as tall as a norren. A short blade hung from his side.

He gestured down the street. "These men bothering you?"

For a moment, relief shot through her veins. Throw him to the attackers and make a break for it. Then she saw the smile on his face.

"Get the fuck out of my way," she said.

The footsteps advanced behind her. The new man gaped. "Ugly language from such a pretty girl! I'm only here to help—"

She drew the sword. It felt as light as the bamboo chairs Gaits had imported from Gallador. Still smiling, the man drew his blade. It was much shorter than hers, the type of dagger favored by those who needed a weapon that was serious yet concealable, but he didn't seem concerned in the slightest about her reach advantage.

Probably because the other three men were now just twenty feet away. Raxa moved to the face of the nearest row house. The four men fanned out across from her. Everyone except the raspy-voiced man now bore a dagger. The tall man tapped his against his thigh.

"This doesn't have to hurt," the raspy man said. In the gloom of the street, she could make out nothing more than his eyes and teeth. "Put down that silly sword and turn around."

She pointed at them with her sword. "You four are friends?"

He laughed throatily. "The best of them. And friends share."

"If you're that close, then it's time to tell each other goodbye."

His cheek twitched. He drew his blade and stepped toward her. "Bad news. It *does* have to hurt."

She shrugged off her pack. It hit the ground with a jumbled, metallic clank. The man took another step forward, putting himself within range. Raxa slashed at him, the blade horizontal to the street. With fluid skill, the man pivoted on his heels, tucking back his hips as he extended the dagger to deflect the blow.

The bone sword clicked into his blade. Steel twinkled as it fell to the dirt. She barely felt the impact. Her sword carried straight into his side. Passed through ribs. Guts. He was still holding the hilt of the dagger and the two inches of steel that remained attached to it and he was looking down at this with the befuddlement Raxa associated with children understanding they've just broken their favorite toy.

The sword wasn't done. It kept passing through, as if she were swiping it through empty air. As if it hungered to cut as deeply as it could. It exited the other side of his body.

The tall man was stabbing at her overhand. She whipped her sword in a backhand. It cut through his forearm with a gritty click of bone. His hand and a sizable portion of his lower arm spun away. His elbow continued swinging forward, spraying her face with hot blood.

As the severed limb thumped to the street, the raspy man slid in half. His upper half struck the ground. He gawked as his lower half toppled beside him.

Everyone was screaming. The tall man clutched his stump. The two unwounded men turned and dashed away as fast as they could.

Raxa picked up her pack and ran.

"I have no words." Gaits stared down at the table. Jewels glittered like stars. And almost as numerous. "Correction: I have words. But compared to this, they're so cheap and mean I don't dare utter them for fear I'll tarnish your treasure."

"The sight of money always makes you so eloquent," Raxa said.

"How did you *do* this?"

"Same way I always do."

"How did you even get in? It's like you can walk through walls!"

She maintained a straight face. "Look like you belong, and you can go anywhere."

He rubbed his jaw, pacing around the table like a stalking cat. "We're rich. *So* rich. Did you pick up anything else?"

"What? A fortune isn't enough for you?"

"This is true. There probably wasn't anything left to steal."

She leaned back in her chair, letting out a long, quiet breath.

"So when do we get paid?"

"Don't tell me you've spent the last score already."

"I just earned the Order enough money to buy a new building. Is it crazy to want to know when I get my cut?"

"The Jerrelec Collection is far too famous to sell here. We'll have to fence it in Dollendun. Maybe even Setteven. It'll take weeks. You let me know if you run short before then."

"Weeks, huh?"

He leaned back, lacing his fingers behind his head. "Don't worry, I've got plenty of other ways to fill your time. Interested in another job?"

"Are you joking?"

A grin pooled across Gaits' face. "Not in the slightest."

In its way, his plan was even crazier than robbing the Sealed Citadel. Seven houses in seven nights. Some of the biggest names in the city. Gaits had already lined people up for four of the jobs. The other three? All Raxa's.

She had two days before the first. She badly wanted to get good and drunk, but that could wait until her personal work was done.

Back home, she collapsed into bed. As soon as she got up, she went downstairs for a cup of tea. Ready to face the world, she went back to her room, reached inside the chimney, and retrieved a long, cloth-covered bundle. She sat on the bed, laying the sheathed sword across her knees. The sapphire on the scabbard winked up at her.

She faced the same basic problem with the sword that the Order had in fencing the Jerrelec Collection: the scabbard was way too obtrusive. She'd never be able to wear it around town without someone recognizing it. Or at the very least, recognizing it was too expensive for the likes of *her*. Couldn't carry it around unsheathed, either. Its white length was even more recognizable than the scabbard. She could dye it, but she wasn't sure that would be enough. Besides, if she turned around too fast and the blade flung wide, she could chop someone in half.

She owned the sword, but she didn't dare use it. And what was the point of a magic sword if you couldn't use it?

But she did have money. The whole point of money was to

solve problems. Could always bribe a smith to keep quiet, but the flaw in bribing someone was that you'd just proved they were dishonest.

What she needed was a copy. One she could make herself. She was no smith, but she had an idea.

She dropped by the Marrigan. Joldy was holding down the bar. Raxa asked and discovered that Vladd was out back. She found him hucking knives at a battered wood target.

"Vladd," she said. "How can I make a mold of a sword?"

He turned, the tip of a throwing knife pinched between his thumb and forefinger. "Why'd you want to do that?"

"To duplicate it."

"You could pack it in clay easy enough. Make sure and oil the blade down good so's it won't stick. Dry the clay and fire it, then cast the sword. Don't think it'll be too pretty nor too strong, but if looks is all you care for, it'll match."

Raxa headed to the masons' district for the clay, brought it home, and followed Vladd's advice, including a generous slather of oil. She gave the mold time to harden, then withdrew the sword as gently as she could, somehow managing to extract it without slicing open the hardened clay.

She took the mold to a smith in the Sharps, paying extra to have it done that same day. Like Vladd had promised, the work was far from pretty, weird swirls and specks marring the dull metal. A flat tang extended from the blade's base. Benner, the smith, had added that without being asked.

Raxa pinched her upper lip. "Can you make me a scabbard for this?"

The smith sniffed. "I ain't even polished it yet."

"You don't have to worry about that. Just get me a scabbard. Nothing fancy. Got it?"

Benner gave her a long look, then shrugged. "It's your money."

"Make sure it's steel. The strongest you've got."

"For the *scabbard*?"

"Like you said, it's my money."

After seeing the color of her coin, he promised he'd have it ready in three days. Not in time for her first job, but that turned out to be a total cakewalk: the Faddegans, the target, were hosting a midsummer ball. All Raxa had to do was bribe her way past the staff—several of whom had been brought on for the occasion, and had no loyalty to the family—then slip upstairs, grab the collection, and dash out by way of the shadows. The whole thing took less than an hour.

The haul was pennies compared to what she'd nicked from the Citadel, but it was still going to make for some fat pockets. And she'd have her cut in days, not weeks.

Late the next morning, she wandered past the Pridegate. Herrick was out in his yard hammering scraps of lumber into something that might pass for furniture. Seeing her, he laid down his hammer and picked up his shirt to swab off the sweat.

"Raxa," he muttered. "Come to make sure I'm playing nice?"

She stared at him. "Are you?"

"I been working him hard." He tossed down his shirt. "But I ain't touched him. And the good news is he *has* been workin.'"

"Is he around?"

Herrick stuck his fingers in his mouth and whistled. Footsteps padded from around the side of the house. Fedd was as shaggy-haired as ever, but the dark bruise around his eye had faded completely.

He grinned up at Raxa. "Whadja bring me?"

"My love. How's it going?"

The boy shrugged. Like his foster father, he was shirtless, and though he was filthy, it looked like the grime of honest labor.

"Okay," he said. "Dad's showing me how to build chairs and stuff. It's pretty neat."

At his use of the word "dad," Herrick abruptly turned away. He reached for his shirt again, dabbing his eyes and brows for several seconds. Raxa chatted with Fedd until Herrick cleared his throat and turned back around.

She winked at Herrick. "Keep up the good work."

From there, she returned to Benner, her smith in the Sharps. He was in the back banging away on something metal. She was afraid he was still going at her sheath, but when she called to him, he came out carrying a curved black scabbard.

"Leather wraps," he said warily. "When most people go metal, they want to show it off, but you made it sound like you wanted it as plain as Aunt Janne's thumb. But don't you worry. There's hard steel underneath."

She smiled and took the sheath. It felt solid. Weighty. Smelled like fresh steel and leather. Good things.

"You made the right call." She unhitched her belt and fed it through the two hoops attached to the scabbard. "This is perfect."

"There's just one problem."

Raxa kept her expression neutral. "What's that?"

"You ain't got any grip on your blade!" He laughed. "Want me to take care of that, too?"

She exhaled. "Appreciate it. But I've got something else in mind for that."

He brought her the copy of the sword. It inserted smoothly into the sheath, the tang sticking out like a fractured bone. She settled her accounts, including a tip that was generous, but not so far out there that he'd get suspicious. Heading home, she did her best not to run.

Inside her room, she bolted the door and went to the fireplace. A piece of her was certain the sword would be gone, but it was right where she'd left it. She pulled the copy from her new scabbard, removed the bone sword from its case, then eased it into the new sheath as gently as if she were lifting a man's purse or deflowering her true love.

The crossguard clicked into place. The fit was perfect. She drew the sword back out as carefully as she'd inserted it, then brought the scabbard to the window and inspected it. No sign of damage. She sheathed and unsheathed the sword a few times in a row. The scabbard held.

She was tempted to the roots of her being to carry the sword outside with her then and there. To never go without it again. Problem was, she ran with an entire tribe who made their living through light fingers and sharp eyes. Sooner or later, someone would notice.

Missions only, then. When she'd be alone and exposed. Besides, it wasn't just the risk of being seen by the wrong person that made carrying such a sword dangerous to the owner. With a weapon like that, you'd start to think you were invincible. The instant you began to believe you were beyond harm was the instant you signed your death warrant.

Her next job was Rolligen House. She took the sword, but the grab was even easier than Faddegan Manor.

"This is too easy," Gaits said on her return, standing over the loot like a man who'd bet everything on the turn of the dice and rolled kingsies. "Why weren't we doing this years ago?"

"You tell me," Raxa said. "How have the others been going?"

"Selly landed himself in the clink trying to take down the Jeddelics."

"I could have told you that would happen the second you told me it was Selly."

"Yes, well we can't give *all* the jobs to you. We have a guild to run here."

"So what's going to happen to him?"

Gaits tried on one of the sapphire rings she'd brought back. "Generally speaking, the process is that he'll be kicked around until the authorities' feet grow tired, after which he'll be dumped into a cell and largely forgotten until he dies, or they need room for a more recent criminal."

"We're not going to spring him?"

"That's not in the interests of the guild. If something went wrong in the attempt, it would implicate the entire Order of the Alley. You know this."

"Sure do," Raxa said. "But I figured we're so damn rich now that we could spend a little more to look after our people."

Gaits smiled crookedly. "Don't worry. I'm sure we'd do whatever it takes for *you*."

At her final job, they'd tripled their guards. Word was already getting around. Didn't matter. As long as rich people kept living in stone houses, she'd always be able to walk through their walls.

But they had a guard in the strongroom, too. Still in the shadows, Raxa stared at the silvery curve of his neck. All she'd have to do was become real for a split second. Jerk her sword through his neck. So far, though, they'd kept the latest string non-violent. Any murders, even of the help, could stir the heavy hand of the

Citadel. She hit the bedrooms instead, grabbing whatever was obvious and getting out before her hold on the rope connecting her to the netherworld pulled her back into the open.

Word came down from on high. Except for ongoing jobs and maintaining territory, the entire Order was on furlough for the next few weeks. They'd just thrown eight stones directly into the hornet's nest. It was time to let the buzzing die down lest someone get stung.

Fine by Raxa. She'd done her job.

The soldiers were everywhere. Garbed in the black of the Citadel, the White Tree of Barden blazing from their chests. They stood outside the manors. They marched through the Sharps. They came by the Marrigan, where they interviewed Gaits, Gaits' counterparts Anya and Ackley, and then—in a move that had the building gossiping for days—the soldiers went to see the bossman: Kerreven.

Word was they threatened to haul him bodily from the Marrigan. His response—again, according to rumor—was that if they wanted to search the building, they could do so. And if they didn't turn up any of the missing goods, he'd go on to search their bodies, one organ at a time, as he removed them from their bodies.

Time played on. The days got hotter. Raxa wanted to spend more time out, but she felt safer at home with her sword. Then, word from Gaits. He needed to see her at once.

Leaving her sword in the chimney, she walked swiftly toward the Marrigan. There, two bulky men escorted her upstairs to Gaits' offices. He was waiting outside.

"Raxa," he said, bowing his head. "What I'm about to show you is going to change your life. But I want you to make you a promise: you won't let it change you."

"Something wrong, Gaits? You talk like you're about to toss me out on my ear."

"Far from it," he said. "It's the Citadel heist. It's been fenced."

He swept the fabric from the table. Gems and metal shimmered in the candlelight. Necklaces. Rings. Stacks of coins. And —even looking right at them, she couldn't believe it—three bricks of silver the size of her forearm.

"Careful with those." Gaits grinned toothily. "They don't look so big, but they weigh half as much as you do."

She stared in something like awe. Forget *like* awe. She stared with the awe the gods must have felt when they'd forged the stars.

She gestured timidly, as if afraid that stirring the breeze would blow the gems and silver blocks away. "How much is this?"

"More than you could spend if you lived to be nine hundred."

"I don't know. I could get used to this."

"Forgive the pointiness of my nose," Gaits said. "But do you have any thoughts as to what you're going to do with it?"

"Be rich?"

"I'm serious. Are you going to leave it here? In the Strongbox?"

"Do you have a better idea?"

He wandered from behind the desk, circling around the shining bars set out on the table. "What've you got in front of you? Coins? Jewelry? Ingots? If I take one of these pretty silver bars out of here, whose is it then?"

She set her hand beside the dragon's hoard. "Mine."

"How are you going to prove that?"

"Because you keep records of everything you pay us."

"I could say you were paying your debt," he said. "Or I could take it to the nearest smith and have it melted into strips. At that point, it could have come from anywhere. Same with the jewelry. Sure, you could make records of it, leave them with the Hall. But gems can be recut. No one in Yallen cares who owned a ring taken from Narashtovik. Hell, that's how we make half our money."

"Do you have a point somewhere in all those words?"

"My point, Raxa, is that everything you've taken for yourself in the last month can be taken away from you just as easily. When you had little, there was no point keeping it safe. But now that you have a fortune? You need to get a hell of a lot smarter. Before some sly young thing grabs it out from under you."

He was right. That didn't stop her from being annoyed. "What do you suggest?"

He looked her in the eye. "Buy a house. Better yet, buy land. As much as you can afford."

"Land."

"There's a reason it's called *real* estate. The only ones who can take land away from you are your debtors—or Galand himself."

She ran her finger over the cool silver. Strange that an ounce of metal could buy an acre of land. Good thing, though, because she was very good at stealing pieces of metal. And if she had a house—better yet, houses—then the kids she plucked from winter's door would never have to worry about being turned out into the street again.

"Two conditions," she said. "First, I need someone you trust. Someone who's used to working with our kind."

"Agreed. And the second?"

"When the time comes? You help me carry this stuff downstairs."

"So." Gaits leaned out the open shutters, facing the wind blowing in from the bay a half mile to the north. "Does *this* one meet your standards?"

Keller turned enough to watch her without looking directly at her. He was Gaits' contact in this realm. According to Gaits, they'd done dozens of deals together—the Order, as it turned out, was involved in a surprising amount of legitimate business. Nobody had ever told her. Because she'd been uninterested? Or had she been too small-time to be worth showing?

Gaits' voice carried an edge. They'd been traipsing around town for three days. The first plot they'd taken her to had been three blocks from the Marrigan. Convenient, and stately enough, but it had only had three rooms that could serve as bedrooms.

When she'd mentioned this drawback, Keller had raised an eyebrow. "How many of you will be occupying the home?"

"For now?" she'd said. "Just me. But I plan on having a big family."

After that, the fixer had tried her with several places outside the Pridegate, where many homes remained empty. Hence big and cheap. But she'd eventually decided it was too far from the city's heart. She was looking for a home, not a country manor.

Next had come a string of houses in quieter sections inside the Pridegate. They were all fine, but they blended together. Didn't grab her. Nothing that felt like the place she'd spend her next forty years. Finally, in desperation, Keller had brought her here. He'd warned her how much the property would set her back. That she'd need to dress better to blend in with the neighborhood. That she might not feel at home.

Then she'd seen the rooms. And the bathtub. And the view of the bay that stretched away to the north forever, reminding her how vast the world was and how there was always somewhere else you could go.

She stared out at the ocean and she smiled. "I'll take it."

The next few days were among the worst of her life. It turned out it was incredibly difficult to give someone vast sums of money for a hunk of land they no longer wanted. The titles. Interviews. Barristers. By the end of it, she was starting to think the nomads had the right idea.

As Keller had prophesied, it sucked down most of the fortune Gaits had told her would last a lifetime. But that fortune hadn't been lost: it had been converted into a different kind of treasure. One that could never be taken from her.

The next few days were a mess of cleaning, meetings with woodworkers for furniture, and visits to the tailor. Not her idea of a good time. She was beyond relieved when a messenger arrived from the Marrigan. Gaits wanted to see her that night.

It was a hike from her new house and she set out early. Nine o'clock and the sun wasn't yet down. The high summer evening was sweltering. By the time she neared the Marrigan, she felt like she was swimming in her own sweat.

Smoke hung in the dead air. She didn't smell any roasting meat. Strange. Way too hot for anyone to need a fire. The odor had a second tang to it: whitewash. Angry shouts sprung up ahead. A prickle went down her spine. She dropped into a jog and turned the corner.

Directly ahead, the Marrigan was on fire—and beneath it, drawn swords glinted in the flames.

8

They hiked down a steep escarpment, black rocks tumbling away from their boots. Dust clung to the sweat on Dante's arms. The rocks ranged in size from walnut-sized rubble to slabs big enough to serve a formal dinner. The larger chunks felt sturdy enough, but if one slipped down on them, they'd be crushed like the grapes the basin was famous for.

The rocky scree quit, ushering them onto a slope of sagebrush and dead grass. Crickets whirred. They were a few miles north of the butte that hosted Collen. Ribbons of canal gleamed in the withering afternoon light. A blue haze hung on the horizon, darker than the sky, but it was too distant to tell if it was mountains or some form of weather.

They made their way to the nearest canal. Frogs croaked from its banks. Against the dust of the desert, the smell of the water stood out like a ship's lanterns at night. Blays led them east along the shore beneath fragrant trees. Around the waterway, trellises of beans and grapes curled in the sunlight. Small houses and large barns scattered the landscape.

"There it is." Blays pointed to two sticks jammed into the bank to form an X. He moved down to the canal's bank, indicating a fist-sized spiral shell resting in the mud.

Dante kneeled beside it, picking it up. It smelled tartly of rotting snail, but the meat was gone, a few small scraps clinging to the interior.

He glanced up. "This is it?"

"Sure is," Blays said. "You might recognize the shaden by its distinctly shaden-shaped shell."

"Are there any others?"

"This is the only one we could find."

"You realize we're looking for hundreds of these. Possibly thousands. We already know they're in the area. What does it prove to find one empty shell?"

Blays lifted his index finger. "The emptiness is the key to its use. The meat has all the shadows in it, right? I was thinking it's time for you to use your bloodhound impression. Use the bits of nether left in the shell to trace it back to the meat."

"And thus to where it was used," Dante said slowly. "And where all the other shaden likely are, too."

"Unless you have a better idea."

"One question. Why drag me all the way out here? Why not just bring me the shell?"

"I didn't want to disturb the scene. Anyway, *we* had to hike all the way out here. Fair's fair."

Still kneeling, Dante moved his mind inside the nether tucked beneath the shell's hard surfaces. It was far denser than it was in most living things and it was a trivial task to gather it up and reach out to the other shadows still linked to it. Pressure bulged in Dante's head. He turned in a slow circle until the sensation peaked.

"Got it," he said. "North-northeast."

Blays clenched a fist in triumph. "How far away?"

"Good question. Let me consult the map they were kind enough to inscribe inside the shell."

"I was wondering if it felt closer to one mile or one million."

Dante gazed blankly, exploring the pressure in his mind. "It's neither very close nor terribly far. It might be a few days' walk from here."

"We'll need provisions," Blays said. "As long as we're out here, we may as well ask Mrs. Fielder if she knows what lays between us and where we're going."

Mrs. Fielder turned out to be the owner and chief farmer of the land on which they'd found the shell. Blays and Naran had first met her in town, where a chance conversation revealed that she'd recently found a few large black shells along the ditch that watered her property. In Dante's experience, farmers fell into one of two distinct shapes: implacable barrels, and animated twists of rope. Fielder was one of the ropy ones.

"Been showing up here and there the last few weeks." She stood on her shaded porch, watching the three of them flatly. "Knew they weren't from the river."

"Do you know anyone else who's seen them on their land?" Dante said.

"Far as I know, I'm it. What are they?"

"It's probably best if you don't know. Let's just say the Mallish brought them and leave it at that." He pointed in the direction of the pressure in his brow. "What's out that way?"

She scratched the back of her neck. "A few farms. Then a whole lot of nothing. Then the Spiderfields."

Blays frowned. "Tell me that's just a name."

"It is," Fielder said. "For a field filled with giant spiders."

"How giant are we talking? Giant like the size of a plump grape? Or giant like the size of the deposit we'll leave in our trousers upon seeing them?"

"Wouldn't know. I make it my business to have no business there."

After a few more questions, they thanked her and went on their way. Faced with the prospect of spending multiple days in the wilds, they returned to Collen to settle their affairs at the inn, then headed down the switchbacks to the town at the butte's foot, where they'd found provisions to be cheapest.

Despite their thrift, by the time they'd bought enough food for a week, they found themselves down to their last pennies. Dante used his loon to check in with Jona, but he and Fenk didn't have enough cash to their name to justify the trip to Collen.

"We're looking at a problem when we get back," Dante said as they hiked through the town. "The nights are warm enough for us to sleep outside. But we won't have anything left for food and supplies."

"When we were kids, you used to rob people in the street,"

Blays said. "Too distinguished for that now?"

"It's less a matter of being too distinguished and more a question of not wanting to be arrested and jailed by the people we share an enemy with."

"All right, new plan: when we find the Mallish, we rob *them*."

They made their way through the housing at the base of the butte, striking out north-northeast. A dirt path took them through a few miles of farms, quitting at the edge of the uncultivated desert. As the sun set, they cleared rocks from a square of earth and laid out their blankets. It was not the most restful night of Dante's existence. At every sensation on his skin, he sat up and slapped at it, convinced he was being overwhelmed by spiders.

At daybreak, they got back on their way, hiking through the low hills. Ahead lay nothing but wasteland: black rock, gray dirt, yellow grass, and pale green spiky plants, some of which grew ten feet high. It looked forbidding, but they covered their heads with cloths to shade them from the sun. And if their water grew short, Dante knew he could reach down into the dirt and draw up as much as they needed.

Good thing. The pressure in his head had only increased slightly since starting out. They had a long walk ahead of them, with no roads to ease the journey.

"While you were at the library, I've been doing some research of my own," Blays said after several minutes of silent hiking. "Starting with that damned wheel of theirs. Know what it's for?"

Dante stepped over a striped bug the size of his thumb. "Making you look foolish?"

"Combating heavily armored infantry. The club end is normally an iron ball. Will smash right through anything you've got on to protect you. In battle, the Collenese infantry keeps a tight formation, then the wheelers dart out, smash up everything they see, and fall back into cover. Then the front ranks advance to stab whoever the wheelers knocked down."

"Sounds effective against infantry. What do they do against cavalry?"

"Naturally, they retreat to the buttes," Naran put in. "And watch the Mallish burn their fields."

Blays shrugged. "Yeah, but the Colleners are fanatical about keeping their granaries stocked in case of blight or siege. From what I've seen, the farmers pull far more respect than the warriors."

"What warriors?" Dante said.

"Like Cord." Blays tapped his right elbow. "With the ribbons. They're all attached to a different temple. They live and train there. Totally taken care of. Some earn money on the side serving as Arms, but whenever the Mallish come calling, they're expected to serve in the army."

"Cord's ribbon was gold. Does she serve Barrod?"

"That's right."

"Barrod's the smith. What does he have to do with fighting?"

"This isn't the Celeset you grew up with," Blays said. "These people have been under constant war for a thousand years. *Everything's* about fighting."

Once or twice a mile, an abandoned building stood on a hillside, as conspicuous as the last tooth in an old man's mouth. The day was cooler than the few before it. Even so, they used twice as much water as Dante had expected. By the time they bedded down for the night, they'd only seen two other people trudging through the dust.

Before going to sleep, Blays tapped the middle of his forehead. "Any progress?"

"Getting stronger," Dante said. "Another day, maybe two."

"I sure hope I'm right about this. If we spend a week out here with no shaden to show for it, I'm going to be very mad at someone."

"Yourself?"

"What good would *that* do?"

As the next day of travel began, the landscape was no different than the day before. As the morning wore on, though, the land grew flatter. Abruptly, tree trunks projected from the dust, bleached white by sun and time. The soil was matted with dried matter that crackled underfoot with small puffs of dust. Rodents scampered across the flats, ducking into holes dug through the matting.

Dante gazed northeast. Mountains hung on the horizon, little more than a blue wall. "Does this remind you of anything?"

"Yeah," Blays said. "That I never want to do this again."

Dante was going to mention Morrive, then remembered Blays had never been there. "Let's take a quick rest. I'd like to look around."

"Yes, you wouldn't want to miss any of the rats. Or the dead trees."

Blays and Naran sat on a rotting log. Dante wandered away, tapping the dead tree trunks, producing hollow thuds. When he tested a branch, it snapped off in his hand. It felt incredibly light. He tossed it aside, then thought better and picked it back up. He crouched over and used it to scrape through the gray blanket covering the ground.

The substance shredded like old rope, revealing dirt beneath. Dante grabbed hold of the edge of the matting and walked back, tearing away a swath. It was vaguely reminiscent of dried thatch. He kneeled beside the exposed earth and sent his focus within it.

The nether there lay in thick pools, swirling at his touch. Most dirt was homogenous, studded with the occasional stone which he could manipulate as well, but as he'd suspected, there was much within this soil that he couldn't move at all.

He softened the dirt, pulling it aside. The hole breathed a smell of rot so faint it was like exposing the corpse of a ghost. The pieces of earth he hadn't been able to move turned out to be twigs, branches, and leaf mulch. He reached down with his stick and gave them a poke. The mulch collapsed into fragments, scattering on the light breeze.

He sat back, examining the trees. There was a lot of space between each one. Some trunks were slanted, broken off a few feet above where they stuck from the soil. He moved back to the hole, widening it. Dirt flowed like water, exposing more branches and ragged lumps of leaves. An eighteen-inch-wide hole opened at the bottom of his excavations.

Dante felt his way through the nether surrounding the hole. The passage delved downward, branching numerous times before terminating in a round space thirty feet below the surface. Tunnels for the rodents? It seemed far too wide for that. A well or latrine? Some kind of —?

Legs scrabbled up from the darkness. With a shout, Dante jumped back. Spindly legs churned into the light, as thick as his thumb and as long as a bent bow. These were attached to a pale globular body a foot across. Fangs twitched on the massive spider's face as it emerged into the depression Dante had dug in the ground.

Dante tripped on a rock and fell onto the crinkling gray matter. The spider dashed across his excavations and up the side without slowing down. While its body was no bigger than a small dog, its legs spanned eight feet. Dante yanked the nether loose from the earth, shaped the darkness into a spear, and plunged it into the spider's fat body.

Blue ichor spouted to the dry earth. The spider collapsed, legs waving like storm-tossed boughs. Feet drummed across the ground as Blays and Naran arrived, swords in hand. Dante blasted a second spike into the spider's head, stilling it.

Blays gawked. "Tell me that's not what it looks like!"

Dante got to his feet. "In that case, it's a nightmarishly large potato bug."

"Holy *shit*!" Blays shuddered, stalking in a circle. "I always knew you were going to open a portal to hell one of these days."

"These must be the Spiderfields. Would have been nice if your farmer friend had warned us what they look like."

Naran poked the oozing corpse with an extremely long branch. "I've sailed halfway around the world and I've never seen one a quarter this size. What can they be eating?"

"Rats?" Blays pointed his head at one of the rodents perched on a bleached log thirty feet away. The animal watched them with knowing black eyes.

Dante slapped the dust from his pants. "Or maybe they just sleep until prey wanders into them."

"You know what? I don't care how they do it. Right now, all I care about is getting out of here before..."

Dante had turned around to pick up the flask of water that had come untied from his shoulder when he'd fallen. Hearing Blays trail off, he whirled to face the hole.

Legs poured out from it, dragging grotesque round bodies behind them. The spiders emerged into the daylight, writhing hypnotically, stirring the specific revulsion that only a swarm of bugs can invoke. There were dozens of them—and they were heading straight toward the three men.

"Are we running?" Naran called.

"*I* am!" Blays took off like a loosed arrow, twigs flying up from his feet.

Dante fell in behind them. The spiders streamed across the flat, hard-packed ground, limbs clicking.

"They're catching up!" Dante said.

Blays glanced back, mouth half open. "You're the wizard! Do something about it!"

Dante drew his antler-handled knife and held it over his arm, waiting for his steps to smooth out enough to prevent him from mangling himself. Then, coming to terms with the idea that mangling himself was the whole point, he lowered the blade, gashing his arm. The nether leaped to the trickling blood.

Black lances slammed into the closest three spiders, splashing their blue interiors across the gray desert. Ten of their kin stopped to lap up the precious fluid. Dante's stomach flopped. As the next wave closed on his heels, he struck those down, too. More and more spiders peeled off to feast on the easy prey. Yet forty others continued after the humans.

Unhindered, Naran and Blays were outpacing Dante, veering away from a jumbled scree that had formed beneath a low butte. Dante headed straight for it. Rocks turned under his boots. Heading uphill, he felt woefully slow. The spiders rushed on, closing to thirty feet, then twenty.

Dante thrust his mind into the stone beneath the rubble, turning it to mud, then ripping it away. With a roar, the loosened rock tumbled toward the verminous swarm. The spiders disappeared beneath the avalanche.

Dante stumbled a few steps higher, then staggered to a stop, breathing hard. A pall of dust strung out on the breeze. Behind them, the spiders who'd turned aside continued to slurp up the dead.

"Well done," Blays called from his right. "Now if you'll excuse me, I'm going to start running again."

~

They crossed the remainder of the Spiderfields as swiftly as their muscles allowed.

At last, the gray, matted plains gave way to familiar gray hills. By sundown, the bulge in Dante's forehead had intensified to the brink of discomfort. They kept watch that night, more leery of being ambushed by giant spiders than by Mallish forces.

Morning brought nothing unpleasant besides the heat, which Dante was growing used to. Or maybe it was growing less severe as the summer neared its close. In any event, the morning's trek felt easier. Within an hour, Dante crested a low ridge. The pressure in his head spiked. He came to a halt.

He pointed to a butte less than five miles away. "Whatever's left of the shaden we found on the farm, it's over there. Let's just hope the rest of the shells are with it."

They made their way below the ridge so their silhouettes wouldn't stand out, then hunkered down behind a redolent stand of sage. Minutes later, a column of dust approached the butte. Three men on horseback rode up the trail that had been scoured in its southwestern face.

"Mallish," Blays murmured. "Colleners typically think horses are too precious to be ridden. They only use them in fields."

Dante glanced his way. "You're turning into a regional expert."

"With all the time I've spent in Collen's taverns, I've been absorbing a lot more than beer."

"My element is the sea, not the desert," Naran said. "But even I can see that there isn't much cover between here and there. How do you propose we advance?"

Blays swept a bead of sweat from his nose. "We could alway wait until dark and I could get close enough to sneak in. Or Dante could find some unfortunate creature to kill and send in right now."

Dante tramped around the hillside until he spooked one of the rodents. He struck it down with a lash of nether, then reanimated it, ordering it across the plain. It ran tirelessly toward the butte. Once it was within a mile of its target, he sent it to the highest nearby hill to stand on its hind legs and take in the scene, where he could watch through its eyes.

As it gazed at the scattered buildings atop the butte, it was hoisted suddenly from the earth. Wings beat against it.

"Damn it," Dante muttered. "A hawk just grabbed my spy."

Blays chuckled. "Maybe the Mallish have finally learned how to fight back."

Dante scared up another rodent. He'd have had no problem slaying a city rat, but for some reason, killing one in the wild sent a small pang through his conscience. Perhaps it was the desert. In the woods, life was everywhere. Here, it had to fight for every day. Snuffing it so coldly felt disrespectful. He consoled himself with the idea that, if he took away the shaden from the Mallish, it might save hundreds of Colleners.

The vermin zoomed across the plain. This time, he sent it straight to the switchbacking trail up the butte. The path was lousy with the prints of boots and hooves. Horse droppings scattered the dirt. At the top, a wooden palisade had been erected between the ruins of a stone wall. The rodent scooted under the gate.

Crumbling brick buildings baked in the sunlight. Soldiers in blue uniforms moved between the most intact structures. An ox-drawn cart rumbled down what had once been a road. Dante sent the rodent for a closer look. The cart came to a stop near the edge of the butte. There, a team of incredibly filthy men clambered into the cart's rear, took up shovels, and began flinging dirt and loose rocks off the side of the plateau.

"The Mallish are here in force," Dante said. "And they appear to be digging for something."

Blays shifted behind the sagebrush. "Like what? A well? Buried treasure?"

"I'm going to find the shaden, then figure that out."

Separated from the butte by several miles, the pressure in his head was too indistinct to use it to guide him to the shells. His only way to find them was to send his rodent scout through the crumbling city. The wattle and daub houses sported countless holes in their walls, making for easy entry. Most of the brick and stone structures had held up better, but their doors had been hide or wood, and had fallen off long ago. The rat went from structure to structure, sticking its snout through the entry long enough to confirm that it was a barrack or storage before moving to the next.

As it made its rounds, it passed by the dig. Twenty men stripped to the waist jabbed shovels into the dry earth. They'd already excavated a section of ground twenty feet to a side and three feet deep. Dante hid the rat behind a water barrel. A soldier hopped down into the dig, going from man to man. Each man handed over rusting blades, small leather sacks, tarnished silver necklaces, and other trinkets too time-worn to identify.

"I see," Dante muttered. "They're graverobbing."

He described the scene. Naran snorted. "They came all this way to steal from those their ancestors killed decades ago? No wonder the Colleners hate them."

"It gets worse. They're pulling out the bones, too. Gods know why."

He moved the rat along. It soon came to a tall round building whose mortared stone walls were weathered but intact. A closed wooden door revealed that it contained something leadership didn't want the rank and file to have access to.

Dante sent the rodent around the structure's circumference, searching for cracks or a drain. He found no entry. The building bore narrow windows, but these started six feet up the sides and the wall, though eroded, was too slick for the rodent to climb, especially now that it had been rendered clumsier by its recent death.

While Dante was still searching for a way in, a man in a gray robe swayed up to the door, looking sweaty and miserable in his heavy church garb. The priest got a key from his pocket and opened the door. The rodent scooted in behind him.

The door creaked closed. Yellow sunlight illuminated a broad, circular room. At one end, a chalk circle had been drawn on the stone floor. A gray tapestry hung from the wall, sewn with the blue hourglass of Taim. Of far greater interest to Dante were the barrels lined along the wall—and the sharp, brackish odor the rodent scented on the air.

The priest fetched an iron rod from the wall. One end of the rod curved, splitting into three prongs, like a bent fork. The priest went to one of the barrels, removed its lid, and lowered the instrument inside. After a bit of splashing and thumping, he removed a shaden. He turned it side to side, eyeing it, then replaced the instrument on the wall and exited the building.

"Found them," Dante said.

Blays clapped his hands. "About damn time. How many?"

"Hold on." He sent the rodent up the side of one of the barrels. It fell three times before making it to the top. "They have about twenty barrels. It's too dark to see inside, but there have to be hundreds of shaden here."

"What's the situation around them?"

"They're in a secured building. Stone walls. Plenty of soldiers around, but they're mostly occupied by the dig. There's a trail up to the top of the butte. Gated. And guarded. There's at least one priest in the vicinity, probably more. Since he took one of the shaden with him, I'm guessing he knows how to use the nether."

"The nether?" Naran said. "But that's a crime punishable by death."

"Don't ask me. Maybe they make allowances for themselves when they're out of Mallon."

"Don't be naive," Blays said. "The powers that be exist to set strict rules for the commoners. They have no intention of following the rules themselves. That's why they *seek* power. And it goes all the way to the top. Taim couldn't even follow his own rules about infidelity. Most of his compatriots are no better. The holy books paint the gods as such drunken, petty sluts it's a wonder they haven't brought humanity to trial for libel."

Dante regarded him with amusement. Blays rarely expressed much interest in theology, probably because the slant of his opinions would get him hanged in most places where he wasn't best friends with the high priest.

Naran set his chin in his hand. "I suppose it doesn't matter what the laws are. What matters is that a powerful force is standing between us and the shells."

Blays glanced toward the distant butte. "Oh, that's nothing. The building's stone. I'll shadowalk right in."

"Is that so?" Dante said. "Do you intend to shadowalk out with twenty barrels slung over your shoulder?"

"I intend to stuff the shaden in a sack of some kind."

"And you'll have enough nether to shadowalk up the trail, over the gates, inside the building, and then repeat on the way out? What if you get delayed at some point? Or one of these shameless priests notices you blundering around in the nether?"

Blays waved in dismissal. "It's not *blundering*. I'm not running around the shadows drunk. Except when I am."

"Even if you're perfectly stealthy, you won't have enough nether to get in and out."

"Do you have a better idea? Maybe you'd like to fight our way through them?"

"Nope. I'm going to tunnel through the butte—and then straight up into the building."

"That's actually pretty great. But what happens if someone stumbles into us? After you've cut through all that rock, are you going to have any woo-woo left to kill them with?"

"Not much," Dante admitted. "But I'll have the shaden to draw on, won't I?"

"Now that's handy. What do you say, Naran? Want to head in with us? Or would you rather stay out here?"

"If it comes to a fight, I can't offer more than a sword," Naran said. "But if I can speed up our gathering of the shells, we'll be less likely to get in a fight in the first place."

The rodent scout was still perched on the edge of a barrel. Dante ordered it to jump into the water, find one of the shaden, and remove a small piece of its meat. This accomplished, its next task was to climb back out of the barrel.

While Dante waited for the creature to pull that off, he provided the others with a detailed description of what he'd seen so far, especially the building the Mallish were using to house the shaden.

"There's something funny about this," Blays said. "This is an awfully long way to travel to dig up some rusty old chain mail."

Naran brushed a large red ant from his boot. "It's not politically sound, either. Relations with Collen are strained at the best of times. Why worsen matters by digging up Collenese graves?"

"Two possible answers," Dante said. "Either they don't care what the Colleners think. Or whatever they're after is worth so much that it doesn't matter how much outrage they cause."

Once the rodent had escaped the barrel, he sent it scampering up a set of shelves and out one of the windows. It landed in the pillowy dust. Without haste, it made its way beneath the gates, down the switchbacks, and across the miles of open field, stopping often to watch for hawks.

After more than an hour, it reached Dante. He held out his hand. It spat the bit of shaden meat into his palm. He dropped his connection to the shell they'd found at Mrs. Fielder's farm, swaying back at the welcome release of the pressure. He gave himself a minute, then delved into the shadows within the flesh the rodent had brought him. A new bulge sprung in his mind. One that would lead him straight to the storage room.

They planned to make entry after nightfall. With nothing else to do, Dante sent his scout loping back across the fields and up into the butte. He positioned it near the excavation, hoping for a better look at what the Mallish were after. Dirt-smudged soldiers hauled up armor, weapons, packs, and bones, sorting them into piles.

After a few minutes, a gray-robed priest—a different man than the one Dante had seen take the shaden—looked up sharply. Shielding his eyes from the sun, he wandered toward the rodent. Dante retreated the creature into a ruined house. Once the priest returned to the dig, Dante sent the rodent to the shaden storage, where it waited outside until one of the priests entered the building late that afternoon. Dante tucked the scout behind a crate, intending to leave it there so they'd know it was safe to infiltrate.

As the sun advanced across the sky, the three of them shifted around the sagebrush, seeking shade. Only after darkness took the plain did they descend the hill and cross toward the plateau. Smoke rose from the soldiers' camp, lighter gray against the black sky. Dante stopped a half mile from the butte, the rodent perched in the storage room window, watching the grounds. The soldiers had already washed up and eaten. Soon, the men retired to their barracks.

"All quiet," Dante said. "Let's get thieving."

He led the way to the butte, coming at it from the west side, out of sight of the gates. The ground there was littered with loose stones and piles of dirt dumped from above. Tattered clothes and rusty blades scattered the upturned earth. Dante moved to the sheer rock wall, drew his knife, and cut his much-abused left arm. Nether shot up from all sides, unusually dense.

He placed his hand against the rock. It had been hours since sunset, yet the basalt was still blood warm. Stone flowed away like water down a drain, forming a narrow tunnel just large enough for a man to fit through.

Dante climbed inside, sloping the passage upward as he expanded it forward. Fifteen feet in, with the moonlight fading behind him, he got out his torchstone, blowing on the small white marble until pale light flooded the tunnel. Onward and upward, he advanced into the heart of the butte. The pressure in his head intensified with each step, slowly sliding from the center of his brow toward the top of his head. Once it reached the dead center of the top of his skull, he sent the tunnel spiraling upwards.

Minutes later, a pale light shined in the eyes of the rodent. Dante blew out his torchstone and climbed out onto the floor of the shaden vault.

9

Blays and Naran entered behind him, taking in the lay of the room. Dante instructed the rodent to leap out of the window and take up position across from the door. Outside, the plateau was silent except for the song of crickets and the hollow hooting of owls.

Blays grabbed the claw-tipped rod from the wall, moved to the closest barrel, and winced. "Do you really think they'll survive? Buried in the desert for a week?"

"I don't know," Dante said. "But they've lasted this long. There's no other way to do this. We'll come back for them as fast as we can."

Not looking particularly mollified, Blays went to work scooping up shaden and relocating them to a single barrel closest to them. Naran rolled up his sleeves and grabbed other snails with his bare hands. The barrels contained hundreds of them. Highly unlikely to be Mallon's entire stock of shaden, but it might well be everything they'd recently imported from the Plagued Islands. And with the Tauren defeated, the Mallish no longer had a supply to draw on.

Dante pried the lid from a barrel and reached into the dark water. His hand brushed a shell. With some gentle prying, he worked it loose. As he lifted the brackish-smelling creature from the water, silver threads glimmered around its shell before fading.

He frowned, doing his best to follow the silvery tracework. "There's ether in these."

Blays didn't look up from his hook-work. "I thought there was ether in everything."

"This has been shaped by someone. I wonder if this is how they've kept them alive this long."

"It's not connected to anything, is it? Like an alarm?"

Dante blinked and did his best to follow the course of the ether. For him, even that simple task was a challenge, yet he couldn't have done it at all before visiting the islands. He didn't see any tendrils leading away from the shaden. Whatever the ether's purpose, it was self-contained.

He returned to the snails, fishing about in the water and relocating them to Blays' main barrel. Some of the shaden were far more stubborn than others. With Dante's frustration mounting, he stepped back, drying his hands on his pants, and wandered around the room, looking for another one of the hooked rods that seemed so effective at detaching the snails.

One hung on the opposite wall, but the path to it was blocked by stacks of small wooden boxes. With a grunt, Dante lifted a box and set it aside. Its contents rattled dryly. The timbre of the sound was specific. Familiar.

The lid was latched but not locked. He swung it open. The light of the full moon cut through the windows, illuminating the jumble of bones inside. They were marred by streaks of something like blood or dirt. He picked up a rib.

It wasn't blood. Nor dirt. The sweep of the rib was painted with ancient Mallish runes he'd rarely seen and couldn't read. With tingling dread, he moved his mind into the bone's marrow. It was infused with nether.

"We can't leave yet," he said flatly.

"I see that," Blays said. "That's because you're too busy fooling around with old bones to help us with the shaden."

"These bones are covered in runes. When we first came to Narashtovik, Samarand had me make objects just like these. She used them in the ritual meant to summon Arawn."

Blays straightened. "We're not interrupting a god-summoning, are we? I've made it my life's mission to not get on the bad side of any deities."

"Whatever they're doing, that's why they've brought the shaden here."

"Maybe Gladdic thinks he can summon Arawn and then kill him."

"That's what they're digging for," Dante said. "It isn't to loot the pockets of forgotten corpses. It's to take the bones."

Naran put another snail in the barrel. "If all they wanted was bones, why come all the way to Collen? There are more than enough corpses in Bressel."

"Let's get the shaden out of here and I'll see what I can find out."

Dante got the hook from the wall and returned to the barrels. Tedious work, but with three of them, it went fast enough. Once they'd scooped up every snail they could find, Dante secured a lid to the top of the packed container. Drawing the nether from one of the shaden, he dissolved the rock beneath the barrel. It sank into the floor of the building.

As he slowly extended the hole beneath the barrel, lowering it toward the base of the butte, he sent the rodent trotting toward the mass grave the Mallish soldiers had been unearthing. Blays stood beneath a window, face tipped back as he listened to the night. Dante passed Naran the torchstone. The captain descended the spiral ramp Dante had used to get them up into the room.

Outside, the rodent came to the dig. It was now silent. Rotten clothes and leather armor lay in a jumbled heap. All the bones had been removed from the scene. A path had been worn from the site to one of the better-preserved buildings. Dante sent his scout trotting along the trail.

A bolt of white light flashed toward the rodent. Before Dante could order it to dash away, its vision went black.

"We have trouble," he said in the storage room. "A priest just killed my scout."

Blays frowned. "If he exterminated your rat, then he's either going to want to kill us or bill us. Either way, we should get out of here."

Dante headed for the exit in the floor. As he moved, however, he lost his hold on the earth beneath the barrel, which he was still lowering.

He stopped, teeth clenched. "Get to the bottom. I'll be right there."

Blays brushed past, disappearing around the curve of the ramp. Dante withdrew the rock from beneath the barrel as fast as he could. Feeling it come level with the main tunnel out, he stopped, extending a horizontal passage between the two excavations.

The building's door burst open. A blue-clad soldier rushed into the room, sword glinting. A priest followed on his heels. Dante rushed down the ramp, sealing the stone closed behind him.

Wan light glowed ahead. He stumbled from the spiral ramp into his hallway, rushing into the backs of Naran and Blays, who were wrestling with the incredibly weighty barrel.

"Get back," Dante said. "I'll close it up."

"We can't risk them finding the shaden before we can get back here," Blays said. "There's only one way we can go with this."

"We can't destroy them. Do you have any idea what I could do with this much nether?"

"Sure. About exactly as much as the Mallish could do with it."

Dante pressed his lips together. "You're right. Get back."

Blays and Naran retreated toward the exit. Feeling sick with himself—how was it that he could kill any number of humans without remorse, yet harming a barrel of sea snails made his conscience bleed?—Dante moved away from the barrel. He lashed the nether toward it, cutting loose its hoops. Staves burst apart, spilling sea water and shells across the ground. He moved into the rock. A shelf of stone slammed downward with a gut-churning crunch.

"Not our proudest moment," Blays said. "Now shall we get out of here before they add us to their pile of bones?"

With Naran lighting the way with the torchstone, they jogged down the tunnel. As they neared the exit, Naran passed him the stone. Dante blew it out. They moved into the night. Dante sealed the tunnel behind them. Atop the butte, men hollered to each other. Doors slammed. Steel clinked.

"Better hoof it," Blays said. "I'd like to be ten miles away by sunrise."

They jogged toward the nearest hill, meaning to put it between them and any pursuit. Halfway to it, torches flapped from the top of the butte. Faint hoofbeats carried through the darkness. Dante and the other two paused long enough to ensure the riders were going in the wrong direction, then ran up the hill. They crested it, slowing to a jog as they moved downhill.

Dante waited until they'd made it past the next ridge before speaking. "Well, that could have gone worse."

"Is that what you consider success?" Naran said. "We lost all the shaden."

"Correction," Blays said. "We *destroyed* the shaden. I'm sure Dante had visions of using them to brand his name across the sky, but the fundamental objective was to get the shells away from the Mallish. Mission acc—"

He had just glanced behind them. He double-taked violently, tripping through a clump of sage. Dante's heart sank. Behind them, three dotted lines glowed white in the dirt. Each spot of light was a narrow oval about a foot long. They began some hundred feet away from Dante, but as he watched, the lines of light advanced across the field spot by spot, stopping directly beneath their feet.

"Ethermancers," he groaned. "They've found a way to track us."

"We must do something." Naran kicked dirt over the closest patch of ether, but his efforts only brought more light to the stretch of ground he'd just disturbed. "They'll be able to see these for miles!"

"Then I suppose we'll have to bury them." Dante reached into the earth, lifting up a shelf of turf and dropping it on top of ten feet of tracks. His satisfaction with his idea died as the area he'd moved the dirt from began to glow as well.

"Interesting," Blays said. "It appears we're screwed."

"Not so fast." Naran pointed to the hill they'd just descended. As they watched, the furthest footsteps faded, the line of light contracting toward them. "Should we stay here? Wait for them all to fade?"

"The ones around our feet don't seem to be going anywhere,"

Dante said. "But the tracks only last for a few minutes. If we get far enough away, we'll take our tracks with us."

Blays nodded and broke into a run. Dante dropped in behind him, doing his best to overlap his footsteps with the ones Blays was setting down. In a small silver lining, the eerie white light made it better to see where he was going. Blays swung away from the next ridge, opting instead to detour through the low fold where two hills met. The sage was slightly thicker there, and the low elevation would keep their tracks hidden unless a scout crested one of the surrounding hills.

They moved in silence, slowing to a jog after half a mile. The tracks persisted for a few hundred yards behind them. Compared to the vastness of the desert, it was little more than a speck. At night, though, the brightness of that speck was like a lighthouse at sea.

After another hour, eight miles lay between them and the Mallish-claimed butte. Yet after what they'd done to the shaden, Dante wouldn't feel safe until he was back in Collen. They pushed hard, cycling between walking and jogging. It was far more pleasant to travel by night. Dante thought they should have been doing so all along.

Even so, he was starting to wear down. He considered using the nether to wash the weariness from his muscles, but after all the tunneling, his command was shaky. He needed to keep a reserve handy.

When the horn sounded behind him, he knew he'd made the right decision.

"Where is he?" Dante said. "Where's—"

The horn sounded again. Naran's arm jerked forward. Dante followed the path of his finger to a mounted silhouette on the opposite slope. Shadows condensed in Dante's hand. He shaped them into a spike and flung them into the air. The scout was hundreds of yards away and Dante lost sight of the nether almost at once. Seconds later, however, the figure dropped from the saddle.

Dante exhaled heavily. "Time to decide where to make our stand."

"It's all right," Blays said. "We just have to keep running."

"And then outrun the squadron of horsemen that's about to show up? The only reason we've been able to evade them so far is that this place is gigantic. Now that they know where to look, there's no hiding our tracks."

"Then it's a good thing we don't need to. Quit whining and get running."

Dante felt none of Blays' optimism, but often, the only thing required to get tired people moving was for one of them to take action. Once more, he found himself following in Blays' glowing footsteps.

They didn't make it another mile before a second horn sounded. Hooves thumped faintly. Voices carried on the still desert air. White light sprung from a mile across the fields, illuminating at least a score of soldiers. Only a few were mounted.

"Ethermancers," Dante said. "They've been refreshing their soldiers' strength to give them speed."

Blays gazed across the darkness. "Good. Then they'll have less ether to try to kill us with. Come on, then. It isn't much further."

"Precisely what is this 'it'?" Naran said.

Blays didn't deign to answer. They jogged up another hill. Behind them, the riders stuck close to the infantry, yet the circle of light cast by the priest grew a little nearer each minute.

After the next rise, Dante and the others entered a flat plain. Within a quarter of a mile, the ground crackled beneath them. Gray. Matted.

Blays looked down in surprise. "Would you look at that!"

Dante sputtered with the laughter of sudden understanding. "This is evil."

"It's my fault if something bad happens to them? *They're* the ones chasing a group of thieves across a hostile desert in the middle of the night."

They entered a stretch of old dead snags, the branches broken off close to the trunks. Still on the move, Dante sent his attention down into the dirt. In less than a minute, he encountered a tunnel a foot and a half wide. It extended far below the surface, branching repeatedly.

Dante skidded to a stop. He yanked back a wedge of dirt, exposing the tunnel and forming a ramp down to it. The Mallish forces were almost within bowshot. Dante picked up a stone and dropped it down the hole.

"Move back," he said. "Make it look like we're making our stand."

They retreated to a thick stump well removed from the hole and drew swords. Dante made sure to flash his in the moonlight. The contingent of soldiers slowed, drawing weapons.

A man on horseback trotted to the front ranks. "Lay down your arms."

"Then what?" Blays called back.

"Your deaths will be fast."

"You call that a deal? We can take care of that ourselves!"

The man turned to his soldiers, barking commands. A line of troops marched forward, followed by a second. A priest walked behind them, light shining steadily from the point of his staff.

A series of soft crackles whispered through the darkness. It sounded like fallen leaves rustled by the wind, but there was no wind. No leaves, either. The front line faltered as men strained their eyes into the night.

"What's that?" a man yelled raggedly. "Who's out there?"

The advance stopped. Claws crackled through the blanket of dried, flattened reeds. Shadows stretched across the prairie, impossibly thin and impossibly long, their numbers beyond count.

Men screamed with the unique pitch of those who faced a swarm.

Dante turned and ran across the plain. His feet still left shining prints on the ground, but after a few seconds, the light winked out completely. Another few seconds, and the screams stopped, too.

In case a priest had survived, they trudged on for another few miles before finally making camp.

"How did they do that?" Blays gestured back to the east. "Lighting up our footsteps?"

Dante smoothed out his blanket. "It might have been a ward of some kind. Anyone who entered the storage room was marked by it. Left a trail for them to follow."

"You don't sound too sure of that."

"Nether is messy and chaotic," Dante said. "It mirrors life. Ether, though, is a reflection of the heavens—or maybe the cause of them. It's orderly. Predictable. Now, think about what happened. Our footsteps were glowing. And when we tried to disturb them, it only made them glow brighter."

"You're forgetting a key point with this lecture," Blays said. "I know nothing about anything."

"I wonder if the ether gets used to the shape of how things are. If you go on to disturb that shape, the ether might hold fast to that memory for a little while until it's adjusted to the new shape of things."

"An interesting lecture on the properties of the ether. But you know what would be even more useful?"

"What's that?"

"If you'd bother to learn how to *use* it."

"I'd like to," Dante said. "For some reason it's harder for me."

"Maybe it's not that hard. Maybe it's only hard compared to how easy it was for you to pick up the nether."

Any other night, this might have kept Dante up for a while. After the day they'd had, he fell asleep immediately.

They ran into no further problems on the way back to Collen. On the day the city came into view, it had been more than two weeks since they'd left Bressel. If the Wandering Bear clan tasked with traveling to Narashtovik was making all haste, they'd have the loon delivered to the Sealed Citadel in another two weeks.

In the meantime, Dante, Blays, and Naran would keep as quiet a profile as possible. While Dante tried the Reborn Shrine's library for more information, Blays and Naran would take up honest work to earn enough money to keep them fed. Dante didn't have much hope of figuring out what Gladdic had done when they'd tried to attack him in his temple, but there was one mystery he thought he *could* solve. And the rune-inscribed bones the Mallish priest had been creating gave him one more avenue to explore. Even if that terminated in a dead end, once he was in contact with Narashtovik, Nak or one of the other scholars might be able to help him.

To his relief, the plateau on which Collen rested showed no large plumes of smoke nor invading armies. They made their way to the path up its side. They were filthy from the desert, but so were many of the farmers coming and going. As Dante neared the base of the switchbacks, a boy stared at him for three full seconds, then took off running up the road to the plateau.

Blays nodded after him. "You see that?"

"What about it?" Dante said.

"He had the look of a tiny spy," Naran said. "Are you expecting trouble?"

"These days?" Blays chuckled. "Always."

They had no money and thus no reason to stop at any of the bakeries on the way up. Despite hiking steadily, by the time they got up top, they found the road forward blocked by a sizable group of men and women. Most wore colored ribbons around their elbows. Some leaned on wheels. Others had swords hanging from their belts.

For a brief moment, Dante was heartened at the sight of so many people come to greet them on their return. As he was puzzling out how they'd heard about the defeat of the Mallish, the Collenese warriors drew swords.

Dante sighed. He'd been arrested far too often not to know it when he saw it.

10

The Marrigan burned across its top floors. Bodies lay crumpled in the street. Swords clashed inside the building. Armed men poured inside the front doors, blades in hand. Strangers.

In the education of the streets, sizing up a fight was one of the first things you learned. Only fools got in fights they weren't likely to win. Strike that: only fools got in fights they weren't overwhelmingly favored to win. Fools, and the desperate.

The scene before her was beyond desperate. The smoke. The bodies. The animal in her wanted to rush in and start cutting throats. But the human in her—specifically, the human that had been trained since age four to deal with life and death decisions on a daily basis—was telling her that if she stayed and fought, the only thing she'd win was a fresh grave.

Twenty men stood out front, watching for any signs of resistance. Raxa backed away, keeping her shoulder tight to the shadows. When she'd put a row of buildings between her and the Marrigan, she turned to run.

And stopped. She might not be able to turn the tide. But she could at least find out who was trying to burn them out of their home.

Anger welling in her like blood from a fresh cut, she ducked into an alley, pressed herself to a wall, and slid into the shadows. The night streets brightened with stray streams of nether. She ran back toward the Marrigan. Out front, four swordsmen dragged a man out the front door kicking and screaming. The man's voice was warped with pain, but she recognized it as Dink's. A recent addition who'd been showing a lot more guts than brains.

They hauled the boy to the street. He kicked up at one of his captors. A man drove a sword into Dink's shoulder. He writhed. Raxa could only watch as another man moved behind Dink's head, lifted a maul, and brought it down on the boy's forehead. The crunch made Raxa want to sit down. A silver mist rose from the blood pooling around Dink's body.

She was wasting time. She ran toward the attackers. They were hooded, dressed plainly, but she doubted their swords would be so anonymous. Cloaks were cheap. Good blades weren't. Besides, when people went out expecting a fight, they wanted to know they could trust the weapon they carried.

"Help!" The voice speared through the crackle of the flames and the shouts coming from the building. Gaits. "*Help me!*"

A scream of pain followed, echoing to Raxa's left. She broke away from the scene in front of the Marrigan and dashed toward the sound of Gaits' voice. In the alley running along the building's left flank, cloaked men trotted away into the night. Their bodies were dark, but the blood running from Gaits' wounds shined like silver lanterns.

Still in the shadows, Raxa jogged up behind them in perfect silence. Five of them. Gaits was trussed like a goat, slung over one man's shoulders. The other four carried swords. Not expecting any trouble, Raxa had left the bone sword at home. She had her good dagger on her and another three knives, but you couldn't do knifework from inside the shadows. It was like trying to cut a steak with a stick. Things just sort of mushed up against each other.

They walked briskly down the alley. Gaits had gone motionless. She'd have to go visible. At five on one, her odds would be awful. Everything the streets had taught her told her to run.

When you ran, you got away with your life. But that didn't mean you could live with the self you saved.

She jogged up behind them, barely feeling the cobbles under her feet. She drew her dagger with her right hand and a thin-bladed knife with her left. Two men walked in front and two behind, the Gaits-bearer in their middle. The air smelled like smoke and ocean. She moved behind the man walking on the left rear, lifted her knife parallel to his neck, and lurched into that which was real.

She jammed the knife into the swordsman's neck. He shrieked, gurgling, grasping at his wound. Raxa was on the next man while he was still turning toward the disturbance. Reflexively, he lifted his sword high. She leaped forward, driving her dagger in his gut, hugging him close so he'd have no leverage to swing.

He collapsed against her, sword clanging to the pavement. Warm blood soaked her front. She swung behind him, putting his body between her and the other three men, and blinked back into the shadows. In that world, their eyes burned like stars.

"The fuck?" One of the men in front stared at the gutted man, who Raxa was still holding upright. "Bean? What's happening?"

A second man moved toward Bean, grabbing his arm. "You okay?"

Raxa reappeared. Her dagger took the man's throat. She shoved him aside and threw a knife at the man who'd been staring at Bean. It buried itself in his side. To Raxa's left, the soldier carrying Gaits dumped his body to the ground and went for his sword.

Her blade found his heart before he found his weapon.

The man she'd thrown the knife in was the last one standing. He staggered away, eyes wide, waving his sword in front of him. "What the hell are you?"

"Vengeance," she said. She blinked out. He screamed at the top of his lungs. She moved behind him, stepped back into the world of flesh, and cut his throat.

She ran to Gaits. Lying in the alley, his chest rose and fell, but he was out cold. They were only three blocks from the Marrigan. She had to work fast. Raxa moved from body to body, turning out pockets. The alley stank of blood and feces. She supposed it had been too much to ask for a signed order from whoever had sent them, but other than a few iron and bronze coins, the attackers' pockets were empty. Not just of anything interesting. Empty of *anything*.

She checked their hands, ears, and necks. No rings on their hands or ears—but one of them had a slim iron chain around his neck, hidden beneath his shirt. On its end dangled an iron ring bearing a black stone.

She snapped the chain and pocketed it. Despite the work her knives had just done, they felt a little flimsy. She undid two of the dead men's sword belts and strapped them around her waist. She scooped up Gaits and used the wall to help her stand, legs straining. As soon as she'd shifted him over her shoulder, she tottered down the alley.

Raxa was shiny with blood. So was Gaits—and he was leaking steadily. The Order had an in-house physician, but he was out of the question now. They had a backup, too, but at that moment, he'd be overwhelmed with other casualties. And the attack on the Marrigan had been too organized. They might have people waiting to ambush any wounded who went for the physician's help.

There was only one option. She was going to have to see Lady Vara. All the way outside the Pridegate.

Raxa struck southwest, keeping to the back alleys. Gaits' limp body pressed her down with every step. She'd only made it two blocks when footsteps rasped down the tight street. She ducked behind a jumble of wooden crates. Two members of the city watch jogged past, dressed in the black and silver of their station.

When the noise of their boots faded, she cut off the hem of her shirt and Gaits' sleeves, using them to bind the cuts on his arm, ribs, and hip. Done, she picked him back up. Lifting him took twice as much energy as it had the first time. She staggered along block after block. After a mile, she hit the boulevard of Pavvers. Forty feet wide, completely exposed to the night. Detouring around it would take her a mile and a half out of her way. With gritted teeth, she waited for the pedestrian traffic to thin to nothing, then moved across the boulevard as fast as she could.

In the shelter of an alley on the other side, she leaned against the wall. With a quiver, her thighs went out from under her. She slid to the ground, grabbing Gaits' hair so his head wouldn't bang into anything on the way down.

He inhaled with a start. His head jerked back. "Let go—!"

She clamped her hand over his mouth. "Still your tongue before they find us and cut it out."

Muffled by her hand, he said something that might have been "Raxa."

"Yep," she said. "You've been hurt, Gaits. I'm taking you to see a friend of mine, but you're heavy as shit. Can you walk?"

Gaits tested his legs, faltering. Raxa swooped a shoulder beneath his arm. Leaning on her heavily, he shuffled southwest with her.

"What happened?" he murmured dreamily.

"You tell me. When I got to the Marrigan, it was burning like a Falmac's Log. And a group of thugs was hauling you off."

"Thugs," he repeated. "One minute normal. The next, they were everywhere. Flames and swords. They were saying something. Something like…" He gazed forward, head swaying as he walked, eyes as leaden as shadowcut glass. Just as Raxa was sure he'd forgotten what they were talking about, his chin jerked up. "'When the man steps too far, the brother must put him down.'"

"The hell does that mean?"

"Don't know."

"Any idea who they were?"

"No uniforms. Didn't recognize—"

He stumbled. Raxa caught him, pulling him back to his feet. "Save your strength. We've got a long way to go."

Block by block, they advanced through the city. As they neared the Pridegate, she squeezed his arm. "Gate's ahead. Time to play the Ale Game, okay?"

Gaits nodded weakly. As they neared, a soldier in black and silver moved to intercept them. His eyes fixed on Gaits' bandages. "What's got you out so late?"

"Well," Raxa said. "You see—"

Gaits convulsed, retching so convincingly Raxa nearly did, too. The guard scowled and backed off, waving a hand in front of his nose. "Get him home."

Raxa smiled tightly, agreed profusely, and hustled Gaits

through the exit. They soon came to a sturdy wooden house, its dark yard fenced with pine branches. Raxa hammered her fist on the front door. Wood scraped inside. The door flung open, revealing a woman as thickly built as a bull. Her short, slate gray hair stuck from the sides of her head like a rogue dandelion.

Her voice was hoarse with sleep. "What kind of asshole dumps trash on my step in the middle of the night?"

"Lady Vara," Raxa said. "It's Raxa. My friend's hurt."

"I got eyes. And you got three seconds before I slam the door on your nose."

"The Marrigan's been attacked. We've got nowhere else to go."

"Boo hoo."

Raxa bit back a curse. She motioned to the silhouettes of goats and sheep behind the fence. "Come on, Vara. I've brought half your stock in off the streets."

"So you brought me one more wounded animal to save." She swore, grunted, and stepped aside. "Get inside before the watch sees you."

Inside, Vara lit a lamp. Gaits had gone pale and shaky. Raxa led him to the back room and helped him lie down. The boards were well-scrubbed, but blood was the strongest ink there was. The room smelled like fur and manure. Vara entered, kneeled beside Gaits, and unrolled a leather kit. The shiny metal tools inside looked like something between thieves' picks and a torturer's tools.

"You're a physician," Gaits said.

Vara took a slim pair of scissors from her kit. "Bah."

"'Bah'? What is 'bah'?"

"Yes, she's a physician," Raxa said. "Of animals."

"*Animals?* You're a butcher?"

"Don't think so." With a deft swoop, Vara cut through the front of his shirt. "But if you don't hold still, I may turn into one."

She worked with the firm sureness of someone used to holding down thrashing ewes and calves, cleaning, stitching, and bandaging his wounds. Gaits did some gasping and moaning, but to his credit, he didn't scream once. When it was done, he lay panting on the floor.

"I owe you big." Raxa smacked Vara's solid shoulder, grinning at her. "And our boss will owe you much bigger."

The woman grunted, cleaning her tools on a grimy cloth. "You mean to stay?"

"Until he's recovered, if we can. Right now, though, I need to get back to the Marrigan. I'll be back by dawn."

"Raxa!" Gaits sat up and grabbed the leg of her pants, delirious, bloody-handed. "Don't leave me!"

"You might not be the only one who got hurt. Besides, we have to learn more about who did this."

He held fast to her pants, pleading, eyes bulging. Vara rolled her eyes, got a wax tube from her kit, and trimmed off its end. As Gaits babbled on, she dumped milky fluid down his throat.

"That'll snuff him like a candle," Vara said. "Now go see to your friends."

"Thanks again. Vara, if anyone shows up while I'm out? Run and don't look back."

Vara jerked a thumb at Gaits, who'd rolled onto his back, drooling. "What about him?"

"You try to save him then, and you'll both die."

Outside, Raxa took off at a jog. A column of smoke rose from within the west side of the Pridegate. To the east, the spire of the cathedral and the lump of the fortress watched over it all.

She could smell the smoke from a mile away. Before leaving Vara's, she'd changed into one of the woman's spare shirts and left the looted swords in the back room. Raxa now looked like nothing more than an average lowlife drawn by the promise of a fiery spectacle.

Outside the Marrigan, the attackers had vanished. They'd been replaced by a squadron of the city guard. They stood calmly and watched the building burn, passing around flasks of liquor.

When Raxa couldn't stand it any longer, she walked toward the closest soldier. "What's going on?"

The man gave her a glance that started out brief and quickly turned lingering. "Something wrong with your eyes? Someone set the flame to it."

"Aren't you going to try to put it out?"

"What for?" He spat in the street. "The cockroaches are finally being burned out of their hole."

It was a moment before Raxa was able to reply. "Do you know who did this?"

"Rival gang, I'd bet. But whoever it was? They deserve a feast."

She had to walk away before her dagger found itself twitching from his jugular. She made a circuit around the building, eyes out for anyone wounded, or any clues as to who had brought the Marrigan to its ruin. There was nothing left but fluttering ash and drying blood.

The Order had a protocol for an event like this: get out, get safe, and keep your fool head down until you knew what was going on.

In the morning, Gaits looked pained and deathly pale, but he was lucid again. Vara's version of tea involved ten different weeds from her yard and only a sprinkling of good Galladese leaf, but that did nothing to stop Gaits from gulping down half a pitcher of it.

He sat at the table, looking unusually delicate within his bandages. "Right now, everyone who made it out has scattered to the six winds. They're going to stay scattered until we know who hit us—and where we need to hit back."

Raxa took a sip of lukewarm tea. It was bitter. Grassy. "Where do we start?"

"In a situation like this, you always start with the most likely culprit. In this case, that's the Sealed Citadel."

"For the theft of the Jerrelec Collection? I can buy that. What I can't buy is that they'd come after us wearing plain cloaks."

"Why not? It would be easier to sneak up on us that way than to march out in the black and silver."

"Yeah, but when the Citadel rolls in like that, it's to do more than crack a few skulls. They're there to send the message that if you step out of line, they'll use your guts to fertilize their crops. If it had been the Citadel, as soon as they made their attack, they would have shed their cloaks to show their colors. But when I went back last night, they had no idea who'd made the attack."

"Unless that was a cunning trick to avoid retaliation." Gaits frowned. "But that would only make them look afraid of us. Let's say you're right. Who else could it have been?"

"I don't know. A rival gang. Or maybe the nobles we've been robbing took up a collection to hire someone to get back their goods. Whatever it is, I picked up a few things that might point us in the right direction."

As Gaits' eyebrows attempted to take flight, she went to the other room and picked up the last night's harvest. Back in the main room, she clunked the two swords down on the table, following this with the small clink of the black ring.

"Pulled these off the guys who were trying to haul you away," she said. "What do you think?"

His gaze shifted between the swords and the ring. He picked up the ring, holding it up to the light. "Do you recognize this?"

"No. Should I?"

"I don't, either. I'll send you to Telly, our jewelry man. He knows every gem cutter and sigil in the city. If anyone can identify the owner, it'll be him." Wincing, he set down the ring, picked up a sword, and drew it. "Rather plain. What were you hoping to do with this?"

"Figure out who made it."

"Worth a shot. For some projects, we've used a smith named Farben. He might know something about the swords' make."

"I've got my own guy." Raxa stood. "No sense wasting time. Sit tight while I run these down."

Before she left, Gaits penned a quick letter to Telly, folding it once. Raxa tucked it in her pocket, rolled the swords in one of Vara's spare blankets, and exited. It was a warm summer morning and the air smelled like the purple blooms of the gannet trees growing on every boulevard. To Raxa, it still smelled like smoke, blood, and steel.

Telly the jeweler was on the way to Benner's. His was a small shop tucked into a quiet corner of the Emerald District. Telly was silver-haired with a small pointed mustache and eyebrows like inverted V's.

He glanced over the letter Raxa brought him, then looked up at her. "Gaits all right?"

"You heard about what happened to the Marrigan?"

"Way I heard it, everyone who was there is currently at rest in the carneterium."

"If you could trust rumor, every single one of us would be rich, dead, or pregnant."

"True enough." Telly laid a black velvet cloth on his counter. "Let's have a look at it."

Raxa gave him the ring. He held it up to the light, shining it back and forth, then produced a bulging glass lens affixed to a brass handle. Holding the lens over the ring, he muttered to himself, then set down the lens for another look with his bare eyes.

Eventually, he shook his head. "Don't recognize it."

"Seen anything like it?"

"Yes, I've seen darkstone embedded in black iron before. As for the cut of the gem or the scrollwork on the shank here? Never."

She swore under her breath. "Do you know any organizations that use rings similar to this?"

"None." Telly rolled the ring around his palm. "Like me to keep this for you? Ask around?"

"I'll see what I can turn up on my own. Thanks for your help."

She pocketed the ring and headed to the Sharps. Benner was in back at his forge, banging away on a glowing rod. Seeing her, he held up a finger and motioned her back out front. A few minutes later, the clanging stopped. He entered the front room shirtless and sweating.

"You again," he said. "What do you need this time? A dagger without a blade? Or maybe I can interest you in a helmet without a crown?"

"Can you tell who made these?" She set the bundle on the counter and swept away the blanket.

"Doubt it."

"Can I pay you to try?"

Benner curled his lip. "These swords have about as much artistry in them as a privy. Could have been forged anywhere. But if you don't mind tossing your money down a well, I'm happy to take it from you."

He picked up one of the swords. He gave a detached, bored

once-over to the scabbard, then unsheathed the blade with a whisper of leather. His eyes roved down the blade, which was straight and double-edged, and not especially long, short, wide, or thin. When his gaze reached the crossguard, he stopped cold.

He turned the sword over, then set it down and unsheathed the other, examining its crossguard with a keen eye. He laughed through his nose.

"What've you got?" Raxa said.

Grasping the hilt, he extended the sword, indicating its guard. "See that?"

She leaned in. The guard was your typical two prongs of steel, bent slightly upward, away from the bearer. Functional and unadorned. But where it crossed above the hilt, the shiny metal was marred with a small black stain. It was vaguely heart-shaped, but one lobe was larger than the other.

"See what?" she said. "That stain?"

Benner nodded. "Know what it is?"

"The mark of the group that uses these?"

"If it was official, it'd be tidier. No, I think it's a signature."

"Of who? The smith?" Raxa said. Brenner nodded. Raxa tipped back her head. "You guys sign your weapons?"

"Every artist puts their name on their work somewhere. Painters. Potters. Even stonemasons got a signature—they'll lay one specific stone upside down, say. Weaponsmiths got one, too. Some small, deliberate imperfection that marks it as yours. Nothing that weakens the weapon in any way, mind you. Just something to put your stamp on it."

"So every smith's signature is unique. Do you recognize this one?"

"Not offhand." Brenner smiled toothily. "But if you make it worth my while, I can find out."

She haggled out a price, leaving him with one of the swords and taking the other with her. By then, the sun stood directly overhead. Hard to believe it had only been half a day since the burning of the Marrigan. She touched the hilt of the sword she'd taken from Gaits' attackers. Felt wrong to be wearing it. Like marrying your cousin's killer. But if she could use it to take them down...

Like Gaits had said, the Order of the Alley was now homeless. Adrift on the six winds. But Kerreven hadn't structured the institution to be so fragile that it could be torn down in one night of terror. Itching for intel, Raxa headed for the One-Eyed Frog, a pier-side tavern designated for use by the Order if their members ever lost a central location.

Beyond the Frog, women slogged through the mud on the edge of the bay, digging clams and barble shells, whose meat was highly prized, but which Raxa had always thought looked like enormous gray phalluses. She stepped inside the tavern. Compared to the dazzle of the streets and the sea, the interior was as black as a tomb.

Someone grabbed her right arm. Her left hand darted for her dagger.

"Raxa." The voice was Jenker's, Order muscle. "Keep your calm."

He guided her to a back room and knocked a code into the closed door. It swung open, revealing three more Order grunts. Inside, Ackley sat at a table accompanied by a large jug of wine. He was their logistician, a lieutenant same as Gaits.

"Raxa." He kicked out a chair. "Figured you'd be too slippery for the bastards."

She seated herself. Jenker poured her a glass of wine. It was light and summery and tasted like apples. "Does anyone know who said bastards are?"

"That remains a matter of high speculation. But I know this much about them: they're walking dead men."

"Are we in shape to hit them back?"

Ackley drained his mug. "We lost the Marrigan. And a lot of good people. But most of us weren't there last night. Most of those who *were* ran off as soon as they saw it was hopeless. Yet right now, it looks like we're utterly smashed, right? Good. That's exactly what we *want* them to think."

Hearing this soothed Raxa better than any wine could. "What about Kerreven?"

"No one knows."

"He's the boss, Ackley. How can no one know if he's alive or dead?"

"Because if he's dead, he can't talk. And if he's alive, he might want his enemies to *think* he's dead."

"I've got Gaits." She finished her wine. "And a lead on who did this. As soon as I know, you will, too."

"I can't wait." He gave her an appreciative but confused smile. "How did it take them this long to start putting you to use?"

On her way back to Vara's, Raxa took the scenic route, dropping into every pub she passed. Not to drink (though that was certainly a welcome secondary benefit), but to soak up the gossip. As she hopped from tavern to tavern discussing the possibly identity of the attackers, she heard every possibility she'd floated to Gaits along with several she hadn't—including the idea it had been a civilian mob come to flush the scum out of the neighborhood.

At Vara's, Gaits was asleep. The stout woman came in from tending her goats.

"How's he doing?" Raxa said.

"He'll be weak for a while," Vara said. "But unless infection takes him, he'll come away with no worse than a few scars." She watched Raxa. "Who is he? Your bedwarmer?"

"I don't think I'm his type."

"What? Young and pretty?"

"Female."

Vara took a moment, then laughed. "I've had rams like that. Don't have eyes for anything but each other. I don't understand it, but they seem happy enough."

As soon as Gaits fell asleep that night, Raxa walked across town to her new house. It showed no sign of having been disturbed. The bone sword was still where she'd hidden it on top of a rafter in the attic. She greased it down with steelblack, got one of her nicest dresses, and went back to Vara's.

In the morning, she put on her dress and dropped by Brenner's. She'd expected he'd need more time to get to her task, but as soon as she came in, he locked the door behind her.

"Found your signature," he said. "It's Gonson's work. His shop's over on Pennimore."

"How long would it take you to forge fifty of these?"

"Me? A month. But Gonson's got a full house of apprentices.

He could bang out fifty of these inside a week."

She thanked him and tossed him a small but weighty purse. She hoofed it across the city. Gonson's shop was at the edge of the Heights, a ritzy neighborhood on a hill inside the Ingate. Racks of weapons adorned the walls. Gonson was well into middle age, but like most blacksmiths, he looked capable of wrestling down a bear.

Raxa smiled and leaned over his counter. "It's so good to meet you. My friend recently had a sword made by you and I just think it's so elegant. I'd love to commission one for my husband's birthday."

She laid the sword on the counter. Gonson unsheathed it, giving it a long once-over. "Sorry, ma'am. But I didn't make this."

She frowned uncertainly. "You're sure? I'd swear he gave me your name."

"Looks like fine work. I'd love to claim it. What was your friend's name? Perhaps I can find out who made it for him."

"Gaittigan." She took back the sword. "But I'm sure he had one of his servants handle this. I'll have to ask who."

She gave the smith her brightest smile. On her way to the door, a well-dressed man strode inside. Raxa paused to admire a rack of swords on the side of the room. Gonson took down the man's order for a new saber, writing it on a greasy sheet of paper.

She killed the rest of the day going from pub to pub. She was sorely tempted to check in on her rescues, but now wasn't the time to risk being seen with them. Long after sundown, when even the Sharps had gone quiet, she returned to Gonson's shop. The windows were dark.

The front walls were wood. No walking through those. But the forges in back required fireproof housing. She cut down the alley behind the shop, stepped into the shadows, and walked through the wall.

She was afraid the apprentices would have rooms in the back, but the building was deserted. She located Gonson's office, rifling through his drawers. Two of them were locked. She had the first sprung in two minutes. It was full of jewels, presumably for prettying up pommels and crossguards.

The second drawer held his ledgers.

They were sorted in order of date received. She paged backwards. About half were in the same writing—Gonson's, presumably—while the others had been made out by the buyer. Almost all were for single orders or matched sets for a handful of guards. The commission for 42 blades was as obvious as a full moon. Dated sixteen days ago. Right after the Order's seven-day spree through the richest houses in the city. The order had been made by one Hallidan. It wasn't written in Gonson's hand.

She folded it into her pocket, closed the drawer, and jimmied the lock shut.

By the time she got back to Vara's, it was three in the morning. She entered as quietly as she could, but a candle lit as she closed the door behind her.

"Gaits?" She scowled at him. "You should be asleep."

"So should you." He limped toward her. "Which means you must be up to something interesting."

"I found the smith who made the matched blades."

Gaits took it from her, scanning rapidly. His eyes darted up, the liveliest they'd been since the attack. "Who wrote this? The smith?"

Raxa shook her head. "The buyer. But there's no way he was stupid enough to use his real name."

"I'm sure he didn't." Gaits grinned and smacked his index finger into the middle of the page. "But it looks like he was stupid enough to use his real handwriting."

"How does that help us? There must be a hundred thousand people in this city."

"But less than a tenth of them can read. And of those, our master of forgery knows everyone worth knowing."

He insisted on delivering the paper to Ackley then and there. Raxa didn't get to bed until dawn. The next day was dead quiet. The day after that was the same. Unable to hold still, Raxa took the black ring around to three other jewelers, but none could identify it.

Back at the house, Gaits and Vara were arguing so loudly Raxa could hear it from the street. As she walked inside, Vara was in the process of tearing Gaits' shirt off his chest.

"Vara!" Raxa yelled. "What the hell are you doing?"

"This fool you call a friend spent all day running around town." Vara jerked her chin at his ribs, which were trickling blood into their bandages. "Popped half his stitches."

"Then you'll have to redo them. Assuming you can find time away from milking your goats." He swung toward Raxa. "Raxa! I've got word from the Order. We know who paid for the swords."

She grinned viciously. "Who was it?"

"Not my place to say. Kerreven wants to tell you himself."

"He's alive?"

"He's ready to strike back—and he wants you to be his blade."

11

Dante stood with his back to the edge of the plateau. Thirty people stared him down, most of them bearing swords or the deadly wheels.

"That's them," Ked said. "That's *them*!"

Beside him, Cord nodded, well-toned arms folded. "I remember the face of everyone who's bested me."

Blays rolled his eyes. "Do you duel every traveler who comes to Collen?"

Ked spat. "Are you travelers? Or Mallish spies?"

"Definitely travelers."

"Is that why you've spent the last week parlaying with your running dog masters?"

"This is ridiculous," Dante said. "Get out of our way. We don't have to answer to you."

"But you'll want to." A gravelly-voiced man stepped forward. He was at least sixty, but he had the jaw of a bulldog, and if you were to attach his head to a mill wheel, his bald pate looked capable of grinding flour. He wore trousers and a vest the color of dust. "Come with me. And don't try any of your tricks."

A man and a woman stepped to either side of him. They wore pale yellow robes trimmed with red thread. Each carried a dirk, which they placed against Dante's spine.

Naran let his hand hang near the hilt of his saber. "What's the nature of this inquiry?"

The bulldog-jawed man stared him down. "It's no inquiry. It's a trial. To find out how bad you sold us out to the Mallish."

"Sold you out?" Blays laughed. "We're on the same side!"

"So you say."

"I'd tell you to go ask the Mallish soldiers, but when we left them, they were being devoured alive by giant spiders."

The gray-clothed constable held up a meaty palm. "Enough! Save your breath for the trial."

Keeping one eye on the dirk-wielding monks, Dante glanced at Blays. The two of them had been in similar situations often enough that verbal communication was no longer necessary. At the moment, Blays' face was saying two things: first, that he didn't like where this was headed. And second, that he would much prefer to extricate themselves without any whirlwinds of limbs and viscera.

"Will we be allowed to speak in our defense?" Dante said.

The older man glowered. "'Course you will. This ain't Bressel."

"And will we be allowed to call witnesses on our behalf?"

"What did I just tell you? King Charles and his ghouls will march you up to the noose the second they've tortured the answer they want from you. But Collen's a free land. If you're charged with a crime, you get to speak. How else can the gods hear you?"

"I'm glad to hear your land is so enlightened. In that case, I'll need Hodd, a monk of the Reborn Shrine, to be at this trial."

The bulldog-jawed man smiled humorlessly. "Don't you worry. He's one of the chief accusers."

He ordered the ribboned warriors to disarm the prisoners. Blays unbuckled his belt and turned over his swords. "Be careful with these. If they go missing, the crimes I commit in response will have us tied up in trials for the next ten years."

He continued the lengthy process of turning out his many knives. Dante passed over his sword. Its fine steel was worth a year's wages. Not for the first time since getting dragged away from the north, he was glad he'd left the bone sword behind. He felt no strong connection to his current weapon, yet as he passed it over to the ribboned warriors, frustration bubbled in his veins.

If these had been Mallish troops arresting him, he would have simply blasted them into a rapidly expanding red hemisphere. But these were Colleners. Their story wasn't so different from Narashtovik's. Even the enemy was the same.

Narashtovik's ending had been happy—but he feared Collen's story would someday end on a far darker note. He had no wish to contribute further tragedy to their tale.

In all of Dante's travels, jails had taken one of two forms: towers and dungeons. In Collen, the jail was located beneath a squat basalt building outside the keep. The cells had been carved right out of the rock. The doors were the iron grilles commonly seen in such places. The bulldog-jawed man, whose name was Den, motioned them inside a single cell and locked the door.

Blays swiveled his head, taking in their surroundings. "I have to say this is the least musty dungeon I've ever been in. But would it have killed you to give us separate cells?"

"Won't be here for long," Den grumbled. "'Sides, it's your right as accused to be able to speak freely with each other. How are you going to do that from different cells?" He trudged away.

"So," Blays said as soon as the constable's footsteps faded. "Ready for our dashing escape?"

"We're not escaping," Dante said.

"I assumed we only let them capture us so we could get out of this without bloodshed. And that our next step would be to reclaim our well-deserved freedom."

"I don't think that's necessary."

"You know why I'm going to win this argument, then? Because in a few days, you're going to be too busy strangling in a noose to debate me. We already saved Collen from whatever the Mallish were planning with the shaden. Why not tunnel us out of here?"

"Because we need to tell these people about their true history. Anyway, we're not going to get hanged. I know a way to prove we're not in league with Mallon."

"How do you intend to do that?" Naran said. "Charges of treason are as pernicious as heresy. For most lawmen, suspicion is proof enough."

"We'll start by telling them the truth about why we're here."

Blays frowned. "I thought we were keeping that as secret as the king's syphilis. If Mallon gets word of our involvement here, their eyes will turn to Narashtovik."

"They won't be able to harm Narashtovik until they've dealt with Collen." Dante seated himself on a stone bench along one wall. "Collen needs to know what they're up against. That's the only way they can defend themselves."

"But *we* don't even know what they're up against. I thought we'd agreed not to get involved here."

"We're not. Once they cut us loose, my only goal is to figure out how to kill Gladdic. If the answers aren't here, we'll travel back to Bressel. Things will have quieted down since we left. And by the time we get there, our loon will be in Narashtovik, where I'll have access to the complete wisdom of the Citadel."

Blays continued to argue, but they're hardly spoken for another minute before a door creaked and footsteps thumped down the tight stone corridor. Den moved in front of the doors, flanked by his two yellow-robed monks.

"Move your asses," he said. "Time for your trial."

Naran stood, brushing off his pants. "This is rather hasty."

"Every man deserves a fast trial. Would you rather rot in here?"

Den marched them upstairs and outside, where a squadron of colorfully-ribboned warriors awaited to escort them. Dante expected to be taken to the Reborn Shrine, which seemed the natural location for the handing down of divine judgment, but their destination turned out to be a clearing on the north end of the city known as Justice Falls.

The ground was naked stone. It had once been ringed by a semicircle of twelve-foot stone blocks, but many of these had toppled and cracked. Two winding grooves ran from the middle of the ring to the edge of the cliffs. Den ordered Dante, Blays, and Naran to stand between the two grooves. A warm wind buffeted their faces.

Den strode back to the standing stones. Ked, Cord, Hodd, and several other familiar faces were assembled to either side of him. An announcement of the trial must have gone out during their brief stay in the dungeons; two hundred strangers stood outside the ring of standing stones.

"Bring out the waters," Den called roughly. "And let justice water the desert."

Two small carts rumbled forth, pushed by pairs of apprentice monks. The carts each held a large barrel. The vehicles came to a stop at the edge of the grooves. The two monks who'd helped take them prisoner walked forth solemnly, knelt beside the barrels, and flipped open their spigots. Water splashed into the grooves and ran toward the cliff's edge where Dante stood.

"Duset," he blinked. "The sign of Arawn."

Blays nodded at the Colleners watching them. "If they've got Arawn on their side, is it too late to buddy up with Taim?"

The waters flowed past them. And began the long fall down the cliffs.

Den gestured toward the three accused. "These three are said to be Mallish spies and conspirators. Make your case!"

"Hang on there," Blays yelled back. "Aren't you going to tell us how this process works?"

"What's there to tell? The justice will describe your crimes. You'll be allowed to state your defense, if you have any. And at the end..." Den motioned sweepingly to the crowd. "This fine lot will judge your guilt."

"Trial by *mob*?"

"That's no mob. That's democracy!"

"I have to admit it sounds more fair than Whetton," Blays muttered.

Den gestured to the group of witnesses. A squat man strolled forth, his face laced with scars. Muscles bulged beneath his short sleeves. He stopped twenty feet from Dante, turning to regard the audience.

"Den has already stated the crime before us." The man looked like a slab of beef brisket, but his voice was as sonorous as the tropical doves they'd seen in the Plagued Islands. "My name is Bond, and it's my task to prove these crimes are real. I'll let you in on a secret: it's going to be the easiest job I've ever had."

The ad hoc jury tittered. Bond considered them a moment before continuing. "The first matter needs no explanation. This man, Andrew Welborn, is clearly Mallish." He gestured to

Dante; Welborn was the name Dante had provided them to preserve his identity. Too late, it occurred to Dante that he'd taken on the most Mallish name possible. Bond gave the crowd a moment to inspect Dante for themselves, then went on. "The hair. The eyes. The nose and skin and the angle of the cheeks. These are all the same things we see when the armies march forth from Bressel. How do you answer this, Mr. Welborn?"

"I was born in Mallon," Dante said. "But I renounced my loyalty to it over a decade ago."

"So you don't deny you're Mallish." Some of the crowd chuckled. The justice tucked his hands behind his back and strolled closer to the accused. "This isn't a crime in itself. But you came here mere days after a significant arrival of Mallish troops. And when you came to Collen, what was the first thing you did?"

"Stumbled into a group of Colleners being attacked by Mallish soldiers. When I saw one of your citizens was mortally wounded, I went to help him."

"You're speaking of Ked Danzer." The justice gestured to the witnesses. Ked stepped forward, nodding to the crowd. The justice folded his hands in front of him. "Who was Ked wounded by? As you've said: Mallish soldiers. Hence, you took his deathright away. An act of ignorance? Perhaps. Or perhaps it was a deliberate insult. Only the Mallish would be so cruel as to steal a man's deathright."

This provoked a great deal of dark looks and muttered oaths from the expansive jury. Bond gave them time to settle down before continuing on, pacing between the two streams of water, careful not to step in either.

"Hodd of the Reborn Shrine," he called.

The young monk stepped forward from the cluster of witnesses. "Yes, Justice Bond?"

"You told Den that Mr. Welborn came to the Reborn Shrine in search of information. Precisely what was he looking for?"

"Well." Hodd stared fixedly past the justice's ear. "He was looking for books."

"Books concerning which subjects?"

The young monk's olive cheeks flushed red. "Concerning... demons. Arawn. Nethermancy. When I told him the shrine contained no such blasphemy, he continued to look for it in other works. Legends and histories."

Dante's blood ran cool. The earlier charges struck him as ridiculous, but to an outsider, his interest in reading material would sound troubling, if not outright dangerous. To most people, an interest in dark topics was profound proof of a dark mind.

The justice nodded slowly, as if absorbing Hodd's answer. "Do you know *why* he had such interest in banned works?"

"He said he was a Galladese monk devoted to Carvahal." Hodd lowered his head. "But I thought that was strange. If he wanted to know more about Arawn's workings, why not go to Narashtovik? Why travel all the way to Collen?"

"A fair question. Do you have an alternate theory for why Mr. Welborn came to your shrine?"

"I, ah. I thought it might be a trap. A way to find out if our order was still harboring heresy."

"That would be a cunning way for Mallon to justify further arrests—or occupation." The justice raised his eyebrows to the crowd. "Even so, you might be inclined to dismiss it as the occult interests of an eccentric monk. Except that the men before you have spent the last week parlaying with Mallish troops."

This provoked a score of angry curses. Dante uttered one of his own and took a step forward. "If we *were* Mallish spies, you'd think we'd be a little more careful to cover up our meetings with our contacts. The real explanation of our activities is more complicated, but it has the virtue of being true. Your bevy of accusations are nothing but circumstantial—which may be why you have to rely on so many of them to convince your jury."

"Circumstantial?" Justice Bond smiled grimly. "I don't disagree. I was merely laying the foundation for this." He reached into his vest and produced several sheets of folded parchment. He unfolded them, completely unhurried. "This is a letter we intercepted three days ago. It's signed by Gladdic, Ordon of Bressel. It's addressed to Baldren, Spalder of Bressel, commander of the incursion that's made camp many miles to our northeast."

The justice cleared his throat and read, his sweet voice carrying through the outdoor court like a traveling bard earning his keep in an inn. The letter alerted Baldren to be on the lookout for three men who had been dispatched there to assist him in restoring order to the "rebellious province." Though Gladdic used no names, he described Dante, Blays, and Naran in meticulous detail.

Finished, the justice lowered the letter. He gazed sadly across the mob/jury. "Tell me the men described in this letter are not the men you see before you. I beg you. Else every one of us will end the day with blood on our hands."

There was a brief silence. The intake of breath before a shout. The crowd erupted.

"Hang them!"

"Boot them from the cliff!"

"Kill the traitors!"

Blays leaned close to Dante. "We may be new to this place, but I know a bloodthirsty mob when I see one. Got a way out of this?"

"Yes and no." Dante peered down the edge of the butte. They were two hundred feet above the plains below, separated from it by sheer cliffs and murderously steep piles of broken rock. "I can get us down from here. But if they pursue us on horseback, I don't know how we'll get away."

"If you don't get us down there, I suspect these people will lend us a hand in doing so. Or more accurately, a boot in the ass."

Dante nodded. He had no knives, so he was forced to bite the inside of his cheek to draw blood. While they'd been speaking, Den had resumed oversight of the trial.

"—find them innocent?" Den called to the crowd.

No one made a peep. Dante sucked the nether to him and plunged it into the earth beneath his feet.

"And who among you say they are guilty?" Den said.

"Aye!" the mass jury roared as one.

"Then let the gods hear what their people have decided."

Den motioned to the contingent of warriors who'd been observing from behind him. They advanced through the standing stones, gripping their wheels near the weighted base, spear tips held before them. Dante began to shape a long, smooth ramp down the cliff face, its outer edges curled up to prevent them from flying over the side as they slid down it.

"Stop!" Despite the imperative, the voice delivering it was hesitant. Hodd wandered into the clearing of stone, arms held stiffly to his sides, as if he were stepping out onto a ledge and terrified he'd lose his balance.

Den jogged toward him, his tan face going red. "Clear out! Before you get hurt!"

"But I know who these men are!" Hodd shrank on himself as three hundred pairs of eyes locked on him. Throat working, he forced himself to stand taller. "They're not Mallish spies."

"What are you blathering about?" Den said. "Haven't you been listening to the justice?"

"Very closely. When he read the ordon's letter, it jogged something loose in my mind. I've heard two of these men described elsewhere." He turned his back on the crowd and brushed past the halted warriors, coming to stand across from Dante, eyes darting nervously. "You're him, aren't you?"

Dante licked his dry lips. To keep his city clear of any conflict brewing between Mallon and Collen, he'd done his damnedest to preserve the secret of his identity. Exposing himself now might save his life.

And expose his city to war.

He shook his head. "My name is Andrew Welborn. Once of Mallon, now of Gallador."

Hodd lifted an accusatory finger, eyes sparking with the first anger Dante had seen in him. "You lie. You're Dante Galand! High Priest of Narashtovik!"

The gathered people, including the stalwart warriors, burst into confused babble. A few sounded like they were choking. Others laughed in disbelief.

Den's face was now so red it resembled a freshly laundered Gaskan military uniform. "Is this true?"

"No sense denying it," Blays said. "If you do, rumor will spread the story twice as fast as the truth."

"Hodd's right." Dante lifted his voice and gazed across the crowds. "My name is Dante Galand. I was born in Mallon, but if you think I'd help my former country subjugate your people, then you don't know a gods damn thing about me."

"Dante Galand." Den chuckled, sobering rapidly. "If that's true, then what in the twelve hells are you doing in *Collen*?"

Justice Bond began to recover his former confidence, striding about the bare stone. "And why are you here in disguise? Infiltrating our city under a false name? Just what are you hiding, sir?"

"I can answer all these questions," Dante said. "But I'll need two things." He beckoned to Hodd. "I need a book from the Reborn Shrine. *An Account of the Third War with Almers*. By—"

"Flinders" Hodd finished. "Ah, yes. Yes of course."

"Next, we have to go down to the plains. What I have to show you can't be found up here."

Den threw his hands in the air. "We can't leave Justice Falls in the middle of a trial. This ain't how it's done!"

"Are you that intent on punishing us? Or do you want to learn why we're really here—and why Mallon first declared war on you a thousand years ago?"

"We know that front and back. During the blights, our ancestors fed nether to the crops. But rather than growing the plants tall, it killed them dead. When our people turned to taking from Mallish lands in order to survive, the Mallish declared war."

"Wrong," Dante said. "But if that's what you prefer to believe, then you can go on dishonoring your ancestors for another thousand years."

The justice's eyebrows jumped up his scarred forehead. "Den, the gods know there's a time for tradition and a time to break it. This here? This is one of the latter times."

Den looked like he didn't know whether to sigh, spit, or swear. He fixed Dante with an exasperated look. "Where are you intending to take us, milord?"

Dante didn't let the sarcasm embedded in the last word register. "Right outside the lower city. Anywhere that hasn't been farmed recently should do."

"Right then. The sooner we get there, the sooner this day will start to make sense again."

Den hollered orders to all sides. The warriors formed a loose ring around Dante, Naran, and Blays, escorting them from the so-called Justice Falls. The mob followed after them at a safe distance. Hodd scampered off to the shrine in search of the book.

As they crossed the city, Cord made her way to Blays. "If he's Dante Galand, does that make you Blays Buckler?"

"That's right," Blays said. "Heard of me, have you?"

"The Blays Buckler *I've* heard of has never lost a fight." She beamed. "So it sounds like it's time for the bards to start singing the chronicles of Cord Wheeler!"

"Don't get ahead of yourself," Dante said. "Blays has lost dozens of fights."

Blays brushed dust from his shoulder. "And I'm still here, aren't I? That's far more impressive than never having lost."

A steady stream of civilians came out to ask the mob what was happening. Most of the newcomers wound up joining the proceedings. Den barked various commands, which Dante followed without defiance. They descended the switchbacks, crossed through the lower settlement, and walked into the open yellow plain.

A few hundred feet away from the last of the flat-roofed houses, Den called for a halt. The warriors backed away from Dante but maintained the ring around the outsiders.

"Will this place work for you, milord?" Den said.

"I expect so." Dante kneeled in the dust. "I'm going to summon the nether. No tricks. I swear on my life and my city."

Den gestured subtly to his warriors, who held their weapons in hand, including throwing spears and nocked bows. Dante bit his cheek again, wincing, and called to the shadows. He sank them into the ground. The crumbly gray dirt leveled, becoming as flat as a summer lake, then began to drain away.

People gasped. He heard his name whispered among the crowd as doubters became believers. As a teenager, Dante had yearned for such recognition — dreamed of it — but that need had begun to fade as soon as he'd joined the Council. His work had soon become all the accomplishment he needed.

Even so, he twisted the nether in the earth, making it swirl away in pretty patterns that served no purpose other than to bewitch the crowd.

The hole lowered further, revealing branches. Matted grass.

Flattened shrubs. The long-dead foliage was as gray as the soil around it.

Dante stood. "Do you see this?"

"The tolts?" Den's voice squeaked with incredulity. "They're everywhere. Created during the blights. Since those black days, nothing's grown what hasn't been right next to a canal."

"That's what your histories say." Dante pointed into the distance. "The mountains to your northeast. What are they called?"

"The Horned Mountains. What of it?"

"How high would you say they are?"

"How would I know that? Should I asked the ravens?"

"Take a guess. One mile? Two?"

Den shrugged broadly. An old man with a scraggly white beard and sun-creased skin stepped from the jury-mob. "Sone Pass is three thousand feet. The big peaks like Huck and Franken? Ten thousand."

Den turned on him. "How do you know that?"

The man folded his arms proudly. "Took my measures up there thirty years back. The mercury grows the closer you bring it to the ether. Tells you right how tall's the piece of earth you're standing on."

Dante gazed at the blue blur of the range. "So we'd all agree they're mountains. Big ones."

"Is this how you win arguments in Narashtovik?" Bond said. "State the obvious until no one can stand to listen any longer? I think the northern snows have frozen your skulls solid."

"Where is Hodd?"

"Here, sir." Hodd waved his hand from within the crowd. "I mean, milord."

"I'm not your lord," Dante said. "Did you find the book?"

"Excuse me," Hodd said to those around him. "Excuse me?" A path opened. He wedged through it, approaching Dante and holding out the book.

Dante flipped through the pages of Flinders' chronicle of the wars between the early Collen Basin and the long-dead kingdom of Almers. His eyes snagged on a paragraph in the middle of a section describing the terms of the alliance between Collen and Kolody, an independent city that had once existed to the east.

He passed the book to Hodd, tapping the relevant paragraph. "This section, if you would."

"Ahem." Hodd supported the tome in both hands and read aloud. "'Kolody sat almost three hundred miles from Collen on the other side of the Horned Hills. The distance was far, but it was made lesser by that of the River Common, which had long united the two lands through trade. For Kolody's aid in the war, Collen promised it a colony in Almers, and so Kolody was convinced to trade its fine armors. The first Kolodians made for Collen, entering the hills with their great wains. But the Almerians awaited them in the valley of the River Common, and rushed from the forest beside the road, destroying them.'"

Dante nodded, retaking the book. "Horned *Hills*. I imagine the scholars dismiss this as a slip by Flinders, or the fault of whichever monk copied the original text. But he also describes the Kolodians as passing through the hills via a valley that no longer exists. And that the two lands shared a river that also no longer exists. Scholars might dismiss this as a mistake on Flinders' part. After all, he was writing two centuries after these wars were over. Perhaps he simply got it wrong."

Dante turned his head slowly, meeting the attentive gazes of the crowd. "Or perhaps he's referring to facts that have long been forgotten."

"This have a point?" Den said. "What's the war with Almers have to do with Mallon?"

"I'm getting to that. But first, I have to divert to Narashtovik. A thousand years ago, the ancestors of my people had been pushed to the brink of destruction by their mortal enemies. In desperation, my people sought to raise a range of mountains between them and their enemies.

"But they were far more successful than they intended. The mountains they summoned were colossal. In Narashtovik, the existing mountains became the Woduns, the largest range I've ever seen. And I believe they extended much further than the north. From what I've discovered, they reached all the way to Collen—and transformed the Horned Hills into the Horned Mountains."

"Oh bullshit. Mountains don't just sprout from the ground

like a forest!"

Dante gestured to the hole he'd sunk into the ground. "You've seen with your own eyes what I'm capable of. Now imagine a full order of nethermancers bent to the same task—and in possession of an artifact of divine power."

Den's expression softened slightly. "Even if the hills became mountains—so what?"

"This land was once verdant. There were even forests. The evidence is right under your feet. It wasn't your greedy nethermancers who ruined the land. It was the mountains that took away your rains."

The silence that ensued was as stark as the desert around them. Den looked like a child seeing the sea for the first time. Most of the warriors appeared guarded, but some of the citizens' faces had gone stormy. Naran looked almost as gobsmacked as the locals.

The battle-scarred justice was the first to recover. "How could our people have forgotten such a drastic change?"

"It was a thousand years ago," Blays said. "I can't even remember what I had for breakfast this morning."

Dante gazed at the desiccated branches and grass exposed in the pit. "My best guess? You forgot because the Mallish wanted you to. During the first wars with Collen, back in Bressel, the ethermancers of Taim threw out the nethermancers of Arawn. Here, they saw the opportunity to net two fish with one swoop: blame the nether for the disaster that befell Collen, and blame the Colleners for using it."

"And hence the war that followed," Bond mused.

"When Mallon invaded, they burned your histories. And killed everyone who denied their version of the story. The truth isn't like the stars, burning forever beyond our grasp. It's as mortal as the people who carry it."

Den's jaw worked like he was actually chewing on these ideas. "You said Narashtovik's to blame for the raising of the Horneds. Sounds like *we* ought to be enemies."

"If you want," Dante said. "But I think our lands have much in common. Including frequent clashes with Mallon. Far from being Mallish spies, we came here to curtail their ability to wage war on others."

"How d'you intend to stop them from *that*?"

"Telling you that would compromise our ability to get it done."

"Might convenient."

"Even more conveniently, it's true."

"So," Blays said. "Are you guys going to execute us or what?"

Den and the justice exchanged a look. Den tugged at his vest. "We'll have to consider that. In the meantime, it's back to the jails with you."

"Nonsense! I thought that was the mob's decision." Blays crossed the crunchy dirt toward the audience. "So what do you say, mob? Still want to pitch us off a cliff?"

"Nay," a woman said. Her declaration was echoed by the man next to her. Then it poured forth from the throat of every witness, a river of sound in the stillness of the desert.

Half-dazed, the three of them returned to the butte-top inn where they'd stayed prior to their destruction of the shaden. They climbed the steps to their room and flopped in the chairs there, grateful to be out of the sun and away from the crowds.

"Well, that wasn't so bad," Blays said.

Dante eyed him. "Wasn't so bad? They almost executed us as spies!"

"That's not what happened at all. They *almost* got cut into thousands of fluttery little bits to be thrown behind us like confetti as we galloped away from Collen as fast as our legs could carry us."

"That might not be such a bad idea."

"Killing a mob? Has all the sunshine boiled your brain?"

"Leaving Collen. We've convinced them we're not spies, but we outed ourselves in the process. It might be best to get out of here before word gets back to Gladdic."

Naran shifted on his chair. "What do you propose?"

"We can hole up in Averoy with the rest of your crew. Once we're in contact with Narashtovik and have a handle on how to deal with the Star-Eaters, we'll return to Bressel and take down Gladdic."

"One small problem," Blays said. "We're out of food. As well as the money to buy food."

"We can forage on the way."

"Forage? On our way through Collen? I hope you like roast lizard. With a seasoning of sand." Blays produced one of his knives, which had been returned to him following their acquittal. "I suppose I could pawn a couple of these."

"That works," Dante said. "But don't sell any of your favorites. I'd hate for you to die of heartbreak along the road."

Blays departed to buy food for their coming travels. Naran decided to catch a nap. Finding the room stuffy, Dante walked downstairs to one of the covered patios. As he waited outside, Hodd entered the square, neck craned.

Seeing Dante, he trotted up to him and bowed low, one knee brushing the ground. "Milord."

"For the last time, I'm not your lord," Dante said. "What can I do for you?"

"Ah." Hodd rose. "I'm looking for you. But I'm not the only one."

"Tell me Den hasn't decided to slap us with a new set of charges."

The monk blushed. "I brought word of your discoveries to my order. The Keeper of the Reborn Shrine wishes to see you at once—and to repay you for what you've unearthed."

12

Dante tilted his head. "The Keeper of the Reborn Shrine?"

Hodd dipped his head and bent at the knees. "Just so, milord."

"Who is this Keeper and what does he want with me?"

"He will answer all your questions. Please say you'll come with me, milord."

"We were about to leave town," he said, then shook his head to clear it. "Let me tell the others there's going to be a delay."

Dante jogged upstairs and left a note for Blays and Naran in their room. He returned to the plaza and walked beside Hodd on their way to the shrine, pressing the young monk for details. Hodd merely stammered that the Keeper would be much better qualified to tell Dante everything he wished to know.

The shrine's multi-stoned dome hovered over the rooftops. Hodd took him into a room deep inside the main building.

"Wait here," he said. "The Keeper will be with you soon."

Hodd closed the oversized door behind him. Dante seated himself in a padded chair facing the entrance. Five minutes later, a low whoosh sounded from the side of the room. A door Dante hadn't noticed swung open. He stood. An incredibly old woman hobbled inside, supporting herself with a broom that was taller than she was. She eyed Dante with eyes so pale that he initially thought she was blinded by cataracts. Yet after she looked him up and down, he realized they were simply the lightest shade of blue he'd ever seen. She limped forward, sweeping monotonously.

"Pardon the dust." Her voice was a deep croak, as strong as an oak or a glacier, jarringly cavernous compared to the narrow frame of her body. "The monks, they ask, 'What's the point? There'll just be more dust tomorrow.' They're used to it, I suppose. But what would happen if no one swept?"

"Here in Collen? I imagine you'd drown in it." Dante watched her another moment, then returned to his chair.

She crossed the room, the broom's bristles rasping on the stone, marshaling a growing pile of dust. Dante kept his eyes fixed on nothing. He'd grown up as a peasant, then an orphan in a monastery of far meaner status than this shrine. Despite his last decade in the grandeur of the Sealed Citadel, he'd never fully gotten used to ordering servants around as if they were pieces on a Nulladoon board.

With inexorable patience, she swept past him. Her broom was as plain as her dress, but the end of its shaft was carved into a crude horseshoe.

When she was behind his chair, she said, "So you're Dante Galand."

He jolted to his feet, twisting to face her. "Are you..?"

"I am."

"Excuse me. Hodd led me to believe you were a man."

The old woman laughed to herself. "That's because he thinks I am one. I would ask you not to disabuse him of his assumptions."

"If that's what you'd prefer."

"It helps me do my sweeping without being bothered." She stared into his eyes, reading them, then nodded and resumed working with her broom. "Why are you here?"

"Hodd said you wished to see me."

"Why are you here in Collen, you fool?"

"That's a long and winding story. The short answer is that I've been following the trail of Mallish meddling."

"You could follow that trail the rest of your life and still not find its head. Is this visit official?"

"It's personal. And it will remain that way."

The old woman chuckled, the deep rasps bouncing off the walls. "You are your country. When you indulge in a personal vendetta, that vendetta becomes your nation's as well." She came to the corner of the room, reached into a brass urn, and retrieved a small hand broom and pan, which she used to gather up the formidable pile of dirt she'd accrued. "You claimed the blights that ruined Collen weren't our fault. Is this true? Or something you told the mob to save yourself from a swift trip down the cliff?"

"What would you do if it was a lie?"

She straightened, one hand pressed to her back, and stared into his eyes again. "Be surprised."

"When the people who came before me raised the Wodun Mountains, it altered the lands of Weslee forever. There, a region of verdant forest became sandy desert. I believe the same thing happened here."

"And we forgot. Swallowing Mallish lies instead." The Keeper's wrinkled face burned with sudden wrath. "The one thing my line is here to prevent."

"What *is* your line?"

"When Mallon comes, the priests bring knives. Hooks. Fire. Acid. When they turn those tools on a man, there's nothing he can hide from them. The only sanctuary is ignorance. The Keepers know what the common folk can't afford to."

"And how do the Keepers keep themselves safe?" Dante said.

"By making sure the common folk don't know we exist."

"Then why am I allowed to meet you?"

"You've only been here a brief while, but you've already given us knowledge of ourselves we'd lost centuries ago. I don't think your work is done yet. Even so, most times, I'd be content to let you hoe your own way through the weeds ahead of you."

"I'm guessing there's a 'but' on its way."

"Even the stories about you take the form of a storm," she said. "Where you go, chaos follows. Say I stand on a ledge looking at my enemies below. There is a rock that may be poised to set off a slide, but reaching for it would be dangerous. Do I pray that it tips over on its own? Or do I stretch across the abyss and give it a nudge?"

"I have no interest in dragging my people into a conflict with Mallon. But if I succeed in my goal here, Mallon will be significantly less driven to a new conflict with *your* people."

She did her eye-reading thing again. Dante was well used to staring people down, but he found her gaze uncomfortable. Like that of an alligator, or the deep-set eyes of the statues of gods.

"I see vengeance," the Keeper said. "But not malice. Let's loose the arrow and see where it lands." She tapped her broom against the floor. "Before we go any further, I need to warn you. Do you know the prophecy of this shrine?"

"It was one of the first things Hodd told me. When it's reborn for the twelfth time, Arawn will emerge to destroy the Mallish."

She nodded once. "And when he comes, he'll consume all who betrayed the shrine—including its secrets."

"By the time this temple is torn down twice more, chances are I'll be long dead."

"Arawn's realm is death. Do you think being dead would save you from his wrath?"

The Keeper turned to the wall she'd come in through. Its face was adorned with bas-relief carvings of expansive fields of flowers and crops. The old woman lifted her broom and fit its horseshoe-shaped tip into the petal of a flower. A muffled metal click sprung from inside the wall. A door swung into a darkened room.

She shuffled inside and Dante followed. The room smelled like rust. A string of small white stones hung on a hook beside the open door. She picked up the string with a clatter, cupped one of the stones in her palm, and blew on it. Pale light pushed back the darkness. Two dozen torchstones hung from the string. Enough that, even if she had to use their light for an entire day, by the time she exhausted the last one, the first would be ready to use again.

The Keeper touched the edge of the door, which closed of its own accord. The room was half filled with religious statuettes, braziers, and candlesticks, coated in cobwebs and grime. It had the appearance of a forgotten storage room, but Dante wasn't surprised when the old woman jabbed her broomstick into the corner of the room, springing open a hatch in the floor.

Stairs spiraled down into the darkness. They were narrow and steep, but the Keeper descended them without hesitation, coming to a landing of solid stone. She kneeled in the corner, withdrew a metal pin from her gray hair, and inserted it into a hole in the floor, opening yet another hatch. The floor had been Mallish limestone, but the next curve of stairwell was white chalk. They came to another landing, where the Keeper opened a third hatch with the help of a small knife. The third leg of the stairwell was black basalt.

"What's down here?" Dante said.

"Me," the Keeper croaked. "My two apprentices. And the truths our people would be killed for keeping."

At the next landing, she shuffled through a brass door. The light of her torchstone seemed to shrink. Dante followed her through, stopping short as he emerged onto a landing overlooking a twenty-foot drop.

The old woman blew on two more of the stones. White light flared across the room, which was a dark mirror of the library upstairs. Thousands of books crowded the shelves, alternating with racks of scrolls. Dante had seen few libraries to match it.

Something felt wrong, but it took him a moment to place it. "There are no desks."

The old woman gave him a sneer. "Who would use them?"

The library looked simultaneously ancient, yet also astoundingly recent, as if a great arm had reached into the past and drawn the shrine's underground into the present day. The Keeper moved along the railing, coming to a high-ceilinged alcove lined with shelves. This room held a desk as well. Before she sat, she pulled one of four cords dangling from the wall. A bell jangled distantly.

"Sit down," she said. "And tell me what you wish to know."

They took up chairs at either side of the desk. Dante glanced up at the walls. "Maybe it's best if you don't know too much. I don't want to cause any extra trouble for Collen. Gods know you have enough."

"Does it look like we get out much?"

"The monks upstairs have to deal with all kinds of travelers."

"I allowed you down here. If you want to stay, you'll tell me why you came."

He scratched his stubble, then leaned back, exhaling through his nose. "We came here for two reasons. The first was to deal with some powerful objects the Mallish have gotten their hands on. Essentially, they're nether storage devices a sorcerer can use to augment their strength."

"You're talking about the shells."

"You know of them?"

"Farmers have been finding them in the fields for two years. We've had many questions about them. And not so many answers."

"A few weeks ago, we cut off Mallon's supply," Dante said. "A few days ago, we destroyed everything they had here."

The Keeper scowled. "What were they using them for?"

"We don't know. Maybe you can help us figure that out." He explained about the digs the Mallish soldiers had been conducting on the butte. How they'd been disinterring Collenese bodies and painting the bones with nether.

The Keeper looked as though she might spit flame. "I don't know why they want our dead. For all the crimes they accuse us of, their own are nine times worse."

A man padded into the room bearing a small lantern. His face was so pale and soft he looked boyish, yet he was clearly at least a decade Dante's senior. "You called, Keeper?"

"Tea," she said without looking over.

"Yes, Keeper." He turned and exited.

"You have tea down here?" Dante said.

"Does your order forbid it?"

"My order couldn't function without it. But when I last spent much time in Mallish lands, no one knew what tea was."

"Things change, don't they."

Sitting there in the ageless, sealed-off library, he wasn't sure if that was a wry comment or a truth so basic it existed everywhere. The Keeper seemed lost in her own thoughts. Dante's loon tingled—the one connected to Jona—but he ignored it.

The boyish man returned with a tarnished silver tray and two sturdy mugs. The tea inside was cold, and weaker than Dante was used to, but he was grateful nonetheless.

"Does someone bring this down to you?" he said. "Or do you keep it in storage?"

The Keeper gave him one of her looks. "Storage. What's the other reason you came to Collen?"

"Do you know of Gladdic? The ordon from Bressel?"

She snorted. "Do you know of forest fires? Plagues? Less than ten years ago, things were as close to peace as we ever know. Then Gladdic arose from the monkhood. He said Arawn's lies had once more poured out of the north. He said we were as weak for these lies as a drunk for his wine. He asked for all who believed in Arawn's place in the Celeset to come with him to the desert, where he'd show them Taim's miracle. We never saw them again. Since then, Mallish bluebacks are rarely away from Collen."

"Right," Dante said. "Well, I'm here to kill him."

The Keeper grabbed the desk's edge for support as she got to her feet. "He's here?"

"What would you do if he was? Sweep him off the edge of the butte?"

"Never," she said. "I'd make his death much slower than that."

"Too bad, then. Last I heard, he was somewhere north of Bressel."

The wrath faded from the old woman's face. She lowered herself to her chair. "Then if you intend to kill him, it seems to me you're in the wrong place."

"A few weeks back, we made a run at him. However, when we infiltrated his temple, we ran into something...unexpected." He described how Gladdic had shrugged off all of Dante's strikes with the nether, and how, when he'd finally attacked the ordon with the ether, he'd seemed to turn into a shadow of himself—one with bright silver eyes. "I couldn't seem to hurt him at all. But my friends had learned that he'd taken his most recent batch of shaden to Collen. We decided to follow the shells and see if I could learn anything more about Gladdic's ability here, where people have never stopped their practice of the nether."

The Keeper asked a bevy of questions regarding Gladdic's transformation and what exactly Dante had done to try to harm him. At last, she lapsed into silence.

"Enough for now," she said. "Return to me at noon tomorrow. I'll have your books then."

"We're done?" Dante glanced around for a window, but there were none. "It's not even dinner yet."

"I have other things to do besides educate ignorant young men. Such as nap."

"If you're too tired, I could start looking through the archives myself."

"The consumption of knowledge is no different than food, boy. It needs time to digest. Treader will show you out."

The pale man stepped out from the shadows as silently as a ghost. "With me, sir."

He led Dante up the stairwell and through its hidden trapdoors. In the storage room on the ground floor, he peeped through a hole in the wall, then brought Dante to the chamber where he'd first met the Keeper.

Dante exited the shrine and made haste for the inn. Blays and Naran were sitting around the room looking annoyed.

"Where were you?" Blays said. "Saying goodbye to all those friendly locals who've spent the last week dueling, insulting, accusing, and imprisoning us?"

"I left you a note. I was summoned to the shrine." Weary after the lengthy day, Dante dropped into a chair. "We're not leaving. We were right to come here. More than we knew." He explained his meeting with the Keeper. "I'm supposed to see her again at noon tomorrow. She may know more about what the Mallish were doing out there—and how we can deal with Gladdic."

"You're sure you can trust her?"

"Why wouldn't I?"

"She lives in a hole in the ground with no contact with the outside world. For all we know, she believes she's some kind of talking mole."

"She sounds more like a bullfrog," Dante said. "I'll stay wary for tricks. But I think we'd be foolish to walk away from this."

"I wouldn't mind a few more days here. Cord dropped by to invite me to train with her at her shrine."

"Is there anything we can do to help?" Naran said.

Dante ran his fingers through his hair, which had grown excessively greasy during their jaunt into the desert to destroy the shaden. "Be prepared. If the Keeper knows how to kill Gladdic, we'll want to move before he has the chance to cause any more trouble. Which reminds me." He touched his loon, activating it. "Jona? Did you try to reach me earlier?"

Fumbling noises came through the loon. "Ahoy? Dante? Just wanted you to know Gladdic's returned to Bressel. Two days ago, by the rumor I heard."

"Know where he was? Or what he's planning next?"

"The crown's been right miserly about publishing his schedule. But if I hear anything about it, I'll let you know."

Dante shut down the loon. "According to Jona, Gladdic's back in Bressel. Stay ready to move. We may be ready to go after him as early as tomorrow."

Blays had earned a few coins pawning his knives, but they were still hurting for money. In the morning, Dante killed time by treating the wounds and maladies of the inn's lodgers in exchange for a modest handful of iron clinks and silver chucks. His healing involved the open use of the nether, something he wouldn't have done prior to the trial, but the cat was out of the bag. Trying to stuff it back in wouldn't earn him anything but scratched-up arms.

As noon neared, he walked to the shrine. Hodd was out front greeting a group of pilgrims.

Seeing Dante, he handed the pilgrims off to another monk and jogged over. "Did, ah…did you…"

"Did I what? Make it home last night? It was touch and go at first, but then I remembered that I own working legs."

Hodd dropped his voice, glancing to all sides. "Did you speak to the Keeper?"

Dante nodded. "Have you ever met him?"

"Sometimes we receive notes. For supplies and things. But meeting him is forbidden. That way, we can never betray him, even if the Mallish put out our eyes and slice off our testicles."

"Sounds like an enlightened policy."

"May I ask what he's like?"

"Wizened," Dante said. "And tough. Like chewing old leather. You're in good hands."

He returned to the chamber where he'd first met her. After a short delay, the side door opened. Treader brought him down the stairs to the library concealed in the belly of the shrine. The day before, the library had had very little in the way of furniture, but in Dante's absence, someone—Treader, presumably—had been put to work. A redoubt of desks now occupied the largest alcove. Towers of books soared from the desks. A large torchstone hung within a glass bowl suspended from the ceiling, shedding ample, moon-like light over the tomes. Somewhere in the center of the castle of books, a page flipped. Dante circled around the ramparts of parchment, paper and leather until the Keeper became visible, her knobby back bent over a volume that looked as heavy as she was and twice as old.

"So." He sat in the nearest chair. "Have you had time to digest?"

"And to consume even more," the Keeper said. "Be careful you don't step in any of the resulting excrement."

"It looks like you've pulled half your library out. I hope that's the result of a wealth of sources rather than a desperate search for anything remotely close."

"Do you know of the Second Scour?"

"The Two-Part War," Dante said. "Four hundred years back, King Sarl of Mallon led a crusade against Gask, looking to stamp out Arawn's influence there. But the Gaskan winters killed more of his troops than any battle. It left his forces in such a shambles that Gask was able to push Sarl back through town after town. The Gaskans marched halfway to Bressel before agreeing to peace—in exchange for Sarl's promise that the Mallish people would be allowed to worship Arawn as they pleased."

"A promise that lasted eight whole years. But this is not that story. This is the story that explains why Mallon's testicles had swollen to the point that it was convinced it could conquer Gask in the first place."

Her voice was even froggier than the day before, but as she went on, it began to warm up. "Eighty years before the Two-Part War, Kon the White-Haired, greatest nethermancer in the land, was elected absolute despot of Collen. By the end of his second year, he announced the end of Mallish rule in the Basin. By the end of his fifth year, he had made it so.

"The Mallish responded as they always had. But each force they marched into Collen was met by Kon, who commanded at the front of his lines, beating back each charge, smelling out each feint, laying ruin to his foes with hellstorms of nether." Here, she described a number of battles and flashpoints, noting that she was summarizing blow-by-blow accounts that would be tedious to anyone who wasn't a very young or a very old general. "For seventeen years, Kon held them back. Children were born and came of martial age knowing nothing but that Collen was free."

She paused, whispering something Dante couldn't catch. Her eyes went distant in the way he'd recently felt when thinking about whether he'd ever make it back to Narashtovik.

The Keeper glanced at him, then away. She grunted. "Two years of quiet passed since the last army had crossed into Collen and soaked the dust with the blood of its own soldiers. Then came Franric, Eldor of the priesthood, master of ether, who had survived the assassination attempts of Orell, his predecessor, and then supplanted him. Franric marched on the Basin. With one victory after another, he pushed the defenders back to the city of Collen itself. But this was not the first time the Colleners had defended their city, and they dug in on the road through the cliffs, and set archers above, who rained arrows down on the Mallish as the bluecoats made their assault.

"The Mallish stalled on the slopes. With their dead littering the cliffs, they began to withdraw. A cheer erupted from those who defended their land. Then the Mallish drove their engines of war forward. Covered and armored, their wagons took the road, pressing to the gates. There, Kon ordered his nethermancers to the defense. The first siege wagons fell, but Franric and his priests rallied forth. Light and dark formed a storm in the skies. Soldiers and sorcerers fell, never to rise again. And Mallon advanced to the gates.

"The fighting was too ferocious to say where the dark ones came from. The Mallish blamed the Colleners; the Colleners blamed the Mallish. As the creatures stepped forth, both sides withdrew. These things looked like shadows, but they were attached to no men. Their eyes glowed silver. And when they opened their mouths to scream, their throats burned as if they'd swallowed the stars."

"That's them," Dante broke in. "The Star-Eaters."

"As it says in the history," the Keeper said. "At first, the Star-Eaters attacked all they saw. Swords couldn't cut them. The nether couldn't harm them. It couldn't so much as slow them. But the ether stalled them, and in this way, the Mallish pushed the Star-Eaters into the city. While Kon's soldiers fought the Mallish troops, Kon fought the demons with every ounce of his strength. For three days, it could not be said who would prevail. Yet one by one, Kon's sorcerers fell, and block by block, so did the city.

"With his people on the verge of retreat, White-Haired Kon told them that he thought he knew how the Star-Eaters could be defeated. He entered the Reborn Shrine. And then he disappeared, never to be seen again. With Kon gone, the Star-Eaters tore through the city in a matter of hours. Collen fell. The Mallish razed the shrine down to its second basement."

Through this point, it had sounded as if the Keeper had been reciting a passage from a history book. Now, she chuckled, pointing to the ceiling. "That's right above our heads. It's the closest this shrine has ever come to total destruction. Collen was pacified for decades afterwards. Freed of the need to fight us, Mallon soon turned its sights on Gask and the Second Scour."

"Is there anything more? How were Kon and the Colleners able to fight them?"

She nudged a thick book across the table. "Read for yourself. But nothing more is said."

Dante dived into the book to pore over the relevant section for himself, but the Keeper had quoted it nearly verbatim.

"Are there any other works that discuss them?"

"One." She handed him a blue-bound book. "But the reference is thin."

She wasn't kidding. It was contained to two pages, most of that involving the author's speculation that Mallish priests had summoned the Star-Eaters—or "Andrac," as this author called them, using a word from an older Mallish tongue—as the means to finally break Kon's defenses.

Dante swore and slapped the book closed. "Would it have killed them to talk about *where the Andrac came from?*"

The old woman chuckled throatily. "You've already found the answer to that."

He reopened the book, thinking he'd skipped something. The Keeper sat in silence as he reread the passage.

"If there's some secret here," he said, setting the history in front of her, "it's too subtle for me."

"You expect this information can only be found in a carefully preserved book. But you've already seen it with your own eyes."

"Is this a test?" Then he snapped back his head. "The bones."

"It's no more than a guess. But it feels right. The bones are objects of summoning."

"You think Gladdic is using them to draw forth the Andrac. From where?"

"There's a realm like this one. But in it, it isn't these tables and books that are most real." She knocked the desk and one of the stacks, wobbling it. "It's the shadows."

"If this is the same realm I'm thinking of, I have a friend who can enter it. But as far as I know, he's never seen any demons there."

"You think your friend can enter the Shade? What does he see there?"

Dante gestured vaguely. "He says it's like here, but everything's cast in moonlight and shadows. Dark places are often far brighter than we see them. And the nether seems to glow."

"That sounds like a place between. The place I mean, the Shade, looks no more like our world than I look like the girl I was ninety years ago."

"And the bones are a way to reach this Shade."

"The bones act as both signposts and doorway. They open a way out of the Shade and show the things that live there how to take it."

"Can that work in reverse?" Dante said. "The story says Kon knew how to defeat the Andrac—and then he disappeared. Maybe he went into the Shade to fight them there. And died in the attempt."

"That has the smell of possibility."

"Well, there's one thing that *I* know for sure: Gladdic's rediscovered how to command the Andrac. Do you know how to dismiss them? Or how I can fight them?"

"Fight them?" The Keeper hooted. "Before I read the accounts in these books, I didn't know they existed."

"Is there anything else like them? What more do you know about the bones and the Shade?"

Her mirth dried up. She craned back her head to take in the towering shelves of books. "There may be more answers. But it'll take more time to find them. Come back at noon in two days."

"This is the most important thing in my life right now. I can help you search."

"Do you know how these books are shelved?"

"By author? Or chronologically? How many ways can a library be shelved?"

The Keeper hooted again. This time, she was joined by Treader's high-pitched laughter; he seemed to have a second sense for when the old woman wished her guests to be taken away.

"Your help would only slow us down," she said. "Two days, boy."

It was still early afternoon when he came back to the inn. Blays and Naran were out. Dante closed the shutters and sat at the darkened table. The histories claimed that, while ether hadn't been able to harm the Andrac, it had slowed the demons down. He reached into the air and reeled the light to him. A teardrop of ether hung above the table. He fed more and more light into it, expanding it to the size of an apple.

The surface of the ether began to quiver. Dante reached for more, but it bent back from his grasp. The ball collapsed on itself, leaving him in darkness.

He stared across the table. The nether had come to him so easily he hadn't even realized he was learning it. One day he'd been reading *The Cycle of Arawn*, and the next day, he'd conjured a ball of shadows around himself. From there, his progress had been like advancing up a stairwell. The steps were all right there in front of him; all he had to do was climb them.

His experience with the ether was the complete opposite.

He'd been so bad with it that Cally, his master, had quit bothering to teach him after a handful of lessons. From there, it had made sense for Dante to align his efforts with his talents rather than pouring energy into a skill he found so hard to hone. Too many causes called for his attention. That was the core of it. He'd focused on the nether because he had a single life to live—and the drive to become the kind of sorcerer he'd only read about in the *Cycle*. Every day he squandered with the ether lowered the ceiling of what he could achieve with the nether.

At the same time, he'd been utterly convinced of his skill with the nether. That conviction had carried him through challenges that could have killed him. His belief in his ability caused it to come true.

Then shouldn't the same factor be true of his doubts about the ether? What if he was awful with the light because he believed he'd *always* be awful with it?

He was still in pursuit of this thought when the door swung open. Naran and Blays spilled through, laughing hilariously. Their hair hung in sweaty strands. Dust streaked their faces. Their forearms were spangled with fresh bruises.

"What have you two been doing?" Dante said. "Cliff diving? You understand you're supposed to do that into water?"

"We were beating the hell out of each other," Blays said. "What does it look like?"

Naran fanned his perspiring face. "Cord was showing us how to use and defend against the wheel. Invigorating experience."

"I have good news," Dante said. "The thing we fought in the temple in Bressel—it wasn't Gladdic."

Blays clucked his tongue. "Really? It sure looked like him."

"It was an illusion. What we fought was a demon known as an Andrac."

Naran scowled. "A *demon*? This doesn't sound like good news at all!"

"Don't you see?" Dante reopened the shutters; the room was growing stuffy and the two of them stank. "Gladdic's perfectly mortal. We may not know how to kill the demons, but a knife in Gladdic's throat will put him in the ground like anyone else."

Blays got a rag from his pack, toweling off his sweat. "And as soon as Gladdic's dead, we can go home?"

"Are you addressing me?" Naran said. "I agreed to help you in the islands in exchange for your help avenging Captain Twill. If Gladdic's dead, that debt is satisfied."

Blays fell into a chair. "Jona said he's back in Bressel, right? Should we wander over and slit his throat?"

Dante shook his head. "The person I've been speaking to might have some ideas about how to fight the Star-Eaters. I'd prefer to add that arrow to our quiver before we face Gladdic again."

"You sound like you know nothing about these things."

"I don't. I'm not sure if my source is going to have anything for me, either. But it's worth checking."

Naran stood with his hands folded in front of him, gazing at the floor. "When I asked you to vow to kill him, I knew he was a sorcerer. But I had no idea he had command of demons. We've already crippled his plans with the shaden. Perhaps we should consider your honor satisfied."

Dante and Blays looked at each other and laughed.

"Have I said something amusing?" Naran said.

Blays tossed his sweat rag in the corner. "If this was just about our honor, we'd have weaseled out of this weeks ago."

"Then why are you still here?"

"Because Gladdic's an asshole. As long as we're down here, we'll plant him in the ground and pray his successor isn't so awful."

Dante turned his back to the window. "My father spent his life fighting Mallon's efforts to take over the Plagued Islands. He died before I had the chance to see him again. Gladdic took that from me. I aim to pay him back."

When the conversation concluded, Dante interrogated Blays about what he'd seen while shadowalking, but the talk went nowhere. Blays had never noticed anything remotely resembling the Andrac in the netherworld.

With nothing scheduled for the next day, Dante let himself sleep late. A hand shook him roughly awake.

Blays stood over him. "I just spoke to Cord. She says the Mallish soldiers have decamped from the butte to the northeast.

They look to be on their way here. Could be here as early as tonight."

Dante sat up, rubbing his eyes. "How many?"

"Eighty, maybe."

"Are they hostile?"

"You know, I'm not sure," Blays said. "Would you like me to run out and ask them?"

"Whatever they're up to, they don't have the numbers to threaten the city. Keep your ears open. They might be coming here to find us."

As soon as he was awake enough to form coherent thoughts, Dante called up what little ether he could. It could have been his imagination, but the drop of light looked larger than the day before.

After that, he went around to a butcher shop, where he spent some of the pennies he'd earned healing travelers to buy a bag of goat bones that had already had the marrow scraped from them. Back in his room, he laid the bones out on the floor and closed his eyes. In his earliest days in Narashtovik, when he'd been no more than the monks' errand boy, he'd been assigned to prepare bones in the way he'd seen done at the Mallish dig across the desert. But they'd been used to attempt to summon Arawn himself, and when that effort failed, Dante had considered the bones to be a pointless trapping. He hadn't used them since. To his annoyance, he couldn't remember how the process was done.

The soldiers neared that afternoon. Dante sent a moth to observe. They were eighty strong, accompanied by four gray-robed monks. They walked through the streets of the lower town like a winter wind, freezing the farmers and traders around them. As the Mallish moved up the road to the top of the butte, the shops carved into the cliffside closed their doors.

A platoon jogged ahead, taking the top of the butte. The body of soldiers joined them there and marched into the city. Civilians watched, joined by a number of fit men and women with ribbons dangling from their elbows. The Mallish soldiers passed through them in silence, filing into a large stone building with iron-banded doors and slitted windows.

Dante posted the moth outside. The soldiers stayed put all

night. In the morning, they emerged into the streets, traveling in groups of four. They stopped everyone they passed, questioning them briefly before moving on.

"The Mallish are searching for something," Dante said to Blays. "But the moth I'm following them with can't hear a thing. Think you can find out what they're after without getting jailed?"

"Probably not." Blays stood. "But I bet Cord can."

He left the room. Dante continued to watch through the eyes of his moth. He couldn't hear what the soldiers were asking the citizens, but the locals replied almost uniformly with a shake of their heads.

Blays was back within an hour, a funny look stamped upon his face. "You know those soldiers out there? Turns out they're looking for us."

"Us? By *name*?"

"There's no mistaking it's us. They were looking for the handsome Collener, the tall fellow from the southern lands, and the ugly Mallishman."

"How do they know who to look for?"

Blays shrugged. "One of them must have survived the Spiderfields. Went back and told the others who'd done them wrong."

"Too many people know we're here," Dante said. "It only takes one of them to expose us. Then Narashtovik's implicated as well. Even if they don't know exactly who we are, if they find us, we'll have another fight on our hands. How much more of this recent violence do you think Mallon will tolerate before they march on the Basin?"

"Little to none," Blays said. "What are you thinking?"

"We know Gladdic isn't a demon. He can be killed. I say we get out of here before we accidentally set off another war."

"Just so I'm clear on this, your plan is to avert war by assassinating one of Bressel's highest-ranked priests."

"Gladdic seems to be spearheading operations here. Removing him from action could shut down hostilities."

"Or provoke the king into jumping up and down on Collen like an enormous mattress," Blays said. "But I suppose there's no getting around that."

"In any event, Narashtovik will stay in the clear. Get your

things. We should get out of here before the Mallish think to post guards at the top of the trail."

Naran folded his arms. "You mean to leave now? I thought you had more to learn at the Reborn Shrine."

"I don't think she knows how to hurt the demons," Dante said. "As for the bones, they may be irrelevant—and Narashtovik will know how they work. Our loon should be there by the time we've arrived in Bressel. We have to get out of here before Narashtovik's connected to the destruction of the shaden."

While Blays and Naran packed, Dante jogged to the Reborn Shrine, employing his moth to ensure the way forward was clear of soldiers. At the shrine, he wrote a message to the Keeper, which Hodd sent down in the small dumbwaiter they used for such things. The Keeper replied with a note stating that she'd found nothing more regarding how the demons could be fought.

Back at the inn, Blays and Naran had their packs assembled, including food for the trip to Bressel. The three of them left their room and headed through the city, detouring around two groups of soldiers on their way to the switchbacks. By early afternoon, the city of Collen receded behind them. Ahead, the road cut a straight line through the irrigation ditches and the patches of green farms around them.

Dante reached Jona through the loon to inform them they were on their way and to confirm Gladdic was still in the city, which Jona thought was so but pledged to double-check. The season was edging into fall, the sunlight far less brutal than it had been during their trek from Bressel. A steady wind buffeted their backs. Tiny tornadoes spun through the parched and dusty fields.

That night, with the butte far behind them, Dante wondered if he'd left too rashly. Blays and Naran might have kept themselves cloistered in their room while he spent more time in the shrine. But the risk would have remained. As much as he wanted Gladdic dead, Narashtovik had already fought too many wars during his tenure. It was time to finish this.

Two days later, with fifty miles behind them and another eighty ahead of them, they crested a rise and stopped in their tracks. Two miles to the west, hundreds of men traveled east along the road, dressed in uniform, blue banners fluttering above their heads.

Mallon was marching on Collen.

13

The news of the attack on Cobb's Fort was like rain in the desert.

With the Eldor's blessing, Gladdic went straight to Truman. Gladdic took only his secretary Horstad. As usual, the Minister of War attended the meeting with no fewer than a dozen of his generals and advisors. The coterie was supposed to make him appear formidable. As if he commanded armies not only in the field, but within the halls of the palace as well.

Yet to those who saw keenly, his assemblage displayed weakness. The inability to stand by himself. And the irregularity of his numbers—Truman included, they made thirteen—seemed a deliberate piece of hubris. As though his men mirrored the dozen of the Celeset. And Truman commanded them all.

Gladdic seated himself, Horstad taking the chair to his right. Gladdic folded his hands on the table, nodding to each of the dozen men Truman had brought with him. He took his time about it, allowing the greetings to stretch into a silent criticism of Truman's habit of surrounding himself with so many unnecessary bodies, but ensured his expression remained courtly at all times.

"Lord Truman," Gladdic said at last. "Thank you for arranging to see me on such short notice."

Truman wore a trim goatee and a perpetually pained look, as though one of his old wounds had never healed. "It's as they say.

When the Eldor asks, the crown bows."

"Did the Eldor's entreaty mention the nature of today's discussion?"

"Let me guess. There's been more trouble in Collen."

"Would that come as a surprise?" Gladdic replied mildly. "The Colleners carry rebellion in their blood."

"Their blood. Would you say the same of hornets?"

"Hornets, milord?"

"Hornets," Truman nodded. "When one throws a rock at a hornet's nest, one expects to get stung. I begin to dread that our meddling in Collen is no different."

A few of his attendants chuckled. Horstad's quill worked as he wrote this witticism down. Gladdic had the urge to snatch the plume from him and jam it in his ear.

"Hornets are mindless." Gladdic kept the edge from his voice. "The Colleners have minds. Free will. Souls. Yet they choose disobedience. Rebellion. Heresy. This is not a one-time event, the product of poor fortune or a silver-tongued despot stirring them to unwise action. Rather, their warring is as endless and predictable as the Celeset. For such a cycle to persist across so many centuries, I fear their moral failure can only be explained through a flaw of the blood."

"Could be. So what has this flaw caused them to do now?"

"They have attacked a butte known as Cobb's Fort. A number of very important and powerful resources were destroyed. Fifty of our men died in the fighting. Including two of my monks."

"What incited this latest skirmish? Did the wheat-pickers decide you were trespassing?"

"Prior to our encampment, Cobb's Fort had been unoccupied for decades. It held no value for the Colleners in terms of resources or strategical location. And those who attacked it were no mere rabble of farmers." Gladdic paused. He shaped the tone of his next words like a master potter. "They were nethermancers."

This drew alarmed looks from several advisors. Truman grunted, scowling. "You're certain of this?"

"A handful of witnesses lived to tell the tale. As well, the attackers left evidence of their unnatural powers. There can be no mistaking their taint."

The minister ran his thumb over a burn scar on the back of his other hand. He grunted again. "Sounds like a task for your priests. Faced with nethermancers, my soldiers are no more than grist for the mill."

"But you agree it must be addressed. By force, if necessary."

"I *agree* that it must be addressed by those most capable of addressing it. This isn't a military matter, Ordon. It's a religious one."

"All things are of the gods, Minister Truman."

"Including these impure-blooded rebels? And their nethermancers?"

"Indeed," Gladdic said. "They are the work of the god we must oppose with every grain of our soul. It is vital to stamp out every last ember of his faith in Collen. If that is not done, the fire of his blasphemy *will* spread to Bressel. Just as it has done every other time. Horstad. Are you taking notes?"

The portly young monk looked up in surprise. "Every word, Ordon."

Gladdic maintained eye contact with Truman. "Then when the flames reach from Collen to Bressel, it will be noted who lies at fault. And it will be asked why, when faced with the choice of restricting the fighting to Collen, or allowing it to spill into Bressel, that man chose to bring the fight into our home."

The room went as still as a winter night. All except for Horstad's quill, which scratched across his ledger like a puppy outside the door on a cold winter's eve.

"Milord." A man leaned forward, murmuring into Truman's ear.

Truman worked his jaw, glaring at Gladdic from across the table. "How many men do you need?"

In life, there were few things as satisfying as taking that which another man didn't want to give you.

Gladdic had his army two days later. Eight hundred men. Insulting. He deserved at least twice that. It would not have been unreasonable to provide him with *five* times as much. It was clear that Minister Truman had given him the bare necessity to pretend that he took the cause seriously. And arranged matters such that, when the token army failed, blame for that failure would fall firmly on Gladdic's shoulders.

Minister Truman was conniving. Gladdic charged his monks with combing the archives for all mention of past battles in Collen, particularly sieges of the basin's capital, as well as the men required to take it. Before departing, he then assigned Spalder Baldric to draft an essay to the king stressing the difference between what was needed and what Truman had given him. The essay came to the subtle conclusion that Truman was either incompetent at his job—or deliberately sabotaging both the holy duties of the church, and the Mallish military Truman was ostensibly protecting.

This accusation would be undermined by Gladdic's upcoming victory. Yet following Baldric's analysis of the hopelessness of the situation, that victory would be little short of a miracle. The only explanation would be that Gladdic was a tactical genius, or the favorite of the gods—or both. Whatever the consensus, he would use it to seize greater authority to enact his next step.

Their troop left at dawn, striding down the king's road, scouts ranging ahead on horseback, blue banners waving above the infantry. It was ten times the size of the largest force Gladdic had ever commanded. Yet he knew his next command would be ten times larger still.

Horstad rode beside him near the head of the column. The sun was just up and his secretary was already sweating like a pig. Did Horstad drink in secret? That would explain the discomfort on his face.

Gladdic cleared his throat; Horstad jolted. Gladdic said, "Does something trouble you?"

"It looks mighty." Horstad twisted in the saddle, surveying the line of troops. "But will it be enough to seize the city? It's said that with a few hundred men at its defense, the butte can hold off an entire nation."

"Do you lack faith in our mission?"

Horstad sputtered. "I have faith in Taim's cause. And in your leadership. But my faith in the resources provided to you to achieve your mission is…less robust."

"Less robust." Gladdic chuckled. "You're correct, Horstad. We don't have enough soldiers to take the city."

"Er. Then I wonder—and I hope it is natural to do so—why we intend to try?"

"Can you guess?"

The younger man twisted his face. "Because that's what the gods demand of us. It's not our place to question them. Only to obey."

"That is what we tell the soldiers. The congregants in our temple. It is true, of course, and helps sustain our strength through dark times. But battles aren't won through duty alone. What do we have that they don't?"

"Faith?" Horstad sighed. "I'm sorry, Ordon. I have no experiences with armies and tactics and the ways of war."

"That is a good thing, Horstad. War is the symptom of a land broken beyond repair. We are healers, yes. But it's best that the land is never sick enough to need ministrations such as these."

The secretary nodded, bobbing in the saddle. "Still, if these are the times now upon us, I'd better learn to serve you through them. What *do* we have that the Colleners don't?"

Gladdic smiled. "Ethermancers."

"They have no priests?" Horstad squawked. "They truly *are* heretics!"

"They have priests. But none have Taim's bright spark. They're of common blood."

"But all realms produce men with the talent. Is it some kind of curse?"

Gladdic shook his head slowly. "Some Colleners are born with the spark. But those men are promoted to other temples. Bressel, Whetton, Dormand, and so on."

A frown crept over Horstad's face. "Is this removal of talent intentional, Ordon?"

"Are you starting to think strategically, Horstad? This is part of a long-standing treaty with Collen. A chance to educate their brightest minds in places free from the ideas that have corrupted those who came before them. Now, if this opportunity we grant them happens to diminish Collen's ability to resist us…well, they shouldn't be resisting in the first place, should they?"

"That is a very clever arrangement."

"A good ruler solves crises as they arise. A great ruler prevents them from arising in the first place."

Horstad pulled back his chin, visibly impressed. His expression turned thoughtful. "But once we take the city, Ordon. What then? How do we prevent the next crisis? It seems like we're always conquering Collen only for Collen to rebel again as soon as we turn our backs."

"It seems that way because that is the truth." Gladdic was silent for a time. "Have you heard the story of Sedwick and the Five Fountains?"

"Yes, Ordon. It's most interesting."

Gladdic blinked, annoyed. Horstad was far more competent as a secretary than his humbleness implied—and Gladdic would not have taken on an assistant whose grasp of theology was frail—but the stories of Sedwick were one of the obscurities held back by spalders and ordons for the express purpose of humbling younger monks. It irked him that Horstad had discovered them on his own.

"But I haven't heard it in some time, Ordon," Horstad hurried to amend; his sensitivity to Gladdic's moods was one of his chief virtues as secretary. "It would be best if you were to refresh my memory."

Gladdic sniffed and cleared his throat. "Sedwick was a priest in the city of Masdow of the nation of Fellan, in what is now the Middle Kingdoms. He was born 497 years ago and died in his 78th year. Though the Fellanese Celeset differed from fact in unfortunate ways, Sedwick was virtuous enough to devote his life to Taim.

"In Masdow, the city's greatest pride was the Five Fountains. These were centuries old—the precise age is unknown—and had provided plentiful water for the entire city. Sculpted from Heddish marble, their beauty was said to rival the Odeleon. This opinion, however, may have been biased by Fellanese pride, as each fountain had been built by one of the five families who founded Masdow in misty antiquity."

Gladdic glanced at Horstad to confirm the secretary was listening. Horstad wore an appropriately attentive look.

"The Five Fountains were utterly beloved," he went on. "To the brink, perhaps, of idolatry. But after some time, the fifth fountain, built by House Winsten, grew tainted. Those who drank from it grew sick. There were many deaths. Masdow's priests purified the waters and all was well. However, in time, the taint returned, bringing sickness and death, requiring a new purification. Year after year, this process repeated. Offers were made to move the Fountain of Winsten, but it had become too holy to be removed from the other four.

"This cycle of sickness and purity endured for two hundred years, at which time its care fell into the hands of Sedwick. After the first bout of sickness under his watch, Sedwick devoted himself to purifying the fountain once and for all. However, these efforts proved fruitless. When the next illness arrived, spreading to claim hundreds of lives, Sedwick petitioned his order to build a new Fifth Fountain.

"They denied him on the basis that the grounds themselves were holy. Sedwick redoubled his efforts to permanently purify the fountain. After the next sickness, he petitioned his order again, only to be rejected. A third plague came, followed by a third petition—and a third rejection.

"Sedwick went to his temple and prayed to Taim for answers, who rewarded him with a vision of a fountain that flowed more clearly than any stream. This fountain, however, was not the Fountain of Winsten. Knowing what he must do, that night, Sedwick came to the fountain, called upon every mote of ether he could command, and crumbled it to pieces.

"Sedwick correctly guessed that he would be vilified for his crime. He fled the city he had protected for so long, living as a hermit in the wilderness. In Masdow, they built a new Fountain of Winsten. Year after year, it flowed as purely as a mountain stream. The sickness was gone forever. When thirty years had passed without a single death from the fountain, the city's leaders pardoned Sedwick and invited him to return to the Masdow. He did this, and when he died, he was buried in the city. The city he'd loved so much that he chose to heal it and be exiled from it rather than to allow it to go on festering."

Gladdic leaned forward in the saddle, hands folded. "Sometimes we cling to that which is broken because we can't bear to part with it. But it will always be broken. Until someone finds the strength to cast it aside and build anew."

Horstad licked his lips, eyes darting to Gladdic. "You believe Collen is beyond mending."

"It can be mended. But doing so will require faith in our gods and great strength in our heart. You see, Collen is tainted. By the nether that seems a part of the people's very blood. There are times when mercy is cruelty. And there are others—such as when an injured horse is put down—when cruelty is mercy. We've been too lenient with Collen. This has led to nothing but suffering for everyone there. But there is hope on the horizon, Horstad. Today, we bring the solution of the Fifth Fountain."

Gladdic smiled at the road unwinding to the northeast. Sedwick had salved one fountain in one city; four centuries later, his name remained.

How long would Gladdic's name last when he cured an entire realm?

14

Gazing across the hill, Dante's heart squeezed tight in his chest. "Tell me that's not what I think it is."

"In that case," Blays said, "it's absolutely not a Mallish army that's most likely headed to Collen because of our meddling with the shaden."

Naran squinted ahead. "Do you think so?"

"I said it's *not* that. Are those flaps on the sides of your head just something you use to hang earrings from?"

Dante scanned the ranks, making a quick count. "They have less than a thousand men. They can't be intending to take Collen. The citizens would tear them apart in the street."

"They might not have many men," Blays said. "But how many of them are wearing the gray?"

After a bit of sky-gazing, Dante located a dragonfly, knocked it down with a pin of shadows, and reanimated it, sending it toward the oncoming troop. Wary of detection, he kept it some distance from the Mallish priests. But even with the man riding on horseback, he recognized the stiff posture and cadaverous face.

"They've got at least six monks and priests—and Gladdic's with them."

"Gladdic?" Naran spat. "Jona was supposed to warn us of his movements!"

"We haven't had amazing success keeping track of him ourselves," Blays said. "Although now that he's traveling in the company of an army, it might be a little easier to follow him."

Dante rattled off a length of curses colorful enough to raise Captain Naran's brow. "We have to go back."

"To Collen?" Blays said. "The place we're currently in the business of leaving?"

"We have to warn them. If the Colleners have an extra day to fortify the road up to the butte, the Mallish will never be able to break through their defenses."

"What about Gladdic?"

"He's forced our hand," Dante said. "Besides, we can turn this to our advantage. If we kill him during the attack, there will be so much confusion it won't be clear who did it."

"That's in the vicinity of reasonable. But I hope you don't mean to attack the rest of his army, too."

"The Colleners should be perfectly capable of taking care of a few hundred soldiers. They've got more experience fighting the Mallish than anyone."

"They've got experience fighting soldiers," Naran said. "But I doubt any of them has ever faced an Andrac."

Dante swore again. "All I know is that the sooner Gladdic's dead, the sooner the Andrac are gone, too. We're heading back to Collen and putting an end to this here and now."

They retreated over the hill, then broke into a run so they'd get behind the next rise before the Mallish advanced far enough to spot them. After that, they jogged, with Dante refreshing their muscles with nether when they wore down.

"How many times have we tried to leave Collen now?" Blays swept his forearm over his brow. "When we finally make it out to another city, I'm going to drink until the pub runs out of beer."

Dante nodded. "So it will be like any other day, then."

With the nether's help, they made twenty miles before their bodies insisted on real rest. They kept watch that night, but didn't see any scouts. The following day was a brain-numbing passage of walking and running. By afternoon's end, they approached the butte of Collen proper.

"How do you want to spread the alarm?" Blays said. "Cartwheels and shouting? Or were you intending to summon a magical plague of some kind?"

Dante knocked dust from the legs of his trousers. "I think it's time to see the despot."

They climbed the switchbacks to the top of the butte. Dante

hadn't been to the palace before, but the keep was unmistakable, a brutal block of basalt near the north end of the city. With the Mallish as little as a day away, the three of them headed straight to the keep.

Most palaces, including the Citadel of Narashtovik, were guarded by men in trim uniforms bearing oversized, well-polished weapons. In Collen, there was no line of soldiers to either side of the gate, but inside the keep's outer walls, fighters trained outside a shrine, black ribbons tied around their elbows. A few glanced Dante's way without breaking their practice.

The keep had so little ornamentation that the observer's eye was commanded by the few touches it did possess. Upthrust fists were carved into the stone beneath the windows and buttresses. A gold banner hung above the doors, its field emblazoned with a black shock of wheat and one of the warriors' wheels.

Dante swung open one of the bronze doors, releasing the smell of incense and bread, and entered a high hall. Seeing no one, he walked forward. He hadn't made it three steps before a slim man in a dapper black vest barged through a side door and strode straight toward him.

The man stopped in front of him, blond hair slicked back from his forehead. "May I *help* you?"

"We're here to see the despot," Dante said. He fumbled for and found the name. "Jodd the Half-Footed."

The corner of the man's mouth twitched. "Do you have an appointment?"

"That won't be necessary."

"Do you mean to say that Despot Jodd's time is of so little value that it can be claimed by anyone off the street?"

"I mean to say—"

The man shook his head, guiding Dante back to the doors. His fingers hardly rested on Dante's shoulder, yet he had the particular quality of most upper-level servants and majordomos, where it required an act of high will to not go wherever his touch guided you.

The man's voice was hard enough to split lumber. "And now that you see you can't waste the despot's time, you waste mine instead. Out."

Dante planted his feet and turned to stare the man in the eye. "You waste *my* time, sir. And when Despot Jodd learns whose time you've been wasting, he'll throw you off the edge of Justice Falls."

The official rocked back on his heels. Through gritted teeth, he said, "Your name, sir?"

"I am Dante Galand, High Priest of Arawn. And I'm here to warn your ruler of a Mallish invasion."

In an attempt to match the highly revered earthers, most Colleners sported deep tans. This servant was unusually pale, however — and hearing Dante's words, he went as ghostly white as a Gaskan. "Please, milord. Wait right here."

He turned on his heel and nearly ran from the room.

Blays chuckled. "You enjoy pulling rank, don't you?"

Dante found a chair and sat. "It's just a tool."

"A mallet's only a tool, too. It's still a hell of a lot of fun to pound things into the ground with it."

The official returned a minute later. He bowed low, a blond lock coming unstuck from his slicked hair. "The despot wishes to see you, milord. He asks for but a minute of time first."

"Of course."

The man smiled tightly and led them up a carpeted staircase to an antechamber. Voices murmured beyond the inner door. Dante expected to wait for some time. In Royalese, "a minute" lost all temporal bounds; sixty seconds could stretch on for two hundred minutes. Yet in no more than three minutes, the antechamber door swung open and the black-vested official ushered them inside.

The walls of the despot's high room were lined with warrior's wheels. Rather than being shiny and bright, they were scratched and pitted from use. A long table took up most of the room. A fireplace and chairs occupied the far end.

So did a man with a gold cloak draped over the burly shoulders of a farmer. Dante approached. The man stood from his chair. He was bearded, graying, his eyes pale blue. His cheeks and brow were etched with scars.

"Dante Galand." His voice was a gravelly tenor. "I'd heard

you were in my city. What a kindness to finally introduce yourself."

"My manners have been even worse than I normally allow them to be," Dante said. "This was never intended to be an official visit."

"Came incognito, did you? To take in the sights of Collen without the pressure of courtly duties?"

"I came to investigate a serious matter. This would have been compromised if I'd operated under my own name."

The despot sighed. "I gathered it was something like that. Even so, I was disappointed I didn't get to hear about Narashtovik from you."

"Why would you be interested in Narashtovik?"

"You took one run-down city and used it to dismantle an empire that had stood for hundreds of years. A topic so obscure only a scholar could love it, I'm sure, but I thought I might be able to *somehow* apply it to my situation here."

Dante chuckled. "I'd be happy to tell you more shortly. Before I can forget my manners again, these are my friends, Blays Buckler of Narashtovik and Pocket Cove. And this is Captain Naran, of…"

"Wherever the tradewinds take me," Naran finished.

"Five days ago, we left Collen for Bressel. Two days ago, we almost ran right into a Mallish army. They'll be here by tomorrow night. Their force is less than a thousand strong, but it's headed by ethermancers. Including an especially dangerous man named Gladdic."

"Ronn," the despot said mildly. "Get me my generals."

The official bowed low and exited the room. Despot Jodd strolled to a table by the wall, pouring four glasses of dark wine from a copper jug.

"Sounds like we've got talking to do," he said. "Let's sit."

The chairs were unpadded wood, but the wine was among the best Dante had tasted, black cherries and smoke. Jodd, however, seemed to take no satisfaction from the quality of his drink. He leaned forward in his chair, shoulders hunched, running his finger around the rim of the glass.

"I've done everything they've asked," he said. "Even when I

thought my spleen would tear loose from my body in pique, I obeyed. And I was a fool. When the king's men come to tell you the new rules, bowing low doesn't buy you any leniency. It only displays how soft your neck is."

Dante set down his glass. "The type of person who wants to rule is also the type who wants to spit in a conquering king's face. But the type of person who *deserves* to rule remembers the thousands of lives who depend on your wisdom to keep them safe. If I wore your crown, I'd want to defy Mallon, too. But I expect I'd bow every bit as low."

Jodd laughed wryly. "That's the worst part of the job, isn't it? Before you've got it, you think you'll change the world. Lift your sword high and spill so much royal blood that next year's wheat grows blue. Then you take the cape. And you feel the weight."

"At least you've only got a few more years on the throne before the next election." Blays jerked his thumb at Dante. "This poor fool signed up for life."

Dante took a large drink. "You don't shoulder all the blame for the arrival of the Mallish. We may have had something to do with that, too."

Jodd snorted. "Your attack on Cobb's Fort. Reassure me that was necessary?"

"Define 'necessary,'" Blays said.

"It took a powerful weapon out of Gladdic's hands," Dante said. "One that would have been turned on Collen in time."

Jodd had already received most of the details following their public trial, so Dante filled him in on the rest.

After, Jodd sighed through his nose. "These must be very important dealings, given that I don't understand half of them. But I know enough to know where I stand. Thank you for provoking the Mallish into marching."

"You're *thanking* us?" Blays said. "I was afraid there was a good chance this meeting would end with a frank exchange of swords."

"Then you must not know the history of Cobb's Fort. I won't hold it against you, since Collen's military historians are the busiest people in the basin. Three hundred years back—or was it was four?—Mallon sieged Cobb's Fort. Rather than losing even more lives, the defenders chose to surrender. But when the Mallish entered the city, they massacred everyone there.

"So when Gladdic's people dug up those bones, they weren't only digging up our dead. They were digging up people they'd betrayed and massacred." Jodd stood, his face going red except for the pale lines of his scars. He pointed to the southwest. "They want to march on *my* city? Good. Because I'm itching to wash my hands in their blood."

As they moved on to their second cup of wine, the doors swung open. Ronn held them wide for four women and eight men. Most of them were at least middle aged, but even the elderly among them looked as fit as the warriors drilling inside the keep's walls. Each wore a different-colored ribbon on their elbow.

"Gentlemen," Jodd said. "These are my generals."

Introductions followed, which went in one of Dante's ears and out the other. He was far more interested in the fact that each general was head priest of one of the city's twelve shrines of the Celeset, in personal command of a legion of soldiers. In Mallon and Gask, the priesthood was separated from the military. Even in Narashtovik, which was ruled by a council of priests, the military ran its own command structure.

In Collen, however, war was as much a part of basic life as religion.

Jodd told his generals that a small army was on the way. That its intent was unknown. Some looked upset by the news, but others bore it with a stoicism that bordered on serenity.

"You don't bring an army unless you're ready for a fight," Jodd concluded to his generals. "After what they did at Cobb's Fort, I'm ready to fight back. Question is, are you?"

They made a quick tally of hands. The count was nine in favor and three opposed.

The despot grinned wolfishly. "Then the city will be closed to them. They want inside? They'll have to climb a staircase of their own dead."

Blays screwed up his face. "You *vote* to go to *war*?"

"I know you kings, queens, and mighty priests get to wave your hand, invoke your god, and do whatever the hell you like.

One man decides the fate of tens of thousands? Doesn't seem so divine to me."

"What happens if you disagree with the vote?"

"A lot of yelling." The generals got a good laugh from that. Jodd grew sober. "You came to warn us. You might have saved us. But if it comes down to it, will you stand on the front lines with us?"

"We can't wade into battle with you," Dante said. "I can't put my own people at risk like that. But if Gladdic moves on the city, I'll make sure he won't walk away."

"I don't like the news you brought," Jodd said. "But I thank you for bringing it. I have much to discuss with my generals. You're welcome to stay in the palace."

Ronn showed them out and brought them to their guest quarters. After the last days of hard travel, Dante longed for a bath. Instead, he walked straight to the Reborn Shrine and asked Hodd to see the Keeper. After a few minutes, Treader arrived to escort him downstairs.

"The Andrac," Dante told the old woman. "There may be one in this city within two days. Have you found anything to help me fight it?"

"There is nothing," she croaked. "Except one mention in a scroll with no author and no date. It is said: 'When the shadows came, and took man's shape, Gott lifted his sword, shining, and drove the beast into the mists.'"

"That's it? He whacked it with his sword, and no more demon? But *how*?"

The old woman shrugged her narrow shoulders. "I can't give you what I don't have."

Dante started to swear, then caught himself, uncertain if she was the type to be offended by hard language. "When I get home, I'm going to tell my scholars to write down every detail they ever hear, no matter how tedious. Somewhere in the future, it's going to save someone a lot of trouble."

He read the scroll for himself, but there was nothing else remotely related to the Star-Eaters.

"Please keep searching," he asked the Keeper before he left.

"It is searched," she said. "If Andrac come, you'll have to find weapons of your own."

Night had fallen, but on his way back through the city, the streets thronged with people. Word had spread. Many were on their way to the trail down from the butte, looking to find safety in the countryside, desolate though it was. Others packed themselves into shops to buy dry goods and supplies. Few faces showed signs of panic. Rather, most bore the annoyed look of someone whose plans have been disrupted by an unplanned errand.

In the morning, Dante awake to the news that Jodd's scouts had found the Mallish camped a half day's march from the butte. Outside, the streets bustled as the army made its way across the plain. Soldiers gathered around the road leading down from the butte. Archers drilled on bales of hay. Most of the infantry carried swords and short spears, but gold-banded warrior-monks drilled with wheels, shafts clacking, their sandals kicking up dust.

As Dante watched, Cord glanced his way. She stepped back from her sparring partner, pressed the tip of her thumb to her brow in Collenese salute, and jogged toward Dante.

"Do you come to fight?" she said. "Or are you just here to watch while others fight for you?"

"Seems to me like if I don't join in, more of you will have the chance to die on Mallish blades. Isn't that what you want most?"

The tall woman closed her eyes and inhaled deeply. "I dream of it. Sometimes, I can smell it. But why hurry? Some day, the Mallish will kill me. Until then, I mean to kill as many of them as I can." She grinned and clapped his shoulder. "That way, when they send me to face Arawn, I'll have company!"

Dante blinked. "You believe that when you die, you'll stand before Arawn? Not Taim?"

"Don't you?"

"In Narashtovik, that's what most of us believe. But I've never heard a Collener openly say the same."

Cord laughed and gestured to the soldiers around them. "If the Mallish are on their way to kill us for our beliefs, why not finally speak them out loud?"

She rejoined her peers. A messenger dressed in palace yellow found Dante and informed him the despot wished another audience. An open-walled carriage awaited. Its team of horses were among the first Dante had seen used for travel. At the palace, Ronn whisked him upstairs to the high hall where they'd first met.

Jodd stood over a table blanketed with papers and maps. "Yesterday, you sounded hellbent on snuffing Gladdic's candle."

"Nothing's changed. You won't have to worry about him."

"We're preparing for a fight. But could be they're only here to give us a scare. Or maybe they're passing through on their way to bedevil someone else for once. If we aren't to fight, you aren't to go after Gladdic. Not here."

"I'm not here to cause trouble for Collen. If this isn't war, I won't start one."

The despot looked up from his maps, eyeing Dante. "I've heard you're the type to grab your goals no matter what the cost to others. Give me your word."

"If you can't trust me, how can you trust my word?"

"I can't. But if the gods give a damn, it'll be one more thing to punish you for in hell."

Dante laughed. "I swear it. If I hurt him without your permission, may I be damned by Arawn himself."

"Wonderful." Jodd nodded to the door. "See you in the field."

The sun climbed, slow but steady. The advance of the Mallish was as methodical as the sun's ascent. The city streets were now as silent as the desert floor. Most of the citizens had remained—rather than fear, the primary response to the approaching army was outrage—but they'd shuttered their windows and bolted their doors.

At the cliffs above the path, though, over two thousand soldiers waited with weapons in hand.

"This is a new one," Blays said, looking down as the Mallish troops entered the fringes of the town below. "The besieged outnumber the attackers?"

Dante homed in on Gladdic near the head of the enemy column. "In older times, it was common when the attackers had sorcerers and the defenders didn't. A wall can't keep you safe from the shadows. A handful of ethermancers can collapse your flank in seconds. That's why Mallon and Gask worked so hard to bring the sorcerers under the court's control."

"Like you do any different in Narashtovik?"

"We need them for defense. Besides, they serve freely. Not like those caged bears in Gask."

As the army neared the base of the cliffs, a trickle of citizens ran up the switchbacks, seeking shelter in the city. The gates remained open. Gladdic came to a stop three hundred feet below. Jodd walked to the edge of the cliffs, flanked by four of his generals.

Gladdic stepped forward from his troops, tall and lean. He was joined only by a portly young man, also in gray robes.

"I am Ordon Gladdic of Bressel." His voice cut through the dry air like a freshly stropped knife. "I come on behalf of two kings. Charles, regent of Mallon. And Taim, regent of the heavens and all that lays below them. Both of my masters will be displeased to hear that I have been met by a hostile force."

Jodd stared down at him. "I don't care who you are. Don't care why you're here. You want to talk, come on up. But your army stays down there."

"Your refusal to let us enter a city of the king's own realm will be considered an act of war."

The despot planted his hands on his hips and laughed. "An act of war? What do you call marching a thousand men up to my gates?"

"Insurance that justice will be done." Gladdic bit off each word. "You will step back from the gates. You will lay down your arms and let us inside. You will then turn over all weapons longer than the king's forearm. You will also turn over all those associated with the attack on Cobb's Fort, and assist our investigation of the matter. If you satisfy each of these conditions, then you will preserve peace with Mallon."

"Preserve peace. I'd like that. But there are others who don't think that'd be an honorable deal."

"Who could question the decision of the despot?"

"The ancestors whose remains you defiled at Cobb's Fort!" Jodd bellowed down the cliffs, the cords in his neck as taut as the strings of a lyre. "The only way you're entering this city is on a corpse wagon, you arrogant son of a bitch. Now get back to Bressel before you get sunburned."

His soldiers cheered, hoisting spears and wheels. Far below, Gladdic stared upward, head tilted back, motionless. Dante was wearing plain clothes and had been careful to keep himself separated from Jodd, but he now wished he was peering from the cover of a shuttered window.

In time, the cheering dwindled. Gladdic spoke. His voice wasn't loud, yet it made its way to the top of the cliffs. "Take the city."

Jodd turned to his generals and nodded. They hollered orders to their troops. Squads of infantry descended the top of the slopes, joined by the gold-ribboned wheelers. Archers took position on the bends in the road.

Blays nudged Dante in the ribs. "If Gladdic hangs back, do we have a plan to get at him?"

"He'll have to stay close to support his infantry. If he stays out of range, his army won't last long. We'll follow his retreat and take him on the road."

Below, Mallish soldiers in blue advanced, shields and boards held above their heads. The archers, who bore armbands of orange and silver — devotees of Jorus and Carvahal — fired a smatter of arrows, testing range.

"I don't like this," Naran said. "Gladdic doesn't strike me as one to be goaded into an attack he can't win."

Blays loosened his swords in their sheaths. "Meaning he's planning to get ugly. Sorcerer stuff. You'll probably want to stand back."

Naran stayed put. Dante wasn't sure if that was to his credit or demerit.

Near the bottom of the road, a man screamed. The first casualty of the day. The Collenese archers upped their rate of fire, but the enemy was on the move and far enough downhill that few arrows came close. Most were caught by Mallish shields.

Once the bluecoats had made it past the first few turns, the archers slowed, conserving fire. The Mallish trotted onward, dressed in chain and boiled leather studded with iron. They advanced a quarter of the way up the road, then halfway.

As they negotiated the turn there, the archers loosed a sudden, concentrated volley. Below, a sergeant barked out. The Mallish stopped, hunkering down, shields locked above their heads. Arrows rapped into their shields. As soon as the volley ceased, the soldiers stood and rushed forward. The Colleners fired again. Again, the Mallish turtled up. A single man fell. They moved on.

Over the course of the next leg of the trail, the archers staggered their fire, forcing the bluecoats to slow, then come to a complete stop. The attackers pressed closer to the rock, hampering the archers' angle of fire, then moved on. The archers plinked away at them, but the Mallish were now moving single file. Sticking close to the cliff wall, they left little for the archers to fire on except when they came to the next turn in the road. There, their cover shrank to nothing, leaving a hectic scramble to get behind the next ledge of rock.

Two-thirds of the way up, with the wounded and dead littering the trail behind them, the Mallish stopped their advance, tightened ranks, and lifted an interlocking shield wall over their heads. Four beads of light arced from the soldiers, blinding and terrible.

Dante gawked. "The monks are disguised as soldiers!"

The lights whipped forward, punching through the bodies of four archers. Vivid red viscera spattered the rock wall behind them. The Colleners returned fire, but the arrows thunked into the shields without drawing a single scream.

The priests launched a second volley of pearly light, then a third. One archer after another fell, blood soaking into the dust. Collen had no sorcerers of its own. Nothing to stop the awful light from piercing its soldiers. Dante had to clasp his hands together to prevent himself from tearing into the priests with all he had. He needed to save every drop of his powers for Gladdic.

The archers jogged higher up the trail, seeking angles of fire through the shield wall. Lights spun and slew. Without warning, the archers broke into a run, fleeing uphill.

"Lasted longer than I thought they would," Dante said. "But no one exposed to sorcerers can stand firm for long."

Blays tucked down the corner of his mouth. "You almost

sound proud of that."

With the archers in ragged retreat, the Mallish infantry rushed onward. Collen's generals called orders. A column of swordsmen moved downhill and stopped, digging in. The disguised ethermancers turned their attention to the infantry, blasting soldier after soldier to the ground. The front lines wavered.

"Gods damn it." Dante unsheathed his knife and slashed his arm. Nether rushed to his hands. He slung a ball of shadows downhill, intercepting the priests' incoming volley. Nether and ether twinkled away in a blast of sparks.

The priests fired again. Again, Dante swatted it down. One of the sergeants yelled out to Gladdic, who remained with his advisors at the base of the road.

Blays socked Dante on the shoulder. "I thought we weren't going to get involved!"

"If we don't stop the priests, they'll punch right through the defenses. They'll enter the city uncontested."

"But they'll run out of light eventually, won't they?"

"Before or after they've slaughtered every Collener standing on this road?"

Blays grimaced. "Did Collen just forget that it was a good idea to have a few sorcerers kicking around for situations like this?"

"It is illegal here," Naran said. "If someone shows the talent, and wishes to pursue it, they must do so in Mallon."

"Leaving their homeland vulnerable to anyone who can pull a few sparkles out of the air. That's a fiendish little setup."

After some yelling back and forth, the Mallish priests fell back. The bluecoats climbed upward, shields and swords in hand. The ribboned Colleners planted themselves, spears out.

The Mallish picked up speed, roaring as they charged. The two sides met with the clang and swash of steel. With the Mallish halted, the Colleners withdrew their front ranks. Wheelers jogged forward, spinning their long weapons. The weighted iron ends clubbed aside Mallish shields. Spears darted through the gaps. With the shield wall in disarray, the wheelers backpedaled away and the Collenese infantry surged forward, hacking and stabbing.

The Mallish retreated to reform their lines. In the space

opened by their withdrawal, a ring of bones lay in the dirt, their pale surfaces painted with black sigils.

Dante's eyes went wide. He turned toward Despot Jodd and yelled, "Pull back your soldiers! Pull them back!"

Beside him, Blays whispered a curse. On the road between the two groups of soldiers, a man's shadow stretched across the dirt—but no one was there to cast it.

The Andrac pulled itself from the ground, eyes shining like two fragments of a lost moon.

15

On the slopes, both Mallish and Colleners fell back as the Andrac stretched its thin arms wide. Long claws spread from its hands. It opened its mouth. A light shined within its throat, silhouetting triangular teeth as black as pitch.

It swiveled its head between the two groups of soldiers, considering, then lowered its arms and charged the Mallish bluecoats.

"A demon!" Gladdic's clear voice cut through the clamor like a shard of broken glass. "The defilers bring a demon to bear against us! Retreat!"

As his soldiers galloped away, he raced up the switchbacks. Blinding light swirled from his priests, striking the Andrac and winking out in flurries of sparks. The ether didn't so much as slow it. It raked its claws across the back of a Mallish soldier. The man wailed and dropped. Black steam gushed from his wounds.

The demon's long strides easily overtook the retreating soldiers. It lashed about, felling five men in a span of seconds. Wherever it struck, the wounds blackened, belching smoke.

"Right," Blays said. "Now I'm *very* glad we ran from the first one of those."

Dante stared, mouth hanging half open. "It's going after the Mallish. How much control over these things does he have?"

The Star-Eater carved through the laggards, men limping from injuries sustained during the skirmish with the Colleners. It stopped to tear apart the bodies and fling the pieces on the soldiers flowing down the switchback below it. The soldiers parted to allow Gladdic through. He stopped thirty feet from the Andrac. His priests stood a safe distance behind him.

"Demon!" Gladdic lifted a white rod, a crystal glinting from its tip. "Vile summons. Incarnation of filth. How dare you stand here in the sunlight of men?"

The demon stood from the remains of a corpse, blood sizzling from its black claws. It flexed its arms and stepped toward Gladdic.

He thrust the rod forward. "Turn on those who brought you here! Turn on those who would use Arawn's horrors to profane their fellow men! *Turn!*"

With this last word, white light gushed from the rod. It bathed the Andrac, outlining it in witchfire. The demon swayed, fading to mist-like insubstantiality. Then its form hardened, black as a hole cut through the fabric of reality. It lunged straight up the steep slopes. Before the Colleners had the chance to scream, it slashed the first of them down.

The city's soldiers turned and fled. A vanguard of wheelers formed before the Andrac, jabbing with their spearpoints. These slid right off its blank black surface. A woman wound up and swung the clubbed end with all her might. When it struck the demon, the weapon's shaft broke into splinters.

The beast lurched forward. Bodies spun away from its claws, tumbling down the hillside in puffs of dust.

Down the hill, Gladdic smiled. He spread his arms to his men. "I have turned the darkness against its master! Sally forth. We will purify the city of this awful taint."

His soldiers cheered, waving their swords high. They regrouped and jogged up the road in the company of the priests.

"This was a stunt," Dante murmured. Like a knife on a whetstone, anger made each word sharper and sharper. "He summoned the Andrac, then made it attack his people to make it look like *we'd* called it here. And he had no problem sacrificing a dozen of his own men to put the blame on the Colleners."

Blays grunted. "Most of the soldiers he sacrificed were already wounded. No good in the fight. That man's mind is as cold as an iceberg."

"We already know Gladdic's soul is lost," Naran said. "And if we don't stop that demon, this city will be forfeit to him."

Dante turned to run toward the despot, but Blays grabbed his sleeve, pointing downhill. "Look!"

Cord stood alone on the road, wheel angled behind her body. Her laughter boomed. "Come then, demon! If you kill me, I die for my people. But if I kill you, what have *you* died for?"

The Andrac moved toward her, shoulders swaying.

"Cord, you idiot!" Blays cupped his hand to his mouth. "Dying down there won't do anyone any good!"

She showed no sign of having heard. With the demon nearing, Dante reached into the road, softened the rock to mud, and let it slide downhill with a great whoosh, opening a deep gash between Cord and the Andrac.

Cord looked uphill and down. "What sorcery is this?"

She jogged backward from the gap. The demon crouched its legs and jumped. Cord's face went stony. As it sailed toward her, she turned and ran straight up the hill, rocks sliding from under her feet. The Andrac followed in bounds, closing quickly. Dante yanked away the rocks beneath it. Small landslides clattered away. The demon slipped repeatedly, but each time it looked ready to fall downhill, it found a small foothold and leaped upward again. The Collenese infantry flooded back onto the butte.

Despot Jodd strode up beside Dante, flanked by generals and advisors. "What is that thing?"

"It's just as Gladdic said," Dante said. "It's a demon. Your soldiers can't harm it."

He ran his hand down his beard. "Can you?"

"We're about to find out."

The Andrac came to the top of the cliff. It paused there, arms extended from its sides, and flexed its claws. The Colleners withdrew, forming a wide ring around it. The Mallish had advanced most of the way up the road behind the creature, but they kept their distance, too.

Dante gathered fistfuls of nether to him. He fired it at the Andrac in little needles, probing. The Andrac slowed and brought its arms closer to its body. Every scrap of nether that touched its body disappeared. As if the beast was drinking it. The demon flex its arms and bounded forward.

Heart pounding like a war drum, Dante conjured every speck of ether he could condense from the air. He formed an icicle of light sharper than any spear and thrust it at the demon's heart.

The point punched through the demon's chest. The Star-Eater reeled back, shrieking like tearing metal. A two-inch hole gaped through its chest, the desert visible on the other side. The city seemed to hold its breath.

The Andrac lowered its chin, regarding the wound. The patch of desert on the other side of its chest began to shrink. Bit by bit, the hole contracted until the demon's chest was a seamless patch of darkness.

"Oh," Dante said. "We're screwed."

Blays unsheathed his swords. "My turn."

The demon took a step forward. Dante grabbed at Blays' elbow. "You can't possibly think you can hurt it with steel!"

"According to that story of yours, Gott took on an Andrac with his sword." Blays strolled toward the demon. "Besides, you said they come from the shadows, right? Let's see how it likes being fought on its home turf."

Blays disappeared mid-step. As always when people saw him shadowwalk, the crowd gasped. The Andrac jerked back its head and fell into a fighting crouch. It skipped back a step. The air around it rippled. It swiped at the disturbance, then yanked back its arm, shaking it. The demon circled, slashing repeatedly, then darted to the side with preternatural quickness. Step by step, it backed toward the cliff.

Without warning, it sprung forward, claws whisking through the air as it made attack after attack. Sometimes its arms stopped mid-strike, arrested by an invisible sword. After a ferocious exchange, Blays was dumped bodily back into the visible world. He staggered backward. Blood coursed down his left arm.

"You're hurt!" Dante ran toward him, waiting for his arm to blacken like all the others the demon had harmed.

Backing away from the creature, Blays touched the scratches on his arm. "That thing fights like a demon!"

"What happened? It looked wary of you!"

"I was hurting it. But it was healing too fast for me to take it down."

The demon rushed the nearest formation of soldiers. Archers fired, their arrows skidding off the Andrac's black skin. The front line fell before the Andrac's claws. The soldiers behind the dead broke, fleeing toward the buildings behind them.

Mallish soldiers poured from the road to the top of the butte. Seeing a target they could actually engage, the Colleners ran to meet them. Metal crashed on metal.

"Galand!" Jodd called. "Can you bring down the demon?"

Dante sprinted toward him, joined by Blays and Naran. "Do you have anyone here who can wield the ether?"

Jodd questioned his generals, but none of them had a warrior talented with the light.

"I've already burned through what little I can use," Dante said. "Blays, you just fought it. Is there any point in trying again?"

Around them, Collen's soldiers held their ground wherever they faced a mundane enemy. But before the Andrac, or the priests now taking the field, they fell back step after step.

"I can't kill that thing. Not by myself." Blays spun the grip of his left-hand sword. "But what if we kill the guy commanding it?"

Dante's eyebrows shot up. "That could work. If a nethermancer dies, so does any animations under his command."

Jodd glanced between them. "You're talking about removing Gladdic."

"We need your people to fall back. Let the Mallish get a short way into the city. Enough that Gladdic will feel safe enough to come up here."

"We have no choice *but* to fall back. That thing is ripping my soldiers to pieces!"

"What a prick," Blays said. "Don't worry, I'll keep him distracted."

"When Gladdic exposes himself, I'll engage him," Dante said. "Shadowalk up behind him as fast as you can. Whichever one of us he turns on, the other will cut him down."

Jodd and his generals left to relay orders. Naran went with

them, saber in hand. The Collenese soldiers battling the Mallish began an orderly retreat. Blays jogged toward the Andrac, which had stopped killing for a minute in order to shred apart the bodies of its victims, an activity it appeared to relish.

Blays ran faster, hunched low, and vanished. The demon planted its foot on a corpse, grabbed its arm, and yanked it from the socket. It twirled the limb above its head and slung it twenty feet away. It bent down to grab a leg, then shot upright, whirling to slash at Blays somewhere within the shadows.

Keeping one eye on the duel, Dante backed away from the square. Dozens of bodies were strewn across the setts. Many wore the blackened wounds of the Star-Eater. Across from the demon, Blays flickered into being, rubbing a gash on his chest. He skipped backward. As the demon advanced, Blays lifted his blades and disappeared again.

"Come on," Dante muttered. "Your supposedly immortal pet is getting stabbed repeatedly. Get up here and give it a hand."

The duel carried on. Just as Dante was about to go to the cliff's edge for a look, Gladdic ascended the butte, accompanied by a few soldiers in blue. The ordon's eyes locked on the Andrac. Light glittered around his hands.

Dante jogged toward him, shadows flowing in dark storm clouds. Gladdic glanced his way and stopped on the dusty stones. The priest's mouth bent in a frown.

"Dante Galand." His tone was musing. "I thought this stank of your involvement. It is always nice to be proven correct."

"You're a liar and a hypocrite," Dante said. "You're the one who brought the demon here. And used the shadows to do so. What will your Eldor do with you when he hears that?"

Gladdic's face reddened. His words were clipped, precise. "He will support me against the latest of Collen's lies. My soldiers saw me turn the monster against its true master."

Dante glanced at the Andrac, which continued to duel its invisible foe. "That's what you'll write down as history, too. Assigning Mallon's crimes to Collen. Just as you always have."

"Why do you insist on endangering your own kingdom? You have fought so hard to restore Narashtovik to its former glory. I can't say that I approve—your beliefs sicken me—yet I'm confused why you'd cast everything aside for this barren desert."

"Because," Dante said. "I always win."

He hurled a wave of shadows at Gladdic. Gladdic spread his feet and opened his hands, deflecting the darkness with a deft thrust of light. Sparks faded around him. The priest's smile was almost benevolent. He unshouldered a bulky pack and flipped it over, dumping a pile of bones onto the ground. Light flashed from his hands. On the ground, a man's shadow appeared, but there was no one there to cast it.

A second Andrac collapsed in reverse, unfolding to a height of seven feet. It stared at Dante and flexed its limbs.

Dante felt the blood drain from his face. "Blays!"

The demon trotted toward him. Dante drew a globe of shadows around his fist and slammed it into the ground. The earth wrenched apart, the cracks shooting toward Gladdic's feet. Dust boiled into the air. Screams went up from around the plaza. Even the Andrac stopped to watch.

Mist glowed around Gladdic's hands and rained to the ground. Dante could feel the cracking stone suddenly yearning to retake the shape it had just lost. The advance of the crevice, once lightning-fast, slowed to a crawl.

Gladdic stepped aside, dust sifting onto his robe as he considered the cracks. "Are you proud to destroy? Is that why you are here? Not to help, but to start a war and watch everything burn?"

Dante turned and ran.

Gladdic splayed his hand. Light winged toward Dante's back. He batted it down with a clumsy lump of shadows. Across the plaza, Blays popped back into being, drenched with sweat and covered in cuts. His swords were spotted with black stains. He dovetailed to meet Dante.

"Well that didn't work," Blays said. "What now?"

Dante glanced over his shoulder. The new demon was sticking close to Gladdic. "I'm currently executing the only idea I've got left."

Across the square, the Colleners were being pushed back into the buildings. Jodd was near their front, calling them to hold against the swords and ether of their foes. As Dante watched, he fell, lost within the melee. The first Andrac loped to join the battle.

"The city's lost." A cold weight sat in Dante's stomach. "We have to get out."

He veered to his right, where a small group of wheelers and infantry were engaged in an all-out fight with a group of bluecoats. As Dante neared them, he brought the nether flocking to him like silent ravens. His fury forged the shadows into blades and spears which he hurled into the backs of the Mallish soldiers. Limbs and heads fell in piles.

The Colleners cried out in shock, scrambling back. Dante's hold on the shadows was now shaky, close to depleted. But striking down the Mallish was the first time he'd felt good that day. Among the wheelers, Cord looked up from the bleeding pieces to stare at Dante.

Sweaty strands of blond hair swayed across her face. "I thought it was my day to die."

"Not quite yet." Dante glanced back toward Gladdic, but the priest had stopped near the road to the butte and was engaged in a vigorous argument with a blue-clad officer. "Jodd's fallen. The city won't last much longer. We have to get out—but there's work for us to do first."

"I will die before I give my city over to the Mallish!"

She was taller than him and her shoulders were broader, but he stepped in her path, putting his face a foot from hers. "Collen is lost. Nothing you can do here will stop that. Die, if that's what you wish. But if you live and help me, we *will* return. And we will kill every last one of the invaders."

Cord planted the blunt ball of the wheel on the ground. "What do you need?"

"To get the Keeper of the Reborn Shrine out of here. We'll need a guide. A little extra muscle won't hurt, either."

"The Keeper." She gazed across the plaza. Her face and armor were spotted with blood. "He's real?"

"And we need to get them out of here. Send your friends to evacuate whoever else they can."

As Cord relayed orders to the other soldiers, a figure ran toward them from the cover of the buildings. Naran was limping, blood trickling down his left leg. Dante escorted him behind a row of shops.

"Gladdic lives," Naran said sadly.

"Time to ensure we do the same," Dante said. "Are you strong enough to walk?"

Naran didn't so much as glance at his leg. "I've suffered worse."

"I need to conserve what's left of my powers. But you tell me if you can't go on."

Blays and Cord came around the corner and jogged toward them. Cord's eyes smoldered like twin forges. "This way. Before I have the chance to remember my honor."

She broke into a loose run. The others followed. Blays glanced at Naran's leg, then turned to Dante. "This hasn't been our best day, has it?"

"One of my least favorite this year," he said. "But it's going to get a lot better as soon as we're away from the Andrac."

Screams echoed behind them, increasingly distant. Within a minute, the streets grew so quiet that two people standing at opposite ends of the block could have held a conversation without raising their voices.

"Cord," Dante said. "Is there another way out of here besides the road?"

She chuckled humorlessly. "Do you think this is the first time someone in the city has had to sneak past an invading army?"

When they were halfway to the shrine, boots pounded down the street. Their group took cover beneath a raised porch. A platoon of bluecoats ran through the intersection, swords drawn. As their steps receded, Cord rolled from beneath the porch.

Her jaw jutted forward. "There were only eight. We could have killed them in less time than it took to hide."

Blays glanced back. "Could we have killed them before their screams alerted the demons to our whereabouts?"

She went silent and led on. Dante's mind churned. After Gladdic had summoned the second Star-Eater to protect him, he should have sent the first after Dante. Instead, it had pursued its own aims, chasing after the Colleners, giving Dante and the others the chance to light out. Maybe Gladdic was so confident in his conquering of the city that he thought he'd be able to hunt Dante down at his leisure.

But maybe his command of the Andrac wasn't total. Maybe he couldn't point them at a specific target, but only in a general direction. Overall, it hadn't made a difference to the course of the battle, but it had absolutely saved their lives.

The Reborn Shrine was deserted. The bronze doors were locked. Dante pounded on them until his fists grew sore. Just as he was summoning the shadows to cut through the lock, the latch clicked and the door cracked open.

"Dante." Hodd's eyes darted between those who stood on the steps. "Er. Is the battle over so quickly?"

"And we lost," Dante said. "I have to see the Keeper before the Mallish get here."

Hodd shrank away from the door, as if he could deny the unwelcome news from getting inside. "But if they come here...will you protect the shrine?"

"If we could protect the shrine, we wouldn't have to, because we'd have already kicked their asses down the cliffs. Hodd, there's no time to waste."

The young monk nodded, then again, harder. He allowed them inside and brought them to the inner room where Dante had first met the Keeper. Hodd withdrew to send the message that there were visitors. Rather than being met by Treader to be escorted downstairs, the Keeper herself entered through the side door.

Her pale blue eyes moved between each of them. "You shouldn't be here."

Dante stepped toward her. "Neither should you. Mallon's taking the city. Their soldiers will be in this shrine by night's end."

"The Keeper stays. That's how it has always been. They destroy the shrine. And the Keeper lives on."

"Gladdic's going to rip this place to the ground. He's far too cunning to miss what's concealed beneath it—or who."

"I must stay. That is my vow. To renounce it is to renounce my people."

"I don't think they'll consider themselves renounced by your departure after you've helped to save them."

"How will I do that?"

"You might not know how to destroy the demons," Dante said. "But we can figure that out together. We'll break Gladdic's weapons and take back the city."

The Keeper drew back her lips, revealing gaps between her yellowed teeth. "The Keeper is supposed to stay outside of the events of the world. That is what allows her to remember those events clearly, without the distortions that arise from participating in them."

"And the High Priest of Narashtovik isn't supposed to involve his people in wars that have nothing to do with them. Yet here I am."

She closed her eyes. "I always promised myself that if they found my rooms and burned my books—our land's own history—then I would burn with them."

"That's an awful promise," Blays said. "Let's break it at once."

"Destroying the Andrac won't destroy the armies of Mallon. I see four people before me. I know the famed Dante Galand is a great sorcerer. But as today proves, even he can't defeat an army by himself."

"I can't." Dante glanced at Cord. "But I'm guessing the other towns in Collen will contribute to the cause."

Cord bared her teeth. "Any true Collener will drop their plows and take up the sword."

"While we pursue that, I expect to be in touch with my city any day now. I'll bring down more sorcerers. Troops, if we need them. Collen doesn't have to be alone."

The Keeper frowned at him, the skin sagging from her ancient neck. "Why would you do this for us?"

"Because I'll do whatever it takes to keep Narashtovik safe. After what's happened today, if Mallon takes Collen, they'll come for us next." Dante held her gaze. "But I don't think they'd ever reach our city. The real reason I'm here? Your people are in the same place mine were with Gask. I'll burn Bressel to ashes if that's what it takes to free you."

She stared back—then began to laugh, the frog-like sound bouncing off the stone walls. "You prey on people. Find their deepest wish and promise to make it come true, knowing they'll follow you off a cliff to pursue it." She tilted back her head to take in the high arched ceiling. "Wait here."

The Keeper shuffled through the door to the lower levels.

"So much for staying uninvolved," Blays muttered. "Promising to set Collen free from Mallish rule? I'm starting to think we should never leave home."

"*I* wanted to stay put," Dante said. "You're the one who convinced me I had to go see my father before he died. If we hadn't gone to the Plagued Islands, none of this would be happening."

"You're right. Once again, devotion to family has ruined everything."

Cord gave them an impressed look. "You were in the Plagued Islands?"

"That's what brought us here," Dante said. "We may have fought a sort of…war. Mallon had turned the locals against each other in order to extract the islands' treasures."

"That news wouldn't surprise a blind dog. Mallon's eyes are restless for whatever they can take."

"How do you know about the islands?" Blays said. "Last I checked, Collen was a little short on oceans."

"That is the point!" Cord grinned, throwing her arms wide. "The basin is landlocked, yet home to one of the most honored sea captains. Collen always finds a way."

Naran rolled his lower lip between his teeth. "Which captain is this?"

"Mariola Twill, captain of the *Sword of the South*. She's bedeviled the royal navy for years!" She glanced between them, grin fading away. "Something is wrong."

Naran lowered himself to one knee. "I served with Captain Twill on her ship. When she fell ill with the Weeping End, Dante saved her life. In exchange, she provided these men passage to the Plagued Islands. For this crime, Gladdic arrested her—and executed her with his own hand."

Cord's hands curled into fists, face darkening like the clouds above Arawn's Mill. "This filth is in our city and we're *running* from him? The gods will spit on our backs."

"We've pledged to kill him in revenge," Dante said. "That's what brought us here in the first place."

"Then I'm glad I didn't claim my deathright today. I can't die happy until I've seen Gladdic's corpse rotting in the sun." She drew a knife and cut her palm, allowing her blood to drip down her fingers to the ground. "As my blood waters the earth, this oath waters my soul. I will help you kill Gladdic—and if I reach him first, I'll kill him myself."

Blays clapped. "Excellent. It'll be a race, then. Except when one person wins, we all do."

After another minute, the side door reopened, revealing the Keeper. "My apprentices choose to remain here. Thus if I don't return, there will be a new Keeper." She headed toward the main doors, then glanced back at Dante. "What are you waiting for, promise-maker?"

Dante jogged to catch up with her. On their way through the main hall, Hodd wandered out from a cell, blinking at them. "Where are you going?"

"We're leaving the city," Dante said. "The invaders will come for this shrine tonight. We'll return when we're ready, but until then, you have to keep yourself safe."

"Ah. Safe. How do I do that?"

Dante hesitated mid-step. "I don't know."

Hodd was still staring as they exited the shrine. In the courtyard, the Keeper drew to a halt, lifting her face to the setting sun.

Dante glanced up. "Something the matter?"

Her nostrils flared. "I haven't felt the sun or smelled the open air since I made my vow to the Pastkeepers."

"You're a talented woman. Walk and smell at the same time."

She gave him a barbed look, then honked with laughter. "And I haven't had someone speak to me that way in almost as long."

She tottered forward. Cord took the lead, head swiveling to all sides. Naran's limp had worsened, but the Keeper was no faster.

Dante made himself match her pace. "Cord, how far are we from the other exit?"

"A long mile. It'll be even longer if we run into a patrol." She turned to the Keeper. "Are you one of those stuffy priests whose dignity is more important than doing what you need to do?"

"I preserve the truth," the old woman replied. "As long as it outlasts me, my dignity means nothing."

Cord kneeled in front of her. "Then climb aboard."

The Keeper climbed her back, hooking her bony heels around Cord's hips. Cord stood, shifted the Keeper on her back, and stepped into a light jog. Naran kept up, swinging his wounded leg stiffly. The first time Dante saw a rat, he slew it with a needle of nether, then reanimated it and sent it bounding forward. After half a mile, it spotted a formation of bluecoats marching down the street in the general direction of their group. Dante alerted Cord, who changed course.

As twilight took the city, Cord brought them to a structure that resembled the bones of a temple or shrine, with fifteen-foot stone posts supporting graceful arches. It was roofed in stone, but there were no walls besides the posts themselves. Cord crossed beneath an arch. On the other side, a wide stairway descended into darkness. The air flowing up from it was cool and smelled equally of mustiness, aquatic rot, and fresh water.

"This way," Cord said. "Don't slip."

She set the Keeper on the ground and moved down the stairs, holding lightly to a rope on the wall that served as the bannister. With each step they took down, the arches above loomed higher and higher.

"What is this place?" Blays whispered.

"The town well," Cord said. "The rains are as fickle as young lovers' hearts. They stay away for months at a time. When they do come, we have to be ready to catch them."

During the first twenty feet of the descent, the steps were dry and gritty. As they moved beneath the overhanging rock, the steps grew slick with mold. The air smelled like a stagnant pond. Ahead, the stairs split two ways. Cord took the left fork. Dante got out his torchstone, lighting the way forward. After another set of stairs, a pool of green water spread before them.

Blays leaned forward and sniffed, scowling. "This is your reservoir? No wonder you people drink so much beer."

"Better to drink this than cups of nothing." Cord kneeled and touched the water's surface. "At the bottom of this pool, there is a passage. It leads to another pool inside the butte. Past that, a dry tunnel leads to the caves on the road up the cliffs."

"We have to swim?" Dante said. "How far are we talking?"

"No more than a few hundred feet."

"No more than enough to repeatedly drown us?"

"You complain about having to swim in the dry season?" Cord tipped back her head and laughed, the noise echoing loudly. "After the winter storms, swimming to the other side can only be done by those whose lungs are as big as their hearts."

Naran leaned on his good leg. "Are you sure the other side is clear?"

"Am I dripping water everywhere? Do I look like I've been to the other side today? As with all things, to know, you must do."

With admirable swiftness, Cord stripped down until she was wearing nothing but her smallclothes and a long knife. She flexed her copious muscles and waded down the steps into the pool. She swam to the far edge of the water, inhaled deeply several times, and plunged beneath the surface.

Dante nudged Naran's shoulder. "I think it's time I healed your leg. Would hate to lose you down there."

"I always imagined it would be the water that killed me." Naran eyed the stagnant pool. "But in my imagination, it was the ocean, not the town well."

Nether lay thickly in the moss and mold. Dante brought it to the gash on Naran's leg, sealing it back together until no more than a light scar remained on his skin.

Ten minutes later, with no sign of Cord, Dante was beginning to think she'd succumbed to the waters. As he contemplated finding a minnow to kill and send to look for her, bubbles popped on the surface of the pool. Cord emerged, gasping, water spattering from her body. She carried a rope in her hand.

"The path is clear all the way to the road." She cast down the rope. "Follow the rope, and it'll show us to our freedom."

She gathered her clothes and weapons, including her wheel.

"Okay, I'll say it," Blays said. "Four of us are young and healthy. One of us, however—while no doubt wise and charming—is a ninety-year-old woman who had to be carried here. You expect her to hold her breath all that way?"

Cord shrugged her damp shoulders. "So I will carry her again."

"Ah. And where would you like your remains to be buried? Or should we just leave them at the bottom of the pool?"

The Keeper waved her gnarled hand. "I've taken care of myself for more than a century, you numbskull. I can take care of myself for a few minutes more."

Blays blinked, thoroughly rebuffed. Light glowed around the Keeper's fingertips, the ether condensing like warm wax. She spun it between her fingers, then inhaled. Tiny sparks fluttered into her mouth. Cord grinned and swam to the back of the pool, holding onto the rope all the way. Blays followed her out. Dante came third, with Naran fourth and the Keeper bringing up the rear. The water was jarringly cold. Fully dressed, with a sword on his hip, Dante found it hard to stay above water.

Then again, he wasn't supposed to.

Cord and Blays took deep breaths, then plunged under the water. Dante clamped the torchstone between his left ring finger and pinky and followed them down. Bubbles fluttered past him. He pulled himself hand over hand along the rope, kicking his feet. Beneath him, Cord and Blays disappeared into a tunnel at the bottom of the pool.

Dante hauled himself after them, entering a tunnel of unknowable length. Behind him, Naran kept pace, but the glow of the Keeper's hands grew dimmer and dimmer. With his pulse thumping in his head and his lungs beginning to burn, Dante had no choice but to press on.

By the time his lungs began to scream, Cord and Blays vanished upward. The tunnel opened into a broad pool. The torchstone's light shimmered on the underside of the water. Dante kicked his way up and surfaced.

"Lyle's balls," he said, spitting water; Naran swam up beside him. "Couldn't you have made your secret escape route a little less murderous?"

Cord scoffed. "That sounds like a fine way for the Mallish to find it and use it against us. Now get out of there. That water is for drinking, not swimming."

Dante waded ashore and stripped off his shirt, wringing it dry. The four of them stood at the pool's edge, watching the water for signs of the Keeper. At last, white light shined from the bottom of the pool.

The old woman slogged up the stony bank, her robes trailing heavily behind her. "I will remember this day. I haven't swum in even longer than I've felt the sun."

"This way," Cord said, striding down the only way forward. "The top of the cliffs are filled with the enemy, but the bottom is unguarded."

The passage led out to a silent cobbler's shop. As the others gathered around the door, Blays shadowalked out for a look at the cliffs.

He reappeared within a minute. "It's like Cord said. Nothing between us and the desert."

Outside, night had fallen over the land, taking the warmth with it. On his way down the switchback, Dante shivered in his damp clothes. They reached the bottom of the road without drawing any shouts or alarms. The town at the base of the butte was eerily silent. They hurried through it, taking a southern fork in the road toward a town called Tanner, which Cord said was only a few miles away.

Once the last shacks of Collen were behind them, Blays turned, grunting. Atop the butte, fires crackled, casting sheets of smoke across the bare sky.

16

Raxa walked through the city. It was early afternoon and Gaits was at her side, but being in the company of others from the Order only made her feel less safe. The people who'd burned down the Marrigan were still out there.

But when Kerreven called, you answered.

Gaits led her to a tenement on the fringe of the Sharps. They climbed to the fourth floor, where two men played dice in the hall. Seeing Gaits, they nodded—Faddie and Jenker, muscle from the Order.

Gaits knocked a code into an unmarked door. It opened, revealing two more of the Order's brutes. They took Gaits and Raxa to a back room. There, a man sat at a small wooden table. He wore plain, loose clothes, but his long black hair and trim beard looked like something you'd see on a wealthy merchant or minor noble. His eyes, though—these were as brown and hard as two agates.

He jerked his chin at the chairs across from him. Raxa and Gaits sat.

"Raxa Dosse," Kerreven said. "Do you know this? You've earned more for me in the last two months than most of my people have made me in their entire lives. Shouldn't we have met already?"

"I didn't need an audience with you." She scooted her chair an inch forward. "Just my cut of the cash."

He chuckled. "Gaits said you were like this. Pure alley."

"That a bad thing?"

"For me? I always need people who don't look any further than the end of their knife. For you? Depends if that makes you happy."

Raxa held his gaze. Kerreven's words carried a slight Setteven accent. According to the story, he'd grown up there as a lesser noble, moving to Narashtovik and eventually taking control of the Order a few years before Galand and Callimandicus had revived the city. Beyond that, Raxa didn't know much about the man. Nothing she'd swear to. Rumors flew like flocks of starlings, though, which Raxa suspected was intentional. When people had to choose which rumors to believe about you, they normally went with whatever sounded scariest.

Which meant your average thug off the street thought that Kerreven liked to dine on stray dogs while lutists he'd blinded played him songs on instruments strung with the guts of his foes.

Raxa thought the truth was more humdrum. For one thing, though his was the three-syllable name of an aristocrat, she'd once seen a bundle of letters in his quarters. They'd come from Setteven, but they were addressed to someone named Karr Vanes. Gaits sometimes made offhanded comments about his boss as well. Piecing these together, Raxa had the idea that Kerreven had grown up like her and most of the others in the Order: streetside, no money or honor to their name.

Which meant that somehow, he'd gone from an urchin in Setteven to the most powerful figure in the Narashtovik underground.

"You sound," Raxa said, "like you're about to make me an offer."

Kerreven sat back, smirking. "Here's what we know. The swords you tracked down? They were made for an outfit called the Army of Crows."

"They sound familiar."

"They should. Mercenary outfit that formed up during the Chainbreakers' War? For a while, they were selling their swords in Gallador. Backing merchants against their rivals. Then they got greedy. Stole from a caravan they were supposed to be guarding. Do you know what they do to people like that in Gallador?"

"Part their bones from their skin?"

"And then sell both bones and skin to the highest bidder. Rather than be sold for soup stock, the Crows took flight. They've been roosting here for a few months. Did you know the attackers lost seven men at the Marrigan? Do you know where the bodies were taken?"

She shrugged. "The nearest sewer?"

"The carneterium. I paid a monk to get one of our people inside. She identified two of the bodies as Crows."

"I thought you'd linked the swords to the Crows."

Kerreven gave her a skeptical look. "We're talking about war, aren't we? Would you go to war without being damn sure you were fighting the right enemy?"

The man had a habit of peppering his speech with questions. On the surface, it was intended to get you to think your way through the answer. To Raxa, it felt more like he was leading you down the precise path he wanted you to follow.

She leaned forward. "So who hired the Crows?"

"The obvious question. We've done some digging. The leader of the Army of Crows? A man named Bennel. Would you believe me if I told you Bennel's cousins with Vart Dracks?"

Raxa's jaw dropped. "Lieutenant for the Little Knives?"

Kerreven nodded deeply. "I think they're making a run at us. But we need more than that to declare war. I need to be sure it was the Knives."

"What do you want from me?"

"I want you and Gaits to pay Vart a visit. Search his house. And bring him to me."

"I can do that. What do I get out of it?"

The man snorted. "Do you think they're done with us? What do you get out of this? You get to survive."

When they were back down in the street, Gaits glanced up at the fourth floor, then at her. "Well?"

"Well what?"

"You just met the man who runs one of the five most powerful institutions in the city. Did you leave that encounter with any particular impressions?"

"I liked his beard," Raxa said. "Now let's work. We know who did this. Every second they're alive is a second they don't deserve."

The carriage rolled toward the two guards dressed in black and silver. Raxa straightened her back, the starched collar of her dress rubbing against her throat. The dress was supposed to be the height of the summer's fashion, but some idiot had cut it to reveal her belly and a dangerous portion of her lower ribs, requiring her (and everyone else who had to keep up with the season's trends) to also wear a tight-fitting shirt (of contrasting color—again, as per trend) in order to maintain her modesty.

She would admit it looked dashing. But given the summer heat, the dress and its multiple layers had obviously been invented by someone who'd never had to wear the gods damned thing himself. As the carriage passed the city guards, sweat trickled down her brow. Not the look she was looking for.

The soldiers watched, bored, as the vehicle rattled past.

"Told you," Gaits murmured. "Want to be rich? All you have to do is dress the part."

The carriage turned, hooves smacking the cobbles. Manors rose on both sides, separated by small but impeccable yards. The air was dense with the smell of flowers, but she couldn't have named most of them.

Gaits nudged her hip. "That's it. The small one."

In this case, "the small one" meant the manor's main wing was only two stories rather than three, though a steep-roofed turret provided its residents the same view as its neighbors. A gated iron fence protected it from unwanted traffic. They continued past to the north. Three blocks away, they rocked to a stop.

"Take your time," Gaits said. "In this fine carriage and equally fine suit, I'm a man about town. Nothing for the city watch to be concerned about."

Raxa nodded. Lars, the driver, dismounted and opened her door. He swung down the hinged steps from the running board, offering her a hand. Once she'd gotten outside, she tugged her dress straight and continued north. She was presently on Denner Street, known proverbially as Make-Good Lane for its reputation as a place where those who'd built their wealth in disreputable ways spent it to buy reputability.

During her search for a house, she'd looked at Make-Good Lane herself. And discovered that, while its residents liked to put on a good face, they also maintained a back alley. The kind you'd use for the delivery of anything you didn't want visible on the main street.

She turned down the alley. The dress' airy skirts fluttered behind her, only rarely snagging on the scabbard strapped tight to her thigh. She counted down houses until she stood behind Dracks'. Its rear was gated the same as the front. Raxa stepped into a cluster of tall, conical shrubs. Amidst the citrusy smell of their blossoms, she entered the other world.

Silver shined from the shadows of the shrubs. She moved to the gates and climbed them easily; in the netherworld, she felt so light she wasn't sure her feet would leave prints in the snow. She landed in the yard and approached the manor.

She'd tried walking through every substance people had thought to make buildings out of. Wooden boards. Plaster walls. Metal doors. All of it was as solid and impassible in the shadows as it was in the normal world. Thank the gods that the rich liked to build their houses out of solid stone. She walked straight through the wall.

And into a sitting room. The house was dark, quiet. Hidden in the shadows, she ran from room to room. Two men sat in the hall beyond the foyer. Swords on hips. The rest of the lower floor was empty. Upstairs, a young girl and a young boy slept in separate rooms. Dracks snored in his bed. No sign of a wife.

With time ticking down, she ran to the hall downstairs, unsheathed the bone sword, and moved behind one of the men. A moment of remorse tugged at her guts. These men were just pieces shuffled across the board by the players. No different from her.

They just happened to be on the wrong side.

Raxa cocked the blade and shifted back into being. She swung. The edge clipped through the man's neck. Across the table, the other bodyguard jerked back against his chair. Raxa jumped onto the table. As the bodyguard fumbled for his sword, her angled downward stroke cleaved through the right side of his neck and exited his left shoulder.

The bodies slumped to the ground. Blood unspooled over the stone floor, leeching into the patterned rug. She stared up at the ceiling, listening. The house was as still as ever. She cleaned and sheathed her sword. She took the loop of keys from the belt of one of the guards, unlocked the front door, walked to the gate, and keyed it open. Gaits and Lars walked through.

Gaits raised an eyebrow. "Well?"

"Had to stiff two guards," she said. "There's two kids upstairs. Dracks is sleeping alone."

"Lars, watch the upstairs hall. Raxa, you're with me."

They headed upstairs. Raxa pointed out the kids' rooms to Lars, who leaned against the wall and got out a length of thin rope. Gaits drew a narrow-bladed sword. Raxa got out a dagger. Gaits opened the door to Dracks' room.

The man didn't wake until Gaits leaned over his bed and put a hand over his mouth.

"Mr. Dracks," Gaits said. "You will notice I have a sword. My partner is likewise armed. I am going to take my hand away from my mouth. You may scream, if you like, or try to fight us. And then you're going to bleed to death in this incredibly nice bed of yours. Or! You can be quiet, and live. Do you understand?"

Dracks nodded. Gaits removed his hand, keeping the point of his blade on Dracks' chest.

"Who are you?" Dracks said.

"We are your transporters. We know nothing, but we'll be taking you to someone more than capable of answering your questions. We're going to search your house, then we'll take you on your way."

"I'm not leaving. Not without—"

Gaits rolled his eyes. "Mr. Dracks, you appear to be under the mistaken assumption this is a negotiation. You're coming with us. The only choice available to you is whether you're going to do so like a gentleman, or like a trussed pig."

Dracks' throat worked. "Gentleman."

"Very good." Gaits stood, keeping his sword pointed at Dracks. "You can stand, if you'd be more comfortable."

Dracks slid out of bed. He was wearing a gauzy gown.

"Watch him," Gaits said to Raxa.

She sidled across from Dracks. She didn't like the look on his face. "Keep quiet and your kids will live to see adulthood."

"A generous offer." Dracks cupped his hands to his mouth. "Help! Guards! I'm being—"

Raxa cocked her fist and drove a right hook through Dracks' jaw. His head wobbled side to side as he collapsed to the rug.

Gaits sighed extravagantly. "Oh, for the gods' sakes. Well, truss him up."

Raxa gagged him, then bound his wrists and ankles. While she kept watch, Gaits and Lars made a sweep of the house, gathering up papers and dumping them into a satchel. Neither of the kids came out of their rooms. When the search was done, Gaits and Lars picked up Dracks, who was doing an admirable job of staying unconscious, and carried him outside to the carriage. They rattled away.

Dracks woke halfway to the tenement. He tried to speak, wild-eyed and sweating hard. Raxa stared at him until he shut up. Once he calmed down, he watched them carefully. She thought she saw recognition in his eyes.

At the tenement, Lars jogged upstairs, returning with two more men. As Lars drove the carriage away, the others grabbed Dracks and carried him bodily up the stairs. Inside Kerreven's quarters, they tossed Dracks in a windowless room and locked the door.

"Grab some sleep," Gaits told her. "But stay here."

She folded her arms. "Don't tell me there's more fun on the agenda."

"Dracks is about to be...questioned. I'm going to go through his letters. If we turn up any evidence linking the Little Knives to the Crows, Kerreven isn't going to want to wait to make his next move."

"How does that involve me?"

Gaits shrugged. "I've got a feeling, that's all."

Raxa found a back room with a cot. The bedding smelled like stale male sweat, but it had been a long few days, and she was too tired to care.

A hand shook her awake what felt like minutes later. Gaits stood over her, his grin flashing in the moonlight. "You're going to want to hear this."

"Hear what? That you're going to let me go back to sleep before I knife you?"

He handed her a cup of lukewarm tea. Head aching, she sucked it down, then followed him to Kerreven's room. The doors to the balcony were open. A candle burned with the pleasant scent of melting beeswax, but there was an ugly smell lurking beneath it.

Kerreven sat at his table, looking three times as haggard as when they'd delivered Dracks. He didn't look up. "Does she know?"

Gaits gave a small bow. "I saved that honor for you."

"Gaits, have you ever considered you may be in the wrong line of work?"

"Sir?"

"With such a refined sense of courtliness, I think you'd make a better knight than a thief." Kerreven turned to Raxa. "We went through Dracks' letters. Two were from Bennel. We questioned Dracks. He confessed. The Little Knives hired the Crows."

Raxa blinked. "Why? What did we do to them?"

"Say you're a..." He cast about. "Butcher. The town you work in supports five of you; you're all good enough at what you do. None of you are rich, but none of you will ever go broke. Then, one day, one of your rivals learns a new trick. Suddenly, everyone in town is going to them for meat. And you're starving. What do you do?"

"Find a new line of work."

"But you're a butcher. Do you think butchers mind getting their hands dirty?"

"We'd gotten too good. They were afraid of us. They knew they couldn't compete, so their only choice was to take us out of the picture."

Kerreven opened his palms. "In a twisted sense, it's quite a compliment, eh? In their position, I might have done the same."

"What's going to happen to Dracks?"

"Well." Gaits steepled his hands. "Now that he's dead, I imagine his next order of business will be to rot into various colors of goo."

Raxa grasped the back of a chair, leaning on it. "So we're at war."

"That's right," Kerreven said. "And wars need soldiers."

She waited, silent.

"You have a unique talent for getting into places without being discovered. So far, we've used that talent for larceny." He tilted his head forward, holding her gaze. "You've never had anything against taking jewels. How would you feel about taking lives?"

"You want me to turn assassin."

"Do you have something against that?"

"Not if it means taking down the Little Knives."

Kerreven thumbed his beard. "How much are you capable of?"

"I can take care of anyone you want. But there are restrictions. I work alone. And nothing in public."

"But public is the best way to send a message."

She shrugged. "After the Little Knives are dead, I think the message will be loud and clear."

"Why solo? Wouldn't you rather have a good man at your back?"

"Take it or leave it."

He sighed and leaned back in his chair until it clicked against the wall. "What choice do I have? I'll take it."

"Wonderful." Raxa's heart began to beat so hard she was sure both men could hear it. "There's one more condition. I want a share."

Kerreven smiled in disbelief. "A *share*?"

"Gaits has one, doesn't he?"

"Gaits has been a vital wheel of the Order for years."

"And I'm about to wreck our worst enemy," she said. "If you can do that on your own, you're free to keep your money."

Kerreven slapped his hand over his eyes, rubbing his brow.

"Why did I encourage you to be ambitious? One twenty-fourth. Don't you dare ask for more."

She forced herself not to smile. "I'll want that in writing."

"I'm sure you do. Now go get to work."

"I've barely slept."

"And now you own a part of the business." He gave her a sardonic look. "You'll soon learn that, when you run the store, every minute you're not working is a minute you're not earning."

Between the sword and her skills, it was almost too easy.

She slept through most of the day. By the time she was up, Gaits had her first target: Jain Winks, one of the Knives' lieutenants. She was holed up near the docks with two of the Knives' muscle. Raxa took the three of them down without earning a scratch.

She wasn't the only one out for the Little Knives. Wanting to take down as many of the enemy as they could before the Knives knew what was happening, Kerreven declared open war. Offered street bounties, too. Including Raxa's hit, by the end of the first night, they'd notched eleven Knives.

By morning, the streets had dubbed the conflict the War of the Gutters. Gaits had a new assignment waiting for her as soon as she woke up. A tenement not four blocks from where Kerreven was holed up. The walls were pinewood harvested from the outer city during Narashtovik's recent renaissance. With midnight behind her, Raxa crouched in the shrubs across the street, waiting for someone to enter. After an hour, she got up, went to the front door, and picked the lock.

The inside smelled like musty urine. She climbed to the third floor and counted down to the seventh door on the left. She knocked on the door with the code Gaits had given her.

Footsteps shuffled on the other side. "He left one hour ago."

One hour ago. Code that her knock was a day old. But if they were using the code, that meant she was in the right place.

And in another second, if she didn't knock the right code, they'd know she was in the *wrong* place.

She drew her sword. It cut through the door's hinges like they were made of parchment. She burst inside, hacking through the man stumbling away from the splinters of wood. Three others jolted to their feet, playing cards fluttering from their hands as they drew swords. Hers cut right through the steel. The men fell in halves, mouths gasping like fish as their heels kicked the floor.

The apartment went silent. She blew out the lantern and slipped into the shadows, silver light springing around her. Two minutes later, the back door swung open. A man crept forward, eyes wide, dagger in hand. Raxa walked up to him, emerged, and swung her sword through the crown of his skull.

The second night of the War of the Gutters claimed the lives of eight Knives and three members of the Order of the Alley. Their people reported that the city guard's presence in the rich neighborhoods had doubled, but that they'd vacated the poorer areas altogether. No surprise. Thieves paid no taxes.

They'd taken down two lieutenants, but so far, the Little Knives' king—Cane Dreggs—remained out in the wind.

"I want the job," she told Gaits.

He chuckled. "I want you to have the job. The problem is that Cane is highly motivated to allow none of us to have it."

"Then do your job better than he does his."

He dropped to one knee before her. "I swear to do my best, Lady Raxa."

On the third night, she walked through a manor's walls and found it empty. The Knives had abandoned it. The story was the same across the city. Realizing silent war had been declared, they'd withdrawn from their houses and gone underground, same as the Order. That night, neither side suffered any casualties.

On the fourth night of the War of the Gutters, Gaits fed her the location of one of the Knives' new safehouses.

"This is different from what you've done before," he said. "Are you up for this?"

"Have I failed you yet?"

"Against noblemen who think their gates and locks can keep out the rabble? You're invincible. But this time, they'll have guards. Eyes open all night. Whatever black magic you've been using to steal jewels and stab men in their beds isn't going to work this time."

She made herself laugh, doing her best to sound natural. "There's no blood rituals or human sacrifices, Gaits. Just a hell of a lot of patience."

"Be sure that patience doesn't slip away from you. Better to fail lightly and try again later than to let your frustration get you killed."

The Knives' hideout was deep in the Sharps. Three-story row house. Wooden walls. She'd have to get in the old-fashioned way. That afternoon, she made up her face and hair like a Galladese merchant, then killed time in a teahouse across the street from the safehouse. During the two hours she spent watching, no one came or went.

With twilight on its way, she left to change and arm herself. She didn't return until after midnight. Gaits had located a neighboring row house whose resident was happy to let someone up to the roof in exchange for a pouch of silver. Raxa knocked and was allowed inside. She ascended to the third floor, got out her grappling hook, and slung it up to the roof. She swung out onto the side of the building and climbed the rope.

As she rolled onto the rooftop, she dived into the shadows, uncertain if the Little Knives had a spotter up top. She got to her feet, trotted up to the peak of the roof, and took a quick jaunt in both directions. Nobody but a pair of pigeons. She flattened herself to the roof, returned to the world, then went back for her grappling hook.

Stepping lightly, she came to the eave above the Knives' safehouse, grabbed the gutter, and stuck her face over the ledge. The windows were dark. She secured the hook to the gutter and lowered the rope down the side of the building. The third-floor shutters were closed. Given the heat of the summer night, this would have been suspicious if Raxa hadn't already known the house was full of thieves, thugs, and killers.

Fortunately, the safehouse was a piece of junk. The shutters were as warped as the rest of it. Supporting herself against the wall, Raxa got out a length of wire and bent a hook into its end. She stuck it through the gap between the two shutters and felt around until it bumped into the shutters' hook latch. She snagged this with the wire and jimmied it open.

She swung apart the shutters, entered the shadows, and leaped through the window. The room was filled with empty cots. A few cups were scattered around the floor. Most still had moisture in the bottom, glinting silver from within the nether.

Drawing her sword, she moved to the door and exited the shadows. Pressing her ear to the door, she heard nothing. She tossed open the door and winked back into the nether. There were three other rooms on the third floor. Like the first, there were signs they'd been recently occupied, but they were now empty.

By the time she'd cleared the second floor—it was the same story as the top floor—she was starting to feel the weight of the real world increasing, trying to drag her back out of the darkness. Raxa descended to the first floor, which housed the kitchen, a pantry, and a communal room.

And no people.

"The hell, Gaits?" she muttered. She made a second circuit of the ground floor, poking around for trap doors or secret panels in the walls. Nothing doing. Was she in the right house? Had to be, she'd counted the windows from the spot where she'd climbed to the roof.

One explanation: someone had tipped them off. Rather than walk out the front door and straight into whoever was waiting for her, she went back to the stairs. As soon as she stepped on the first tread, something whipped past her head and clapped into the wall. She dropped her feet from under her. Pain seared across the top of her shoulder; another arrow smacked into the wall. She tumbled to the ground and rolled away from the doorway.

Her shoulder was bleeding. Deeply grazed. On the stairs, men yelled to each other. Multiple steps of shoes thumped around. Her shin burned where she'd scraped it on a step. Ambushed. An unknown number of the enemy alert to her presence. And she was low on shadows. She turned and bolted for the front door. As she threw it open, an arrow rattled into the wall beside her.

Raxa sprinted outside and into the nether. As she neared the end of the block, it felt like her feet were sliding beneath her. She barely made it into an alley before she was ejected back into the mundane world.

Footsteps rang out behind her. She crouched behind a set of stairs and drew the bone sword. Two men jogged north past the alley, swords flapping on their hips. Others called to each other, voices distant. She backed down the alley. As it fed into the next street, she put away her sword and walked west, meaning to put the Sharps behind her and find a tavern to hunker down in for a few minutes.

After two blocks of walking, steps echoed from the intersection ahead. She moved into the shadow of a building and watched a pair of men jog past. The two men who'd passed her in the alley. But they weren't looking down side streets or questioning the drunks sitting against the sides of buildings. They were just running.

They weren't hunting for her. They were going somewhere.

That late at night, there weren't many other people out. Her boots would be as loud as hammers. She unlaced them and yanked them off, allowing the two men to get another another block ahead. She followed them at a jog, staying as close to the buildings as she could. Dressed in her thin hose, her feet made no sound at all. She watched the back of their heads like a hawk. Each time one of them glanced over his shoulder, she stopped.

Four blocks later, as they came to the door of a tenement not unlike the one Kerreven was hiding out in, she still hadn't been made. She took a seat against the front of a rug shop and watched them knock on the door. A candle lit on the third floor. A few seconds later, the door opened and the men went inside.

Keeping one eye on the tenement, Raxa rolled up her sleeve. The cut on her shoulder oozed blood. She unrolled one of her hose, brushed off the worst of the muck, and tied it tight around her shoulder.

Five minutes later, the door reopened and the two men walked back the way they'd come. One glanced at Raxa, then moved on.

She sat there another hour. No one else came or went. She got up and returned to Kerreven's tenement.

Gaits was still awake, waiting for her. Seeing her, he grabbed her forearm. "Are you all right? What happened?"

"Ambush," Raxa said. "Who else knew where I was going?"

"No one but Kerreven and myself. Do you think we have a mole?"

"They were waiting for me. You tell me."

"I'll make sure no one else knew. Did they hurt you?"

"Just a scrape. There's something else. I need a spotter." She gave him the address.

He cocked an eyebrow. "What've you got?"

"I don't know and I can't find out until tomorrow. Just get someone to watch the door."

Exhausted and sore, she went to bed. The next afternoon, she waited for Gaits to come back from the streets.

"No one else knew about your job," he said. "Unless the Knives have someone hiding in our floorboards, there's no way they knew you were coming."

Raxa moved to lean against the wall, but her shoulder twinged. "After the last two attacks, they knew they'd be in for more of the same. They purposely tipped us off to where they'd be last night. To make sure I'd walk into a trap."

"I can buy that. If so, your next move should be to take a few days off. Break up the pattern."

"Maybe," she said. "Anything from the spotter?"

"Quiet all day. Ready to tell me what's in there?"

"I'll find out tonight."

"Careful out there, Raxa. You're our blade. If we lose you, we'll be trading punches with the Knives until one of us drops."

He smiled, but like everyone, he looked battered. Weary. Raxa felt it, too. For the first few days there, she'd thought they'd chew through the Little Knives like a bowl of hominy, stomping them out with no more than a handful of losses. But the Knives were getting smarter. It was about to get ugly. Both sides trapped in a bitter war that could take months to shake out. At the end, even if the Order of the Alley won, they'd be crippled by it.

Raxa met the spotter in the late hours of the night. He'd seen a few people come and go from the tenement. She grilled him for descriptions. None stood out, but that was exactly what she was looking for.

She paid her way up to the tenement's top floor and climbed to the roof the same way she'd done the night before. This time, there *was* a spotter hidden among the chimneys. Raxa popped from the shadows and cut him in half. She secured his pieces against a chimney, then stuck her head over the ledge. The room where she'd seen the candle light up the night before was dark now, but the shutters were open.

She drew her sword and swung inside.

A man sat in the darkness. His eyes shined like silver coins struck fresh from the mint. "You're him. The Ghostmaker."

"Hi, Cane." She took a step forward. "So you've heard of me."

"They said you were a man." The leader of the Little Knives laughed dryly. "Then again, you've killed everyone who ever got a good look at you."

"Doesn't bode well for you, does it?"

"I'll be fine. You won't be killing me tonight."

"Afraid that's my job, Cane. And I'm very good at it."

"Wrong, woman. Your job is to kill those who wronged the Order." Cane tilted back his head. "You have the wrong man. I didn't hire the Army of Crows—and I have proof."

17

As towns went, Tanner wasn't especially big. Likely no more than four thousand people. Dante had seen dozens larger. However, Tanner was far and away the *narrowest* town he'd ever seen. Across its lengthier dimension, it was a good mile long. Yet across its meager dimension, it was less than a bowshot wide.

The cause of this irregular shape was the canal that ran down its center and watered the town. To either side of Tanner's tips, farms fought the desert for survival. The green fields had staked a small claim, but against the wide miles of gray and yellow, they didn't seem to have much hope.

The morning of their arrival, Cord set up a meeting with the Small Senate, the town's governing body. As their group of five walked to the shrine, they drew any number of looks from the locals. Unlike the unfriendly stares Dante had gotten on first coming to Collen, these ones were questioning and grim. They'd heard of the attack, then.

The shrine of Tanner stood on a low hill. A T-shaped structure of basalt, its long end was open-walled, black pillars supporting a high roof. The six members of the Small Senate stood inside on a dais carved with the twelve sigils of the Celeset.

"Senators of Tanner!" Cord approached the dais. With her wheel angled across her back, she drew her sword and cast it to the ground. She kneeled beside it. Tears slipped from her eyes. "Collen has been taken."

"We heard the news last night." The speaker was an older woman, though across from the Keeper, the woman's sun-weathered face and graying straw-colored hair looked positively youthful. She gazed across the others. "I am Ana, Senator of Tanner. Before we go further, I'll know who we're speaking to."

They made their introductions. Dante and Blays used their real names, but out of the desire to keep herself safe from being hunted by the Mallish, the Keeper had asked to travel under the moniker of Senna. Dante hadn't asked if that had been her birth name.

"Dante Galand." Ana spoke his name as if she were tasting it — and uncertain what she thought of the flavor. "What interest does Narashtovik have in the troubles of Collen?"

"That's a convoluted story," Dante said. "Mostly, it's because we share a common enemy. I want Gladdic dead. You should, too."

"You're *mostly* here for Gladdic? And why else?"

"Because I want the same thing for Collen that we achieved in Narashtovik. Freedom. Independence from an empire that's done everything it can to keep us on a leash."

"Very noble," Ana said. "Do you think we can't fight our own battles?"

"Narashtovik never could have stood against Gask alone. We needed the help of every ally we could make. I know I look like one of them. And I know that Collen is an extremely proud land — or it never could have resisted the Mallish for so long. But when you're lacking steel, you can't afford to turn away a good sword."

"Lacking steel." Ana exchanged looks with the other senators.

A man named Madd squinted at Dante. "You want an alliance, eh? And what do you want to do with it?"

"What else?" Dante nodded toward the butte of Collen, a vague gray plateau on the horizon. "Drive the Mallish right back to Mallon."

"Hah!" He laughed, whacking his palm against his thigh. Despite his theatrics, he didn't sound too pleased about his conclusion. "Can't be done."

"I promise you the situation isn't as bad as it sounds. The

Mallish have less than a thousand men in the city."

"Right. And how'd they take Collen with less than a thousand men?" Madd spat on the shrine's floor. "*Demons.*"

This drew mutters from the other senators. Ana looked nauseated. "Arawn's turned against us. Sent his demons to murder us."

Dante held his arms wide. "Why in the world would he do that? You're the ones who still believe!"

"Because we failed him! We let ourselves be cowed into silence, keeping our faith secret. Letting the Mallish haul off anyone who showed the heart to speak out. The demons are our punishment."

"The demons aren't from Arawn. They're from Gladdic. And they can be beaten."

"That right?" Madd said. "It's so easy to defeat them, eh? That's why you're here, pleading for our aid, rather than waving the despot's banner over the city?"

"We fought the demons and lived. Soon, I'll learn to kill them."

"And I'll learn to grow wheat from the crack of my ass." Madd shook his head. "We've heard more than enough to vote."

"Those who wish to fight?" Ana said. No one moved or spoke. "And those who wish to make peace before the demons are unleashed on Tanner."

All six lifted their hands.

Cord had remained kneeling during the entire conversation. At the senate's verdict, she stood, her glare hot enough to melt iron. "I was there when the Mallish came. I fought on the front lines, eager to claim my deathright. I gave it up because I believed the fight wasn't over. You look like Colleners, but you have the hearts of rats!"

Ana's jaw tightened. "Against men? We would fight. We have *always* fought. But if we lead our people against demons, every one of us will die. And the Mallish will finally win."

"You know one of the other towns will choose to fight. When they do, you'll join them on the field, and you will be shamed."

Madd laughed. "They've all heard the same news we have. If you think any of them will fight, then I've got a fine patch of dust to sell you."

Ana dismissed the hearing before it could grow more heated.

Dante was too frustrated to speak until he was halfway down the path from the hill. "I can't believe this. Do they think Gladdic won't come for them next?"

"Not if they surrender," Blays said. "That's what surrendering's for."

"*Surrender.*" Cord grasped her right fist in her left hand. "May the word blacken their tongues from this day to the grave!"

"You know, we really ought to have seen this coming," Blays went on. "We might be used to doing battle with sorcerers and killer beasts, but these are farmers. Weavers. Cobblers. If they were beating down our door to go battle the demons from beyond the mortal world, I'd be more afraid of them than the Andrac."

"Then what's the solution?" Dante said.

"Solution? Oh, I don't have any of those. Other than going home and enjoying a well-deserved retirement."

"Don't tell me you're ready to give up. You're the one who always insists we 'do the right thing.'"

"We've been away from home for months. I'm starting to wonder how much of the world we can save before our luck runs out."

Dante lapsed into silence. A few days ago, he would have brushed the notion off as defeatist. Now, though, they faced more than Gladdic or his pet Andrac. They faced an army. One that might not have come if they hadn't attacked Cobb's Fort and destroyed the shaden. Morality was a form of arrogance. Who were they to wade in and risk Collen's security on the gamble that they could make it better? He now felt obligated to counterattack the Mallish invaders, but what if that failed, too?

And provoked the arrival of a second army?

"Cord," Naran said. "You made it sound as if, should another town choose to fight, Tanner would join them. Why?"

Cord glanced back at the shrine. "There are five other towns in the basin with Small Senates of their own. Each is bound to the Code of the Wasp. If one town votes for war, the others must join them."

Blays frowned. "Even if they think it's crazy?"

"Total unity is the only way we've ever been able to last against the Mallish. To refuse the call when the horn is blown?" She laughed in disbelief. "Such a thing has never happened. The traitors would be eaten by earwigs in hell."

"If all it takes is one town to blow the horns, that sounds like a fine way to guarantee you'll *always* go to war."

"What about the city of Collen?" Dante said. "Doesn't the despot decide when the basin's going to fight?"

Cord crinkled her face in affront. "Why would the city of Collen get to decide what the town of Tanner must do?"

Blays scratched his stubble. "Because it's much bigger and it's run by a tyrant?"

"The system may be crazy," Dante said. "But right now, that's to our advantage. Cord, do you think one of the other senates will agree to war?"

"The vote was unanimous. It's like their spirit has been sucked from their livers. I fear the others will be as weak-willed." Cord's face brightened. "But we must try, yes? She who lets her fears defeat her carries the enemy's banner for them."

The bounce returned to her step. Dante's mood remained as chilly as the Woduns. The next town, Dog's Paw, was only ten miles away, but they'd fled Collen with no more than their weapons and the contents of their pockets. Before they left Tanner, they stocked up on provisions, using most of the money Dante had earned treating various maladies in the inn at Collen.

The road to Dog's Paw was a rutted dirt path running alongside the canal that bisected Tanner. The waterway diverted around hills and depressions, but ran in a straight line wherever possible.

"This canal had to be built after the rains stopped coming," Dante said to the Keeper. "Have you ever read anything about their construction?"

Her pale blue eyes swiveled to the sluggish water. "It is written that after the nether ruined the land, and Mallon conquered it, the king brought engineers to build ditches so that farming could resume in his new territory."

"Such generosity," Blays said. "Suppose they were just looking after their investment?"

Dante nodded. "Or claiming credit for somebody else's work."

The Keeper's pace wasn't exactly blazing, but they were able to reach Dog's Paw by sunset. Tanner's houses had been built almost exclusively from wattle and daub, along with a few fieldstone structures. By contrast, Dog's Paw had been carved out of the face of a box canyon. Hundreds of doorways stood in the face of the basalt, some showing wooden doors while others were enclosed with leather hides. Trails criss-crossed the slopes. As their group neared, people stopped to stare down at them.

A woman hollered, "Got news?"

"Collen is fallen," Cord yelled back. "And Tanner refuses to fight."

The woman clapped her hands. "Then there's hope we won't have to face the demons!"

"That's not encouraging," Blays muttered. "Maybe you should conjure up some illusions to travel with us, Dante. Make it look like Gladdic's not the only one with demonic friends. You know, for their morale."

"Good idea." Dante wiped dust from his brow. "As the old books say, there's no better way to rally the commoners to your cause than by leading a pack of monsters into their town."

A massive, three-story shrine had been carved into the middle of the cliffs. Its columns were square-sided, with narrow rectangular fluting running between their capitals and bases. Lights flickered within, carrying a smell like oily sage. Cord led them past the shrine to a tall wooden door gone gray with age.

This turned out to be the entry to the town's inn. Inside, faint light slanted through slits cut into the stone, but with twilight approaching, most of the illumination was provided by gnarled sticks stuck in shallow clay pots. The source of the oily, sagey smell, the sticks burned with preternatural slowness. Dante had seen the shrubs growing on the way to Dog's Paw.

He pointed to one of the stalks and elbowed Blays. "Remind you of anything?"

Blays cocked his head. "Candlefruit?"

"I got the impression nethermancers traveled to the Plagued Islands after the last time Cellen appeared. They might have taken these plants with them. Harvested them into something that would grow in the tropics."

"Am I supposed to find this interesting?"

"That depends on whether your skull contains a brain or just more skull."

Past the foyer, a damp copper bowl sat on a stone pedestal. Cord made a show of pouring some of her own water into the bowl. This appeared to signal the proprietor that they were worthy of being sold a room. The common room was filled with a blend of blond Colleners, dark-haired Mallish, and a contingent of brown-skinned men with shaved heads and yellow robes—it took Dante a moment to recognize them as being from Parth, an inland territory to Collen's southeast that Mallon had always considered too barren to bother conquering. Everyone in the room seemed to be bartering with each other.

"What is this place?" Blays said. "A crossroads?"

Cord glanced over her shoulder. "Dog's Paw doesn't care for laws. It cares even less for Mallish laws. If anyone has the liver to stand up to Gladdic, we'll find them here."

In their room, the tall windows were enclosed with sun-beaten leather skins rather than proper shutters, but the openings were so narrow a person would have to make an effort to fall through them. The Keeper sat on a chair in the corner, massaging her knees.

"I will go to the shrine," Cord said. "It's late, but the senate will answer."

Blays nodded his assent. "And I will go to the common room. It's early, but the beer will heed my call."

"I'll join you," Naran said. "Dante?"

Dante found a chair. "If the senate's too important to meet us tonight, I'll join you then. For now, I'd like to talk to the Keeper."

The others headed downstairs. The old woman continued to rub her knees.

"Are they sore?" Dante said.

"At my age, everything is sore."

"Why not use the ether?"

"Do you always make things easy on yourself?"

"I'm one of those strange people who doesn't enjoy pain."

She smiled to herself. "Pain hurts less the more you face it."

"When we escaped from Collen," Dante said. "You used the ether to help you breathe underwater. How skilled are you with it?"

The Keeper shrugged her bony shoulders. "How can I say? I have nothing to compare myself to."

"How much light can you summon? A single star? A constellation? Or the entire night sky?"

"Don't speak to me like I'm a child unless you want childish answers."

"I'm sorry," Dante laughed. He held out his hand and drew as much ether as he could from the dry air, forming a marble of light little bigger than his torchstone. "This is as much as I can do. What about you?"

She held her hands a foot apart. Opalescent light formed between her palms. Held in this way, the ether was as bright as the sun, but it cast almost no light on its surroundings.

She let the ether dim, then disappear. "Why do you ask?"

"In Collen, Blays and I fought the Andrac. We lost, but we didn't come away empty-handed. Ether hurts them. The problem is they heal moments later. I can't summon enough to kill one, but I wonder if you can."

"I've heard enough of Gladdic to know his mind. He isn't one to commit himself recklessly. Or to hinge his plan on a weapon so easily defeated."

"Have you ever heard of natural philosophy? It's the process of observing the world, testing its properties, and drawing conclusions from its outcomes. We learned a lot in our encounter with the Andrac. If we apply what we've learned to another encounter, we might formulate a solution to destroy them."

She narrowed her eyes. "Now I see *your* mind. And I don't like where it's heading."

"We don't have to fight one of Gladdic's. All we have to do is summon one of our own. You said that's what the bones are for. Do you know how to use them?"

"The bones form a doorway. The shape of the doorway determines what can pass through it. If you know the arrangement, using the bones is as simple as a game of taps."

"I saw Gladdic use them on the road up to Collen."

Dante closed his eyes, remembering the scene. It had barely been a full day since the fight, and like all times when his life was on the brink of ceasing to exist, his memory of that moment was so strong it felt as if he could walk right into it. He stood to get a quill, but he'd left his in the inn at Collen. The Keeper didn't have one, either. Holding the image in his mind, he ran downstairs to get ink, a quill, and a page from the proprietor. Rather than parchment or vellum, the page seemed to be made of rough, pressed fibers, but that didn't stop the innkeep from charging him a ludicrous fee.

He took the materials upstairs and drew the shape he'd seen on the cliffs. It resembled a hexagon, with bent flanges extending from three of the hexagon's outer points.

The Keeper examined the drawing. "These were human bones?"

"Possibly the ones he took from Cobb's Fort. They had markings on them, too. I wasn't close enough to make them out."

"The name of the thing you wish to find. And directions for it to follow. But these are standard."

"Meaning you can replicate them."

She stared balefully. "If you brought one here, you would be tempted to turn it against the Mallish."

"Yes," he admitted. "But I won't give in to that temptation. The Andrac are too dangerous. Even Gladdic doesn't have perfect control over them. If I tried to use one in war, I'd be afraid of it slaughtering my own people."

"Then your idea is to bring one here—and try to kill it."

"Between you, me, and Blays, I think we'll have the strength. If we can figure out how to be rid of them, we won't even need to convince the Small Senates to go to war. The citizens of Collen will be more than enough strength to boot Gladdic out of the basin."

The Keeper folded her hands, gazing across the room, then shook her head. "This can't be done. Once it's here, we have no way to send it back. It's one thing to risk our own lives. But if we die fighting what we've summoned, we will have unleashed a new demon on the basin. One with no one holding back its reins."

"If we fail, the basin's lost anyway."

"That thought might be enough to salve your conscience. But I won't be a part of a plan that could unleash terror on my land."

There was a firmness to her voice that suggested pressing her would only harden her opinion. Dante rubbed his temples. Would she have the same reservations if they traveled into Mallon and summoned the Andrac there? The trip would take several days on both ends—and they'd need to buy a mule for the Keeper to ride or it would take much longer than that—but until they had a solution to the demons, there was no hope of reclaiming the basin. Not unless Dante summoned every ethermancer in Narashtovik.

He was still thinking on the problem when Cord banged into the room. "Stir your feet. The senate agrees to see us!"

After the meeting they'd had that morning, Dante was significantly less cheery about their prospects than she was. But if they exhausted their options with the town senates, the Keeper might be more prone to try his ideas. They headed downstairs, rousted Blays and Naran from the bar, and crossed through the early evening to the shrine.

The shrine's interior was an expansive natural cavern, with additional spaces carved into the walls for seating and prayer. Incense mingled with the sage of the burning shrubs used for light. A monk seated them in the main hall. A few minutes later, six men and women walked in behind them and took position on the chamber's small stage.

The senate of Dog's Paw was run by a man named Serta. Like the traders in the inn, he looked Parthian, including his shaved head, but he wore the elegantly plain jacket favored by Colleners of importance. If he had an accent, Dante couldn't detect it.

"You fought the Mallish," Serta said. "We're honored to have you."

Dante inclined his head. "We did fight them—and we're a long way from done. But the Mallish aren't going to evict themselves. We need your help."

To head off their fears at the pass, he gave a detailed recap of Gladdic's attack, stressing the point that Gladdic had been the one who'd summoned the Andrac, and furthermore, that Dante and Blays had been able to combat it.

When Dante finished, Serta hooked his thumbs into the pockets of his jacket. "I hear many things. But no answers to the demons."

"We're working on that now. But as soon as King Charles hears the news of Gladdic's victory, he'll dispatch more troops to strengthen his hold on the basin. We can't afford to delay."

"'Afford' is a good word. Everything has a cost. If we resist Mallon now, the demons will be sent to Dog's Paw next. How many lives will that cost us?"

"I couldn't say. What I can tell you—"

"I *can* say." Serta tipped back his head. "It will cost every single life we have."

"You think this is wisdom," Cord said. "But I call it cowardice! The Mallish offer you your deathright and you turn it away?"

"I would be happy to claim *my* deathright. I won't commit every man, woman, and child in my city to do the same."

She clenched her fists, as if ready to surge forward, then sagged, head bowed. "I dedicated my life to fighting them. Now, when the talents of those like me are most needed, we're too afraid to use them. Have I wasted my life?"

Serta lowered his gaze. "It was never a waste to make Collen strong. But this is beyond the strength of any of us." After a moment of silence, he looked to the other senators. "Are we ready to vote?"

They nodded. He asked who wished for war. As in Tanner, not a single senator raised their hand.

"I'm sorry," he said. "Keeping my hand lowered makes me want to hack it off at the shoulder. But if I were to raise it, I might as well use it to draw a knife across my throat."

Cord nodded. As if in a daze, she turned away and wandered from the shrine.

Outside, the air was sweet with dew, but the mood was as sour as a farmer's beer. They stood beneath the cliffs, gazing up at the lights flickering from the windows carved into the rock.

"Look on the bright side," Blays said. "If they won't fight, we can't lose."

Dante booted a black pebble across the dust. "If we leave now, we *have* lost. Gladdic won't forget Narashtovik's involvement. Maybe it'll take a year, maybe it'll take ten. But he'll come for us."

"My heart's as heavy as a millstone," Cord said. "But there are four more towns with the power to declare war. We must try them all."

"Both votes have been unanimous against us," Dante said. "To get war, we need four votes from a senate, right? Unless something changes, we're operating on hope alone."

"Hope makes thin gruel." The Keeper's deep voice was almost a moan. "You wish to race for answers. But I garden the past. Victories are like great trees. They don't leap to their full height overnight. They are grown and tended over the course of years."

"What are you suggesting? We step back and wait for Gladdic to do something so heinous that the senates have to react?" Dante took a sharp breath. "Maybe we don't have to wait. Naran. Cord. Do either of you know where exactly Twill was from?"

"Oh no." Blays' jaw dropped. "That's *sick*!"

Naran wrinkled his brow. "Have I missed something?"

"He wants to use her death to provoke her hometown into declaring war. Thus forcing the rest of the basin into it, too."

"I'm not going to make anyone do anything," Dante said. "They should have all the information available to them before they make their decision. Including how Gladdic executed Twill for helping to free the people of the Plagued Islands. This is the *moral* choice."

"Convenient that the moral choice happens to be the one that will inflame the locals against our enemy."

"That sounds like Gladdic's fault. Naran, you knew Twill best. What do you think?"

Naran pressed his fist to his chin. "There is no doubt whatsoever. Twill would have wanted her people to fight back."

Cord punched the air. "A great woman has died. Her family must know the truth."

"Where can we find them?" Dante said. "Please tell me it's not in the city of Collen."

"Where do you think she found her thirst for trade? Mariola Twill grew up right here in Dog's Paw."

"About time something broke our way. It's time to stop trying to sway the senators and speak to the people the senators answer to." He turned to the Keeper. "The people's support will be meaningless if we don't know how to defeat the Star-Eaters. We have to find new weapons against them. You're afraid of summoning one of the demons? Then teach me to be able to hurt them. Teach me to use the ether."

18

"The ether," the Keeper repeated. "But I am not a teacher."

"So what?" Dante said. "At this point, I'd say you're well beyond the authority of the Mallish priesthood."

"Do you think I'm concerned about being caught teaching their secrets? I didn't say that I wouldn't teach you. Only that I'm not a teacher. And you will make an awful student."

"Because I know too much already?"

"Definitely not the problem," Blays said.

The old woman shook her head. "You will never have the talent you want."

Dante got up from his chair and began to pace. "What makes you so sure?"

"When a man is born without legs, does he ask why he can't run?"

"But I can already summon the ether. All I need to do is get better at using it. Why is that so impossible?"

"I am the Keeper of the Past. I have read all there is to know of six different lands. I know every sorcerer whose name was worth writing down. And you are no ethermancer."

"Obviously there's plenty you don't know. Or else we'd have beaten the Star-Eaters at Collen."

The Keeper snorted. "Explaining this requires that you understand the ether. I doubt you even know that much."

Dante did his best to keep his tone neutral. "Have I done

something to offend you?"

"I don't get out much," she said. "Am I too blunt? If the truth is too hard to swallow, should I feed you soft lies?"

"Tell me whatever you think is true. But I'm still going to try. Even if I'm such a terrible student that they run out of wool before they can finish knitting my dunce cap."

"Then tell me what you know of the ether."

Dante cleared his throat. He could have quoted passages from the *Cycle* word and verse, but wanting to show understanding rather than rote memorization, he paraphrased.

"In the first days, Arawn's Mill hung in the heavens where it ground the ether. The ether filled the sky with stars and the earth with life. There was no sickness. No death. But in time, the world groaned with so much life that it toppled, knocking Arawn's Mill down to earth. Arawn set it back in the sky, but it had cracked in the fall. After that, rather than ether, it ground nether. And for the first time, people died—but that was the start of the cycle. Life was born, but in its time, it also died. Since then, the earth hasn't toppled again."

"That is what's told outside of Mallon, yes. So what is ether and what is nether?"

"Ether's light and nether's shadow. But that doesn't mean ether's good and nether's bad. Just that they're different substances. Like salt and pepper."

The Keeper waved a hand. "I'm not a Mallish priest. You don't have to convince me that the nether isn't an abomination. The only thing I want to know is that you understand the difference."

"They're both a form of energy. If you're asking for something more precise than that, then maybe I don't understand."

Blays chuckled. "That's the best you've got? Apparently they'll make anyone High Priest these days."

"Do you really have nothing better to do?"

"Than watch you fall on your face? This is better than bear-baiting."

The Keeper waited for them to finish. "The breaking of the mill taught Arawn that perfection is only possible in the Celeset. Not among mortals. He altered life to include death. To become a cycle that could renew itself each time it became degraded. Taim rejected this lesson and cast Arawn out. But the perfection of the first days had been lost forever.

"Those of us who work with the primal substances must accept the lesson Taim couldn't. Ether is the ideal. In this realm, it might last for a time. But the ideal can't survive in our world forever. In time, it is always broken. However, the nether is the matter of our world. It may crumble. It may break. But death becomes life once more, and the cycle goes on."

"I see," Dante said.

"By which you mean that you don't. Here is another way to perceive it. The nether is shadow. The object casts a shadow. But it is the ether that casts the object."

"I think," Blays said, "my brain just melted."

The Keeper looked amused. "They aren't my words. They're that of Stathus the Wise."

"Let me offer a piece of hard-earned advice. If you never tell anyone when you're quoting somebody, everyone will think you're a genius."

Dante leaned against the wall. "I think I get what you're driving at. So what does this have to do with me?"

The old woman stared into the distance. "Ethermancers come from people of ideals. Nethermancers come from people of the world. I have seen you, Dante Galand. I have read of who you are and what you've done. You don't bend the thing to the ideal. You bend the thing to what *is*."

"You mean I'm practical? What about Gladdic, then? He's a skilled ethermancer, yet he's a violent hypocrite. He doesn't give a damn for his ideals. They're nothing more than a way to cover his grabs for power."

"He cares far more deeply than you believe. He cares so much that he'll warp those ideals if that's what it takes to achieve them. I fear for Collen."

Dante crossed his arms. "I'm not sure I buy this. There are plenty of sorcerers versed in both skills."

"How many of them can match your skill with the nether? Answer me this. How did you first learn to use the shadows?"

"By reading *The Cycle of Arawn*."

"Which you stole from a temple," Blays said. "After disposing of the guards there. After which you hired me—with money you got robbing people—to keep you safe while you learned."

The Keeper belched with laughter. "What ideals were you fighting for when you killed these guards and robbed those people for the sake of your own curiosity and power?"

"I was young," Dante said. "I didn't care about anything but becoming something greater. You know, I tried to learn to wield the ether from my first teacher, too. His explanation was nothing like this."

"Who was this first teacher?"

"Callimandicus of Narashtovik."

The Keeper bent double, eyes glittering like ice in the winter sun. "Ha! I should have guessed!"

Blays smiled in disbelief. "You knew Cally?"

Her pale eyes twinkled. "As closely as a man and a woman can know each other."

"You're kidding!"

"When we were much younger, he came to Collen help us resist the Third Scour. We were drawn to each other from the start. Fighting the Mallish together only tempered the steel of our passion. He talked of marriage, and so did I. I dreamed of children who'd carry our talents combined within them. Sorcerers who could point their finger and send the towers of Bressel crumbling to the ground."

Blays took a seat. "So what happened?"

"When our movement was ready, we took the palace in Collen, routing the baron and all his men. For two weeks, we hung onto the city. Then King Winsten sent his men from Bressel. Hired sellswords from Larkwood. In the siege, many Colleners claimed their deathright. My brothers were captured. Burned alive for treason and heresy."

The Keeper's deep voice caught. She smiled, a small thing that acknowledged the heartache of the past, but also that it was in the past, as far from her now as her youth itself.

"In time, the Mallish drove us from the palace. Cally argued that we couldn't stay. That Collen would always be stomped beneath Mallon's boots. I thought he was right—I still fear that he was—but I couldn't leave my people to that fate. When I stayed, Cally did as well. But he was too loud in his opinions. Too prone to strike down any Mallish soldier who harassed a citizen. If he'd stayed in Collen, it would only have been a matter of weeks until his temper would have seen him burned alive like the others. So I joined the Undershrine. The one place my Cally couldn't follow me."

"So he left Collen?" By now, Blays was gawking. "You gave up a normal life to save his?"

The old woman shook her head. "I gave up a normal life the instant I watched Mallish priests burn my brothers. After that, it was only a matter of the shape my new life would take. I chose the one that would save the person I loved from the swords of the enemy."

"It worked," Dante said. "After that, he lived for more than a hundred years."

"He's gone now?"

"He died fighting in the Chainbreakers' War. Without him, the norren people would still be in chains. So would half of the former Gaskan Empire. And I wouldn't be here—or half the man I am today. Still, I'm sorry."

"I'm glad I chose this life. But I'm also glad to be reminded of the one I had before. Thank you for telling me where his life took him." Blue eyes as wistful as a nursery rhyme, she stared into the distance, as if she could see into the past itself. She exhaled, then turned to Dante, focus returning to her gaze. "Show me how you bring the ether."

Dante drew his chair to the table, turned up his right palm, and sent his mind into the air. Specks of light condensed and swooped to his hand, forming a small shining sphere.

"Bah," the Keeper said. "You treat ether like nether."

"How should I be treating it? Ideally?"

"That is so. Ether doesn't wish to come like a flock of crows or a swarm of bees. Ether wants to come together like the ribs of a cathedral or the facets of an emerald. Once it's together, it doesn't want to swirl like water or breath. It wants to be a sphere. A cube. A representation of perfection that reality can only hope to imitate."

Dante dismissed the light, took a few breaths, then imagined the vaults of the Cathedral of Ivars in the air above the table. Rather than coming in a storm of disjointed flecks, the ether flowed down eight separate channels, joining in a single point in Dante's hand. As the sphere grew there, the channels quivered, then shattered like glass wine flutes.

But the glowing sphere remained in his hand.

"Better," the Keeper said. "Now practice. The closer you come to summoning it as it hopes to be summoned, the more of it will heed your call."

He did as she commanded, summoning, gathering, and releasing the ether. Each time he brought it forth, he did so in a different pattern, hunting for the ideal even as he trained himself to become more familiar with the ether's movement. But each time, his grip on the ether grew weaker. Within five minutes, he was too shaky to go on. After some discussion of the day's meeting with the senate and tomorrow's effort to speak with Twill's family, they went to sleep.

At dawn, a thunderous boom rolled through the open windows. Dante sat up from sleep, heart pounding. The boom repeated.

Blays scrambled to his feet, moving to the window and grabbing his swords from the chair he'd looped his belt over. "What the hell is that? Are we under attack?"

Cord sat up from her cot, rubbing her eyes. "These are the drums of dawn. They're sounded in Dog's Paw when all is well."

"Then I'd hate to hear what your war drums sound like. Couldn't they just pound them when things *aren't* well?"

"The drums show the watchers are vigilant! Here, the sound is one of safety."

Dante went to the windows. "Do they really expect to be invaded every morning?"

"This isn't about invasion." Cord glared out over the parched earth. "People come to Dog's Paw to trade what the crown has taxed. The drums tell them that none of the king's vultures are here to arrest them for exchanging their own property."

"You don't believe in taxes?"

She boomed with laughter. "How can the king demand money for what isn't his? If I slay a buck, then come to the city to sell the meat and skin, what piece of my hard work has King Charles earned?"

"Apparently he's given you a city that's safe enough to trade in that you'll get a higher price for your pelt than if you tried to sell it out in the wilderness."

Cord patted the sword on her hip. "When I step into a street, *I* make it safe. *I* should be taxing *him*!"

"Can we have this argument another time? Like never? We need to see Captain Twill's family."

"First, we eat. No one is reasonable before breakfast."

Blays hunted for his boots. "At last, something we can all agree on."

They headed downstairs and ate a breakfast of flatbread, spiced squash, and a thick lentil stew. Cord ate what the Keeper couldn't.

Finally finished, Cord stood and stretched her arms above her head. "The day looks much brighter now. I'll seek an audience with the Twills. Stay here, yes? The people of Dog's Paw welcome strangers, but not to their doorstep."

She walked outside, leaving the four of them to pick at the scraps remaining on the table. Aside from the plentiful wines and beers, the beverage of choice in Dog's Paw was a strong tea that tasted similar to the way their sage-lights smelled. Dante couldn't decide if he liked it.

Blays set down his mug. "Is this really our next step?"

"Do you have another suggestion?" Dante said.

"Try the four other senates?"

"The first two beat us down like we'd stolen their shoes and were trying to sell them back to them. What makes you think the next ones will be any different?"

"Because they *are* different?"

"The Andrac have these people so scared they're literally jumping at their own shadows. It'll take us at least a week to go get rebuffed by each of the other senates. That's more than enough time for Mallon to bring a second army into the basin."

"So what? As long as they've got the invincible demons on their side, it doesn't matter if they've got a hundred men or a hundred thousand." Blays brightened and snapped his fingers. "That's your plan, isn't it? After we use the tragedy of Twill's death to light off a war, the gods will be so disgusted with us they'll turn *us* into demons. Then we can fight back as equals!"

"Let me ask you this," Dante said. "Do you think Twill's family should be kept in the dark?"

"They have the right to be told. But the timing's fishier than a fishwife's explanation of why she smells like the neighbor's cologne."

"So we agree they should be told."

"And not so much on every other part of this."

"Then here's my deal," Dante said. "You do all the talking."

Blays narrowed his eyes. "Why would I want to do that?"

"So *I* won't manipulate them into agitating for war."

"Leaving them to do with the information as they will. That's…reasonable. Why are you offering me this?"

"Because we're friends," Dante said. "And I want to keep it that way."

Blays picked up his mug of sage tea. "You've been leading too long. You're finally starting to get wise. What say you, Naran?"

"Agreed," Naran said. "Provide her family with the information they have the right to, and leave it to them to decide how to use it. That will respect Twill as she deserves."

Cord returned an hour later. Her default expression was to look pleased with herself, but that morning, she looked ready to marry herself.

"The Twill family will meet us," she said. "I promised we'd return with all the swiftness of our legs."

The Keeper struggled to her feet. "Then I hope you warned them of the limits of mine."

"Would you rather stay?" Dante said. "If you don't feel safe, I'll stay with you."

"And miss your meeting?"

"That will make it much easier for me to keep my mouth shut."

"I have already broken my vow to never leave the Reborn Shrine. I might as well get the most of my fall from grace."

Cord led them outside. Rather than climbing up to one of the houses dug into the hillside, she took them around a trail into the scrub.

"Can you tell us more about the Twills?" Blays said. "Like whether they're the type to shoot the messenger?"

Cord swung her arms as she walked. "I don't know anything more than what's said in the pubs. Do you know what we say of a true Collener? That they've eaten so much dust they have mud for blood. That is what they say of the Twills."

"She didn't speak of her family much," Naran said. "But I know they're merchants, as she was. Some more legitimate than others."

"But they all do business," Dante said. "As a family."

Blays snorted. "Perverse, I know. But some families *like* each other."

Dante shut his mouth. He'd been afraid the Twills might be an old man and his wife trying to coax a few shoots of asparagus from the dirt. Instead, they sounded like a minor institution. When people of means got angry, they tended to have no compunction against browbeating the nearest official into doing their will.

The walk took them over a low hill and into a stretch of land where patches of grass tried valiantly to maintain their green color. A coalition of black stone buildings stood across the field. Cord approached what looked at a distance to be a small shack, but as they grew closer, it resolved into the hull of a compact sailboat propped on a scaffold.

"They're trying to build ships out here?" Blays gazed across the desert. "No wonder Twill left for Bressel."

As they neared the structures, three small figures jogged outside holding bows and nocked arrows. Two girls and a boy, the oldest no more than fifteen. They crouched behind shrubs.

"Who's there?" a girl called.

"Ho!" Cord lifted her left hand straight in the air. "Is this how you greet friends of Boggs?"

"He's 'specting you?"

"I am Cord, and these are my friends. If you don't fetch Boggs, you'd better hope my partners have more patience than me!"

The girl straightened, peering at Cord like one of the rodents

Dante occasionally saw out in Collen's fields, and scampered back to the house. The other two kids kept their bows trained on Cord. After a minute, the front door banged open. A man in his early thirties stalked outside.

He turned to face the delegation. His tanned face was ruddy with exertion, anger, or both. What wasn't ruddy was scarred.

He tipped his chin at Cord. "These're your people?"

"I can't call them mine," she said. "But for now, they walk with me."

"You said they had news about Mariola." He squinted at Naran. His voice softened a touch. "You're Mr. Naran? She talked about you in her letters."

Naran bowed his head. "I'm honored she thought to do so."

Boggs laughed. "Yeah, she said you were a stiff one. So what drags you out to our little slice of hell? Where's Mariola? Slippin' one past the royal navy?"

The children watched them closely. Naran nodded to the door. "Perhaps we should speak inside."

"It's barely morning. Don't tell me you got your fill of sun already." Seeing the look on Naran's face, Boggs curled his lips. His face went ashen. "Something happened. She's dead, ain't she? Who did it?"

"Are you sure you want to have this conversation in front of the children?"

"You mean am I afraid they might accidentally learn how the world works? That Colleners are planted in the ground every day 'cause Mallish pigs think they own this land and everyone on it? Why do you think I got these kids their bows as soon's they had the strength to draw them?"

Naran exhaled through his nose. "You're correct. Several weeks ago, Captain Twill was executed in Bressel by a priest named Gladdic."

"We're used to not hearing from her for months on end. That's the life at sea. But this time...I had a feeling something wicked was on its way. I wrote to her. Asking when she'd be home next. Hoped I could get her back here before whatever was coming did its damage." A pair of tears dropped down Boggs' face. He made no effort to wipe them away. "Tell me more about who's the bastard I'm going to stab."

Naran relayed the tale. Blays added a few details Naran hadn't been present for, but Dante held his tongue the entire time. Boggs asked a handful of terse questions.

"I can't express the depths of my sorrow," Naran said after he'd finished. "Captain Twill was my mentor—but also my best friend. I can never hope to replace her."

Boggs nodded, shoulders hunched tight around his neck. "Tell me if I'm hearing what you're saying. Mariola died taking you somewhere none of you was supposed to go?"

"Correct. The king shut down passage to the Plagued Islands in order to make sure Mallon's business wouldn't be interfered with."

"In other words, if you lot hadn't been sticking your nose in it, she'd still be here."

Naran's eyebrows shot up. He quickly smoothed his expression. "Don't blame these men. Twill agreed to help them because Dante cured her of the Weeping End. Then, after what Gladdic did to Captain Twill, the crown claimed her ship and press-ganged most of our crew. Dante and Blays freed them and recaptured Twill's ship. In exchange for my further aid in the islands, I made them promise to help me kill Gladdic. They could have abandoned their promise at a dozen different points. For that matter, rather than risk their lives against a terrible sorcerer, they could have killed me and walked away and no one would have been the wiser." He gestured to Blays and Dante. "Yet here they are."

Boggs looked away, teeth clenched so hard the cords on his neck flexed like rigging. "You're still after the asshole that done it? Gladdic?"

Dante glanced at Blays. Blays said, "Even though it's starting to feel more and more suicidal. Not that that's stopped us before."

"So why's he still above ground?"

"There's been a complication. Involving demons."

Boggs swore. "So's I heard. Hoped that was nothing more than fools believing foolish things. So that means you can't get at him. Sneaky, isn't you?"

"How's that?" Blays said.

"I may live out in the desert like some poor mouse, but that don't mean I'm dumb. I know you spoke to the senate last night. And I know they tossed you out on your ear. Today, you come to tell me the last thing I want to hear. You angling to set the Twills on the senate's throats?"

"We just learned you lived here last night. We thought you deserved to hear what happened from those of us who were there."

"So you say." Boggs spat in the dust. "I make my living trading with people who don't want me to know how much they've got in their pocket. I know an agenda when I see one."

"I wanted to talk you into pressuring the senate," Dante blurted. "But Blays and Naran thought that would dishonor Captain Twill's death. And they were right."

"Then why in the twelve hells *are* you here?"

"Your sister was fearless. If we couldn't come here to tell you what happened face to face, then we learned nothing from her."

"Mister Naran said you saved her life. Cured her of the Weeping End."

"Just so she'd take us to the islands," Dante said. "It was entirely for my own ends. I'm no saint."

"None of us is." Boggs stared across the hardpan. "Let me show you something."

He stalked around the side of the house. Dante shrugged at Blays, then followed, as did the others. Boggs headed past the house and several shacks and climbed a low ridge, stopping at the top. Below them, roofed, open-walled structures housed a great deal of lumber. Past this, the desert went on.

"What do you see here?"

"Desert," Blays said. "In plentiful supply."

"Not Mariola. When she looked out here, she saw potential. Great big gobs of it. Mister Naran, do you know what Mariola was doing with her money?"

"She always said she was investing it," Naran said. "But when I or the crew asked what she was investing in, her answer was always 'our future.'"

Boggs chuckled. The sound was almost resentful. "She was

gettin' our aunt into the dredging business. Keeping the canals good and deep. Hard work, but fine money from the earthers. Mariola weren't in it for the coin, though. See, Parth ain't too far southeast of here. No further than some of the canals we already got. My sister wanted to dig a new canal. All the way to Parth. Her idea was we could use the waterways to trade back and forth. Travel, too. Much cheaper than draggin' wagons across the desert. Build right good friends with the Parthians, too."

He nodded to the piles of lumber. "She was just gettin' started on the first barges this year. Was going to send them up and down the canals we already got to show everyone how easy it'd be. Earn a pile of cash and convince others to invest in the new canal she wanted. See, my sister had *vision*. She went to sea because she knew that was the only way to get the seed money — and to learn boats, too. And now she's dead."

Dante kept silent. So did the others. The only sound was the wind; with no leaves to rustle, the gusts were hollow, untextured.

"She saw further than anybody I knew. Don't know why nobody had the idea to use the canals for trade before her. Maybe it seemed too expensive. Maybe it's 'cuz the currents are so sluggish, and with the winds always blowing the wrong way, a caravan would always be faster. Even so, she was going to find a way. But that's what Mallon does, don't they? They take away our best and brightest. And all that's left is fools like me."

Dante itched to speak up, but forced himself to stick to his promise.

"A canal to Parth," Cord mused. "That would be a sight."

"It's gone now," Boggs said. "Once Mallon's through here, we'll be too busy rakin' up the mess to waste any work on a canal. What am I supposed to do? How am I supposed to deal with something *none* of our people's ever been able to set straight?"

Blays toed the dirt. "If you can't answer that, I don't know what hope *we'd* have. All I can tell you is we're going after Gladdic."

Boggs stooped for a rock and slung it as hard as he could. It struck one of the tarps strung over the lumber, punching right through the fabric.

"Stay in town," he said. "It'll take a few days to bring the rest of the family around."

"What are you going to tell them?" Dante said.

"That Mariola's gone. And if we give a damn for her memory, we can't let Gladdic take the *next* Mariola."

The five of them trudged away from the ridge, leaving Boggs to gaze at the desert. Around him, the children fired arrows into a raggedy bale of wheat stalks.

"I'm impressed," Blays said. "I figured that as soon as you heard he was looking to build a canal, an offer to dig it would erupt from you like the gases in a dead man's belly."

Dante stepped over a protrusion of basalt. "Maybe if I pretend to have ideals, the ether will like me better. Besides, now isn't the time to spend my talents digging ditches. We've got demons to slay."

The next few days were quiet ones. It was good to have time away from the stresses of battle, diplomacy, and travel, but it was hard to feel like they weren't wasting vital time. Every day Gladdic had control of the city was another day for him to tighten his hold on it. And for fresh soldiers to arrive from Bressel.

Dante put his time to use continuing to practice the ether, summoning it as the Keeper had instructed. If he was making progress, it wasn't obvious. Maybe the Keeper was right about him. Then again, he'd once thought he'd never be able to use the ether at all. Perhaps the fact it had required a trip into the afterlife to unlock that ability was proof he would always be limited at it, but there was no sense turning things into a self-fulfilling prophecy.

His skills were limited enough that he was only able to practice them for a quarter of an hour a day. After that, he sought news down in the common room or at one of the merchant stalls set up along the cliffs. According to rumor, the city of Collen remained closed. No one entered or left. No reinforcements had arrived yet, either. Dante assumed Gladdic was doing the same thing they were: laying the groundwork for the next move.

"Let's say Boggs convinces the Twills to pressure the senate,"

Blays said one afternoon after returning from the pub. "And the senate is convinced to go to war. Triggering the Oath of the Wasp or the Code of the Honey Badger or whatever these people are sworn to. All of a sudden, the basin's got a new army to play with. What do we do with it?"

Dante rubbed his eyes. "Coordinate with them to liberate Collen. For all that's happened, I'm still hoping to limit our involvement. If we can take out Gladdic and the demons, we can leave the Colleners to take and hold the city. The question is, what happens if Gladdic isn't the only priest who can summon the Andrac?"

"Then the world is much scarier than I thought it was."

"We may have to summon a few monks from Narashtovik," Dante said. "They can keep the city safe from further demons and do their best to train some of the locals into sorcerers."

"Sounds great. But you know what I'm going to ask next."

"No. We still don't know how to take down the Andrac."

"Right," Blays said. "Then I'll get back to drafting our defeat speech."

Dante spent what was left of the day discussing the ether and the Star-Eaters with the Keeper. Between them, they turned up exactly zero new insights regarding the demons. As Dante dressed to go downstairs and get drunk in disgrace, the loon in his ear tingled.

He activated it. "Hello? Jona?"

"You're alive!" The voice was familiar, but Dante couldn't quite place it. "Greetings from Narashtovik, wayward leader."

Dante grinned. "Nak?

"In the voice. Now what trouble have you gotten yourself into this time?"

19

"You've got proof you didn't hire the Crows?" Raxa snorted at the man seated in the chair. "Let me guess. It's sheathed in that scabbard by the door."

Cane Dreggs shook his head slowly. "It's here between my ears. You're right about one thing. It was the Army of Crows who attacked you. But why do you think I hired them?"

"The Crows are run by a man named Bennel. The same Bennel is cousins with your lieutenant Vart Dracks."

"So what? Are cousins incapable of doing business with anyone but each other? In that case, I'm retiring from the underworld to convince King Moddegan he has a long-lost branch of the family tree."

"They talked," Raxa said. "We found their letters."

"Which ones?"

"The ones Bennel sent to Dracks."

Cane shrugged one shoulder. "Ah. Those letters. I'm sure Bennel came on very strong. He was the one who approached Dracks. He was extremely interested in striking a deal to declare war on you. If all you recovered were the letters in Dracks' possession, I assume you have none of the ones he sent to Bennel—including those where he turned Bennel down, repeatedly, in no uncertain terms."

"Wrong. Dracks confessed."

"Did he? And how much torture did *that* require?"

Raxa gripped the haft of the bone sword. "If this wasn't your war, you sure seem interested in fighting it."

"Why would we want to start a war with you? Look around. Right now, who's winning?"

"I'm armed and alone with the leader of the Little Knives. I'd say the Order is about to carry the day."

"Wrong. We're *both* losing. We're out there gutting each other. Bleeding each other dry of everything we've fought to build. The winners of this war will be everyone who's not fighting it. When it's over, it'll be a race for the others to loot our bodies."

"Then why not tell Kerreven this days ago?"

Cane sputtered with laughter. "He'd look at my claims as a ruse. A chance to buy myself breathing room to dig in my troops and hit back. If I was in his position, that's how *I'd* see it. I know we didn't hire the Crows, but the only way to prove that is to find out who *did*. Which I'm in the process of accomplishing right now."

"So you don't know who did it."

"Oh, but I do."

Raxa edged nearer, lifting the sword. "Spill."

Cane wagged his finger. "That information is my insurance against you slitting my throat. Take me to see Kerreven and I'll tell him everything I know."

"How about I cut it out of you instead?"

"Sure. I'll make it easy for you." Cane tugged down the collar of his doublet, exposing his throat. "Kill me. That will end the war with my people. But it won't give you the justice you've been fighting for. And your enemy will still be out there."

Raxa held the sword pointed at his chest. She could cut him in half with a flick of her wrists. But if he was right, she didn't think killing him would actually end the war with the Little Knives. Instead, it would ensure the Knives never stopped fighting the people who'd wrongly killed their leader.

She dropped the blade's tip two inches. "How many people are here with you?"

"Six," he said. "I'll order them to stand against the walls. If any of them rushes you, you'll have plenty of time to cut my throat."

"Are you armed?"

He crossed his legs at the knee, extended his top leg, and tugged up his trousers, revealing a slender knife. He unstrapped this, dropped it to the ground, and kicked it her way.

Cane stood, lifting his arms above his head. "Feel free to search me."

Doing so required she sheathe her sword in favor of a knife short enough to put to use if he tried something while she was close. He was clean. Of weapons, anyway. After days cooped up in the tenement, his clothes smelled like they'd have to be cut free from his body.

She put away her knife and got out her sword. "I'm going to put this to your neck. You're going to walk us out of here."

Cane nodded and stood in the middle of the room. Raxa got behind him and set the blade to his throat. Careful not to make any sudden moves, he walked to the door.

In the room beyond, four men sat at a table playing dice. Seeing Cane's state, they shot to their feet and went for their swords.

"Get against the wall." Cane's voice was as authoritative as a hurled brick. "I'm on my way to end the war. Make a move, and she ends me instead."

At his word, they drew and dropped their swords. He called the other two men into the room and ordered them to disarm themselves as well.

"Mr. Dreggs," one of them said. "You're sure about this?"

Cane laughed softly. "Not exactly. But I'm sure what will happen if I don't go with her."

Raxa stared them down. "If your boss is telling the truth, you won't try to follow us."

Cane moved to the far door. Raxa's ears strained for the first sound of motion, but the men held as still as if they were decorative. Cane opened the door into a hallway and led her to a stairwell. They descended to the first floor.

"Stop," she said before they exited into the foyer. "We're switching things up."

She drew her knife, put away the sword, and wrapped her knife-arm around his waist, slipping the blade under his doublet and putting its tip to the underside of his ribs.

Cane glanced at her hand in amusement. "We're posing as

young lovers?"

"Wrong. You're not that young. Now walk."

He opened the stairwell door and crossed the musty foyer to the exit. On their way down the stoop, he winced, sucking in air. The knife had nicked him. Raxa didn't apologize.

The walk to Kerreven's tenement felt as long as a full night of dreaming. Every person they passed seemed to lock in on Raxa's hand. A few of the grimier-looking men sized them up—couples were a favorite target; men would usually rather turn out their pockets than risk harm to their wife/mistress. Seeing the look on Cane and Raxa's faces, the thugs frowned and walked on.

"They tell stories about you, you know," Cane murmured. "Some say you're a demon. That you pop right up from the floor to drag men down to hell. Then again, when they don't know the truth, they make up whatever stories are the most fun to tell."

"So I've noticed."

"Me, I don't care for stories. I like facts. How *do* you do it?"

"I make myself so thin I can walk right through the walls."

He chuckled, then winced as the knife jabbed his side. "I understand. Trade secret. Maybe you can tell me after we both retire."

As they neared the entrance of the tenement where Kerreven was holed up, the drunk man slumbering against the wall popped to his feet and goggled at her.

"Raxa?" He drifted forward. "Is that *Cane*?"

She nodded. "He's got something Kerreven will want to hear."

The spotter dashed up the stairs ahead of them. On their arrival, the apartment was abuzz with rumor. The muscle took Cane into the back room. Kerreven emerged from his quarters, gave Raxa a nod, and went into the back, closing the door.

"Cane Dreggs." Gaits chuckled, shaking his head. "Where in the world did you find him?"

"In the room where he was staying."

"Allow me to rephrase: *how* did you find him?"

"After they ambushed me last night, a couple of the Knives ran off. Figured they were either going for reinforcements, or to let someone in charge know I'd gotten away."

"Let me guess, he's ready to wave the white flag? Funny how

being captured by one's foes will turn the most bloodthirsty man into a pacifist."

"It's bigger than peace," Raxa said. "He claims it wasn't the Knives who hired the Crows."

Gaits reached out to support himself against the wall. He tried to speak but choked on his own spit. "Bullshit. Transparent effort to save his own skin."

"Could be. I figured I wasn't the one to make that call."

"I expect Kerreven will agree with you. All right, I'll bite. Who does he claim really hired the Crows?"

"He wouldn't tell me. Only Kerreven."

"Right move on his part, too," Gaits muttered. "Though if we were betting, I'd say he wouldn't tell you because he hadn't come up with the right lie yet."

They took a seat, speculating with the other men about who else could be behind the Crows, what Kerreven's reaction would be if Cane was telling the truth, and what it meant for them. Wine and rum were produced and consumed. There were no screams or thumps from the back room. Just the steady murmur of male voices. When her companions exhausted new areas to speculate on and turned back to who'd really hired the Crows, Raxa found a cot and went to sleep.

She woke to the gray light of dawn. She wandered into the kitchen to see if anyone had made tea. Yesterday's kettle was cold, but she wasn't choosy. As she poured a cup, Kerreven entered the room without so much as a creak of the floorboards.

He eyed her puffy face. "Are you awake enough to talk?"

She shrugged. "We can find out."

He led her to his room. Gaits was there, ensconced in a chair, chin propped up on his palm, snoring heavily. Kerreven bumped his chair. Gaits snapped awake, dabbing drool from the corner of his mouth.

Kerreven took a seat, gazing at the ceiling. The bags under his eyes were big enough to feed a destrier. "Do you know the silver lining of a crisis, Raxa?"

She took a gulp from her mug. "Definitely not the quality of the tea."

"When it's bright and sunny, it's hard to notice a new flame.

But when the lights go out? That's when you get to see who burns brightest." He smiled tiredly. "Now that we have Cane? One way or another, the war will end. Because of you. If you hadn't already talked your way into a share, I'd be giving you one now."

"Thanks."

"Are you uncomfortable with praise?"

"I'm uncomfortable with this hangover. I'm guessing you didn't wake me up this early to clap me on the back."

Kerreven chuckled. "Did you find Cane's story compelling?"

She tapped the side of her mug. "Enough to bring him back here."

"I'm glad you did. He's still alive. Know what that means?"

"You think he's telling the truth. Who does he think hired the Crows?"

"An outfit called the Black Star. By the look on your face, I'm guessing you've never heard of them?"

"Nope."

"You're in good company. Cane doesn't know who they are any more than you or I do. He was in the midst of trying to find that out when you brought him in."

Raxa rubbed sand from the corners of her eyes. "So what do we do now?"

"What would you do?"

"Ask you why you're not making that decision yourself. After that, I'd negotiate a truce with the Knives, keep Cane here for insurance, and work to confirm his story."

Kerreven smiled and laced his hands together. "Which is exactly what we're doing."

"You're not afraid he's playing you?"

"Am I afraid this is a trick? Of course. But you know what I'm afraid of more? Continuing to fight a war against the wrong enemy."

Raxa drained the last of her tea. "Makes sense. What can I do to help sort this out?"

"For now? Sit tight. You're one of my most valuable assets. I'm not going to expose you to any more danger until we're certain who the target is—whether that's the Black Star, or the Little

Knives."

By the end of her first day being kept in reserve, Raxa was as restless as the evening winds that blew off the bay.

Gaits came and went from the apartments with news from the informants and street rats, but the Black Star remained nothing more than a name. As for the Knives, they were less than thrilled to hear their commander was being held prisoner. It looked like the truce would collapse before it could begin.

Cane wrote a letter to his people confirming he was alive and asking them to help the Order of the Alley run down any leads. Morning brought the news: for the first time since the war had begun, during the last night, there'd been no new attacks, injuries, or deaths.

But there was no fresh intel on the Black Star, either. Nor the day after that. The third day of the truce, Raxa went to Kerreven to ask to go back into the field, but he told her to stay put.

Later that same morning, he called her back into his room.

"Glad you changed your mind," Raxa said. "I'm being wasted kept in this room."

Kerreven waved his hand. "You're not going into the street. You ran into a group of Crows during the attack on the Marrigan, didn't you? Did you take a ring from them?"

"I did," Raxa said. "But no one could identify it."

"Still have it?"

"It's at my house. Want me to grab it?"

"Please," he said. "But don't wander off, okay? Now that we don't know who the enemy is, we're in more danger than when we were at open war."

It was a long walk to her house. With all the time she'd been spending away, she'd had to keep it locked up. The interior was hot and smelled like a mouse had died somewhere inside. Kerreven had made the ring sound important, but not urgent. Raxa tossed open the windows and doors, found the ring, then spent an hour hunting down the source of the smell, which turned out to be one dead mouse and one larger and deader rat. She tossed these out back, closed the house up, and returned to the tenement.

There, Kerreven's door was closed. The rank and file sat around a table playing dice with Cane.

"Care to join us?" Cane nodded to his pile of croutons they were using in place of money. "These friends of yours may be fine thieves, but they're awful gamblers."

She pointed to Kerreven's door. "He in there?"

Jenker nodded his head, the fat bunching under his chin. "Yup. And nobody goes in."

"Who's he talking with?"

"One of Cane's—who says he knows the Black Star."

Raxa took a seat to prevent herself from pressing her ear to the door. Dice rattled on the table. Behind the closed door, a table crashed to the ground. Feet thumped back and forth.

Everyone bolted to their feet. Kerreven's door swung open, revealing a man in black. He held a bloody dagger in his hand.

Seeing Cane, he stood straight and saluted. "Milord. It's done."

He raised the dagger and slit his own throat.

Jenker grabbed Cane and wrestled him into a headlock. "Check the room!"

Raxa and two others ran inside. Kerreven lay in a pool of blood. He was blinking, but he was too weak to put a voice to the movement of his lips. After a few seconds, his face went slack.

Raxa staggered out to the main room, spots dancing in her eyes. "He's dead."

Jenker tightened his arm around Cane's neck. "By this bastard's assassin!"

"It wasn't me!" Cane sputtered. "I've told you nothing but the truth!"

Raxa stared into his eyes. "Let him go."

Jenker bared his teeth. "Don't tell me you believe him! That was his man. He *vouched* for him. He killed Kerreven!"

"Let him go," Raxa said. "So I can cut him in half."

She drew her sword. Jenker laughed and shoved Cane to the ground. Cane raised his arm to protect his head, but Raxa's blade passed through his hand like it wasn't there, cleaving through his skull.

Jenker was first to speak. "What now?"

"Get the body out of here." Raxa kneeled and cleaned her blade on Cane's shirt. "And get our forger in here. Cane's got a letter to write."

When Gaits returned and heard the news, he closed his eyes and dropped to one knee. "We've been so stupid."

"This was my fault," Raxa said. "I should never have listened to him."

"You can't blame yourself. Kerreven believed it, too."

"What now? We go back to war?"

"I don't know."

"I called in Ferrey to forge a letter from Cane telling his people that all's well. We could have him write a second letter calling for a meet with the Knives. And when they show up?" She drew her finger across her throat.

"None of us has the authority to make that decision." Gaits rose, eyes bright with tears. "So the first thing we do is elect someone who can."

"You're talking about a..." She had to hunt for the term. "The Midnight Coronation."

"Ridiculous term. But yes. If we resume the war with the Knives, things will get very messy very soon. If we don't have a leader with the authority to declare how to clean up that mess, the Order will fracture. Then we aren't just looking at war with the Knives—we're looking at war with ourselves."

He sent word to every member of the Order hidden across the city, instructing them to assemble the following night. Gaits didn't say why they were meeting—if their enemies learned Kerreven was dead, they might be emboldened to attack—but he did warn them that anyone who didn't show up would be expelled from the Order on the spot, be they the lowliest lowling or Kerreven himself.

They removed the bodies from the tenement. They scrubbed up the blood. Then they left, too, relocating to a tumbledown manor outside the Pridegate. The mood in the house that night was grimmer than anything Raxa had felt since the Gaskan empire had sieged the city at the end of the Chainbreakers' War.

In her room, alone except for the weak flickering of an odorous tallow candle, she turned the black-stoned ring over in her hand. Kerreven hadn't told her why he wanted to see it. Gaits hadn't recognized it. Neither had the jewelers she'd taken it to. She inspected the shank of the ring, but the scrollwork there meant nothing to her. Whatever Kerreven had found was lost.

The house's mood in the morning wasn't much better than the night before. The hours dragged past like a cricket with its hind legs torn off. Most of the men drank rum until they could nap. Night came. When the ninth bells of Ivars pealed across the city, they set out from the crumbling manor.

To avoid spies, strangers, or the possibility of running into their enemies, Gaits had called the Coronation to meet outside the city. The late summer night was lukewarm, but as they left Narashtovik behind them, Raxa felt a hint of cold in the air.

They took the western road, crossing a mile-wide field of stumps, grass, and evergreen saplings. Then the pine forest took them. Sheets of brown needles slid underfoot. Low, drunken voices carried on the night. Vagabonds. The wilds outside Narashtovik had fewer than most—years ago, the city had offered the plots of land abandoned on its outskirts to anyone willing to farm them—but some people wound rather roam the woods and hills than work the same square of dirt every day for the rest of their lives. Under different circumstances, Raxa might have been out there with them.

Jenker glared at a campfire burning in the distance. "How far is this place?"

"Several miles," Gaits answered.

"But there's a perfectly good forest right here."

"We are holding the first Midnight Coronation in nearly two decades. We're not going to hold it in the middle of a *forest* surrounded by a bunch of *brigands*."

"But we're brigands."

Gaits couldn't speak for three full seconds. "We aren't brigands. Do you see us sleeping next to our latrines? Rather than choosing our targets based on how much we're likely to acquire from them, do we simply mug everyone who steps out on the road? We are civilized, Jenker. We can't hold the ceremony under the nearest pine tree. A short walk is a small price to pay to honor Kerreven and whoever succeeds him."

At a fork in the road, they headed north down a narrow dirt trail. Raxa found her hand drifting into her pocket. The ring there was cool, its stone smooth. She dropped a step behind the others and took it out. As she did so, one of its prongs caught on a loose thread. The ring tumbled to the ground.

Raxa dropped to her knees, heart bumping. The layer of loose pine needles was an inch thick. But the dark metal glinted in the moonlight. She picked it up. Within the black stone mounted in its center, the light of the moon blazed in a four-pointed star.

Her mouth went dry.

"Raxa?" Gaits called. "Something wrong?"

She palmed the ring. "Boot came untied. I'll catch up in a second."

She pretended to finish lacing her shoe, then slipped the ring in her pocket and moved after them. She didn't push herself harder than a jog, but her heart raced like she'd been running for her life. Had Cane been telling the truth about the Black Star? If so, why had he killed Kerreven? Opportunism? Revenge for what the Order had done to his people? And what did it mean that Raxa had killed him?

She still had no answers by the time Gaits stopped and gestured down the path. "And here we are."

The trail fed into a bowl-shaped clearing. At its far end, low cliffs rose, clefted in the middle. A high stone wall had once protected the gap, but it was now in a state of ruin.

Jenker scratched his cheek. "What's this place?"

"Most people call it Drennecad's Keep," Gaits said. "But we call it Carvahal's Wall."

"Carvahal built this place? Looks pretty crummy."

Gaits gave Raxa a pained look. "I'm risking a guess on my part, but I'd bet good money the god of trickery had better things to do than build himself a keep in the middle of nowhere. Now please, hold on to the rest of your questions. All will be answered at the Coronation."

Twenty members of the Order had already gathered in the clearing. It was the most of her friends Raxa had seen in one place since the attack on the Marrigan, and despite the nature of the meeting, it felt good to be back together.

Then again, most of them didn't know why they were there.

More members trickled into the clearing. Gaits left to circulate. Gurles, the bouncer at the Marrigan, made his way beside Raxa. He was as tall as some norren with a beard and muscles to match.

"He's dead, ain't he?" he murmured.

Raxa didn't look up. "What makes you think that?"

"He ain't here—and all the rest of us are."

"Keep it to yourself? Let's not ruin the mood until we have to."

Gurles eyed her, then nodded and moved off. Over the next hour, the ranks swelled until sixty people were standing in the grass in front of the wall.

"It lifts my heart to see so many of you here." Gaits' voice rang from the top of the wall. Every head swiveled toward his silhouette. "That means you've survived the single worst set of troubles the Order of the Alley has ever faced. Others, though, have given their lives so we'd still be here." There was just enough moonlight to see him lower his head. "Kerreven is dead."

People shouted. Grabbed for each other. Questions and curses fired from all sides.

"He was killed yesterday," Gaits yelled over the hubbub. "Murdered by an assassin sent by the Little Knives. The assassin's dead. So is Cane Dreggs, the Knives' leader. Very soon, we'll send the rest of his crew to join him in hell." This drew gruff cheers. Gaits waited them out. "The Order of the Alley existed before Kerreven. And it will continue to exist after him. Tonight, we summon the Midnight Coronation to determine who will lead us against the Knives and into the nights beyond."

He walked along the top of the crumbling wall, heading closer to its middle. "In the days before days, humans knew nothing of fire. When night fell, we lived in darkness, shutting our doors tight against the wolves and the snakes. Taim wanted to keep us this way, but Arawn, who controlled the fire of the north star, defied him. With his brother Carvahal, he hatched a plan to bring the fire down to us mortals.

"But Carvahal betrayed him. He locked Arawn behind a starry wall and took the fire for himself, ensuring the glory would always be his. It was the greatest theft of all time."

White fire sprung from his hand. Raxa knew the effect was from a spitwand, a tool people of their kind used to incite confusion, panic, or misdirection. Even so, her eyes told her it was magic. With the flame already fading, Gaits pointed it at the top of the wall beneath his feet. Orange fire blossomed from a bundle of kindling laid there.

"In times of peace, the Midnight Coronation is a contest to see if anyone can match Carvahal's feat. Challengers have a week to pull off a heist. Those who bring in the best hauls become the nominees for the crown. But we are at war. There's no time for a contest. Tonight, we vote."

He dropped from the wall, landing in a low crouch and rolling into the grass. Up on the wall, another figure emerged. Even before he stepped into the light, Raxa could tell by the silhouette of his upthrust hair that it was Venk, Kerreven's head enforcer. She was glad to see he was still alive.

"As written by our founder, Witta the Shadow, here's how this goes down." Venk had a thick Sharps accent and always sounded as disappointed as if he'd just caught you urinating on your own shoes. "Process is simple. It's got to be, if *you* fools hope to follow it. First comes the Listing of the Few. You think somebody would make a good leader? You call out their name. And no, smart guy, there's no nominating yourself. Next comes the Declarations of Worth. If your nominee accepts the offer, then you get the honor of standing up and telling us why you think they'd make such a fine chief. When all the speeches are done, we vote to decide the Midnight Coronation of the Grand High Chief of Street and Knife. You got me?"

He was answered by a number of nods and ayes.

"Supreme," Venk said. "Then I hereby begin the Listing of the Few—and if one of you shit-for-brains nominates Stapp, may the gods have mercy on your soul."

Most of the crowd laughed hard, with the notable exception of Stapp and a couple of his friends. But Stapp was the type to wear a cape even in the height of summer and to brag that he could swipe the glasses off a man's face even though it was well known he didn't meet quota half his months. He deserved whatever came his way.

The members of the Order fell into a lull, eyeing each other like gamblers at a table. Raxa did the same. Until that moment, the idea of replacing Kerreven had been just that: an idea. With minutes, it would be fact. One way or another, their future would never be the same.

She called out, "Blackeyed Gaits."

Cheers bounced from several corners of the clearing. Gaits grinned at her and winked. "Fine selection."

Her nomination broke the dam. Someone hollered out for Anya, the Esteemed Countess of Logistics and Material Acquisitions. Mind like an architect. Good choice. One of Stapp's friends offered up his name and was met with a chorus of groans. Someone volunteered Ackley only to be informed that Ackley had died in the streets several days ago.

A silence washed over the clearing, broken by the nomination of Farnan, the Order's oldest member at 71. Raxa wasn't sure if the nomination was for his experience, or a token nod toward his seniority. After that came suggestions for Kenna, Darvid, and Johan, each of whom was popular, competent in the street, and relatively young. And, to Raxa's mind, completely unexceptional.

The clearing grew quiet again. Venk watched from atop the wall, face lit by the unsteady flicker of the fire.

"Last call," he said. "You jokers remember that whoever you choose tonight, you're living with that choice for what could be the rest of your career. Haven't heard the name you want? Belt it out now — or keep your gob shut when some other bastard wins."

"Raxa Dosse," Gurles' voice boomed forth. "The Ghostmaker."

Raxa almost replied. But he wasn't looking to talk to her. He was nominating her. A few people looked surprised. A few others clapped.

Venk took a final look around. "Then I declare these nominations closed. Do any of you so named wish to decline the burden of leadership you've been volunteered for?"

Raxa scowled, ready to decline. There was no point getting in a fight you couldn't win. Ten feet away, Gurles caught the look on her face. He set his jaw and shook his head. Raxa couldn't help smiling.

Venk chuckled from the wall. "Then there's no wriggling out of it now, you poor sods. Onto the Declarations of Worth! First to nominate is first to speak. Raxa, speaking for Blackeyed Gaits."

Raxa tipped back her chin to the stars. "If any of you need to be told why Gaits is the best and only replacement for Kerreven, then we're in far worse shape than I thought." This drew more laughs than she'd expected. "It's too bad he can't speak for himself. Gaits was *born* to speak. He could talk the gold out from under a dragon. He could talk the scales off a fish or the claws off a lion. You know what a leader needs most? Diplomacy. The chops to talk down a war before it begins."

She paused to think, but the words were already there. "But this goes way past talk. Gaits has been Kerreven's right hand for years. He knows this city from bay to forest. He knows every one of us. Our strengths. Our weaknesses. How to use the former and protect the latter. He'll get us past this war. And once he does, he'll make us all rich beyond our dreams."

She stepped back. Applause and whoops sprung from the audience.

On the wall, Venk nodded. "Next! Olac, speaking for Anya the Web-Weaver."

Olac took a swig from a leather flask. "Sure, yes, Gaits is a fine choice. *If* you think a silver tongue is all it takes to make a decent chief. But half of us here could talk the robes off a Council priest. So what makes Gaits so special? Not much, says I. Not in that department. You want experience, though? That's Anya."

He rattled off her list of qualifications. This took so long the crowd started to murmur. Olac flashed a grin. "See? She's done so much you can't stand to listen to it all. You want a chief? A *real* chief? The kind you trust your life to? Then the last thing you want is a guy whose words are so sweet you could eat them on toast. You won't know that guy's lying until it's far too late. What you want is somebody who's been there. Done that. If Anya walked away tonight and started a new business tomorrow, she'd own half the city by next summer. Guess what? Once the fighting's done, we're going to need to rebuild. *I* want the guy who can do that in her sleep."

Olac's nomination hadn't drawn much of a response. His speech, though—that got cheers. Maybe more than Raxa's.

Stapp's friend got three sentences in before the boos came out. People listened respectfully to the case for Farnan, but the applause at the end didn't go any further than "polite." The Declaration for Kenna was surprisingly strong, but couldn't match Gaits or Anya. Raxa forgot the speeches for Darvid and Johan before they were over.

"So we reach the end," Venk said. "Gurles, want to speak your piece so we can all get drunk?"

In the moonlit clearing, Gurles stood perfectly still, eyes making a slow sweep of the crowds. If he wanted to, he could bark like a mastiff. But when he began to speak, his voice was as quiet and precise as an archer drawing a bead on an elk.

"Lot of talk about the future." Gurles stared into the fire burning on the wall. "About what these people will do for you after the fighting's over. You're gambling with tomorrow's wages. You talk like war is a storm. Like all you have to do to get through it is close the shutters, lock the doors, and wait for the sun to come back out.

"War ain't a storm. It's *war*. If you don't have the guts, the cunning, and the know-how to swing a sword, then you get planted in the dirt. Don't think so? You think we'll win because we're the good guys?" Gurles spat at his feet. "I'd much rather be the bad man. That's who's going to win the fight against the Knives and Crows. If we choose the leader we want for the future, none of us will make it out of the now."

He fell silent. The fire snapped. Venk shifted his feet on the rock wall, then cleared his throat. "You done, Gurles?"

"I want you to close your eyes," Gurles said, pausing a moment to let them do so. "Picture yourself walking down a dark alley. There's footsteps behind you. You pick up your pace, but the steps keep coming. You reach for your knife, but it ain't there. Ahead, the alley stops cold. There's no way out. You turn around to meet your pursuit. Who's the last person you want to see coming for you, knife gleaming in their hand? Whose face is staring back at you from the darkness?

"That's who's going to save our miserable lives."

He crossed his arms. This time, there were no whoops or applause. Just a sea of somber faces.

"Right then," Venk said. "Now we vote."

This turned out to be much more sophisticated than ayes and nays. During all the nominating and speechifying, Venk's team had been busy. Atop the wall, he held up seven clay pots. Each was marked with the name of one of the candidates—and an accompanying symbol for the illiterate, which was most of the crowd. The pots were lowered to the other side of the wall.

"Each of you gets three stones," Venk said, as his men passed out three small black rocks marked with a dab of white paint. "That's three votes. Each of which has to go to a different person. My men will be watching. You try to cheat—put more than one stone in a pot, or try to cast more than three—and you'll get walled up just like Carvahal did to Arawn. You got me?"

One at a time, they filed through a gap in the wall. Rocks clinked from the voting chamber. It seemed to take forever until Raxa's turn. Inside the chamber beyond, Venk and two others watched as she allotted her stones. One to Gaits. One to Anya. And one to herself.

As soon as the last vote was cast, Venk and his men brought the clay pots outside. Standing back from the pots, Venk made a display of stripping down to his smallclothes, then turned in a circle, arms upraised to show he had no vote-stones hidden on his person.

Starting with Gaits, he dumped out the pot and counted the votes. Gaits totaled 41 stones. Next, Anya came out at 38. Farnan and Kenna tied at 13. None of Stapp, Darvid, or Johan cleared ten.

Last, he sorted Raxa's pile. A handful of her stones were still waiting to be counted when he tallied her 42nd vote.

"Raxa Dosse," Venk commanded. "Climb the wall and take your throne."

EDWARD W. ROBERTSON

20

Dante dropped the boot he'd been about to put on. Speaking in Gaskan, he said, "I never thought I'd say this, Nak. But it's so good to hear your voice."

Through the loon, Nak chuckled. The sound was as clear as if they were in the room together. "I will do my best to take that as a compliment. As for Olivander, I'm not sure whether he'll be happy to hear you're alive, or furious that you've been out of contact for so long."

"That wasn't entirely my fault. On my way to the Plagued Islands, our other loon broke. Apparently there's a limit to how far they can be separated from each other."

"Well, that explains the lack of communication. Now what about the fact you've been missing for months? The norren who delivered this loon said you were in Bressel. I thought you were going to the Plagued Islands!"

"We did. Didn't you get my letters? I sent one to you and Olivander."

"We haven't heard a thing since you left."

Dante cursed. "In less than an hour, these loons will run out of nether. If they're not shut down before then, the connection will break permanently."

"I'm aware of how loons work," Nak sniffed.

"Then you'll understand when I tell you I don't have time to explain everything that's happened right now. Is Olivander near?"

"Oh, I'm sure he's around here somewhere. Shall I have him contact you once I've found him?"

"Shut down the loon until then. When you find him, stay with him. I need to speak to you both."

"Then I look forward to resuming our conversation!"

The loon went dead. Dante bugged his eyes at Blays. "The loon made it to Narashtovik!"

"Oh good," Blays said. "I was starting to fear you'd gotten so desperate for answers you'd started talking to the gods."

The Keeper tilted her head. "How can you speak to someone in Narashtovik when you're standing in an inn at Dog's Paw?"

"Er." Dante racked his brain. Speaking to Blays, he'd thoughtlessly switched back to Mallish; if he'd stuck to Gaskan, the others would have remained ignorant. Though he'd figured out how to make them on his own, the loons were a norren invention. Even if he'd felt comfortable sharing their existence with the Colleners—which he wasn't, given how often Collen wound up invaded, captured, and tortured by the Mallish—he didn't feel it was his secret to share. "I can't think of a good lie, so here's the truth. It's a secret I've sworn not to reveal."

Cord touched her chin. "This sounds like a mighty weapon."

"That's why I can never allow it to be discovered by anyone else. Like Gask—or Mallon. I need you to swear you'll never mention it."

"I've never liked oaths," Cord said. "They hold you down like chains. Or a bad husband. But for one who fights for a land that isn't his, I'll make that vow."

The Keeper considered her gnarled hands. "This is something I would like very much to know. But keeping secrets is my job. I swear to preserve this one as well."

Satisfied, Dante paced about the room, doing his best to sort through and prioritize the vast amount of information he needed to convey to and extract from Nak. His ear tingled.

"I'm here," Dante said. "Olivander?"

"He's right beside me," Nak said. "And he says he's very relieved to hear you're alive."

"Then I'll apologize in advance for the fresh distress I'm about to cause him. But we've got limited time to talk today. I'm going to dive into what I need from you, and then I'll explain why."

"This ought to be interesting."

"We're currently in a battle with beings known as the Andrac. Star-Eaters. To the best of our knowledge, they're netherdemons." He described them, along with their encounters with the creatures and everything they'd learned to date. "I need you to search the archives, Nak. Find me everything you can that mentions the Andrac. And don't limit your search to Narashtovik. Dispatch someone to the oracle at Houkkalli immediately. They've kept records of events the rest of the world forgot centuries ago."

"I shall do so this very day. In the meantime, Olivander has a question. It's a pretty good one, in my opinion. Why do you feel compelled to do battle with *demons*?"

Dante sighed. "I'll give you more details when we're less pressed for time. For now, here's the abridged version. Blays and I made it to the Plagued Islands. There, I met my father—but he was an impostor who dragged us into a civil war. Turns out that their war was being driven by the Mallish, who lusted for the island's sea snails."

"I'm sorry," Nak said, "but did you say 'sea snails'?"

"They're called shaden. They're repositories of nether that allow you to use much more than you could normally summon. A Mallish priest named Gladdic was gathering as many of them as he could get his hands on. Well, we put a stop to that. After that, though—"

"Hold on a minute. That sounds like a tale and a half. You can't skip right past it with 'we put a stop to it.'"

"Nak, I promise I'll give you the full account later. Right now, all you need to know is that we came back to Mallon to destroy the shaden and kill Gladdic. This, in turn, took us to the Collen Basin. We got rid of the shaden, but eliminating Gladdic has proven gods damn difficult. He's the one who's summoning the Andrac."

"Well, that does sound troublesome. Ah! Olivander has another question. He'd like to know if you're *deliberately* provoking the greatest power in our corner of the world into declaring war on us?"

"We're doing everything we can to avoid that," Dante said. "But before we get into that, there's something else I need to tell you first. You know how there's a netherworld?"

"The place where Blays goes when he deploys his unique skill."

"Well, there's an etherworld, too. And it's the afterlife."

Nak made a thoughtful noise. "How did you formulate this theory?"

"Because I've been there."

"You…died? I'm sorry, Dante. I don't care how long it takes, I refuse to conclude this conversation before I've heard *that* story."

"Lyle's balls, I'm talking to you, aren't I? I didn't die. In the islands, they have a flower that puts you into a sleep so deep you can reach the other side."

"What a silly mistake, assuming that only dead people could reach the land beyond the living. I should have assumed you used a magical flower."

Dante squeezed his temples. "My understanding is based on a combination of what the Kandeans told me and what I saw for myself. First off, as far as I can tell, the entire afterlife is made of ether. There are three layers to it, each of which reflects a different ideal. The first layer, the Dream, is what we believe is ideal for ourselves. That doesn't mean it's paradise. Along with our wishes, it invokes our worries and fears. Everything that's at your core becomes your life there. But you're alone. There may be other people there, but they're not real. They're figments of your own mind to keep you trapped in the Dream. Some people get stuck there, playing out the same dreams and nightmares over and over. But if you break loose, you enter the Mists.

"The Mists seem to be the ideal version of our world. The one we could build together if we set aside all our petty divisions and fears. There are other souls there living in peace. They understand where they are, and while some stay for decades—or even centuries, if they're not done with the ways of the mortal world—eventually, everyone passes into the third layer: the Worldsea.

"I didn't go to the Worldsea. The living can't travel there. To the best of my understanding, it might be *the* ideal. As in the ideal realm the gods have always intended for us. There, you lose your sense of self. But you become a part of the whole."

Dante went on to explain as much as he could remember about the particulars of the Dream, the Mists, and what the dead had told him about the Worldsea.

"This is so interesting I never want you to stop talking," Nak said. "But why are you telling me this?"

"First, the Andrac seem to be from the netherworld. A better understanding of the etherworld might help you understand the demons. And second, if I don't make it out of this, I don't want this knowledge to die with me."

Nak tsked. "Well, we're not going to allow that to happen, are we?"

"Glad you agree. Then I'm going to need a few things from Narashtovik. Primarily ethermancers. Eight to ten of them, including two Council members. We need horses, too. Twenty pounds of silver to grease the skids. And I need the sword of Barden."

"Ah. The bone sword. You're going to laugh about this: it's gone missing."

"It's *missing*? Why would I find that funny?"

"Because it's a priceless artifact. Such things have a way of going missing, don't they? I'm sure it's around here somewhere. In the meantime, this will only add to its legacy."

"I don't know how I've gotten by without your optimism. Find me my sword and get me my reinforcements."

There was a pause. "I would like to do that, but Olivander has just informed me that if I were to try, he will reassign me to the Citadel's smelliest dungeon cell. Perhaps I should let him explain."

Muffled scrabblings came through the loon. Nak's up-and-down tenor was replaced by Olivander's measured baritone. "Dante? Before our argument begins, it's important to me for you to know that you've been missed. Not only by myself, but by all of Narashtovik."

"I've missed it, too," Dante said. "But what is there to argue about?"

"I'm not sending an army of sorcerers to the Collen Basin to fight a war against Mallon."

"Two objections. First, I don't need an army. Only enough to help me kill the demons. The second objection is my fault, really, so don't take this as a criticism of yourselves. But apparently I've been gone for so long you've forgotten *I'm the High Priest of Narashtovik whose word is the law.*"

"And in your absence, I am the steward. Whose foremost responsibility is to keep our people safe."

Dante paced to the windows. "Thank you for taking your duties so seriously. But I'm not absent anymore, am I? We're speaking right now."

"Perhaps," Olivander said slowly. "But how do I know you're you? For all I…"

Olivander's voice cut out. Dante sent his focus into the rat bone stuck in his ear. Inside it, the nether binding it to the other loon was down to its last drops.

"Olivander? Are you there?"

"I'm listening. Are you?"

"We don't have time to argue. Compromise. Put together the team and all the equipment I've asked for, but don't send them out of the city yet. We'll discuss this more tomorrow. Agreed?"

"Agreed," Olivander said. "I look forward to hearing your rationale for this senseless fight."

Dante switched off his loon. He'd been walking about during the entire conversation. Abruptly, he felt how sore his legs were. "Narashtovik is going to hunt for everything they can find relating to the demons. When I talk to them again tomorrow, I hope to have reinforcements on the way, too. Ethermancers. But they won't be enough to retake the basin by themselves. We'll take out the Andrac. It'll be up to the Colleners to take out the Mallish."

Cord scoffed. "Banish those doubts or burn your tongue."

"I don't doubt you or your people. I'm laying out what you'll have to do for yourselves."

"How is Narashtovik, anyway?" Blays said. "Still there and everything?"

"I didn't have much time to ask, but it seems to continue to exist. Although they've lost my sword."

"What, the bone one? What idiot loses *that*?"

"Someone who wants to learn what its edge feels like, that's who."

"I mean, that's almost as dumb as leaving on an extended trip without it."

Dante rolled his eyes. "I didn't have it with me when the letter came from the islands. When we went to Gallador, my agenda didn't include getting sucked into two different nation-wide conflicts."

"Then let this be a lesson to never leave it behind again." Blays clasped his hands together. "Now make no mistake, the loss of a sword like that is a tragedy to make grown men wish they'd never been born. But tomorrow, if there's time, do you suppose I could give them a message for Minn?"

"We'll make time. Even if it means waiting another day to hear about the Andrac."

"Are you serious? Because I was serious about your sword."

"Neither of us meant to be gone this long. I'm sure Minn's as worried about you as you are about her. Just don't take too long, okay? I've got a lot of yelling at Olivander to do."

Prior to the loon from Narashtovik, Dante had been about to descend to the common room to drown his sorrows regarding their lack of progress. Now, he descended to the common room to float his hopes on a sea of good beer.

In the morning, he intended to sleep late, both to minimize the repercussions of the previous day's celebration, and to decrease the time he'd have to spend awake waiting for information from Nak. But the daily morning drums woke him bright and early, and shortly after a long struggle to get back to sleep, a knock at the door dragged him from bed.

It was Boggs. "Spoke to my family. And the senate."

"Well?" Dante said. "Are they in?"

The man grimaced. "I need a drink. You want to talk, meet me downstairs."

Dante and the others joined him in the public room. Dutifully, Dante ordered and sipped a beer so dark and stout it could have served as breakfast by itself.

"Family met up yesterday," Boggs said. "I told them what you told me. Once they had the truth in their heads, they agreed to lean on the senate." He stuck his elbows on the table and stared into his drink. "It *would* take the death of Mariola to get my family to agree on anything."

Blays took a hearty drink. "That conversation sounds as fun as squeezing your balls through a wedding ring."

"Had to be done, didn't it?"

"What did the senate say?" Dante said.

Boggs sipped his beer. "We flipped Tonn Ralon. Weren't so much because of who we are or what that Mallish bastard did to Twill. Think he wants to go to war, but he didn't dare because he didn't think there was any public support."

"But he's the only one?"

"Might be able to flip Ella if we put our backs into it. But no point when that'd still leave us two votes short."

"Question." Dante kept his voice low. "When something happens to a senator, how is their replacement chosen?"

Boggs grinned crookedly and cracked his knuckles. "I heard you was a rough one. Thinking of liquidating the outfit?"

Blays smacked his forehead. "Nobody's liquidating anything. Unless it's wheat into foamy beverages. These guys are only trying to do what's best for their people."

Dante tapped his mug. "But what if that means the loss of the Collen Basin—and all the people in it?"

"Notice how that sentence ends with a question mark? That's because we don't know the answer to it."

Dante lowered his voice. "I'm not talking about mass murder. We only need two more votes. And *you're* the one who jumped right to assassination. These people are politicians. They're as weak to blackmail and bribery as normal people are to swords."

"Advocating for complex skullduggery over simple murder? That's the *real* sign you've been leading for too long."

"You were the one wailing like a widow about the thought of a little blood."

"The senators are Colleners," the Keeper said. "They can't be killed. Not even for the sake of other Colleners."

Dante gripped the handle of his mug, glancing across the

room. It was largely empty and no one seemed to be paying them any mind. "Let's get back to the question. If a senator leaves their post for any reason, how are they replaced?"

Boggs rubbed his index finger across his upper lip. "Popular vote. All citizens of Dog's Paw."

"I was afraid of that. Then unless the populace wants to fight badly enough to elect two pro-war senators, there's no sense replacing anybody."

"Never know. If there's one thing you can count on about people, it's that you can't count on them. They could change their minds."

"In which case the senators, being politicians, will change their minds too." Dante drained what was left in his cup. "Keep working on the Small Senate. We'll see what we can do to make the people believe it's worth fighting back."

Back in the room, he practiced his etherwork. On the day after the Keeper's lecture about how ether wished to be drawn forth, Dante had summoned as much as he could into a small sphere, then lowered it through a piece of paper until the sphere was bisected. At that point, he'd traced it.

He'd repeated the process each day. Each day, the sphere had been the same circumference as his original tracing. That morning, however, the ball of light enveloped the circle of ink completely. Dante traced a new ring and let the ether fade. The new circle was only a fraction of an inch wider than the original, but Dante felt like he'd reached up and grabbed the moon.

The Keeper had wandered outside for some fresh air. As Dante went to the door to go find her, his loon tingled. "Nak?"

"Hello again," Nak said. "How's the day found you?"

"Contemplated murdering a few senators. Pretty typical. Have you found anything on the Andrac?"

"Nothing concrete. However, we do have some promising leads. I hope to have our initial research ready for you tomorrow."

"The sooner the better." Dante reached for his loon. "We'll talk more in a minute. Before anything else, Blays needs you to take down a message."

He handed the loon to Blays, who took it into the hall for five minutes, then returned.

"Thanks," Blays said. "Now let's try to win the day, shall we? Minn's much less likely to toss me out on my ear if we've been spending all this time saving the world or something."

After confirming Nak had nothing for him yet, Dante asked to speak to Olivander.

"So," Dante said. "Come to your senses yet?"

"Come to my senses." Depending on how you were feeling that day, Olivander's voice ran somewhere between deliberate and plodding. Normally, Dante appreciated Olivander's thoughtfulness, but on that day, he was outright slogging. "What kind of sense does it make to take martial action against Mallon?"

"Do you know what's going on in Mallon these days?"

"I haven't been keeping up with Mallish politics very well, as it seems the leader of Narashtovik has absconded, leaving me the responsibility of keeping it in order."

"Hilarious. Olivander, I think we're in the middle of a Fourth Scour. Colleners are being hanged and burned on suspicion they believe in Arawn. Even those who like Carvahal too much are being dragged in for heresy."

"Carvahal? But he imprisoned Arawn."

"Yes, but he's Arawn's brother, which must mean he has to be cast down too," Dante said. "That's how crazy it's gotten here. They're occupying the city of Collen. I expect the entire basin will be next. Before traveling here, we spent some time in Bressel. While we were there, I got the impression that all of this is a reaction to Samarand's failed war on Mallon. You were a part of that—and so was I. We whipped up a storm, and now it's crashing down on Collen."

"That makes my heart heavy. We were only trying to do what was right. To free the Mallish to worship as they wished." Olivander's tone shifted from regret to concern. "And it only made things worse, didn't it? If we meddle in Mallon again, how do you know it'll be any different this time?"

"I don't. But I don't think walking away solves anything. After all, that's what we did when we set the stage for the very first war between Mallon and Collen."

"I don't know my history like you do. What did Narashtovik have to do with *that*?"

"Collen used to be a fertile plain. When the Rashen raised the Woduns, it didn't just effect Weslee. It turned Collen into a desert." Dante explained how, as the Colleners had starved, they'd started raiding Mallish farms and villages. "Because of what our ancestors did, the two lands have been in conflict ever since."

Olivander's sigh was that of a warrior who doesn't know how many more times he'll be able to lift his sword before his strength gives out. "How much longer will we keep paying for the same crime?"

"Until we break the cycles it created. I'm not sure how to do that yet, but I know things can't get better here until Gladdic's gone. If he conquers the entire basin, I'm afraid of what he'll do next. I'm not asking for an army. Just a few good ethermancers."

"Do you know what I haven't missed? Your relentless ability to talk me into doing things I don't want to do. I'll send your people."

"Thank you, Olivander."

"I fear I'm making a mistake. Then again, the history between our lands seems to be nothing but mistakes. So what will be any different?"

Olivander suggested sending the party with a loon, which would allow him to keep up on their progress and relay it to Dante. With a small band on horseback, he thought they'd be able to reach Collen within a month.

"We'll try to keep our heads down until then," Dante said. Before severing the connection, he asked to speak to Nak again. "Nak, there's a story in the *Cycle* about Kennen and Vanya, the apprentices of Stathus the Wise. Kennen winds up summoning a being that sounds a lot like the Andrac. Can you look into that for me?"

"Funny, I never expected you to have any trouble locating a copy of the *Cycle*. Your skills in that department are what got us into this mess in the first place."

Nak found this uproarious. Dante laughed, too. But once he closed the loon, leaving him alone with his thoughts, he wondered how much easier his life would have been if he'd never seen that first copy of the book.

Two days later, the loon twinged. Dante touched his ear. "Yes?"

"I think," Nak said, "you owe me a promotion."

"You're already a Council member. The only step up from there is my job. Would you really want that right now?"

"Oh, it doesn't have to be a *real* promotion. Something like 'the Loremaster' would do. Or perhaps 'Grand Librarian.'"

"Tell me what you've found," Dante said. "Then we'll discuss your title."

"There is very little that we can find regarding the Andrac. What we *have* found largely treats the idea of the demons as a joke no more worth believing in than dragons. But there is one exception. The document is short, but it regards the Andrac directly and with startling clarity. It's called *The Last Confession of Kon the White-Haired, Despot of Collen*."

Dante shot to his feet. "Did you say Kon the White-Haired?"

"Ah! Do you know the name?"

"He was a powerful nethermancer and a towering figure in Collen's history."

"Well, he is also the author of this document. It's dated 482 years ago. According to the author's introduction—which is extremely brief—he penned it during the middle of a battle. Which I'm inclined to believe, given the stains. It's like these pages were illuminated by a monk with a nosebleed."

"I'm going to need to write this down." Dante got out his writing supplies and took a seat at the table. "Whenever you're ready."

"I must say, I'll be very excited to hear your response. Unless I'm mistaken, we've really got something—"

"The sooner you read it, the sooner I *can* respond."

"Apologies and amends." Nak cleared his throat. "Every word that follows is that of the author, which I shall read in the original Mallish. Ahem.

"In my quest to save us, I have doomed us.

"I lack the time to relate my folly in full. If I return from the shadows, I will explain then. For now, I write the facts clear and hard, each one as it happened, and entrust them to the Keeper. So that if I fail, it will be known that it was not for lack of effort.

"I was tasked with the defense of my realm. To fulfill my vow, I drove the Mallish from Collen at the points of swords and wheels. They came back to break us, but I held the line. Their soldiers cracked the dust I'd sworn my life to defend, and I pushed them back whence they came. It was said I could not be fought any more than the wind can be fought; that I could not be defeated any more than death can be defeated. For seventeen years, this was true.

"Then came Franric. Town by town, he fought me through the desert. He was as ruthless as a scorpion. For the first time since taking my vow, I tasted defeat. As the last towns began to fall, I knew Collen itself would come next. I retired to my tower. There, I pursued my weapon. The one secret not even Franric could stand against.

"It is known that when a person dies, the soul goes to Arawn's field beneath the stars. But what is not known—what is known only by myself—is that when a body dies, it leaves a trace in the shadows. These traces can be touched. Manipulated. Put enough traces together, and you have a new body. But not one of flesh. One of darkness. Except the eyes and throat, which glow like a star.

"As Franric marched on Collen, I shaped my weapons. My Andrac. My Star-Eaters. The battle for Collen began. At first, I had no need for the Andrac. But as Franric's ethermancers struck down my servants and soldiers, and his army climbed past my defenses, I brought forth that which would end it.

"The Andrac brought an end: but not the one I sought. They turned on me. Dropped my people as blackened husks. I tried to turn them back against the Mallish. I failed. I tried to banish them back into darkness. I failed. Then I thought to destroy them. But in seeking to defeat the Mallish, I had created the one thing more insidious and invincible than my enemy. How does one harm that which has no flesh? How can one destroy the eternal nether?

"If I can't undo what I've done, the demons I brought will slay the people I love. I have an idea. I will not speak it—I can't risk the enemy finding this confession—but I will see this idea through. Will I fail? Or drive the Mallish from Collen for the last and final time? History will see."

Nak went quiet. The sound of glugging water came through the loon.

"Is that it?" Dante said.

"That's where the confession ends."

"After this, Kon the White-Haired went into a Collenese shrine and was never seen again. Whatever his idea was, it must not have been very good."

"So," Nak said. "About that promotion?"

"Where did you find this?"

"Well, the tale of *that* is every bit as epic as your current imbroglio. First, I mustered a great host of monks, archivists, and apprentices. Then we marched on our leather-bound foes. They put up a ferocious fight, snarling our passage with an endless labyrinth of words and obscurities, but after ransacking each shelf and cubby, our prize was delivered."

"You need to get out more," Dante said. "What about the story from the *Cycle*?"

"There doesn't seem to be much there. No description of how Kennen summoned his dark servant. Nor was there any mention of a glowing throat. If it helps, though, Vanya banished the servant in a flourish of light."

"I think I have enough to move forward. But keep looking for more information. Otherwise, I may have to do something very stupid."

He shut down the loon. The others were away from the room in a discussion with a woman named Gena, one of Dog's Paws most prominent farmers. Trying to convince her, and thus all the other farmers, that it was a good idea to fight back. This was a tricky proposition, given that marching armies tended to treat enemy farmland with the courtesy of a swarm of locusts. But Blays had hit on the idea of presenting that outcome as an inevitability—unless the towns banded together to keep the Mallish confined to Collen.

The four of them trooped into the room two hours later, their clothes dusty, their faces long.

"No luck?" Dante said.

Blays flopped into a chair. "Gena's afraid of the Star-Eaters, too. If we're going to talk anybody into picking up their swords, we're going to have to rename the demons something with less nightmarish associations. Like...'shadowbunnies.'"

"I heard from Nak. He found an incredible source. It was an account of the Andrac from Kon the White-Haired himself."

Dante read the transcribed confession out loud. When he finished, he looked up with a grin. Rather than sharing his excitement, the others looked alarmed, glancing between him and the Keeper.

After so many decades in the basement, the Keeper's face was far paler than the average Collener. Now, it was flushed red with wrath. "Why do you have Kon's confession in Narashtovik?"

"I don't have any idea," Dante said. "Surely you don't think we stole it?"

"Of course you did. It was our story. Thus for you to have it means you stole it!"

"But how can you steal a *story*? They don't belong to any one person. They belong to everyone who wants to learn from them. The best ones are so eager to be heard they seem to spread themselves."

"This is wrong." The Keeper hobbled forward, pale blue eyes burning from her wrinkled cheeks. "This history isn't an insect to be dissected by scholars in Bressel and Narashtovik. It's a piece of Collen's heart. To be kept in the body of Collen."

Dante pinched the bridge of his nose. "I can't tell you why we have this piece of your history and you don't. For all I know, Cally took the confession for his research when he was living here. I can't change what's happened, but I promise you, once this is over, we'll make you a copy of every book and scroll relating to Collen we've got in our archives."

She murmured wordlessly. Deep as her voice was, it sounded like the growl of a dog. "You don't understand. These are our secrets. The Mallish ply us with torture to learn them and use them against us."

"You say this knowledge was stolen." Cord's back was to the

windows, leaving her face shadowed. "But *I* say it was hidden. Kept safe in a vault much like what you do in the basements beneath the shrine."

"Kon said he was leaving his confession to his Keeper. His writings couldn't have gone missing unless they were stolen."

Cord's shoulders bounced with wry mirth. "Unless the one who watched over them didn't want anyone to know the truth: that the great Kon the White-Haired called the demons that killed his own people."

"A Keeper would never betray her oath to preserve our history!"

"Just as she would never betray her oath to leave the Reborn Shrine?"

The Keeper sagged. At once, she looked every day of her vast years, her face crinkling on itself until it looked as gray and withered as the trees buried beneath the dust of the Spiderfields.

"Our vows are supposed to make us strong," she said. "But we are too weak to uphold them. We think we are ether, but everything turns to nether, doomed to rot and ruin."

"No!" Cord's voice rang like a clap of hands. "Only an honest woman is shocked by dishonesty in others. As for your vows, to hell with them. Why would you wish to hobble yourself? Walk free and carry a long sword, for sometimes steel is the only thing hard enough to cut through the lies."

"We can only guess why the Keeper of that era covered this up," Dante said. "But if I'd been in her position, I wouldn't keep records of a weapon the Mallish could use to destroy me. I would have burned them."

The Keeper nodded vaguely. "Perhaps she couldn't bear to destroy it. And sent it to Narashtovik, where Mallon could never reach. That, I think, is what I would have done."

Silence fell over the room. Naran found Dante's eye. "You seem enthralled by this information. But I don't see how it changes our circumstances. The Andrac remain as invincible as ever."

"The confession told us how the demons were formed," Dante said. "I can use that to figure out how to destroy them."

"By reversing the process?"

"I wish it was that easy. Hope you're ready to get your hands dirty. Next, I have to create an Andrac for myself."

21

Blays gave Dante his most dubious look. "Your big idea to eliminate the demons is to make a bunch more of them? How well does it normally work out for you sorcerers when you summon terrible beings you're not sure you can control?"

"I'm not going to try to use it against Gladdic," Dante said. "I'm going to kill it."

"You want to create a demon. And then kill it. Here's an alternate suggestion: why don't you cut to the chase and not summon the demon in the first place?"

"Because then we'll never learn how to destroy them."

"This seems extremely dangerous. Then again, I suppose it's less dangerous than trying to learn how to fight them while also fighting Gladdic and his army."

"Exactly." Dante gazed at his transcription of Kon's confession. "We do it in a controlled setting to minimize risk."

Naran laced his fingers together. "If you wish to minimize risk, shouldn't you wait until your priests arrive?"

"That would minimize the risk of getting hurt while learning to fight the demons. But it increases the risk that Gladdic will make his next move before our reinforcements arrive."

"In all things, it's best to act with vigor," Cord said. "Smite or be smited."

"We're going to need a graveyard," Dante said. "Or a battleground. Anywhere that's seen death."

The Keeper laughed unpleasantly. "Do you forget where we are? Every inch of this land has seen death."

"Will you help me fight it? We're going to need every drop of ether we can muster."

"I am not supposed to fight. Then again, I've recorded history my entire life. Perhaps I've earned the right to finally make some of it."

"Our first step is to isolate these 'traces' Kon mentions. Once I figure out how to combine them, then we'll have our test subject."

"Hold on." Blays began to walk in a ponderous circle around the table. "Kon didn't actually summon any demons, did he? He had to make them himself."

"That's exactly what I'm talking about doing."

"Bear with me. This is about learning to fight them, right? If I'm looking to learn how to fight people, and I walk into a bar meaning to set off a brawl, who should I start with? The blacksmith with the shoulders you could build a castle on? Or the kid who isn't tall enough to see over the bar?"

"Obviously, you should beat up the kid," Dante said. "What are you getting at?"

"Kon wanted the mightiest demons he could get his hands on. Monsters that could shred the Mallish into sandwich filling. But *we* want the wimpiest demon we can get."

Dante tapped his upper lip. "So I should make the smallest, weakest one I possibly can. Sounds like a plan."

Despite the Keeper's claims, the Collen Basin wasn't actually paved with the bones of the dead. In need of bodies, Dante consulted with Cord and the Keeper about where he could locate and potentially experiment on a number of corpses without grossly offending the locals—or Cord and the Keeper themselves. After some discussion, they struck on the idea of using a site where the Colleners had won a decisive victory over the Mallish, meaning most of the bodies at rest would be Mallish as well, and hence no one would care if they got a little desecrated.

The nearest such site to Dog's Paw was known as the Bloodlake. Two hundred-odd years ago, a Mallish battalion had been on the way to Dog's Paw only to run into a rockslide across the road. Rather than clearing it, which would have taken all day, they diverted through a game trail nestled between two hills.

And found themselves ambushed by the combined forces of the towns of Tanner, Kaline, and Darstow. After the last Mallish soldier had fallen, the blood was said to be so deep you could catch fish in it.

Dante struck out with the others on the following morning, taking the road toward Franks, which the ill-fated Mallish battalion had been marching from. It was a rare cloudy day and the desert was quiet and still, as if afraid of scaring off the clouds before they'd dropped their precious rain.

"I've been thinking," Dante said to no one in particular. "If Gladdic's using the bones to summon the Andrac, then it's unlikely he can create them himself. That means he must have a limited supply."

Blays waved away a fly. "I thought the idea was to limit his supply by limiting his existence."

"That's Plan A. But if we've learned anything, it's that it never hurts to have a backup."

Four miles outside Dog's Paw, the road cut through a line of hills. Cord examined the landscape, then took them off the road to a trail running between two of the hills. This brought them to a small bowl-shaped valley.

Cord stopped and stamped her right foot. "This was the Bloodlake. A great victory. Let's see that what lies here makes the fuel for the next one as well!"

Dante wandered among the shrubs and the dense, thorn-filled balls the Colleners called tumbleweeds. He sent his mind down into the soil. The dirt ran deep. A few feet below the surface, it was filled with hard, jumbled objects. Bones.

Dante nicked the back of his arm. The nether appeared in his hands of its own accord; there *had* been death here. And that, according to Kon, was what left the so-called traces behind. Dante inspected the shadows he'd collected for irregularities, but the moiling streams of nether looked the same as they always had.

He sent them into the earth, drawing the soil back layer by layer. Once the pit was eighteen inches deep, the first of the bones broke the surface. Some were held together by mummified flesh or desiccated uniforms. Others were alone, forever parted from their old bodies. As the dirt continued to sink, the bones on top lowered with it until they covered the surface in a solid mat.

Dante withdrew from the shadows. Beside him, Naran looked thoughtful while Cord looked proud. Dante shaped a ramp into the side of the excavation, which was a circle four feet deep and ten across, and descended. As he reached the bottom, several bones snapped beneath his feet.

If there was any stink of rot, it was faint enough to be masked by the pleasant smells of damp earth and the coming storm. He picked up a skull and closed his eyes. The nether within it appeared perfectly normal. He summoned it. Its flow looked as typical as its appearance. Were the traces mobile, like the rest of the nether? Or did they get stuck fast to the body they'd once lived inside? He drew out every drop of shadows from the skull, then peered inside its crannies. No nether of any kind remained.

He released the nether and set down the skull. Where would the trace left by death be found? The ribs, the house of the heart? He separated a rib from a jumble of bones and sought the shadows within it. As with the skull, the rib's nether was unremarkable, and when the bone was wholly drained, no traces of darkness remained in its marrow.

He tried four more ribs, a pelvis, a femur, another skull, then a large collection of the delicate bones of the digits, which always seemed to contain a disproportionate amount of nether to their size. None revealed any secrets.

He sat back, knuckles resting on the span of a femur. "I'm not seeing any of these traces at all. Then again, I've worked with the nether every day for the last ten years and I've never seen a 'trace' before."

Blays climbed down the earthen ramp. "Or you've seen them so many times they've become completely unremarkable to you. Much like how I'm now able to look at that beard of yours without bursting into tears. Here, let me have a try."

Dante observed as Blays moved into the nether lodged in a clavicle's marrow. Blays pulled the darkness this way and that, stretching it so thin you could almost see through it, then letting it snap back. This accomplished—if "accomplished" was the right word—Blays tugged out a black lump and batted it around like a cat with a spider.

Dante frowned. "What are you doing?"

"Punishing it for being part of an invading soldier. What does it look like? I'm trying to see if anything's hidden inside it."

"I hope I'm not as clumsy with a sword as you are with the shadows."

"No, you're all right with a sword. With women, on the other hand…"

Blays returned to his attempt to beat the answers out of the nether. Dante could barely make himself watch, but Blays' unorthodox methods often worked where traditional routes failed.

After a couple of minutes, the nether in Blays' hands grew fuzzy. Black streamers trailed away from the gob he'd been working with, returning to the bones he'd taken them from.

Blays snapped the rib he'd been using, then looked surprised with himself. He gently set the two pieces back on the ground, patting them. "Sorry about that, old dead soldier. No hauntings, please."

"Nobody's going to come haunt you."

"We've been to the actual afterlife. Are you telling me you don't believe in the ghosts we saw there? Including the ones we talked to? Like your dad?"

"What I doubt is their ability to come here. When we went into the Mists, our physical bodies remained in the Plagued Islands. But these spirits don't have a body, do they? They left that behind when they died. They're just a soul."

Blays screwed up his face. "What's the soul made out of?"

"I don't know. It's just a soul."

"But everything in the Mists was made out of ether. The people there—wouldn't they be made of ether, too?"

Dante tipped back his head and gazed up at the gray sky. "When we die, we awake in the etherworld. A part of us must travel there. But whatever comprises that part, we know it isn't *all* of us. Our body remains here. What if a piece of us travels to the netherworld as well?"

"What if that's the trace?"

"Then it's not necessarily going to be in the physical remains. Or even visible in the earthly realm." He pressed his fist to his forehead, which felt like it was about to burst. "Is this completely crazy?"

"You're the gods' authority on Earth. You tell me. Maybe when we die, a piece of the ether in us goes to the afterworld. And that's our soul. Carrying us with it away from this world."

"If our soul is ether, what part of us becomes the trace?" Dante glanced up at the Keeper. "What do you think? Are we talking nonsense?"

She gazed down from the lip of the excavation. "I think you've seen things no living soul has witnessed. Set aside what others have told you and trust what your eyes have shown you."

Dante gazed down at the carpet of bones. "There's a certain symmetry to it. Ether to ether, nether to nether, and the body to the dust."

"Question," Blays said. "Are we figuring out the secrets of the world right now?"

"That depends on whether we're right."

"A followup to the question. If *are* right, that means the books of the gods are wrong."

"The books of the gods were written by mortals," Dante said. "And if there's anything mortals do right, it's be wrong. Anyway, we already know the holy books have…holes in them. For instance, there are multiple accounts of the same events in the *Cycle of Arawn*. They can't all be correct."

"So we've flown past questioning and crashed right into heresy. If Gladdic could hear us, he'd skin us alive. And then knit our skin into demon-mittens."

"Let's get back to the traces. Across the wars, we've seen thousands of people die. Have you ever seen anything leave their bodies?"

"You mean besides blood and feces?" Blays picked up a jawbone and turned it in his hand. "We haven't seen any ether depart them, either. But we know it must. I mean, unless our souls are already up in the ether hanging out without us."

Dante racked his memory for anything unusual he'd seen during the deaths of others, but nothing sprung to mind. Not that this surprised him. If it had been anything that obvious, then someone besides Kon would have noticed it long ago.

Dante frowned at Blays. "Kon's confession says that death leaves a trace in the shadows. Could he be talking about the place you go when you shadowalk?"

"If so, we won't be able to test that out until tomorrow. I've already burned myself out for the day."

"For Minn's sake, I hope you're not always that fast." As Dante considered his next move, isolated drops of rain began to fall from the sheet of clouds. Wherever a droplet struck the faded dust, it plumped into a slate gray hemisphere, like a dark mole against the lighter skin of the soil. "I'm going to keep searching for the traces. There's no need for the rest of you to stay here."

Naran lifted his face to the rain. "I'll pretend it's the mist from the prow. It's been too long since I felt the water on my face."

"You think you know long?" the Keeper said. "I haven't felt the rain in ninety years."

He extended his elbow to her. "Shall we take a stroll?"

She laughed. If Dante hadn't known better, he'd say a touch of red brushed her cheeks. The Keeper accepted Naran's elbow. They turned away from the dig and meandered across the little valley.

Ozone, dust, and sage: rain had never smelled sweeter than that day in the desert. Dante let himself enjoy it for a minute, then returned to the bones, methodically making his way across the excavation in search of any shadows that stood out from the others. Finding nothing, he moved across the valley, found another mass grave, and opened the earth above it. But the shadows there looked the same as everywhere else.

By early afternoon, with the rain still falling, he packed it in and returned to Dog's Paw. There, people of all ages danced together in the rain while drummers kept rhythm from beneath the cover of oiled canvas strung along the base of the cliffs. Dante's mood was far from good, but he stopped to watch the locals celebrate the arrival of the water. Coming from Narashtovik, where when it wasn't raining it was snowing, it was beyond odd to see people throw an impromptu holiday for a bit of a drizzle.

Yet it felt good to listen to music, to watch them laughing, to hear the slap of their bare feet on the damp rock. Even in the midst of an enemy invasion, people found ways to be happy. Dante didn't know if that was stupid of them or inspiring. Probably, it was both.

When he'd had his fill, he went to their room in the inn and looned Nak to ask if there was any record of a trace of nether left behind by death.

"A trace left behind by..?" Nak sounded so baffled Dante could envision the wrinkles on his bald scalp. "I've never heard of any such thing. But to anticipate your next question, yes, I will happily devote the next leg of my life to this matter I didn't know existed until just now."

The next day, the rain had stopped, but the clouds remained, stretching from one end of the sky to the other. Dante contacted Nak, who'd found nothing. Along with the others, Dante returned to the Bloodlake, where most of the moisture had already been wicked up by the ground, leaving it crackly and hard.

"So," Dante said. "Ready to find the traces?"

Blays glanced about the site. "Any new tips as to what I should be looking for?"

"You know everything I do. Try the bodies first, but don't restrict your search to them. If the trace is left by death, then it might remain on the spot where the soldiers died. Or it might have migrated somewhere else altogether."

"In other words, the traces could be anywhere, including the nethereal equivalent of the Worldsea, which we don't know exists, and couldn't get to even if it did."

"Is that going to be a problem?"

"I suppose we'll find out." Blays took a step and exited the visible world.

"Ha!" Cord clapped her hands. "How does he do that?"

"I don't understand it completely," Dante said. "But it seems to be the opposite process of how the Andrac enter our realm."

"What power! If he can move around like the wind itself, then why isn't he already drinking from Gladdic's hollowed skull?"

"Unfortunately, his talent doesn't work so well against sorcerers. We learned that lesson the hard way."

In much the same way as he could hear someone moving around a dark room no matter how stealthy they tried to be, Dante was vaguely aware of Blays' movements through the nether. Blays spent a few minutes down in one of the pits, then climbed out and made a slow zigzag across the valley floor.

As Blays neared the hill's slopes, he reappeared, hands on hips, and glared down into the charnel pit. "Right. This is one of the worst jobs I've ever had. And that includes the time we had to climb up a Galladese toilet."

Dante jogged over to stand across from him. "Nothing?"

"Nothing. Unless, of course, I was staring right at it and didn't know it, because I have absolutely no idea what it is."

"Until we *do* know what we're looking for, we could search for months without finding a trace." Dante's eyebrows twitched up. "We could always kill someone. I'll watch the nether from out here while you watch from in there. That way, we can see exactly where the trace goes."

"You realize I have no way to tell if you're joking."

"It wouldn't be at random. We could take someone who deserved to die. Like a Mallish soldier."

Blays scrunched his mouth to one side. "That's a curious ethical question, isn't it? If a Mallish soldier has helped seize Collen, but at the moment he isn't doing anything in particular—say he's sitting around playing cards in the city square—does he still deserve to die then and there? Or does that only kick in when he's actively committing violent crime against our friends?"

"How about we use an animal? Do they have souls? No one gets mad when I kill a rat."

"Unless it turns out they *do* have souls."

"This is the classic scenario where taking one life can save many. Except in this case, it's made even easier for us, because we can choose to take a specifically bad life in order to save thousands of innocent ones."

Blays pressed the knuckle of his index finger against his chin, scratching his neck with his thumbnail. "So basically, since we're too stupid to work out a real solution to find a trace, our only choice is to murder someone in cold blood. Don't think I can accept that one."

"Then get thinking."

Blays turned in a circle, taking in the hills ringing them in. "First of all, these traces could be as small as flyspecks. It's going to help if I know I'm looking in the exact spot where people died. There's plenty of bodies here, but I assume they were moved to be dumped into mass graves. Cord, Keeper, is there any mention in the stories about any specific battle sites within the Bloodlake?"

Cord tipped back her chin. "It is said that in the end, the last Mallish tried to surrender. But the Colleners wouldn't have it. The bluecoats gathered on Snake Rock to make their last stand. There, they fought so well that the Colleners left their bodies under the sun."

"Do you normally honor the dead by leaving them out for the vultures?"

"How else can the gods see their triumph?"

"Snake Rock?" Dante said. "Please tell me this isn't going to be a repeat of the Spiderfields."

Cord scoffed. "How can you fear snakes? They don't even have arms."

She strode to the east side of the valley where Snake Rock was said to have been. Pocket-sized though the area was, the "east side" covered a tract some three hundred yards across, but after a few minutes of poking around, they discovered a jumble of bones, armor, swords, and spears jutting from the dirt around a shelf of rock large enough to host a dozen men.

There, a five-foot snake sunned itself, its tan body patterned with dark brown diamonds. It looked like a rattlesnake, and did its best to convince them of that by vibrating its tail against the rock, but Cord dismissed it as a gopher snake, chasing it off into a crevice.

"Looks last-standy to me." Blays pointed to the edge of the rock, which terminated in a four-foot drop. "Right there."

He blinked away. During his absence, Dante poked around the nether, but once again, none of the shadows looked any different from the others.

Five minutes later, Blays rematerialized, seated on the edge of the miniature cliff. "We're sure this is Snake Rock?"

Dante sighed. "Still nothing?"

"Nope. Not that I can see, anyway. The thing about the netherworld is it's terribly dark. Except for nether, which stands out all silvery. So if the traces are here, they should be as obvious as your attempts to flirt."

"Your torchstone," the Keeper said. "Give it to Blays. Blays, bring it into the shadows."

Dante drummed his fingers on his upper arm. "The torchstone? Why?"

"Do as you're told."

Equal parts amused and annoyed, Dante passed the torchstone to Blays.

Blays eyed the Keeper. "Anything in particular I should be doing with this?"

"Turn it on and look around," she said.

Blays gave a little bow and disappeared. Dante's frustration at the Keeper's lack of explanation was overshadowed by his ongoing anger that he couldn't walk into the shadows. What was Blays seeing? When the ether trapped in the torchstone touched a land made of nether, was there anything like it in all the world?

Less than a minute later, Blays returned, torchstone gleaming in his hand. He looked like he'd just rolled out of bed only to realize an instant too late that he'd spent the night in the bough of a tree.

He blinked at the Keeper. "How'd you know?"

She gestured to the sky. "When you light a candle by day, the eye is so overwhelmed by sunshine you might never know the candle was there. In a land of shadows, how can the eye pick out one shade of darkness from another?"

Dante moved toward Blays. "What'd you see?"

"Well," Blays said. "Probably easier to explain it like this."

He crouched on the edge of Snake Rock, torchstone extended before him. In the strong morning light, the stone didn't do much to brighten the basalt beneath it.

Yet some portions didn't brighten at all. Black. Star-shaped, just two to three inches from point to point. Two were currently visible in the torchstone's glow, but as Blays slowly swept it across the rock, it illuminated a handful more.

"This is impossible," Dante said. "If these are the traces, and they can be seen by ether, someone would have discovered their existence a thousand years ago."

The Keeper stood over a star. "Blays, how much of the rock did you inspect?"

Blays motioned to the ledge. "Just here, where it drops off."

"Stay in the light and shine the torchstone across the rest of the rock."

Blays moved across Snake Rock in a crouch, keeping the glowing stone close to the surface. He swept from one end to the other, but didn't see any new stars.

The Keeper nodded. "Now return to the shadows and look again."

Blays walked back into the nether. Dante felt him creeping across the rock. Two minutes later, he reappeared.

"I'm not going to be able to do much more of that today," he said.

The Keeper shuffled forward. "You may not have to. Did you find more marks?"

"More than a dozen."

"Now stay in the light and shine the ether on the rock again."

Blays crouched near the middle of the wide slab and shined the torchstone over its surface. The last time he'd done so, it had been blank. This time, it showed a black star.

Dante's mouth drifted open. "Expose it to ether in the netherworld, and then ether can illuminate it here. But why would exposing it to ether make it visible?"

"Shadows can't be seen without light to cast them," the Keeper said.

"But we're not talking about literal light and darkness. The ether and nether are distinct substances of their own."

"You ask and I do my best to answer. These matters might not be understood by anyone alive."

Blays traced his finger along the outline of one of the black stars. "So it makes sense why nobody knows about this. After all, only the very greatest of us can walk into the shadows."

Dante placed his finger on a different star close enough to remain illuminated. "Then we'll have to do as the Keeper just did and figure this out through trial and observation. Blow out the torchstone."

Blays puffed on the stone. The light winked off. So did the black star beneath Dante's finger. Dante sent his focus into the nether laced throughout the rock. Now that the ether had exposed the star, Dante could feel the border between it and the darkness around it. Like slicing the fat from the belly of a buck, he trimmed the nether from the edges of the trace. Once it was isolated, he moved his mind inside it.

As soon as he touched the star, it shrank back. Dante stumbled back, too.

"Afraid it'll bite you?" Blays said.

"If this is what the Andrac are made out of? A little bit, yes."

"It isn't alive *now*, is it?"

"I have no idea whatsoever. But when we die, if the soul goes with the ether, what stays with the nether?"

Dante approached the trace again. Carefully. Like he was walking up on a strange dog. Normally, the nether was never completely at rest: depending on its mood, it rushed like spring rapids, swirled like gusty rain, or gently expanded and contracted like the tide of a lake. Since jerking away from him, however, the shadows of the trace had gone as motionless as a frozen puddle.

Or a predator the instant before it strikes.

He moved his mind toward it, then beyond its outer edge. This time, it stayed put. Typically, nether felt cool to the touch, and substantial yet weightless, not unlike a wintry ocean mist. The trace (if that's what it was) felt similarly misty, but also warm. Not as though it were producing heat itself, but more like a rock that's lain in the sun all day that still bears its warmth after the sun has set.

Dante shook his head in wonder. How was it possible they knew so little about the workings of life, death, the heavens and the worlds beyond? Was truth that hard to find? Or did people not want to find it? There was an afterlife, as the books all promised, but in his experience, it was nothing like what those books described—unless, of course, it *had* looked that way to those who'd seen it. Its manifestation seemed like it varied from place to place in ways Dante didn't understand. In any event, in the best case, someone *had* glimpsed the afterworld and written down their vision faithfully.

They presented that vision as if it were universal. In truth, the experience was unique to the viewer—or a narrow slice of a much greater truth. Because that slice was the only one available to scholars, priests, and laymen, it was taken as the one truth—and the entirety of it.

Yet so much more was out there.

It was men like Gladdic, wasn't it? People who needed to control the source of knowledge for themselves. With no new discoveries to correct their course, the beliefs of such men continued down their crooked path, drifting a little further from the truth every year. And the further off course those beliefs got, the harder it got for such men to admit they'd been traveling in the wrong direction. Until the day came when Gladdic would rather burn you alive than risk discovering he'd spent his life believing in a falsehood.

Surely that wasn't what the gods wanted from their creations. They'd made the world so big because they *wanted* it to be explored. If so, to search and to learn was to worship.

Dante nudged the fringe of the star-shaped patch of nether. It didn't budge. He summoned it to him. Again, it stayed still. Keeping one eye on the shadows, he drew his knife, rolled up his left sleeve, and scratched his biceps.

The trace sprung from the ground like a spooked pheasant. As it swerved toward him, Dante scrambled back, tripping on a rock and landing hard. Beside him, ether sparked in the Keeper's hands.

"Wait," Dante said. A band of darkness circled his left arm where he'd made the scratch. He tried to draw the trace away, but it held fast.

Blays laughed. "That thing's like a dog whose master just came home from war. Or me when I finally get to see Minn again."

Naran's face looked like he'd bitten into an undercooked drumstick. "Something separated from what it used to have for so long it thought it would never taste it again."

After several more fruitless attempts to get the trace to move to his hand, Dante jabbed the pad of his left thumb. As soon as the first bead of blood bulged from his skin, the trace rushed toward his thumb and stuck there like pine sap.

"Seems to have a thing for blood." Dante watched it a moment, then moved to the next dark star emblazoned on Snake Rock. "The *Confession* said Kon simply combined traces until he had an Andrac. Based on the size of these, it's going to take at least a hundred until a demon forms. Let's see if I can combine two."

Blays rested his hand on the hilt of his sword. "You know, if at some point that *does* turn into a demon, you probably don't want to be holding it in your hands. Just a thought."

Dante kneeled on the shelf of rock and dabbed his blood next to a spot of flat orange lichen. At his command, the trace slid to the fresh blood. There were some two dozen black stars scattered around Snake Rock, but doubting that would be enough, Dante summoned plain nether to the trace he'd managed to manipulate. Typically, you could add as many shadows to each other as you had the skill to summon, but these ones slid off the trace without the slightest bit of mingling.

"I don't think you can make an Andrac from raw nether," Dante said. "Only the traces. I suspect they've been changed by their contact with a soul."

He moved on to a second trace, using a drop of blood to coax it from its spot on the rock. As soon as it touched the first trace, the two melded together like drops of oil in a warming pan. The shadows flowed into a circle, edges rippling as they expanded, then became still again.

"One down," Dante said. "Gods know how many to go."

Using the torchstone to light the rock, Dante located a third star and brought it to the larger circle. It combined as readily as the first two. Advancing along the edge of the short drop where the doomed Mallish had made their final stand, he came to a cluster of three stars. He joined them together, then led them over to the first group. They swirled into a single whole. The pool of nether was now the size of a small plate. Dante moved along the rock, bent low, sweeping the torchstone around to reveal the next trace.

"Dante," Blays said. Dante reached out his bloody thumb to press it against the rock and draw a trail back to the conglomeration. Blays socked him on the shoulder. "Dante!"

Dante straightened. Blays drew his swords with a rasp. Previously, the others had been watching from the flattened ground where Snake Rock protruded from the slope. Now, they were scrambling uphill.

Dante followed their gaze to where he'd gathered the traces. There, a black silhouette no more than nine inches tall spread its arms, flexed its tiny claws, and tipped back its head to the sky.

22

Raxa stood in the clearing before Carvahal's Wall. Her ears roared. Her heart thumped. Her feet felt like they weighed a million pounds. On top of the wall, Venk beckoned her forward. She couldn't make herself move.

"What's the matter?" Grinning, Gaits gave her a shove toward the wall. "Are you so used to taking things that aren't yours that you don't know how to treat something that *is*?"

She creaked with laughter and lurched forward. The crowd parted, funneling her toward the wall. Venk tossed a rope down from the top, but climbing walls was one of the first things you learned as a lowling, and the crumbling, ancient wall had so many hand- and footholds that a two-year-old could have scaled it. She heaved herself up next to Venk.

Solemnly, he watched her. "Raxa Dosse, the legions have chosen you as Grand High Chief of Street and Knife. Do you accept their decision?"

She still wasn't certain this was real. Or that it was what she wanted. She'd joined the Order for the freedom. As its leader, she'd be tied down by responsibilities. Politics. And the position itself: once you crossed from soldier to general, you didn't get much time at the front lines.

But Kerreven had been right about her. She was meant to be much more than a foot soldier. She would build the Order of the Alley as high as the Cathedral of Ivars or the Sealed Citadel.

And she would stand on top of it.

She winked at Venk. "Yes."

He nodded. "You swear to protect those the city would hang? To fear no midnight? To carry the knife against priest and king?"

"I swear it."

He smiled crookedly. "Then the Order of the Alley is yours to command."

As if from nowhere, he produced a black iron crown. Its points were the tips of daggers. He lowered it over her head. It was heavy, but the weight felt good.

She turned to the faces below her and lifted her right hand. They thrust up their fists and cheered. As the cheering died out, they continued to watch her. Expecting.

Out of the corner of her mouth, she murmured, "Give your new regent a hand?"

Venk lowered his face to peer up at her from beneath his eyebrows. "A speech is traditional."

Raxa cleared her mind, then her throat. She lifted her voice. "You brought me up here to win a war. Tomorrow, we bring out the blades. Tonight? We get out the cups and we drink. To Kerreven. To all who've fallen and all who will fall before this is done. But most of all, we drink to each other. Our family in the night. The Order of the Alley!"

She was tempted to blink away. Just for an instant. Enough to make them think their eyes were playing tricks on them. Add another whisper to her legend.

But secrets were power. Only fools gave them away.

Raxa hopped down from the wall and rolled into the grass. As she popped to her feet, Gaits thrust a flask in her hand. The rum burned her throat, but some things were meant to burn.

Hunched over like everything hurt, Gaits limped into the room and settled into the seat across from her. "Keep us up all night drinking, then call us to order first thing in the morning? A rather cruel start to your reign, Raxa."

"Who's worse?" Anya said from beside him. "Her, for dragging us in here so early? Or you, for making us wait?"

"Clearly not *my* fault. When someone cuts you with a knife, you don't blame the knife, do you? If so, we're going to need to revise the nature of the war."

Raxa spun a coin on the table, flicking its edge to keep it going. "Do you know why they chose me to lead?"

Gaits turned to her and snorted. "Please tell me you didn't drag us in here to fish for compliments."

"They chose me because one of the toughest men in the Order made the best speech of his life. If Gurles hadn't piped up, one of you two would be sitting in this chair. So as long as I'm in it instead, I want you both in the room with me."

"Whatever the Order needs," Anya said.

"Indeed." Gaits rubbed his temples. "With the caveat that vital Order war councils are never again scheduled for the morning after a vital Order party."

Raxa smiled. "If you don't want any more councils of war, then figure out how to win this one."

"That's relatively simple, isn't it? At the moment, the Little Knives are unaware their leader is deceased. It is incumbent upon us, then, to render the rest of them deceased before they know we're back at each other's throats."

"That's most logical," Anya said. "Think of their ignorance as a resource to be exploited. If we cause the Little Knives to believe we're going to hand their leader back to them, then we can ambush them."

"Good idea." Raxa had kept the coin spinning all the while. She arrested it with a fingertip and clamped it to the table. "One problem. We can't go after the Little Knives."

Gaits watched her for signs of a joke, then leaned over the table, a pained look on his face. "We can't go after the people who burned down the Marrigan. Killed our friends. And assassinated our leader."

"Was that the Little Knives?"

"You seemed to think so when you nearly cut Cane Dreggs in half!"

"I have reason to believe I was wrong about that."

"Oh, what an unfortunate error. Shall we endeavor to sew him back together?"

"Leadership isn't about pretending your mistakes don't exist," she said. "It's about staring them in the eye. And taking them down."

Gaits looked to Anya for help.

Anya rested her fingers on the table. "Do you have any evidence it wasn't the Knives?"

Raxa waved her hand over the coin she'd been spinning, palming it. "Why would Cane send an assassin against Kerreven? Cane was in our custody. He had to have known that we'd blame him. And kill him for it."

"He could have assumed we had no intention of letting him out alive no matter what. That rationale would be consistent with his behavior."

"I don't think Cane felt that way. He thought Kerreven believed him. That it wasn't the Knives who hired the Army of Crows."

Anya's eyebrows twitched. "What is the evidence for that?"

Raxa stood and closed the shutters, draping the three of them in twilight. Anya watched blankly; Gaits' eyes followed her impatiently, waiting for Raxa to finish with the theatrics.

"Cane said the Crows were hired by a group—or a person—called the Black Star." Raxa returned to the table, picked up the candelabra, and lit the central candle. "One problem: I don't think he knew who the Black Star is."

"Convenient," Gaits muttered.

"The night they burned the Marrigan. When I took down the Crows trying to carry you off, I found a ring. Do you remember?"

"It had a black stone." Gaits looked up and frowned deeply. "That's *quite* a stretch, Raxa."

Raxa slipped the ring from her pocket and held it up to the candlelight. A four-pointed star shined within the ring's stone.

"I think the Black Star is real," she said. "And if we go after the Little Knives instead, I think the Star will finish us off."

Gaits tried to catch Anya's eye, but the other woman was staring at the ring. Gaits looked back at Raxa. "Our task, then, is to unmask an unknown enemy while somehow preventing the people we presumed to be the enemy from discovering we've murdered their leader."

"That is an accurate description of our situation," Anya said. "I am suddenly glad to have lost the election."

"There's a way out." Raxa blew out the candle. "To find out who hired them, we go after the Crows. And to keep the Knives off our backs, we bring them on our side."

Gaits' impatient look returned. "I'm sure they'll be climbing all over each other to take us up on that offer."

"We tell the Knives their leader's dead—and the Crows killed him for getting too close to the truth."

"You expect them to swallow that?"

"Sure do. Because the Crows killed our leader, too."

Gaits stopped in the middle of the dark street. His face looked like he'd awakened to find a dead rat under his sheets. "You're sure this is the place?"

They stood across from a three-story stone structure that was difficult to look at. Not that it was ugly, or reflecting dazzling beams of light—the midnight bells had rung a few minutes back—but because its facade was broken into strange planes and angles. Blocks of stone extended and receded without reason. Ivy dangled over asymmetrical gaps that may or may not have been windows. When you looked straight at it, it was hard for the eye to make out the building's depth, or even its specific shape. Most people, after a few frustrated seconds of trying to figure out what they were looking at, glanced away.

"Sure enough," Raxa said. "The temple of Urt."

"And why are we meeting at the temple of Urt?"

"You'll have to ask Vess."

She moved back a step, drawing out of Gaits' peripheral vision, then slipped into the shadows. The very next moment, she returned. She was gone so briefly that even someone staring right at her in full sunlight might not have noticed. But that instant she spent in the other world left the nether's brightness dancing against the inside of her eyelids. Examining it, she saw no trace of people lurking in the temple's windows or ivy.

"Come on, man," she said. "If we're about to die, there's no hiding from Arawn."

She continued toward the temple. The meet was leadership

only and she and Gaits were alone. Anya had wanted to come too, but if the Little Knives were intending to ambush them, Raxa had no intention of putting the Order in position to be decapitated in one fell swoop.

A trellis overhung the approach to the front doors. It was as crooked as a stomped-on snake, its slats choked with thorny vines. The doors turned out to be false: painted onto the wall, shaded to give them depth. Raxa moved past the impostor entrance and located the real doors, which were set at an angle to the path and painted to match the basalt wall they were set into. A big nasty bug like a cross between a dragonfly and a cockroach was painted above them. She put her hand on her sword's hilt and opened the door.

This opened into what appeared to be a blank, closet-sized room. Under harder light, the doorway in the right-hand wall might have been invisible, but the dimness cast a shadow revealing the way out. The door took them into a blessedly straight hallway that led to a high-roofed, partially enclosed chamber that was either a courtyard or an indoor garden.

"Are you two it?" A woman's voice slipped between the leaves and trunks. The accent sounded south of the Dundens, though Raxa didn't know Mallon and those places well enough to pin it down.

Raxa stopped, eyes roving the darkness. "I'm Raxa Dosse. This is Gaits. We're alone."

A stout, well-muscled woman emerged from the shadows. A dark scarf wrapped her blond hair. She would be Vess, the acting leader—or so she claimed—of the Little Knives. And the three not-so-little men behind her would be the bodyguards she wasn't supposed to have brought.

"Good you came alone," she said. She held her thumb and forefinger an inch apart. "Now this much chance you're not a killer and a liar."

Raxa stared pointedly at the bodyguards. "Does that mean there's no hope for you?"

"You're the one's got Cane captive. Just making sure you don't try to do the same to me."

"Excuse me if my ignorance is offensive." Gaits turned up his right palm and made a slight twirl of his wrist, indicating the walls. "Why here?"

Vess smirked. "Three reasons. For first, it's holy ground. Maybe that won't mean nothing to you. But you be damn sure it means something to the god whose ground you stain. Second, you all think Carvahal and his one eye keeps watch over his children in the streets. Maybe true. Me, though, Urt's the only one to keep *my* secrets safe."

"And the third reason?"

"The monks here, they live in barrels 29 days out of the month. They come out before they're supposed to and they get their heads beaten with sticks. They won't never know we were here."

"Aha," Gaits said. "Very astute."

Vess sniffed and looked back to Raxa. "We made hellos. Talked pleasant. You want this talk to go any further, you tell me where to pick up Cane."

Raxa's heart quickened. "I can't do that."

Vess pressed her lips into a thin line. "Then I can't stop these mean bastards from slitting your throat."

"I can't give you Cane because Cane's dead. And so's Kerreven."

The blond woman's hand jerked. A stiletto appeared in her grip, its tip aimed at Raxa's heart. Behind her, the three men drew long, thin swords.

Raxa made no move for her weapon. "You don't want to do that."

"You think you can see my heart? You better look again."

"Kerreven sent me to kill Cane. I was in Cane's room. Alone with him. Ready to cut his throat. Then Cane told me your people weren't behind the attacks. I believed his story enough to bring him in alive. When Kerreven heard what Cane had to say, he believed it, too. We were working on figuring out who the real attackers were when the assassin came for them."

"Bullshit." Vess took a shuffling step forward, body turned sideways. "You kill Cane, then try to bury your crime by lying that Kerreven's dead, too."

"Someone set you up to take the fall—and set us up to take

you down. Kill me tonight, and you guarantee they win."

"Why would that someone do this?"

Raxa shook her head. "Has to be an up-and-comer. A minor gang looking to clear the decks above them. Get the Order and the Knives to kill each other off, then swoop in and scoop up our turf. And all it costs is the money to hire the Army of Crows."

Vess bared her teeth. "Or you're the worm looking to wriggle off the hook."

"You know your people didn't attack us. Cane thought the culprit was a group called the Black Star. You want to pick this fight up again later, that's your call. But they *want* us to destroy each other. Do you want to play their game? Or do you want to make them pay for what they've done to us?"

The other woman eased her posture a fraction of an inch, but the stiletto remained a thrust away from Raxa's heart. "How did it happen?"

Raxa shut her eyes. "Cane thought he had a songbird. Brought him in to tell us what he knew about the Black Star. Instead, the bird put the knife to Kerreven. Then Cane. Birdie cut his own throat before we knew what was happening."

One of the men behind Vess cursed. Raxa reopened her eyes. Vess was staring at her, stone-faced. "This story. It could be believed, but how do I know it's true?"

"You don't."

"So I got nothing to go on but my own judgment. Son of the *bitch*. How you mean to dig into the Black Star? Start hauling in Crows?"

"That's the idea. After they burned down the Marrigan, they went to ground. From what I hear, they're starting to trickle back into the city."

Vess scoffed. "Full pockets and an empty head. They should be drinking in Dollendun, not coming back to wallow in the crime. If their discipline's that bad, it won't take no time to crack the answers out of them."

Gaits cleared his throat. "Does that mean we're leaving here as allies?"

"I came here to cut you a second smile. But I know Cane was onto this." At last, she put the stiletto away. "Fuck me, let's go murder some Crows."

Quiet-like, they put out the word. Two days later, the word came back. Lately, a man by name of Bastya had been slumming the pubs in the Sharps. And when he got sloshed enough, he liked to beckon those he'd been speaking with closer. Tell them he belonged to a certain group—one that had reduced the Order to ashes in the wind. And promise they were always looking for good men, should the listener consider themselves up to the task.

Vess picked him up. Questioned him. He confessed to working for the Crows, but swore he'd never give them up. After Vess clipped his fingers knuckle by knuckle, he was ready to give up the Crows, his mother, and Father Taim himself. According to him, a Crow lieutenant was holed up in a hotel on the fringe of Stodden Hills.

But when they sent a scout to the room, it was empty. The proprietor was happy to take their bribe—and explain the room had been rented weeks ago and left vacant ever since.

"Makes no sense," Vess said. "Why pay for a room you ain't going to use?"

Raxa shook her head. "They *are* using it. For situations like this. They're watching the hotel. And now that they've seen us sniffing around, they'll go back to ground. We might not see another Crow for months."

Gaits exhaled slowly. Defeated. Resigned. "We should keep our eyes and ears open regardless. But if they're truly gone, I don't see another option besides returning to business as usual and awaiting their return."

Vess' eyes narrowed. "This is piles of convenient for the Order. 'Aw shit, the Crows flapped away. Guess we better forget them for good and move on like the last many weeks never happened and we never killed any Knives at all.'"

"We won't forget what they've done," Raxa said. "We're not done hunting them, either. But we can't go after them. They're too skittish. We have to make them come to us."

"Oh yeah? How you make the salmon leap into the bear's mouth?"

"We don't. We treat *them* like the bear. Lure them into a trap."

Vess' suspicion remained, but it was now matched by interest. "Like how?"

Raxa hadn't been working with any hard ideas. Just concepts. She glanced at Gaits, ready for his hawk-like mind to spit out an answer, but he looked glassy-eyed and tired.

"They're mercenaries," Raxa said. "No matter how much the Black Star paid them, they'll blow through it soon enough. Then they'll need more work."

Vess clicked her tongue. "So we say, 'Hey, we're looking for rough boys. Got a job needs jobbing.'"

"Right. We're a potential client impressed with how they handled the job on the Order. We're looking for them to do something similar for us."

"Who is this proposal supposed to come from?" Gaits said. "If they're so cautious as to give out false information to their foot soldiers in order to protect their leaders, they'll smell a rat from a mile away."

"Naw," Vess said. "Not if we use a Blindy."

"A what?"

Vess gestured searchingly. She jabbed her assistant in the ribs. "You know what I mean. Guys what take their own eyes. Urt's people, like at the temple."

Her assistant, a middle-aged man named Jennis with the baby fat of a eunuch, rubbed the rib where Vess had poked him. "I infer that you refer to the Bonded."

"The Bonded," Gaits said. "Expensive. But not a bad idea."

Raxa considered this. The Bonded Messengers of Urt, usually called Bonded, or sometimes "Urtists," were exactly what the situation called for. Every one of the Bonded was blind, a condition they reportedly inflicted on themselves during their training. The point was to be the ultimate safe courier. Incapable of identifying those who hired them, or of reading the messages they were entrusted to deliver.

Not that they couldn't figure out the contents of a note by handing it off to someone who *could* see. But they took a vow, too. The strength of which was represented by the self-inflicted blindness. Servants of Urt, they believed that exposing the secrets they carried would result in their eternal damnation. And that as long as they carried their secrets faithfully, no harm would ever be allowed to befall them.

Raxa had heard enough about the Bonded to know this wasn't strictly true. On rare occasion, someone had tried to extract their secrets through the usual means. Supposedly, none of the Bonded had ever given in. Somehow, the kidnappers had always been found. Whatever torture they'd inflicted on the Bonded had been returned tenfold.

The scariest part? Nobody knew who was watching out for the Bonded.

"It's worth the cost," Raxa said. "Speaking of rats and their smells. The person we send to hire the Bonded—we'll get them to wear the perfume of the Jalladins. They've been feuding with the Paddimores for years. At first, our messenger won't say *who* he's with, but the Bonded will smell the perfume. Later, when our messenger gets into details with the Crows and reveals he's working for the Jalladins, the Bonded can back up his story."

Gaits chuckled darkly. "Gurles was more right than he knew. You take to this work a little *too* easily."

Vess shifted in her seat. "You want to trap the bear, you got to make the meadow look sunny. We can't let the Crows know we're working together."

"I wasn't planning to tell them," Raxa said dryly.

"We got to make sure their own eyes don't tell them, either. The Order and the Knives? We got to make it look like we're still fighting. We need to arrange a run-in. And you want to do this right, then our people can't know we're *not* at war."

Raxa had no doubt who Vess meant to sacrifice to this gambit. The Knives' lowlings. Young teens, mostly, along with a few older types who hadn't shown any skills more advanced than the ability to fetch. The idea rested in front of Raxa like a corpse in her bed. She wanted to walk away from it, but if she tried to deny the reality of it, she'd only make it worse for herself.

She stood. "Set it up. I'll arrange things with the Bonded."

This was a greater pain in her ass than she anticipated, requiring her to hire one go-between to hire someone else to pose as the "client," and then to hire yet another agent to get in contact with the murky organization that oversaw the Bonded. Worse, she also had to find a Crow. Or at least a way to get in touch with them.

While she worked these angles, report came in of a brawl between Knives and the Order. Lowlings. No deaths. Comforting. But one of her people, a fourteen-year-old boy named Vadem, had lost an eye to one of the Little Knives' namesakes. Raxa paid him a bonus out of her own pocket and promised him he'd always have a job with the Order.

After that, for the first time in too long, she went around to see her kids. They looked good. Excluding a few scrapes on his hands and elbows, Fedd didn't have a mark on him.

When she got back to her makeshift offices in the Sharps, a message was waiting for her. It turned out the Bonded already knew how to get in touch with the Army of Crows. This made good business sense, but Raxa found it mildly disturbing how much the Bonded seem to know.

Regardless, she authorized the delivery of the initial message to the Bonded. With it, they'd establish contact, then arrange a meeting between the Crows and her agent who was posing as a member of the Jalladin family. At that meet, they'd grab up whoever showed up for the Crows—who, if they were negotiating for their outfit, were either leadership, or knew how to get in contact with them.

And would thus be able to lead Raxa and Vess directly to the Black Star.

This was the plan. But after the last few weeks, Raxa didn't have much faith left in plans, no matter how foolproof they sounded. Thanks to her agent, she knew where the Bonded operated from (a warehouse half a block from a temple of Urt) and what the individual couriering their message looked like (thin-bodied man; aquiline nose). When night rolled around, and their agent made his way to the Bonded, she followed.

The agent entered the warehouse. Raxa waited in the darkness outside. Not two minutes later, the agent departed the building. Half an hour after that, so did a thin man with a bent, prominent nose.

The Bonded moved down the street with the aid of a lightweight cane made of...what did you call it, that stuff Gaits liked his chairs to be made out of. The wood from Gallador. Bamboo. And when he walked, his face was rarely pointed in the same direction as his feet. Instead, he tilted his head like a sparrow, or let his chin drift in a series of slow, aimless loops.

Despite his blindness, the man walked as fast as anyone else. People said that, in exchange for the sacrifice of their eyes, Urt had given the Bonded other senses. Like second sight. Or the ability to feel the presence of other people in the room with them. It was said that no one could follow the Bonded without the Bonded knowing it.

As the man passed by, Raxa stood and shifted into the shadows. She rose from her cover behind a stoop and entered the street. Watching the Bonded with every drop of her attention, she matched pace. After three blocks, without so much as a twitch or flinch to indicate he felt something amiss, Raxa closed to within half a block of him. Then a hundred feet. Then fifty. At ten feet away, he still gave no sign he knew. Either his extra senses couldn't reach into the shadows, or he was such a good actor she'd never know that he knew she was there.

His path through the city was winding. Circuitous. Often, he took a meandering back alley when there was a perfectly good thoroughfare. It took Raxa until the end of her shadow juice to understand why: even at night, the thoroughfares could be noisy. But in the alleys—where, as Bonded, he didn't have to fear any brigand—he could hear every footstep.

The rope connecting her to reality grew taut. Pulling her closer and closer to the edge of the shadows. As the Bonded neared the corner of Hodder and Venn, Raxa moved into a dark doorway and let herself sink from the world of darkness and silver. She seated herself and watched the Bonded trundle down the street. After he disappeared around a bend in the street, she got up and went back to the Order's temporary office.

By morning, a message had come in from the agent. Raxa and Gaits convened with Vess and Jennis. The message—which was unsigned, and offered no confirmation it was from the Crows—wanted to know the specific target, as well as the scope of the job. The four of them replied that they wanted to move against the Paddimores. As thoroughly and mercilessly as the Crows had during their last job.

That night began as a repeat of the one before it: the agent headed to the warehouse, response in hand. Three minutes later, the agent left the warehouse. This time, it took nearly an hour before the thin blind man emerged, but within six blocks, it was obvious his path was the same as the night before.

Hidden in the shadows, Raxa dashed past him. Once she was several blocks ahead, she found an empty side street and walked back into the real world. There, she hustled to the corner of Hodder and Venn.

Ten minutes later, the Bonded strolled past her, cane sweeping the air before his feet. Raxa returned to the shadows and fell in behind him. The Bonded jagged down two miles of alleys and connecting roads before Raxa had to exit the shadows outside the cathedral of Phannon.

Another morning, another response from the Crows. They wanted to know if the strike against the Paddimores should be public or private.

That night, Raxa went straight to the cathedral of Phannon. It took two hours for the Bonded to walk past, cane swishing through the air. Like the previous two nights, she followed along in the nether, but once more had to stop before the Bonded had delivered the message.

The next morning, the Crows asked for payment.

"Son of a bitch." Gaits' voice was strained. "They have no intention of meeting us in person. The Bonded are *too* safe. The Crows mean to conduct the entire negotiation through them."

Vess got up from her chair, stalking jerkily around the table like one of the tall brown birds that patrolled the bay's mud flats at low tide. "So how do we get to the Crows?" She stopped, grinning madly. "Ah! We already set the table. We pay them to attack the Paddimores. And as they flee the crime, we attack *them*."

"Are we certain that's wise? If there's a single witness, they'll link us to having incited an attack against one of Narashtovik's wealthiest families. We may find ourselves in the same position as the Black Star: hunted down by a relentless foe."

"We're going to haggle," Raxa said. "I'll take care of the rest."

That night, she picked up the Bonded's route where she'd left off the night before. In time, he arrived and wandered onward, Raxa trailing a few steps behind him as he weaved his way through the city. By now, she had a good idea what was going on. The Crows' drop was specific to them. Blind, the Bonded followed a memorized route to that drop. But in order to make sure no one was able to shadow him to it, he made his route as crooked as a pubic hair. There was no way to follow him without being exceedingly obvious about it.

Not through the real world, anyway.

The Bonded made his way to a main street and crossed to Shepherd Lane, a squiggly alley running through a quiet neighborhood in the textile district. For all Raxa knew, the Bonded had another ten miles on his route—but less than a mile after she started dogging him, he made a turn and came to a blank wall. In perfect silence, he tapped his fingers along the wall, dislodging a small brick. He extracted the brick, withdrew a folded note from his satchel, placed it in the wall, and put the brick back in place. This done, he left the alley.

Back on Shepherd Lane, Raxa hurried to a doorway in the opposite direction from the way the Bonded was now headed. Safe in the darkness, she rocked back into reality. Ten minutes after the blind man had left her sight, she popped into the shadows, ran into the alley, and confirmed the note was the one they'd sent to the Crows.

The morning brought a counteroffer from the Crows.

"We can, of course, counter again," Gaits said. "But we need to determine an end game. We're only going to be able to stretch out negotiations for so long before they start to get suspicious that we don't want to reach a deal at all."

Raxa suppressed a grin. "We only need to make one more counter."

"Don't tell me you intend to actually hire them. The last thing we need is another enemy."

"I know where the Bonded is making the drop. Last night, I saw the Crows' man pick up the message. Tonight, I'm going to follow him back to his leadership."

Silence clamped down on the table.

"Er." Gaits' eyes shifted side to side. "How do you know where the Bonded is making the drop?"

"Because I followed him."

Vess pursed her lips and tipped back her head. "Nobody can follow the Bonded. They sniff you out like a hound."

"You can keep telling me I can't have done it," Raxa said. "Or we can put together a plan to grab the Crows' leaders tomorrow."

Vess began to laugh. "You done it, didn't you? One more night. Then we learn which children of bitches tried to set us at each other's throats."

They made plans to send the agent back to the Bonded at ten that night. Raxa would stake out the drop, follow the Crows' messenger back to the nest, then return and report their location to the others. From there, they'd make strike plans. Toughest part would be getting their crews close enough to prevent an escape without tipping off the Crows to the closing of the noose. On the plus side, the Crows couldn't have many of their troops in the city just then. Not if they wanted to stay hidden.

By the time the meeting wrapped up, it was still two hours until noon. Following the Bonded to the drop had kept her up past two in the morning. Feeling beat, Raxa walked home. In the quiet of her manor, she warmed water on the stove and pumped it to the tub, mixing the simmering liquid with room temperature water and a great deal of soap chips, leaving the surface bubbly and opaque. An extravagance, but what the hell. She ran the Order now. Besides, it never hurt to be able to hide beneath the surface.

Once everything was in place, she disrobed, hung her clothes on the hooks on the wall, and stepped into the tub. The water was good and warm. She sank to her chin and exhaled, bubbles popping around her neck. For the first time since the burning of the Marrigan, she relaxed. She rested her head against the rim of the tub and closed her eyes.

A light thud woke her from a doze. She sat up, sloshing lukewarm water around the tub. Her head felt as thick as congealed butter. How long had—?

Feeling eyes on her, she swung her head toward the door. Three men stood over her. One of them was Gaits.

"Lyle's balls, Gaits." She lowered her shoulders back under the water. "Just because you helped get me this place doesn't mean you don't have to knock." She eyeballed his companions. One was a brawler, hulking and veiny. The other looked feverish, eyes burning within a gaunt face. "Who are they? New hires for tomorrow?"

"They," Gaits said, not taking his eyes off her for a moment, "are the people I've hired to make sure you don't pull any of your tricks. Not that I expect you to, Raxa. Because I have your kids—and if you try anything, they won't live to see the end of the day."

23

"I did it!" Dante laughed in disbelief. Ten feet away, the pint-sized Andrac—it was hardly taller than the length of a man's hand—curled its claws and stalked toward him. "Oh shit."

"Er," Blays said. "Should we step on it?"

"Stay there," Dante said to the demon. It continued to advance. "Stay!" He held up his palm and mustered his most wizardly voice. "You will come no closer!"

Blays backed up a step. "Want me to try throwing it a bone?"

"Why isn't it listening? They follow Gladdic's orders!"

"Barely. Besides, I thought this was about learning to destroy them, not to boss them around."

Dante skipped away from the tiny Star-Eater, glancing to the side to make sure he wasn't about to fall off the ledge of rock. "They heal fast. Keeper, hit it hard!"

Ether glowed from her weathered hands. Dante called forth what little he could, forming an incandescent sphere. The demon broke into a run toward Dante, forcing him to turn and dash away.

Darts of ether shot from the Keeper and streaked toward the demon's back. The light struck home, nether spraying from the Andrac like a snowball hurled against a stone wall. Black dust burst away, then slowed, hanging in mid-air; holes perforated the creature's back. As Dante watched, the scattered nether drew back toward the demon.

He unleashed a slew of white needles. They shredded through the small black body, staggering the Andrac. The Keeper's second volley slammed into it from behind. The tiny silhouette became fuzzy, indistinct. It sank to what had once been its knees. Another wave of ether pounded into the remainder of its torso.

The Andrac vanished.

Dante's eyes darted to all sides. "Does anyone see it?"

The five of them scanned Snake Rock, then the grounds above and below it. A breeze ruffled the yellow grass. Pure darkness, Star-Eaters typically stood out from the daytime like an anti-candle, but Dante's was nowhere to be seen.

"It's vanquished!" Cord bellowed. "Scattered on the winds like foe's ashes!"

Blays burst into laughter. "You could have fit that thing into your pocket. I almost felt bad for it!"

A frown deepened on Dante's face. "Blays. Check the shadows — and be careful."

Blays sobered, drew his swords into a guard, and stepped into the nether. Dante had burned through all but a pebble of his ether, but he kept what little he had left suspended between his fingers. Fifteen seconds later, Blays returned to Snake Rock.

"It's there," Blays said. "And it's alive."

Dante gritted his teeth. "That's what I was afraid of. It's like we're attacking its reflection. I think the only way to kill it is to come at it from within its own world."

"Well, don't look at me. I've got about another minute in there before I'm done for the day."

"Then we'll have to wait until tomorrow. Son of a bitch!"

"What are you crying about? This is a huge deal! Now we can beat Gladdic!"

"We drive his demons back into the shadows," Dante mused, calming. "Then go for him, leaving the Andrac trapped where they can't hurt anyone." He broke into a grin. "I'd call that a successful day. Let's get back to Dog's Paw and hoist a flagon or ten."

Blays sheathed his swords. "We can't just walk away. What if the demon finds its way back?"

"Then there's going to be some very frightened gophers in this valley."

"You created it, you fool. That means you're responsible for whatever it does."

Dante glanced at the others for support, but their expressions were watchful. "We'll stay here for the afternoon, then reassess. In the meantime, let's try to figure out what just happened. Like why it attacked me."

"Do you know nothing of demons?" Cord's forehead wrinkled with confusion. "They hate the sight of living humans. We remind them of the foulness of their nature."

"But I'm the one who created it."

"The gods created us," Blays said. "Think about what we think of *them*."

Cord chuckled. The Keeper shuffled forward, watching the spot where the battle had taken place. "What does it matter if you can't control it? Don't tell me you intend to wield them as Gladdic does."

"I intend no such thing," Dante said. "But it would be much easier to figure out how to destroy them if I could order them to stand still while we're hacking away."

Blays tugged his lower lip. "Do you think it's even possible to kill them? You can't kill anyone in the Mists. Their souls are immortal. If these traces are the nether's answer to the soul, maybe they can't be killed, either."

"It might be possible to separate a demon back into harmless individual traces. Or to push it into the nethereal equivalent of the Worldsea. Whatever the case, we have four full weeks to figure this out before my monks get here."

Blays checked in on the Andrac again and reported it hadn't left the spot where it had been banished from Snake Rock. While Blays, Dante, and the Keeper remained at the Bloodlake, Cord and Naran headed back to Dog's Paw for provisions and blankets.

During the others' absence, Dante looned Nak and passed along everything they'd gathered from the day: how to find the traces, how few it took to form a demon, and his best understanding of how these things related to the afterworld.

"How remarkable," Nak said. "All these new revelations, you don't find them…upsetting?"

"Why would the truth upset me?"

"Because you preach something different when it's your turn to handle services at Ivars. Then again, you've never been much for tradition, have you?"

"If what I've been preaching is wrong, then it's my gravest responsibility to get it right. What kind of priest would rather save face than souls?"

"Oh my, now that's a wise line. With your recent theological discoveries, were you intending to write a new work? *The Cycle of Galand*, perhaps?"

"Ha ha," Dante said. "I don't understand half of what's going on here. I'm just trying to get it on the record. If our ancestors had bothered to do that, I wouldn't be in this mess right now."

Naran and Cord returned from Dog's Paw without incident. With the evening looking like it might bring more rain, they strung tarps between the sagebrush and dug a small trench up the slope from their camp site, where it would catch the rain and divert it from their bedrolls. That night, they took turns keeping watch. A lantern burned next to the spot where the Andrac had been banished, ready to illuminate it if it found its way back through.

By the arrival of dawn, however, the demon remained locked in the shadows. Dante had created it in the mortal world, meaning it had been able to interact with physical objects and living people. But once it had been forced back into the netherworld, it appeared to be trapped there. Presumably, the only way for it to get back was for someone to summon it, whether through using the bones, or some other method unknown to Dante.

He went about his morning with a renewed sense of determination. After weeks trying to figure out how to dispatch Gladdic's seemingly immortal bodyguards, they'd found an answer. While there remained work to be done—he wanted to learn how to destroy the demons completely, and there was still the small matter of convincing the outlying towns of Collen that they could and should oust the invaders from the basin—knowing that he could finally stand and face his enemy made him feel capable of tearing down mountains.

Which, technically speaking, he supposed he was.

Naran had had last watch. As the day broke, he got out his journal and began to write. The Keeper woke within a minute of Dante and went off to hike about the hillsides, enjoying every moment of her reprieve from the basements of the Reborn Shrine. It wasn't until Cord got up and began to noisily practice her fighting forms that Blays finally stirred.

After breakfast, and a quick check on the Andrac by Blays, they gathered on Snake Rock.

"Fighting it alone is crazy enough," Dante told Blays. "So don't add any more crazy on top of that. If you're hurt, or you're not able to hurt it, come right back out."

Blays bit his lower lip. "If something happens, you have to tell everyone it was ten feet tall. I can't die fighting a demon that's smaller than most cats."

"I know one way to avoid that: don't get killed."

Blays inhaled, rolled his shoulders, and drew his swords. He disappeared into the shadows. Dante could vaguely feel his presence on the other side. Within moments, Blays was dancing about, limbs whirling. Moments after that, he stopped dashing around and settled down into a single repetitive motion that might have been a chop. After about thirty of these, all activity ceased. Right as Dante began to grow concerned, the chopping motion picked back up.

Keeping part of his attention on the disturbances on the other side of the nether, Dante glanced at the Keeper. "Creatures from the shadows can be summoned here through the bone gates, right?"

She nodded. "That is so."

"Is it possible for someone from our realm to use the bone gates to cross into the shadows?"

"I don't know. You wish to join Blays there?"

"I don't like the idea of him facing the demons alone. Especially when it comes time to put down Gladdic's full-size Andrac."

The old woman lifted a white brow. "I think you don't like the idea of not being able to see what's there."

Dante was saved a response by the reappearance of Blays,

who was breathing hard, face traced with sweat.

"I diced it like an onion," Blays said. "But then it flowed back together and took its original shape. Like a very spooky onion."

Naran swore as colorfully as the flowers of the Plagued Islands. "These creatures are harder to kill than Gladdic himself."

Dante twisted his sideburn, giving it a tug. "Ether's the only thing that seems to hurt them here in our world. I wonder if that's what it takes to destroy them in theirs."

Busy staring into the distance, Blays lifted his chin an inch. "Didn't one of the stories say that somebody chopped up the Andrac with their shining sword? Or gleaming blade? Something involving a bright length of steel?"

Dante was about to make a comment about how "shining" was what steel tended to do, then shut his mouth with a click. "You think he used ether."

"Worth a try, isn't it? Smear some light on my swords and let's see what they can do."

Dante had never done such a thing, but after a bit of experimentation and a few words of guidance from the Keeper, he coated Blays' swords in a thin sheen of white light. As long as he concentrated, the light stayed in place.

Blays swept his blades back and forth, the occasional spark sailing away from the metal. "I look like an avenging god. Why haven't we been doing this all along?"

He hopped forward and into the shadows. This time, Dante felt Blays take a single side step, then get straight into the chopping. He stopped after a handful of strikes. After a thirty-second pause, Blays did some more hacking, then waited, then hacked some more.

Blays returned from the shadows, shaking his head. The light on his swords was dimming. "It definitely didn't *like* that. But it also didn't kill it."

Dante tapped his forehead. "If ether can't kill it, then I'm stumped."

"So is it—I cut off its arms."

"Did you notice anything different this time? Any vulnerabilities?"

"You mean like a beating heart? I *thought* that looked suspicious. Want me to go back and give it a poke?"

Dante sighed. "There was no beating heart, was there?"

"The ether hurt it much faster. It was slower to heal, too. But it still healed itself eventually." With the last of the ether fading from his blades, Blays blew on them and sheathed them. "Still, it was worth a try. Sometimes you have to empty your entire quiver before you hit the mark, eh?"

Dante nodded glumly. Across from him, Naran and Cord were in the middle of exchanging a long look.

Noticing Dante's attention, Cord stalked across the rock. "You're like the fox who's chased the gopher down its hole. So intent on watching for it to come back you don't notice the rabbit sneaking past your back!"

Dante stared up at her. "I'm waiting to be enlightened."

"Do I need to draw you a picture? You're so focused on killing the demon you're blind to what you should have learned!"

"Trust me," Blays said. "I know exactly what you're talking about. Dante, however, is a bit...stupid. Mind explaining? For his sake, of course?"

Cord gave Naran an exasperated look.

Naran clasped his hands behind his back and stood tall, as if he was lecturing from the deck of his ship. "Whether on land or sea, war is the art of resource preservation. When you attacked the demon here in our world, it seemed to take a great deal of ether to banish it. What if Blays' enhanced swords are more efficient?"

Dante smiled. "Then we'd stand a much better chance of banishing one of Gladdic's much larger monsters. Keeper, how about we finally put these old bones to use?"

She gave him a stare that could have felled an oak. "I may be old, but I've always done my best to help you."

His face reddened. "I mean the bones of the dead. To resummon the little Andrac into our world."

The Keeper blinked her rheumy eyes, then burst into spasms of laughter.

They gathered the Mallish bones half-buried around the shelf of rock. Between the Keeper's knowledge of theory and Dante's remembrance of the patterns Gladdic had used during the brief siege of Collen, he painted the bones with nether and arranged them on the rock into the shape of a hexagon with a bent arm extending from one point. While he was at work on this, the Keeper slicked Blays' swords with ether.

As soon as the last bone was in place, a hand-sized shadow congealed in the center of the pattern. The Andrac turned in a circle, starry eyes blazing in its featureless face. It tipped back its head in a silent scream, exposing the silver flame of its throat, and tottered toward Blays.

It moved much faster than its finger-sized legs should have allowed, but even so, it was no matter for Blays to dance back and swipe his glowing sword through the demon's torso. The legs kept running forward until Blays flicked the tip of his blade again, severing them from each other. After a few deft hacks, the demon lay in a pile of black tatters. These dispersed like drops of blood dribbled into a glass, then vanished from sight.

"That," Blays said, "was *much* easier."

"The fun part's over," Dante said. "Now there's nothing to do but practice until we can't stand it."

By their fourth day camped in the Bloodlake, they'd honed the Andrac's banishment into an art.

Bones in place, the tiny demon stepped forth. Always, it went for Blays—it seemed to be angry at him for sending it back to the shadows—and always, Blays cut it to shreds with his glowing swords. A few times, Dante and the Keeper attacked it instead, battering it with ether until it disintegrated to the shadows. But the swords proved so much more effective that it became obvious that wielding raw ether in a battle should only be used as a last resort.

It had reached the point where Dante was tempted to forge a larger demon, or to add more traces to the one he'd already created, and allow them to test their skill against it. Then he remembered the Andrac on the switchback. How its claws had torn through the warriors' flesh, leaving their bodies blackened and crumpled like burned parchment. A full-size demon wasn't like an archer's hay bale. It could fight back. And one misstep could cripple or kill them.

Still, he decided to give it give it some thought on the road. Because while they practiced themselves into expert demon-slayers—or, more accurately, expert demon-banishers—they were also running low on food. Dante was sure that Cord and Naran would have been happy to take another trip back to town. While they'd taken their turns attacking the tiny Andrac with ether-infused swords, they'd had little else to do besides swap stories of life at sea and in the basin. But Dante thought a night in a real bed would be good for the Keeper. And a bath would be good for everyone. So, with the Andrac firmly imprisoned in the shadows behind Snake Rock, the five of them headed back to Dog's Paw.

In a little over an hour, the town's cliffs hung ahead of them. Compared to the last time they'd visited during the rain celebration, the plaza at the base of the town was dead quiet. A handful of people watched them arrive, distant-eyed and lackluster. One of the bow-wielding children they'd seen at the Boggs Twill's farm popped out of a bakery and took off running into the desert.

Inside the inn's foyer, Cord ritually splashed some of her water into the copper bowl there, summoning the proprietor. They rented a room for the night along with the use of the bath located in a cozy room carved out next to the kitchen, where an iron barrel of water was warmed by excess heat from the stoves and pumped through the wall via copper pipe.

The innkeeper warned them they'd only have twenty gallons allotted for bathing. By unanimous decision, the Keeper was granted the first bath. The other four found a table in the common room. They'd barely taken their first sips of sour beer when Boggs burst into the room, face red and sweaty.

He beelined for their table, breathlessly angry. "Where you been?"

"Learning how to rid your land of demons," Dante said. "If you can think of a better use of our time, I'm happy to hear it."

"Two days back, the canals started dropping. Senate sent riders around the basin. It's the same story everywhere they went. Another two days from now, they'll be bone dry."

"They're going dry? Does that happen often?"

"No more than once a generation. And when it does, it sure as shit isn't in the middle of the rainy season. Nor this fast. It should take weeks for the waters to drop this low, not days."

Judging by the others' expressions, they were of the same mind as Dante. "This isn't natural. It's Gladdic's work."

"What I figured," Boggs said. "What I *can't* figure is why? None of the towns have invoked the Code of the Wasp. He must have the spies to know the Small Senates would rather eat their own noses than go to war against his demons. So why risk provoking them into a fight?"

Blays flicked his fingernail against the side of his mug. "Have there been any reinforcements from Bressel?"

"None."

"Maybe he's not expecting any. So this is his way of clearing out the basin without putting his soldiers in the field. Cut off the water and wait for everyone to leave."

Cord stood, rattling the table. "We know how to defeat his demons. What are we waiting for? Let's feed his meat to the lentils!"

The curiosity of this saying broke Dante's chain of thought, requiring several seconds of mental mending before he was ready to speak again. "The only demon we know we can defeat is small enough to use our beer mugs as a bathtub. We can't afford to try to liberate Collen until my ethermancers get here."

"You can wait until enough of your friends are here that you're no longer afraid. But this is my homeland. I have no choice."

She stepped away from the table. Dante put himself between her and the door. This was merely a symbolic gesture: if her mind was made up, he couldn't stop her any more than a hedge, no matter how determined, could stop a charging bull.

He planted his feet. "We're not going to wait. We're going to get the water flowing again. As soon as that's done, we're going to lay the groundwork to retake Collen—and we'll need your help."

Cord looked ready to trample her way past him, then drew back to stare down at him from her full height. "Do you swear it?"

"I thought you didn't believe in oaths."

"I believe in them too much, fool. That's why I never make them."

"Your people found a way to make the desert blossom. I won't let Gladdic take that away from you."

She chuckled, wagging her head. "No wonder you're never home. You make more promises than most of us make shit!"

With no response to that, and no desire to think about it, Dante returned to the table. "Boggs, you said the entire basin's running dry? Where can we find a map of the canal system?"

"Same place we plan all our wars," he said. "In the nearest shrine."

Boggs stalked out into the plaza and led them to the shrine where they'd met with the town's Small Senate. They'd barely made it two steps inside when a trio of monks emerged to intercept them.

"Pardon," said the foremost of them, a man whose bald head was pointed on top and broad in the jaw; combined with his heavy freckles, his face resembled a brown chicken egg. "What's your business in our home?"

"Savin' your soft ass," Boggs said. "Now kindly haul it out of my way."

The monk's face became severe. "Such language has no place here." He glanced Dante up and down. "And neither do the Mallish. I must ask you to depart before you profane this shrine any worse."

"You dumb bastard." Boggs pressed his face close to the monk's and pointed to Dante. "If that man wanted, he could kill you by blinking. He's here to turn that power on the Mallish. Kick him out, and I'll water the inn's greet-bowl with your blood."

The holy man blanched, then flushed, then clamped down on his emotions with the skill beaten into all monks. "How can we help you put your talents to use?"

After Boggs explained, the monk led them to the third floor of the shrine. Sunlight poured through the southern-facing windows and skylights carved into the rock. One whole wall was painted with a map of the Collen Basin, bordered by Mallon to the west, the mountains running diagonal from the north to the east, and the cracked wastelands to the southeast, which stood between the basin and Parth.

The six senate-bearing towns and a number of villages were scattered around the city of Collen, which sat roughly in the map's middle. Everything large enough to be worthy of noting sat within spitting distance of a canal. As the canals crossed to the western fringe of Collen, they spread like the thin upper branches of a tree, but they all shared a common trunk, which tapped into the river that skirted Collen to the northeast and vanished somewhere in Parth.

Dante stood beneath the sprawling map. "You're sure the entire basin's drying out?"

"Don't believe me?" Boggs said. "Go on and lick it."

Dante tapped the map where the trunk of the canal departed from the river, tracing it down to its first fork. "Then the blockage has to be somewhere between here and here. How far away is that?"

"Eighty to a hundred miles. And not much in the way of roads."

"We'll need horses. Even so, without roads, it'll take three days. Keeper, maybe you should stay in Dog's Paw."

The Keeper curled her lip. "You think I'll slow you down."

"We have to get out there as fast as we can. Once the canals go dry, your crops start dying."

"And who do you think blocked the canals? Men with shovels?"

Blays put his hand alongside his mouth and stage-whispered, "I think she thinks it was priests."

The Keeper smirked. "Leave me here, if you're sure you can fight them on your own. If not, how much time will you waste coming back for me?"

A lengthy argument ensued regarding logistics and timelines. One side, comprised of Dante, Cord, and Boggs, wanted to get horses as fast as possible and ride off hell bent for leather. The other position, held by the Keeper and Blays, argued in favor of finding a wagon to go with the horses. It might slow them by a day or two, but it would allow them all to make the journey to the area where the blockage must be.

It soon became apparent no one was going to budge. With time of the essence—and both sides busy squandering it—the argument rapidly expanded in volume.

"Boggs," Naran's voice was all but drowned in the storm of squabbling. "*Boggs.*" Naran drew his sword and whacked its flat against the table with an ear-splitting crack. "Boggs godsdamned Twill!"

Boggs blinked. "Uh, yeah?"

"Excuse me." Naran smoothed his shirt. "Mr. Twill. At present, how deep is the water in the canals?"

Boggs shrugged. "Six, eight feet. For now."

A slow smile spread across Naran's often-stony face. "There's no need for horses. Or to leave anyone behind. We'll use the sailboat Captain Twill built at the Twill residence." He sketched a northeasterly path from Dog's Paw along the canals toward the main trunk. "The winds blow out of the south and southwest. With the canals drying out, and no current to fight us, we can reach our destination within a day."

"One small problem," Blays said. "The Twill residence is built on ground. Which is dry. And hence so is the boat."

Naran's face sank. "The canal's close. With a few logs, we might roll the ship there. But it'll take time."

"Sure, if you want to do things the hard way," Dante said. "Or I can bring the canal to the ship."

On the day, Dante had expended almost all of his ether beating up on the Andrac. Yet he had hardly touched the nether.

The canal gleamed in the sun, sluggish and low. Blood dribbling down his forearm, shadows swirling around him like the dust devils that spun about the plains of Collen, he lowered his finger to the earth. A crack opened perpendicular to the canal. It widened swiftly, plunging to a depth of six feet: just enough to let a foot and a half of water pour out of the canal and into the new capillary. Dante expanded the capillary six feet wide, then walked toward the Twill estate, lengthening the new canal branch with every step.

Despite starting with all of his power, and engineering the

auxiliary canal to require the least possible displacement of earth, by the time he came in sight of the sailboat's mast—which was easily the highest vegetation in the area, and currently the site of a ringing argument between Naran, Blays, and Boggs—Dante's hands were shaking. But having to move the boat more than a few feet would take hours. If the main canal system dropped too far in that time, the entire expedition might be rendered obsolete. Breathing hard, he brought the shallow canal right up to the nose of the boat, then staggered back, panting.

Within the rigging, Naran glanced down. "Have you ever thought of dredging canals across *your* land? You'd encourage trade and discourage invaders in one fell swoop."

"It's a good idea," Dante said. "But before I can do that, I'll have to quit sticking my nose into the business of every country I travel through."

Within minutes, they finished rigging the single-masted ship. With some shimming and jimmying, they stuck round wooden rods beneath the ship's flat bottom, then eased it into the water with an impressive splash. It was almost the exact width of Dante's canal, making it an easy matter for Naran to help the Keeper aboard. As the others climbed on, Boggs passed them poles. Blays dug one into the side of the canal, rocking the boat.

Naran gazed down at Boggs, who was remaining in Dog's Paw. "Did Captain Twill ever give the vessel a name?"

Boggs shaded his eyes against the mid-afternoon sun. "Sure did. The *Promise of the Desert*."

"The crew isn't up to her normal standards." Naran winked at them. "Yet I think she'd be proud to see the *Promise*'s maiden voyage."

Boggs held up his hand in salute. The Keeper seated herself on a bench. The other four took up poles. Each push against the banks sent the boat skimming along—and, typically, grinding into the opposite edge of the canal. This sounded much more damaging than it was, however, and they soon had the sailboat out into the much wider main canal.

It smelled like drying muck. The current, not quite dead yet, attempted to push them away from their destination. But even without making use of the sails, a pair of polers could propel the boat along at the speed of a slow jog. In straight stretches of canal, Naran trimmed the sails to the wind, allowing them to conserve strength while using the poles whenever the boat drifted too near to one side.

Dante took his turns with the pole, but had to set it down whenever they passed one of the canal network's prolific forks to check it off on his map, which he'd copied from the shrine. For if the canals had been flowing at normal levels, with the water's surface two or three feet below the top of the banks around them, the chance of getting lost would have been slim to none. Landmarks would have been constantly visible on all sides.

But with the water so low, the banks hung eight to ten feet above them, blocking sight of everything except the closest hills. The only way to get a look at their surroundings was to climb up the mast. Given how light the boat was, and the flatness of its hull, this wasn't a brilliant idea. This made it vital to track their progress along the map—a wrong turn could send them many miles off course. If they were delayed too long, the canal might dry up to the point of becoming unnavigable. The Keeper might well have been capable of presiding over the map, but her eyesight wasn't always reliable. Dante wasn't positive her memory was, either.

Besides, unlike the forks of a tree, which never rejoined after branching away, some of the canals had smaller channels between them, like alleys connecting main streets, which only made navigation more confusing. Consulting with Naran, Dante drew up a course that ought to shave several miles off their journey. In less than three hours, they had already crossed a quarter of the distance to their destination.

After his turn pushing them along with a pole, Naran swapped out, replaced by Cord. As Naran reviewed the map with Dante, the boat jarred hard, wood grinding on sand. The Keeper sprawled from her bench. Dante fell to the deck. Blays tumbled over the front rail, landing with a shallow splash. Dante picked himself up, elbows stinging, and made his way to the prow.

Blays sat in a few inches of water running over a sandbar. "Oops. Missed that."

"I wouldn't say we'd 'missed' it." Dante shaded his eyes. "This section's silted in. The boat's too heavy to portage. We'll have to try to find a path to pole through."

Everyone except the Keeper took up a pole. Between the four of them, they muscled the boat to slightly deeper water, feeling their way forward with their staves. Soon, the silt fell away beneath them, leaving them free to speed along once more.

Night fell. Naran hung a lantern from the prow so Dante could make note of any forks, then struck the sails to ensure they wouldn't plow into any rocks at too high a speed. Now that they were advancing by muscle-power alone, Dante split map duties with Naran so that he could spell the others at the pole. Even with each of them taking turns, by midnight, they were all exhausted. Blays hopped out to tie the boat to a clump of sage up on the bank.

The few hours of sleep they got wasn't nearly enough for their aching muscles, but it was enough to restore Dante's hold on the shadows, allowing him to take care of their pains with the nether. They resumed poling along. When dawn broke, Naran drew the sail tight. It looked like the water had fallen another foot or two since they'd started out the day before. It wouldn't be long before it got too low to sail.

They hit two more submerged sandbars, but between the poles and a bit of earth-moving, they made great time toward the river. Around noon, with less than ten miles between them and their target, Dante slew a dragonfly sunning itself an an exposed, mossy stone, then sent it flying ahead.

They were now deep in the desert, with nothing man-made to interrupt the steppe except for the occasional homestead of a hermit-farmer. Viewing the expanse from above, Dante couldn't help wonder why the Colleners hadn't relocated to the river. Had they believe the drought would end in time, as every other drought did? Had some force, such as the horrors of the Spiderfields, kept them away? Had they simply been too stubborn to leave their homes? Or had the old ones built the canals before the lack of rain forced the residents out?

Or was the land here so flat that they never would have been able to defend themselves against the Mallish?

The river gleamed ahead, a blue ribbon against the plains. The canal that extended from it was muddy and brown. Through the eyes of the dragonfly, the cause of the lowering of the waters was obvious: a dam of stone and earth was even now being extended across the mouth of the canal.

And a small army of Mallish soldiers guarded the work.

24

"The Mallish are damming the canal," Dante said. "A hundred and fifty of them at least."

Cord stood, rocking the boat. "Those scum. We have to go back for more soldiers!"

"Let me take a closer look. We'll want as much intelligence as possible."

He flew the dragonfly over the works. The canal split from the river at roughly a 45 degree angle, quickly curving southwest toward the interior of the basin. Just upstream from where the canal branched off, a moat-like circle had been inscribed into the river's bank, carving out an island roughly forty feet across. A narrow earthen causeway connected this island to the bank. A run-down camp sprawled across the little island, scraps of canvas propped up by old sticks. Across the causeway, a second camp of identical tents was arranged in orderly rows. A large shack or small house stood on its far side.

Of the laborers, only half were in blue uniforms. The others were mostly dressed in rags and chains. Even if they'd been wearing doublets and trousers, their blond hair would have identified them as Collenese slaves.

It was a good-sized work crew. But Boggs had said the canal had started dropping overnight. Dante lowered the dragonfly to the dam. An earthen prong jutted from each bank. Workers moved atop it, dumping wheelbarrows of earth and rock into the narrow gap of water that was still flowing into the canal. The base of each prong was buttressed by squared-off boulders far too large to have been moved by wheelbarrows.

At the side of the works, a man in gray robes watched the Colleners sweat. Two other gray-clad men were talking to each other outside the shack.

"Good news and bad," Dante said. "The good news is that at least half the laborers are Colleners. The bad news is there are Mallish priests here. Looks like they used the ether to carve out the sides of the canal and jam it up with big rocks. The slaves are filling in the rest."

Naran poled the boat to the side of the canal. Once Blays hopped out to tie them up, Dante described the layout of the dig: the slaves held on the island; the soldiers camped across from them on the riverbank; the command shack.

"I can undo the dam in a few minutes," Dante concluded. "But not while I'm being assaulted by a small army."

Blays rubbed his upper arms. "Think the five of us are mean enough to remove that army by ourselves?"

"That depends on how mighty our brains are."

"We're contemplating attacking an army with five people. I'd say our brains are our biggest liability." Blays sighed through his teeth. "Well, there's no way around it. We'll have to kill the priests."

Naran grunted. "I don't follow why that's necessary."

"It's almost impossible to take a sorcerer captive," Dante said. "You can take the swords from a warrior, but you can't take the nether from a warlock. It takes three of your sorcerers for every one of the enemy you want to keep locked down. Even then, if one of your people lets down their guard for an instant, they're all dead."

Cord brayed with laughter. "This is good. I'll grab any chance to cut down one of those sniveling Mallish hypocrites. We slay them first, yes? With no magic to protect the soldiers, the rest will fall like wheat."

"The priests are occupying the shack. If we bust in on them tonight, maybe we kill them instantaneously. But more likely, they hold out long enough to raise the alarm. Then we've got eighty soldiers on our backs while we're still finishing off the priests."

Naran contemplated the sluggish brown waters. "Why not send Blays to walk through their wall and deal with them in his way?"

"No can do," Blays said. "My little trick only lets me stroll through stone."

"How odd. Why is that?"

"Beats me. Apparently my mentors were too lazy to figure out how it works on wood."

Dante drew back his head. "Harvesting allows a nethermancer to manipulate living vegetation. I wonder if it could somehow be applied to shadowalking through wood."

"Interesting thought," Blays said. "But it took me months to learn how to shadowalk. Unless you're okay with sitting in this ditch until next spring, we're going to have to come up with something else."

Naran held his palms a few inches away from each other and moved them back and forth, as if he was rolling out an invisible length of clay. "You can flash in and out of the shadows, can't you? What's to stop you from sneaking through the nether, emerging beside each soldier in turn, and putting them to rest?"

"Another great idea crushed by cruel reality. Moving in and out of the shadows is harder work than staying in them. I'd be lucky to take out fifteen or twenty of them before my juice ran out."

"We need to be thinking about the slaves, too," Dante said. "If one of them calls out while we're skulking around slitting throats, we might as well take a dive onto our own swords."

"Then we need to think like a quartermaster." Naran spoke slowly as he thought it through, each word standing on its own. "And turn liabilities into assets."

Blays cracked his knuckles. "You want to weaponize the slaves."

"Now that's wise," Cord said. "If it was me in that camp, I'd be begging you for my wheel."

"You think the Mallish could capture and enslave you? I think they'd have an easier time fitting chains on a lake."

Dante took another look through the dragonfly's eyes. "I've got an idea or two. But we're not going to be able to draw my plans in ink until we see how the Mallish arrange themselves tonight."

The soldiers were running patrols up to a mile away from the site. The five of them poled the boat to a kink in the canal two miles south of the enemy and pulled into the cover of the small trees lining the ditch. Unless a soldier walked right up on top of them, they'd be impossible to spot.

Both slaves and soldiers worked throughout the day to fill in the dam. By nightfall, the water in the canal was no more than waist deep. Islands of silt projected from the stagnating waters.

As the last light faded to the west, the soldiers fed the slaves hunks of bread. It didn't seem like nearly enough to sustain them. After, they were chained together in groups of four to six. This hardly seemed necessary, given that their legs were hobbled, a small group of guards was stationed on the causeway between them and freedom, and four score more were camped just beyond that. Then again, Gladdic ran a tight ship.

The soldiers settled into their tents. The three priests entered the shack and closed the door. Within fifteen minutes, the grounds were quiet and dark except for a lantern in the camp on the causeway and another on the fringe of the main camp near the shack.

"This plan is going to require each one of us," Dante said. "There's a camp on the bridge to the island. Blays and I will take out the sentries there. As soon as they're down, I'll move to the shack to watch the door and make sure none of the priests get outside. Cord, you cross to the island and wake up the slaves. You're their countryman. They'll listen to you. Blays, if the sentries have keys, bring them to unlock the captives' shackles. If not, take the guards' weapons to the Keeper. She's going to be down in the canal in the boat."

The Keeper looked amused. "You don't think I have the strength to climb up the bank?"

"Once Cord's got the Colleners awake, Naran's going to escort them to you one group at a time. You're going to strike off their chains with the ether. That's going to be very bright. Having you down in the canal will block out most of the light. Meanwhile, Naran will bring you more captives and Blays will bring those captives as many weapons as he can find. Cord, you'll be guarding the causeway with your wheel. Blays, once you've run out of arms to steal, you'll join me at the shack."

Blays nodded. "Where it's priest-stabbing time."

"As soon as we've freed all the captives and armed as many as we can, Naran, Cord, and the Keeper will take them to surround the sleeping soldiers. Blays and I will see to the priests. Once they're dead, I expect the soldiers will surrender without a fight."

"Bah." Cord waved one hand. "There are far too many links in this chain. If one breaks, all falls."

Dante shook his head. "We don't need to make it all the way to the end of the chain. All we need to do is arm the first twenty-odd slaves. That should be enough to rout the Mallish soldiers before they know what's happening."

"And if the priests come out to put a stop to the fun?"

"Then I will fill their backs with shadowy daggers."

"The soldiers we capture," Blays said. "Is the plan to dispose of them?"

"That'd be easier." Dante rubbed the inner corners of his eyes. "But if we've got prisoners, we can use them as a bargaining chip. Maybe not with Gladdic. But after we've gotten rid of him, the Colleners can show King Charles how reasonable they've been toward their prisoners. And how they'd be happy to return the captured soldiers to Mallon if only the king would agree to a truce."

"And another liability becomes an asset," Naran said. "You would make a fine quartermaster."

"I'll hold you to that. If our involvement here turns Mallon against Narashtovik, the wrath of my council will be so intense I'll have to take to a life at sea."

Wanting to wait at least two hours until they moved on the camp, Dante led the boat to an exposed shelf of mud. There, using a stiff reed, he traced a map of the work site, showing them the island, the short causeway, and the location of the soldiers and the shack. They ran through the plan several more times, exploring contingencies.

Once the stars indicated it was roughly eleven o'clock, they began to pole the boat closer to the Mallish encampment. With the canal so low, this was actually slower than walking; the path forward had to be felt out yard by yard. Twice, they had to get out and push the hull over ridges of silt. It was a full hour before they came around the bend in the canal and saw the camp's lanterns flickering a few hundred feet ahead.

"Cord, Naran," Dante whispered. "Once we've removed the sentries, we'll step in front of that lantern twice. That'll be the sign it's safe to proceed to the island."

Everyone but the Keeper climbed up the side of the bank, disturbing the smell of clams and fresh mud. Naran and Cord hunkered down under the cover of thorny trees awash in sickly-sweet pollen. Dante and Blays advanced along the bank, careful not to let themselves get snagged on the branches. On the causeway, three men sat around the tripod of poles their lantern was hung from, playing cards spread on a blanket. Good. So close to the light, their night vision would be compromised.

Dante and Blays stopped two hundred feet away, exchanging a series of gestures. Blays nodded, took a step toward the sentries, and vanished. Dante tracked his progress toward them. Once Blays was fifty feet from the Mallish, Dante nicked his arm with the point of his knife. At thirty feet, Dante called on the nether. At twenty feet, he unleashed it.

Two black bolts soared silently forward. As they neared the card-players, the bolts diverged. A silhouette appeared behind one of the men. Steel flashed. Before the man's partners could even turn their heads, the nethereal spears plowed through their skulls. All three men fell without a word.

The main camp consisted of a score of tents, each one large enough for four soldiers. At the moment, the tents were dead silent except for a few snores. It was temping to reave into them like the proverbial wolf among lambs. But Dante couldn't kill them all at once—or get rid of them all before the priests interrupted him.

Dante held his knife to the moonlight and flashed it at Blays. On the causeway, Blays performed what might have been a dance, stepping in front of the lantern, stepping back, then blocking the light a second time. Behind Dante, Naran and Cord made their way along the trees lining the canal.

Dante circled around the glob of tents. Back at the causeway, Blays was going through the pockets of the dead. Dante came to the shack, which was windowless, and pressed his ear to the only door. Hearing nothing within, he pressed his back to the side of the entrance and waited.

There was just enough light cast on the causeway to make out Cord moving among the prisoners and shaking them awake. Blays passed a small object to Naran—keys—and returned to the land bridge to loot the sentries' weapons.

Naran moved toward the first batch of slaves and kneeled to see to the shackles around each of their ankles. After, he went to the padlock that secured them to a spike driven into the ground. Iron clanked faintly. Finished waking those on the island, Cord took position in the middle of the causeway, holding her wheel vertically beside her body.

After a minute of maneuvering, five prisoners stepped away from Naran and advanced toward Cord. They were no longer bound by the long chain that had locked them together, but their shuffling steps made it clear that the key wasn't the right fit for their ankle bracelets. Holding a bundle of swords and knives, Blays led the five captives away from the camp and along the trees toward the spot in the canal where they'd left the Keeper in the boat.

Blays saw the prisoners to the canal, then turned back to the camp. Faint white light flashed from the trees, lighting the undersides of their leaves. The Keeper, taking care of the shackles. Blays made his way to one of the weapon racks set between the tents. On the island, Naran had freed another group of captives and sent them toward the Keeper. On their way, they passed the initial group, which was now armed and returning to the causeway to join Cord.

The tents were still quiet. So was the shack. Blays made another delivery of weapons to the causeway. The second batch of slaves had been de-shackled by the Keeper and was on the way back toward the island. A third group departed the island, edging around Cord and the armed Colleners who now accompanied her.

As the new group squeezed past, one of them tripped, reeling to the side. The man tried to throw his feet wide to catch his balance, but before he could plant his feet, the chain around his ankles hit its limit, pulling tight. He toppled sideways. And skidded down the edge of the bridge. Locked in chains, dropping headfirst toward the water, he screamed.

Dante sucked air through his teeth. At the causeway, the island, and the trees along the canal, everyone froze. The man landed with a sploosh, cutting off his scream.

Within the tents, a soldier coughed. Another muttered.

"Never mind the screechin'!" Blays called out in his thickest portside Bressel accent; he stood in the middle of the tents, a bundle of swords held in his arms. "Thought I felt a snake in my blanket, that's all."

For a moment, the night was silent. Down in the moat ringing the island, the fallen prisoner breached the surface and thrashed his limbs, fighting not to drown.

Men yelled back and forth. Boots thumped. Soldiers popped from their tents. Other than Blays, none of the escapees had made a peep. But the lantern on the causeway glittered in the eyes—and on the blades—of the slaves assembled there.

"Escape!" a man roared. "To arms!"

Troops boiled outside and took up their swords. On the causeway, Cord took two long strides, as if to make a break for it, then glanced over her shoulder at the dozens of prisoners who remained trapped on the island.

With a growl, she planted her feet and swept her wheel before her. "Come and let me deliver you to your gods!"

The four Colleners who stood with her brandished their stolen swords. Mallish soldiers swarmed about the camp. A group of a dozen assembled and charged the causeway. Cord spun her wheel, the counterweighted spear blurring. She clubbed down the first three soldiers that stepped foot on the bridge. Losing the momentum of her weapon, she danced back to join ranks with the four prisoners. The Mallish charged into them. Swords clashed in the night. Two prisoners and four soldiers fell to the ground. A second wave of Mallish rushed to reinforce their compatriots.

Naran sprinted across the island to stand beside Cord, bearing his saber in one hand and a dirk in the other. He weaved in and out of the Mallish, his strikes as controlled and elegant as his speech. Another prisoner fell, leaving just Cord, Naran, and a lone captive. Facing twenty soldiers, the three of them dropped back a step, then two more.

A figure materialized at the back of the Mallish lines. With a sword in each hand, Blays carved into the unwitting enemy, felling half a dozen men in a matter of seconds. Cord laughed and stalked forward, wheel whirling. The Mallish soldiers hadn't had time to don armor. The metal ball at the end of Cord's wheel snapped their bones like dry branches.

An officer yelled orders. The soldiers fell back to regroup with an incoming batch of reinforcements. In the confusion, the second group of Collenese captives, armed and unfettered, rushed to the causeway. The defenders now numbered nine in total. They were outnumbered nearly ten to one by the Mallish, but the enemy wasn't wholly assembled yet, and with the fighting confined to the narrow strip of earth connecting the island to the shore, it might be enough.

Naran darted forward, snatching up the swords dropped by the dead. Two prisoners joined him. They grabbed whatever steel they could see and rushed back to the line of defense. Arrows thudded into the ground they'd just vacated.

Beside the shack, Dante craned his neck. Heart racing, he spotted four men crouched to the left of the causeway. A line of infantry protected them from any sallies attempted by the Colleners. Nether shot from Dante's hands, wending over the tents, but the archers were already nocking another volley. They loosed on the defenders.

"Naran!" Blays vaulted toward the captain, who had his back turned to the incoming arrows. Blays rammed into Naran's side and bounced him to the ground. As the arrows slashed toward Blays, he blinked from existence.

As the archers readied another shot, Dante's black bolts struck three of them in the back. Two flopped without a sound. The other writhed on the ground. The fourth jumped back in panic, dropping his arrow. But another six archers were already running into position to fire on the causeway. They dropped to a knee and took aim.

Dante wreathed his hands in shadows. As he prepared to sling them across the camp, the door of the shack clapped open. A priest dashed outside, spheres of light whirling between his palms. Reflexively, Dante slammed every drop of nether he had into the man's side. The priest flew sideways, spinning head over heels.

At the causeway, people yelled in pain. Dante turned back, heartsick at what he was about to see.

Silver lightning flared from the bank of the canal and sizzled into the archers. Their screams were the high-pitched keens of those who burned. The glare was so bright Dante had to shield his eyes, but there was no mistaking the work of the Keeper.

The light faded. Cord led a charge from the causeway, scooping up the old woman while the others grabbed more weapons from those who'd died. Mallish soldiers tried to pursue, but were driven back by another flash of lightning.

"Stuart?" a man called from inside the shack. His words carried the accent of Windwill University, which graduated most of Bressel's priests. "Stuart, are you all right?"

Light winked from the island, much dimmer than the ethereal lightning. The Keeper was striking off more shackles. Twenty of the Mallish had been injured or killed. Several Colleners had fallen, but their numbers on the island now equaled their enemy. Most of the prisoners were fettered and unarmed, but the Keeper was working to undo the former condition—and with every soldier they killed, those on the causeway undid the latter. The next few minutes were going to be grim and bloody, but between the Keeper, Blays, Cord, and Naran, they looked like they'd carry the day.

An iridescent lance shot from the shack door, whisking toward the forces on the bridge. A second followed right behind it. Anticipating it, Dante whacked at it with a lobe of darkness, but he was too slow. Both lances of ether flew through the darkness like shooting stars. They arced over the Mallish lines and hurtled into the Colleners, drawing panicked yelps.

In an open field, Dante expected he could take down both priests after a brief struggle. But rushing through an open door into a tight space he couldn't see inside sounded like a good way to stop being a human and start being a puddle of red goo.

Two more white bolts flicked out the doorway. Again, Dante was too slow to bat them down. Another minute of this, and the priests might weaken the causeway's defenders to the point where the soldiers could break through. Dante tensed his legs, ready to roll around the doorway and fling himself inside.

As he pivoted, the dirt ground beneath his boot. He dropped his weight, stopping himself. Heart racing, he plunged his mind ten feet into the ground, then twenty. It was solid basalt, but at his command, the rock flowed away like muddy water. He moved upward in a rough circle twenty feet across. More and more rock fell away, forming a yawning, unseen chasm. Dante crept away from the shack and drew away the last of the basalt.

But a layer of compressed vegetation remained beneath the structure, holding it upright—all that was left of the Collen that had once flowered and bloomed before the cataclysm that had turned it to desert.

Another pair of bolts streaked from the shack, painting the dirt white as they traced toward the prisoners.

The vegetation wasn't the only thing holding the shack up. A thick layer of dust rested between the building and the mat of dried-out branches. Dante yanked this layer away. The shack dropped two inches, smacking into the wafer of compressed branches and leaves. Ancient and brittle, dozens of cracks sounded at once. The building bobbed as if floating on the surface of a lake. As the branches continued to break, the shack dropped from sight.

Three seconds later, it landed with a smash of boards. Dante poured cool liquid rock over the rubble, then swayed backward, dizzy from the massive expenditure of shadows.

Across the camp, soldiers had whirled to stare at the racket of the shattered building. Several were dumbstruck by the complete disappearance of the shack. Before they could regain their composure, Dante outlined his hands with flecks of ether and brought flocks of shadows to swarm around his head.

"I have sent your priests tumbling to hell!" His announcement drew the attention of every soldier who wasn't actively engaged in combat. He made the light on his hands pulse, the shadows above his head dispersing and contracting like a flock of bats. "Fight on, and I'll do the same to you. Or surrender now, and be returned to Bressel."

The soldiers shot looks at each other. Some turned to regard the causeway, which had grown littered with Mallish corpses and armed Collenese prisoners. Others glanced about the camp, absorbing the fact that a quarter of their people were already dead.

A man slung down his sword and lifted his hands over his head. "I surrender!"

He edged sideways from his fellow soldiers. For a long moment, no one spoke. Then three more soldiers tossed aside their weapons and moved to join the first man.

That was the breaking of the dam. Within another minute, every Mallisher followed suit, though a few looked disgusted with themselves for having done so.

The Keeper and Naran moved to release the last of the slaves, who grabbed up the weapons dropped by the Mallish. Dante crossed the camp to the foot of the causeway, which the Colleners had seized.

"That didn't get off to such a great start," Blays said, wiping down his swords. "You dropped the shack down a hole, eh? Why didn't you think to do that from the start?"

"Funny how inventive the mind becomes when it's about to cease to exist. Anyway, if I'd tried to use that much nether when the priests weren't distracted by fighting, they'd have felt it even in their sleep." Dante motioned to Blays. After the fighting, Blays was spattered with blood from head to toe. Most of it appeared to be from unfortunate Mallish soldiers, but his ribs and thigh were damp with his own blood. "You all right?"

"Don't heal these. They need to become scars. Reminders to Naran that, when you're being shot at with arrows, it's generally a good policy to get out of their way."

Naran scowled. "I was distracted by the prisoners. I've already thanked you for interposing yourself between them and me."

"You're both lucky the Keeper can shoot lightning out of her fingers." Dante motioned to the gathering of disarmed soldiers near the riverbank and the unhappy-looking, well-armed ex-slaves beginning to hem them in. "Think we should do something about that?"

Blays nodded. "My nose for atrocity is picking up a strong whiff of vigilante beatings. Let's step in before—"

The front line of Collenese laborers bowed forward, then broke toward the Mallish. The Mallish fled to the banks of the dark river.

"We surrender!" A lone man in blue walked toward the Colleners, hands raised above his head. "Don't hurt these men. You don't know what they've done to help your people.

"Help," a man said, voice drenched with loathing. "Our people?"

A sword flashed. The soldier screamed and fell.

Dante broke into a run. The lines of Colleners roared and ran, too. The bluecoats—most of whom were presently dressed in their underwear rather than the blue of their uniforms—shielded their heads with their hands. Blades hacked into their bare forearms.

"Stop!" Dante yelled. "I promised them we'd spare their lives!"

The former slaves fell upon the Mallish, slashing and stabbing. Cord moved among them, grinning widely as she jabbed the point of her wheel into any man with dark hair. The Keeper stood twenty feet back from the massacre. She watched, but did nothing to intervene.

By the time Dante and Blays reached the Colleners, every Mallish soldier had been knocked to the ground. The riverbank stank of spilled intestines. Prisoners stalked among the bodies, jabbing at anything that moved. Cord kneeled among the carnage, gripping the shaft of her wheel, its weighted base resting in the dirt. Her eyes were closed and her face was streaked with blood.

Dante strode up to her. "What the hell was that?"

She didn't open her eyes. "Have you never seen victory before?"

"Have *you*? What kind of 'victory' involves slaughtering dozens of unarmed men?"

"Cry for them. Cry for these men who worked to turn the entire basin to dust and bones. They're demons, Dante. Would you give mercy to the Andrac?"

"I promised them sanctuary," Dante said. "This wasn't your call."

Cord pulled herself to her feet and gazed down at him. "Did you take this land when we weren't looking? Are we supposed to take orders from Narashtovik now?"

"You're *supposed* to obey the codes of war. Do you want them to respond in kind? To massacre your people like rats in a barn?"

She spat on the body of a man whose broken back was bent at a right angle. "They've always done that, frostlander. Where do you think we learned to do the same?"

Dante returned Cord's glare in kind. The Keeper stood to the side, observing in silence.

He moved to stand before her. "Why didn't you try to stop them?"

The wrinkles on her brow deepened. "That isn't my place."

"That's the best you can do? You're a walking library. History. Philosophy. Right conduct. You should be a leading light for these people!"

"Let the despots be their lights. My duty is to preserve. Without me, our culture would be ash on the wind."

Dante clenched his teeth. "Maybe that wouldn't be such a bad thing."

A hand grabbed his upper arm. He spun, but it was Blays.

Blays smiled to the Keeper and dragged Dante away. Speaking softly, he said, "Will you quit arguing with them already?"

"You're the one who's always trying to spare every life we can. Don't tell me you're all right with what we just saw."

"I'm pretty damn far from all right. But they're not going to listen to a word we have to say. Not right now."

Dante lowered his voice. "Do you think they ever will?"

"I don't think we have half as much control over them as we thought. Maybe this was an isolated case—prisoners venting their spleens on the assholes who were trying to turn the basin into one giant sand dune—but maybe this is only the beginning. Do we want to be a part of that?"

"*Want* isn't the right word. But it's going to be a lot easier for us to get to Gladdic if we've got an army backing us up. For the moment, our interests align with theirs."

"What about after he's dead?"

"We reassess."

Blays scrunched his eyes shut and pinched the bridge of his nose, laughing ruefully. "Until then, I suppose we'll have to try to lead by example. In the meantime, we've foiled Gladdic's evil scheme to starve the resistance out of the Collen Basin. What do we do now?"

"Get these people out of here before I do something regrettable," Dante said. "Then tear down the dam."

Settling on a new course of action had relieved Dante of most of his agitation. He regrouped with the Keeper and Cord.

"I'll take care of the wounded," Dante said. "As soon as I'm done, take these people out of here and bring them back to Dog's Paw."

The Keeper gestured toward the dam. "You will stay to destroy it?"

"I don't think I'll have the strength until tomorrow. You need to get your people far away from here before Gladdic gets wind of his defeat."

Dante burned through the rest of his nether patching up the wounds the Colleners had suffered in the fighting. As soon as he was done, Cord and the Keeper led the former prisoners south along the canal.

The Colleners had gone through the dead soldiers' pockets, but had otherwise left the bodies where they'd fallen. Faced with the choice of cleaning up the grounds or relocating, Dante, Naran, and Blays headed a short way upriver, making camp behind a stand of trees sprouting from the bank.

Before bedding down, Naran spent a long minute staring at the river. "Do you know any incantations against nightmares?"

"Afraid not," Dante said. "Expecting them?"

"I won't be the only one troubled tonight. Such things aren't seen lightly."

"After everything the Colleners have been through, I should have been wary for something like this."

Naran lifted an eyebrow. "You're not of the school that suffering creates virtue in the sufferer?"

"People say suffering is noble to put a silver lining on the horrors they're going through. But how many people do you know who get nicer when they're in pain? Pain doesn't make you a better person. It makes you as hateful as the one who's hurting you."

Dante slept surprisingly well. Morning came too soon. Once his mind was clear enough to work, he walked downstream to the site of the prior night's battle. Flies rippled on the bodies. He wrapped a cloth around his mouth, but it did little to keep out the stench.

The water in the canal looked no higher or lower than the night before. Dante used his knife to trace a red line on his arm, then moved his mind into the jumble of rocks and earth. Gesturing through the air like he was smoothing a rumpled sheet, he turned stones and boulders to mud. Water rushed in from the river, dispersing the mud down the canal. Within three minutes, Dante had cleared the blockage completely. Water sped down the channel. By day's end, the canals would be filled again.

Dante's spirits lifted with the rising water. The Colleners had been more vicious toward the Mallish than he'd envisioned they'd be. But it was the Mallish who had invaded Collen. Who'd tried to wring it dry. The basin's farmers and laborers had always been friendly enough. They were still worth saving.

The sailboat had remained tied to the banks despite the battering of the reopened canal. As usual, the winds blew out of the southwest, the exact opposite direction they needed. If they followed the map, however, the renewed currents would deliver them directly to Dog's Paw. They searched the battlefield for the boat poles—some of the captives had been using them as quarterstaffs—then got on their way. The going was slower than the previous night, but required no physical effort except when they had to use the poles to steer themselves down a fork in the canals.

Traveling at a steady two to three miles per hour, they overtook the liberated prisoners early the next morning. Dante didn't stop to parlay. After two and a half days of drifting downstream, they came to the canal that ran past the Twill residence. They poled the boat into the small canal Dante had built to bring the ship to the water, ending up within a bowshot of Boggs' house.

As they climbed out and tied up the boat, Boggs ambled toward them, grinning broadly. "Guessin' by the fact you sailed back here that you whipped their mangy asses."

"Mallish force nearly a hundred strong," Dante said. "We'll need another audience with the town senate."

They traveled into Dog's Paw. There, Boggs learned the Small Senate was incapable of meeting on account of the fact that two of the senators were currently visiting Tanner. Expecting the pair to return by morning, the remainder of the senate agreed to meet at noon the next day.

Before the slaughter at the river, Dante would have known exactly what he'd say to the senate. Now, he spent most of his waking minutes leading up to the meeting lost in thought.

At dawn, the drums awoke him. Shortly before noon, he took Naran and Blays to meet Boggs in the plaza outside the shrine, entering together. A monk led them upstairs to the map room. The senate awaited them at the table.

Serta stood and bowed his shaved head. "We meet again. Let me guess: you're here to tell us we must fight after all?"

"I'm here to tell you the facts," Dante said. "What you choose to do with them is your own decision."

The man smiled in surprise. "A welcome change from the tone of your last visit. Please, speak."

"As we suspected, Mallish forces caused the canal to drop. They were trying to dam it up completely." Dante relayed a summary of their trip to the river and the ensuing battle. Including the massacre afterward. He imagined he kept his voice dispassionate. "I destroyed the dam. But there's nothing to stop them from rebuilding it."

"The very attempt is a tacit declaration of war on the entire basin." Serta's words were little more than a whisper. He cleared his throat and raised his voice to a normal tone. "But only fools fight a war they can't win. You returned the water to the canal, but maybe we should leave regardless. It makes more sense to walk away than to die at the claws of the demons."

"Our situation has changed. We still don't know how to destroy them. But we've learned how to banish them. I don't have the power to assault Gladdic's army singlehanded, but I've summoned a team of sorcerers from Narashtovik. They should be here within three weeks. At that time, if you want my help, I'll be happy to assist your army in retaking Collen."

"Last time, our answer was simple. This time, I believe we have much to discuss."

The senators began a conversation that swiftly morphed into a bitter argument. Three of them sounded angry enough with Gladdic to declare war on the spot, but the others remained fearful of provoking further aggression.

As the debate wore on, someone whistled from one of the cliffs outside the shrine. The shutters were open, but the curtains were drawn, blocking out the sunlight, but not the sudden buzz of voices down in the plaza. Dozens of feet rasped across the stone.

A senator named Nell sighed testily and gestured at her fellow senators. "I hear a lot of words. Do you know what words are made of? Air. Air can't kill demons."

Blays motioned in a vaguely northern direction. "We've got a demon trapped at the Bloodlake right now. If you want, we could beat it up for you. Prove we know what we're doing. But honestly, I'm starting to feel bad for the little guy."

Her brows bent. "Maybe you can and maybe you can't. But other than the story brought by these outsiders, how are we so sure the Mallish are to blame for the drying of the canals?"

Serta gawked. "Who else would have done so?"

"Maybe it was the Colleners attempting to get us to join their fight. Or maybe it was these men here. Why are they so eager to drive us to yet another war?"

"You want proof the Mallish were involved?" Dante stood from his chair, crossed to the windows, and yanked back the curtains. "Feel free to ask one of the witnesses."

The senators got to their feet. Down in the plaza, close to a hundred armed men and women milled about, wearing the dust of a three-day trek through the desert. Cord moved among them, her laughter booming between the heights of the cliffs.

"Well." Serta had the look of a man who didn't like what he saw for the future. "I think we have enough to vote. All those in favor of war on the Mallish invaders?"

Two senators raised their hands. Then a third. Serta was the fourth. He was joined by a fifth. Nell was the only one who opposed.

The troubled look on Serta's face only grew deeper. "Send out messengers to the other towns. Dog's Paw goes to war on the Mallish—and the Code of the Wasp demands the entire basin does the same."

EDWARD W. ROBERTSON

25

In the dirt outside the shrine of Silidus, two warriors strived and fought, twirling and clacking the long, spear-like weapons they called "wheels." They did their best to ignore Gladdic's eyes, but for all their physical prowess, he could feel them waiting to flinch.

One monk jabbed at the other. His opponent intercepted the attack, then thrust forward, driving the tip of the wheel toward the attacker's chest. Now on the defensive, the former attacker fell back a step, pivoting to remove himself from danger. At the same time, he used his momentum to swing the weighted end of the wheel toward the body of the other monk—who once again blocked and flowed seamlessly into the next attack.

Beside him, Horstad laughed in delight. "Remarkable. It's as if every action they make serves two purposes."

"They call such practice a 'martial art,'" Gladdic said. His voice may or may not have been loud enough for the two monks to hear. "Horstad, in your judgment, does this skill truly qualify as art?"

Horstad thrust out his jaw, extending his chubby neck. "I believe that all skills, when sufficiently advanced, may qualify as art."

"Is that so. Say a shoe-boy shines your shoes. His technique is without flaw. It is the fastest your shoes have ever been shined; never have they shined brighter. Is this art?"

"Er. Perhaps not. Yet if the shoe-boy's motions are graceful enough, it might evoke the feelings one associates with experiencing art."

"I see. Then is a master artist defined by how pleasantly he moves his brush? Or wields his chisel?"

"Of course not. A master artist is defined by the quality of his product."

"And some products, like the shininess of one's shoes, can never be art."

Horstad sighed, deflating on himself. "I suppose you're right, Ordon. Some skills can't be art no matter how fine the practitioner."

"Whereas some skills, such as sculpture, are recognized as art no matter how poor the practitioner. So we have determined that some skills are always art. Some are never art. And some, like pottery, may become art, if the practitioner is masterful enough. Then we return to the original question: is the martial art an art?"

His secretary tucked his chin, watching the combatants leap, jab, thrust, and parry. "It's certainly pleasant to watch."

"Is this pleasure that which one feels watching a dancer? Or is it the type experienced while watching a wolf's stride and muscles as it chases down a deer?"

"Ordon," Horstad said hesitantly. "Is this the type of question where you're about to provide me with the answer yourself?"

Gladdic smiled thinly. "I ask, Horstad, because I wish to know."

The secretary nodded once and frowned at the fighting monks. Gladdic didn't expect the young man's answer to hold much wisdom, but other minds, including ones far duller than Horstad's, could be a whetstone on which you honed the knife of your intellect until it was sharp enough to cut through whatever confusion bedeviled you.

Observing the monks spar, Gladdic was of two minds. He was not troubled by his mental schism. It was rare indeed when the mind was united in singular agreement. More often, it warred with itself, such as when it was faced with a new idea, or the temptation to sin.

Yet at that moment, his mind was not split by the urge to sin.

Rather, it was split by the urge to show mercy. To the *Colleners*, of all things. Had he been corrupted by the dust, sun, and sage? Or by the presence of the Colleners themselves? In that case, his internal corruption must be isolated, extracted, and eradicated before it could spread to those parts of his mind that weren't yet infected.

It remained possible, however, that his urge was rational. Which wasn't to say it was *correct*: only that the process causing his mind to suggest it was sound, and capable of being explored logically. In that case, aided by the whetstone of Horstad, his skeptical mind would interrogate the proposition to within an inch of its life. If, at that point, his merciful mind held fast to its conviction, his skeptical mind would be convinced.

But if it turned out his merciful mind spoke delusions and falsehoods, then his skeptical mind would cleanse it.

"I feel," Horstad answered at last, "that it is more like the dancer. Wolves don't train their skills; warriors do. Secondly, when a wolf hunts, its only purpose is to kill. Martial arts are practiced to teach one to kill, but as these monks before us prove, the arts can also be used to educate and entertain. Just like dance."

There were several holes in this argument—not least the claim that entertainment was equivalent to art—yet Gladdic set the line of inquiry aside.

"Let us accept, for now, that it is art," he said. "Clearly, it is art of the body. This is distinct from art of the mind, such as philosophy, and from art of the soul, such as theology. Surely, of all the arts, those of the body must come last." He lifted his palm, indicating the monks, who were now breathing hard, knuckles bleeding from the rap of their rival's weapon. "Yet in Collen, this is their primary method of worship."

The secretary glanced at Gladdic from the corners of his eyes. "It's said that, through the art of the body, the monks' minds attain perfect clarity. Don't we teach that clarity of mind leads to purity of spirit?"

Gladdic blinked. Anger rose in his gorge. The argument had the whiff of profundity. Clarity of mind *did* lead to purity of spirit. The only angle of attack, then, was whether the practice of martial arts did provide clarity.

"Well stated." Gladdic kept his tone even. "But who claims physical action clears the mind?"

"Why, it's self-evident, Ordon. When you chop wood, or dig a latrine, or go for a long walk, doesn't your mind feel as if it's awakened from a long nap?"

Gladdic couldn't remember the last time he'd chopped wood or dug a pit. He did, however, enjoy his walks, for precisely the reason Horstad had stated. Gladdic could feel his mind spinning, groping about for wedges he could drive into Horstad's argument. There was no denying the *premise*. But perhaps he could prove that martial arts were an inefficient means of finding clarity? How? Compared to meditation? Or perhaps —

A man jogged into the courtyard. He had the dark hair of a Mallish man, but wore the plain jacket of a Collener. A scout. Gladdic summoned the name: Dafid.

"Ordon Gladdic." Dafid's eyes shifted to the dueling monks. "Please, pardon my interruption."

"I assume," Gladdic said, "you wouldn't be making it unless it were of importance."

"Just so, milord."

"Then cease wasting time and explain what is so important that I must be interrupted."

With infuriating deference, Dafid quietly explained that the dam had been destroyed. Along with every trace of Gladdic's forces, priests included. His strategy had been to claim the remainder of the basin without expending troops he didn't have. Instead, in one fell swoop, a tenth of his army had been annihilated.

Gladdic's mind roared like wind through an empty room. Across from him, the monks' weapons clacked on.

"Is it known..." Gladdic's mouth was too dry to speak. He moved his tongue until it moistened. "Is it known who's to blame for this crime?"

Dafid lowered his gaze. "There were no survivors, milord. Most were killed by common arms. But some were burned like they'd been shot through with bolts of fire."

"The dam was composed of boulders. Was there any indication how these were moved?"

"There's no sign of...anything. It's like the entire dam was never there."

"Thank you, Dafid. Now leave me."

The scout bowed and turned to go. Gladdic flexed his hands. His fingers were long. Graceful. Like those of a harp player. He'd always been proud of them. With a thought, lines of light condensed from the air. The geometry was perfect, like the framework of the ideal cathedral. The light poured into a sphere.

His mind felt as clear as windless winter air. He split the sphere in two and exhaled sharply. The two hemispheres swept forward, shifting on the fly into thin, shimmering disks.

The disks swooped through the chests of the dueling monks. The two men flew back, landing in heaps. Blood showered the hard-packed dirt. One of the monks thrashed weakly; the other lay still.

"Ordon!" Horstad blurted. He took a step toward the fallen monks, then stopped with a lurch, turning to gape at Gladdic. "Why..? Were they involved in the attack at the river?"

Gladdic's hands twitched with the urge to summon another sphere and smash it into Horstad's flabby face. He could smell the shower of blood and viscera, feel the thrill of having torn down that which was flawed.

"Ordon," Horstad pleaded. "Help me understand."

Gladdic's eyes twitched. He returned the ether to the sky and stepped over the dying monk. "They dress their practice in cloaks of art and prayer. They say this art is holy. But do you know the true reason they train to fight, Horstad?"

"No, milord."

"So they can fight us."

Enlightenment filled Horstad's eyes. "I see."

"Their treachery runs fouler than that. Dante Galand accompanied those who attacked the dam. He may even have led them. He's the only one who could have destroyed it so thoroughly."

"Then it's just as you said it would be."

Gladdic nodded. During the chaos of the battle for the city, Galand had disappeared. Gladdic had scoured the city for him, using that same search to conduct a census of the residents—and learned that the veins of nine out of ten citizens was overwhelmed with Collenese blood.

His monks had interrogated a great many of the locals. None of them had credible information regarding Galand's location. Somehow, the heretic had escaped the city. Gladdic had given much thought to hunting him down. He'd received reports the nethermancer and his friends had been seen in the town of Tanner. Yet the only ones powerful enough to dispatch Galand were the Andrac and Gladdic himself.

And the city of Collen remained full of warrior-monks like the two that had just enlightened Gladdic. If he brought the Andrac out of the city to bring Galand to justice, he risked his soldiers being overrun by Collenese partisans. If he lost his troops now, King Charles would refuse to provide him with more. For those entrusted with the responsibility of leading campaigns into other lands, patience was more than a virtue. It was survival.

Even if prudence hadn't insisted Gladdic remain in the city, he would have been inclined to leave Galand to run free. As the *Ban Naden* said, "Thieves hang themselves." Left to his own devices, Galand would cause trouble. Foment unrest. Murder the innocent. And cement Gladdic's case against Narashtovik. The destruction of the dam wasn't a setback. It was the next step toward scouring the north of heresy.

Galand's actions had clarified Gladdic's mind better than the most vigorous exercise. Everything the Colleners did, they did in defiance of Mallon and the gods.

Gladdic kneeled and dipped his finger in the blood of the monk, who'd gone still. It looked as red and healthy as all blood did. There was no more nether in it than the blood of the Mallish. Yet he could feel the taint lurking within it.

"The land here is blighted." Gladdic wiped his hand on the monk's blouse. "When blight comes, the only way to save the farm is to burn the crops and start anew."

That same day, he announced the systematic evacuation of the city.

By the middle of the afternoon, four hundred citizens gathered at the top of the road down from the butte. Every single one was blond-haired and blue-eyed. He had decided to spare those who showed Mallish or Parthian features. It would be unjust to punish them for Collen's crimes. Gladdic nodded to his commanders, then turned and walked down the switchbacks.

Dunswell, one of his officers, began to explain that they were relocating the Colleners to outlying towns for their own safety. Gladdic wasn't listening. A third of the way down the road, he entered one of the caves cut into the side of the butte and finalized his preparations.

Gladdic had left the twin doors open, allowing sunlight to slant inside the chamber. Outside, the priests lifted their voices in the Hymn of Good Travels. The hymn was energetic and hopeful, as befitted such moments. Gladdic waited on a short platform laden with candles, pewter statues, and bags of supplies. Before their departure, the Colleners were to be blessed and provisioned.

A team of soldiers in blue uniforms appeared in the doorway. They ushered a column of citizens into the cavern. The Colleners gathered in front of the stage, watching Gladdic, who was the only other person in the space. He stared back, silent.

In time, the last citizen was led into the cavern. The soldiers exited, leaving the doors open.

"People of Collen," Gladdic said. "Today, you set foot on a new journey. One I hope will at last foster peace between our two peoples. In the spirit of that hope, before you leave, I give you a gift."

He extended his hand. A ball of light leaped beneath the center of the ceiling, illuminating the cavern. The people squinted, shielding their eyes.

"As this light rids this room of darkness, so shall I rid your souls of stains."

This time, he thrust out both hands. Across the room, the doors slammed shut. Voices called out in surprise. Frightened eyes turned back to Gladdic.

He let his hands fall. "May you at last find Taim's peace."

A shadow moved from the wall. Its eyes shined silver. When it opened its mouth, so shined its throat.

It fell among the Colleners with the hunger of fire.

Outside, the priests sang louder and louder, drowning out any screams that escaped the cavern. People rushed for the doors and found them barred. Gladdic spent a few moments watching the demon for signs of disobedience, but the more lives you fed them, the more prone they were to listen. After today, the Andrac would be indistinguishable from a slave.

Satisfied, Gladdic returned his attention to the people. Dozens had already dropped to the smooth stone floor, wounds blackening. He watched the rest die with great interest.

In time, the cavern was silent again. They lay on the floor like autumn leaves. The smell was unbelievable. Gladdic moved among them, peering into the darkness behind the surface of the world.

For when a man died, he left not one, but two varieties of feces behind. The first, common and earthly, everyone knew. But the second—Gladdic believed it possible that he alone knew of its existence. A stain. Black and hidden. He believed it was the waste left behind by a life of sin. In death, every single Collener had left such a stain.

Not that this was unique to Colleners. Gladdic had seen a great many Mallish die as well. Each had also left a stain. He had spent years searching for its ethereal equivalent: a shimmer of glory signifying its body's bearer had lived a life of virtue, and would now join Taim in the measure and judgment of the world.

Never had he seen the white mark.

He searched the cavern from front to back and side to side. As always, there was no light. Only darkness. For a moment, he felt the horror implied by the lack of light. Then he exhaled. These were Colleners. As tainted as vampires. If he found no lights among them, that confirmed his path was righteous.

He took another moment to soak in the scope of his vision. He smiled. Just as every martial artist's move served more than one purpose, so did Gladdic's. He would kill those capable of fighting against him. Then he would use their remains to strengthen his defenses.

And he would rebuild Collen with untainted blood.

26

Two days after Dog's Paw declared war on the invaders, the Strong Senate of the Collen Basin convened on the heights of the town. Much like Justice Falls, two shallow grooves had been carved into the bare rock, winding their way to the edge of the cliff. To the north, the butte of Collen was a blue-brown lump on the horizon. Thirty-six senators milled about, exchanging greetings. In a minute or two, Dante would be expected to deliver the Cause of War.

Serta had explained this to him shortly after Dog's Paw had made its fateful vote. The Cause of War didn't sound as much like a speech or a fiat as it did a court case—and Dante would be the one on trial.

"I thought the Code of the Wasp bound them to declare war," Dante had replied. "It sounds like we're seeking their permission."

"No permission is needed. With our declaration, each town is bound to certain responsibilities. They must supply no less than one hundred able-bodied soldiers. They must provide lodging and provisions for these soldiers in the field. In addition to the infantry, they must employ a certain number of scouts. And so on."

"Great. Then why do we have to make a case for war?"

Serta smiled wryly. "The code binds them to war. But how can it bind them to be enthusiastic? When you step into battle next to your ally, do you want him to be fighting with only half his heart?"

"Of course not. I want him to be fighting with every inch of his heart, lungs, bladder, and wiggly gray things."

"The Cause of War is how we fan the flames. We are at war. Why? What is the plan? And how is it in their best interests to support our war with every resource at their disposal?"

"I've got this one," Blays said. "Because the losers of wars tend to be raped, killed, and burned?"

Serta winced. "I recommend downplaying that angle of the venture."

And so Dante had spent the last two days crafting an argument, along with replies to the most likely questions and critiques of that argument. As the senators finished up their greetings and turned to face him and Serta, who stood at the "source" of the miniature river beds carved into the rock, Dante felt more than prepared.

In response to an unspoken signal, Serta tipped a large copper jug, spilling water into the two grooves. When the rivulets of water reached the cliff's edge and trickled over, he lifted his face and smiled at the other senators.

"Colleagues of the Basin. Thank you for answering our summons. Today, we present you our Cause of War. I will be happy to answer your questions as well, but for now, I'd like to leave matters in the hands of our guest: Dante Galand of Narashtovik."

Thirty-five pairs of eyes shifted to Dante. Once upon a time, such attention would have made him feel uncomfortable, but after so many years in the public eye—first as a member of Narashtovik's Council, then as the city's commander—he no longer felt that teenage resentment at being looked at by a crowd.

"Senators of Collen," Dante said. "I'm sorry we have to be here today. But one man—Gladdic of Bressel—has given us no other choice."

He launched into the tale of Gladdic's crimes stretching back to Bressel, layering and arranging the facts to create a narrative of a man maddened by fear of the nether and Arawn. It was just the opening to his argument, and he hadn't made it halfway through before he was interrupted.

"Enough." An older woman stepped forward, straw-colored hair blowing in the wind; Ana, the haughty senator from Tanner. "As I told you before, this is about far more than Gladdic. Arawn himself has turned against us. Unleashed demons we have no hope of defeating. Tanner comes to answer the Code of the Wasp, adherence to which has always kept our people alive. This time, however, it will be our death."

"I don't know the last time I've heard one person be so wrong about so much," Dante said. This drew sharp looks from several senators, especially those from Tanner. He ignored them. "The demons weren't sent from Arawn. They can be created by any sorcerer who knows where to look—which, fortunately for human existence, rules out almost everyone. And they can be defeated by sorcerers, too."

"Is that so? How would you know the workings of the mind of Arawn?"

"Follow me to Bloodlake. It isn't far. There, I created an Andrac. We've defeated it dozens of times, honing our skills in preparation for the battle against Gladdic."

This rocked Ana back on her heels. Dante stood before the others, eyebrows lifted, waiting for someone to take him up on his offer.

"You're sure of this?" said Madd, Ana's fellow senator from Tanner. "You can kill the demons?"

"I'm not sure if they *can* be killed. But we know how to banish them to the shadow realm. Once they're removed from our world, then their master—Gladdic—is left vulnerable."

The three dozen senators took a moment to mull this over.

"And so you've convinced Dog's Paw to invoke the code," Ana said, recovering from her earlier shock. "What's your involvement in this conflict? Exhorting us to war, then moving to the safety of the rear to give us your commands?"

Dante shook his head. "I had nothing to do with declaring war. You've been at war since the instant Gladdic drained the canals. As for my involvement, I'm not here to lead you. I've learned better than to try to give orders to Colleners."

This drew a round of appreciative chuckles. Ana waited for

them to subside. "My question remains unanswered."

"We're here to kill Gladdic and destroy the Andrac. After that, it's your fight to win or lose."

"You say you don't want to lead," said an old man whose white eyebrows looked like squiggles of whitewash on a stone wall. "That's good. Wouldn't be right. But it sounds like you've got some ideas about how this is to be fought. I'd like to hear them."

"You're sure you want the opinions of a former Mallisher?"

"Pah. Only an idiot would turn down good advice just because the advisor was born in the wrong place."

"The truth is, I don't know how we should conduct the fight." Dante paced in front of his audience. "We don't have any idea what's going on in the city. And the people inside the city don't know that we're ready to come to their aid. Our first step will be to address these issues. We'll install scouts in the city. I can help with that. Once we know what's happening inside Collen, we can formulate a battle plan."

"Sounds like you're itchin' to move."

"We'll have three weeks to prepare. That's when my priests will arrive in the basin. Before they get here, we may know *how* to fight the demons, but I fear we wouldn't have the strength to deal with them in open combat."

Dozens of questions followed this. Rather than being critical or hostile, they were practical, oriented toward strategy and logistics. As the conversation went on, Serta fielded more and more of the questions. Sometimes the senators of other towns answered as well.

After two hours, the discussion finally wound down. Serta asked if there were any other questions. No one spoke up.

"Then I have one last question for you." He gazed across the other senators. "Dog's Paw calls for war. To free our brothers in Collen and drive the invaders out of a land they've never belonged in. Are our sister towns prepared to join us?"

The senators thrust their fists into the air. All said, "Through unity, we survive."

Serta smiled, but it was the expression of a man knowing he's choosing the best of a bad lot. "Then to war we go."

~

The butte of Collen stood against the night, a raised shelf that blacked out the stars behind it. They had left the Keeper behind in Dog's Paw, allowing the four of them to travel as fast as the moonlight allowed. They hadn't been this close to the city since fleeing from it, and as they neared, Dante kept both eyes out for scouts and sentries. In good news, the city didn't appear to be on fire or smashed to pieces. On the east side of the city, he thought he spied the intact dome of the Reborn Shrine.

Dante moved beside Blays. "You're sure you want to do this?"

"What's this?" Blays said. "The fourth time you've asked? Or the tenth?"

"It's easy to make a promise when you're miles and days away from fulfilling it. But Collen's right there. So, for the fourth or tenth time: are you sure?"

"Do I *want* to halfway drown myself sneaking into a city controlled by a man whose idea of a good time is a hanging where the noose isn't long enough to break the prisoners' necks? Not really. But Cord isn't exactly the inconspicuous type, is she? If we're going to learn what's going on in there, we're going to need someone who can get around without being seen."

Cord was currently ahead of them, striding through the darkness as if she could find her way home blind. Dante slowed, allowing her to get another couple steps ahead.

"Just don't put yourself in position to get hurt," he murmured. "We're here for Gladdic, nothing more."

"A week ago, you were ready to lead Collen's banners right up to the palace in Bressel. What happened to your revolutionary zeal?"

"It died by the riverbank."

With the butte less than a mile ahead, he quashed the desire to quadruple-check that their paired loons were still working. Earlier that day, he'd sent a dead prairie mouse up to the plateau. Since their hasty departure from the city, Gladdic had built a rampart around the base of the road up to the top of the butte. The cavern whose pool they'd used to leave Collen was halfway up the trail. With no easy way for Cord and Blays to reach it, they were going to have to employ other methods.

The switchbacks were on the south side of the city. Dante led their group to the southeast. The slopes were nearly sheer, hence unguarded and unlit. Yet fallen rocks had accumulated around the base, rendering it climbable. They picked their way up the scree, careful not to dislodge a rockslide.

Soon, they left the loose rocks behind and began their ascent of the wall. Rugged and forbidding though it was, it was studded with shelves of rock wide enough to walk about on. Sage sprouted wherever there was enough dirt to support it, offering handholds. Now and then, Dante carved a stair or three into the rock to allow them to continue upward.

After a long, careful climb, Dante stopped on a ledge halfway up the side of the butte. Making sure his footing was steady, he closed his eyes and sent his focus into the rock, snaking toward the caves set along the switchbacks. Casting about, he located a passage that extended deep into the plateau and opened into a rounded chamber that matched his memory of the one they'd swum through. Once he knew where the passage was, it was a simple matter to open a tunnel in the side of the butte and link them up. The connection was lengthy enough that he had to keep it narrow, but it was wide enough for a grown man to crawl through it without excessive discomfort.

"Let me know as soon as you find anything," Dante said. "But take your time. We've got almost three weeks before we'll be ready to move on the city."

"I've got it all planned out," Blays said. "For my first move, I'll infiltrate the city's pubs. After that, I'll play it by ear."

He ducked into the tunnel. Cord followed. Dante gave them a few minutes to crawl away from the entrance, then sculpted it to be less visible from above or below, leaving just enough space to wriggle through. He and Naran descended to the plain, a much more treacherous journey than the climb, and headed back in the direction of Dog's Paw.

After forty minutes of walking in silence, Dante glanced at Naran. "Once this is over, what are you planning to do with yourself?"

"I've come in possession of a ship, so that makes me a captain," Naran said. "But I don't yet feel like one. I intend to take the *Sword of the South* away from Mallon for a while. Embark on a few simple voyages. The duller, the better."

"I'm sure we'd have plenty of work for you in Narashtovik. Although I can't promise it'll be dull. It seems like I can't turn around without running afoul of a king or an enemy so ancient we didn't know they existed."

"I've never been that far north. They say it's so cold it will freeze your urine before it's departed your body." Naran bobbed his head. "To paraphrase."

"They exaggerate. Though there have been nights when the hairs froze in my nostrils."

"And you people live there on purpose?"

"After seeing the Plagued Islands, I'm questioning that decision as well." Dante stretched his stride over a rodent hole he'd been about to trip in. "My offer's real, though. Narashtovik's always been short on ships."

"A considerate offer. Unless it's merely a way to secure yourself a ride home."

Dante chuckled. "The thought hadn't crossed my mind."

"I'll have to see what the crew thinks. But after what happened in Bressel, it wouldn't be a bad idea to have a new port to call home." Naran looked over his shoulder at the butte receding behind them. "What's next on our schedule? Intelligence?"

"That's right. Everyone's been so terrified about calling down the wrath of the demons that they've kept their scouting to a minimum. We need to get eyes on the road from Bressel. If Gladdic brings in reinforcements, we have to know about it. I'll post one of my scouts at the mouth of the canal, too. Once that's in place, we should work with the Colleners on strategies to deal with the Andrac."

"They're common soldiers. What strategy would that be? To run as fast as their legs are capable of moving?"

"Probably," Dante admitted. "But we could at least *try* to come up with something more."

They made camp on the back of a rise that was rounded on one side and sheer on the other, as if Gashen had grown angry and cleaved it in half with his axe. That night, the temperature plummeted, and was slow to revive in the morning. To warm their blood, they got an early start, spooking any number of mice on their way through the fields. Dante killed and reanimated four, sending two to the road to Bressel and two others toward the canal mouth to watch for another attempt to dam it. Undead, the creatures could run all day and all night; they'd be in position in less than a day.

Back at Dog's Paw, sentries stood vigil on the ridges. People came and went between the plaza and the cave-houses cut into the terraces, but there was a taut energy in the air that Dante recognized at once: the mood of a city before the siege. Many of the senators had stayed in Dog's Paw to coordinate with the other towns. Over the course of the day, Dante was summoned to multiple meetings to answer questions and offer advice.

The next morning, the loon he shared with Blays tingled. Dante activated it. "What've you got?"

"How soon can you march the townsfolk to Collen?" Blays said.

"There hasn't been any change in the timeline. Our ethermancers will be here in another two and a half weeks."

"Right. Then the city's doomed."

Dante waited for the punchline. "It looked fine two days ago. What'd you do?"

"Something big is going on here. A few days before we got in, Gladdic announced he was relocating most of the citizens to the outlying towns. The cover story is it's for their own safety. The real story—supposedly—is that Gladdic's afraid of a rebellion, and is thinning out the town so he's got fewer potential partisans on his hands."

"The senators of the six largest towns in the basin are right here. They haven't said a word about receiving refugees."

"That was my first thought. So I did some poking around. Every afternoon, the Mallish gather up two or three hundred people. Soldiers lead them down the road to one of the caverns to be blessed. An hour or so later, the soldiers escort them back out and off into the desert."

Dante frowned. "Maybe Gladdic knows about the Code of

Wasps. He wouldn't send the refugees to the larger towns if they're going to be drafted into war at any moment. Could he be sending them to live in the hamlets? Or a camp somewhere?"

"I don't think he's sending them to *live* anywhere."

This took Dante a moment. "You think he's leading them out into the desert and killing them."

"No," Blays said, "I think he's killing them in the cavern."

"I thought you said they left the cavern an hour later. And then the soldiers escorted them into the desert."

"That's how it's made to look. After Gladdic has the citizens killed, the soldiers dress in their clothes and walk off. Anyone watching will think it's just as Gladdic says: that they're being led away for their own safety."

"And then what? The soldiers sneak back under cover of darkness to repeat the process the next day?"

"Yep."

Though Blays wasn't there to see him, Dante couldn't help rolling his eyes. "This theory's getting a little elaborate."

"It's less of a theory and more of a thing that I saw."

At that moment, Dante was standing on the "roof" of Dog's Paw, facing southeast. From that vantage point, he'd been surveying the land, trying to work out the feasibility of pursuing Captain Twill's vision of running a canal from the Collen Basin to Parth. Not that his intentions were to nobly help the basin prosper. Rather, if he found a way to strengthen the connection between Parth and Collen, providing the basin with a new ally, it would be much easier to sever Narashtovik's connection to the country.

Hearing Blays, he had to step away from the edge lest he topple down into the plaza below.

"What do you mean," Dante said, "you saw it?"

"I mean I was physically present in a way that allowed my eyes to witness it. Gladdic brought them into the cavern, said something prayery, then set the Andrac on them. It killed them all within five minutes. After that, the soldiers stripped the bodies and put on their clothes. I had to shadowalk out before they were done, but I watched from up top as they walked down the road and left town. They came back that night dressed in their uniforms."

"You're absolutely sure that's what happened?"

"Unless I went insane from witnessing a demon slaughter three hundred people."

Dante's stomach twisted. "How long has this been going on?"

"Three days. There's another one scheduled for this afternoon."

"You said these were citizens, right? Not monks?"

"Right."

"He was trying to drain the canal to drive out the towns. Now that that's failed, he's decided to murder everyone in the city instead. Only he doesn't have the troops to do it all at once. Instead, he's chewing through them bit by bit. Quietly. So no one will know the truth until it's done."

Blays tried to speak, but his voice caught. He cleared his throat. "That's my read on it, too."

Beneath Dante, the wasteland seemed to stretch on forever. "I've read about things like this in the histories. But I've never seen it myself. The viciousness of it. It's insane."

Across the loon, Blays sniffed; the sound was muffled, as if he was holding his hand over his face. "I could hardly believe what I was seeing. We can't wait on this. We have to stop it."

"If we could do that, we'd have already counterattacked. We have to wait."

"So we act like nothing's different? Twiddle our thumbs until your sorcerers get here?"

"At that point, there will still be thousands of citizens alive in the city. If we rush in now and lose the fight, he'll butcher everyone."

"And if we wait, we guarantee he'll kill thousands. Three hundred people per day, Dante. I don't think I can carry that weight."

Dante licked his lips. "I should talk to Nak. See if we can't get our sorcerers here any faster."

"I haven't told Cord yet. But I can't keep this from her. If she hears you're withholding it from the senators, she'll take the news straight to them."

"And they'll march on Collen on the spot. What happens if we attack the city now and we lose?"

Blays' voice had been weary. Now, it hardened with resolve. "Then we lose trying to stop the greatest atrocity we've ever seen."

"I'll tell the senate," Dante said. "Tell Cord what's happening. It's your job to stop her from charging into the Mallish lines to claim her deathright."

"How do you expect me to do that? Chain her to a rock?"

"Tell her we'll be there in three days—and if she wants to end this, we need her to have her troops ready to fight."

When he broke the news to the Strong Senate, it was all he could do to stop them from charging the city then and there.

Once they'd been talked around to mounting an attack in a non-idiotic fashion, Dante lapsed into silence, letting them argue through their anger and pain. This took such a long time that, by the time they finally quit yelling at each other, he'd formulated a fully formed battle plan. Yet even with Serta's help, it took two minutes before Dante could get the senators' attention.

"Gladdic thinks he's being cunning," Dante said. "But his scheme has left him vulnerable. Every day, he sends three hundred troops out of the city. So you set up an ambush for them. Right outside the city, where Gladdic can see it unfold. This leaves him with a choice. Either he stays put, and your soldiers cut down a third of his men. Or he sends down reinforcements—and leaves the city defended by a skeleton crew."

Serta's eyes glimmered. "Which Cord and the resistance can sweep through from within. Not much of a choice for Gladdic, is it? It's like a fox with its leg caught in a trap: he can chew through his own leg, ensuring that's all he loses. Or he can try to wriggle out, and risk losing everything if the hunter comes back before he's freed himself."

Ana waved her palm side to side, batting down the idea. "Even if Gladdic sends down nine-tenths of his remaining troops, the city *won't* be undefended. Surely he'll leave some priests and Andrac behind."

"Probably," Dante said. "But my team will already be inside the city. And we'll be waiting."

The discussion resumed as intensely as ever, but it soon became clear that the Colleners intended to use the basics of his tactics. While they went over the finer details, the Keeper motioned to Dante, drawing him aside.

"You're sure this is wise?" she croaked. "What if we waited until the rest of your sorcerers arrived?"

"Then five thousand innocent Colleners would be dead."

"We've suffered worse. Those five thousand would be happy to give up their lives to guarantee the others would be saved."

"You've asked them, have you?"

She regarded him with her pale blue eyes. "I know my people well enough to not have to ask."

"It's not my decision." He nodded to the senators. "You want to convince them to wait? Have at it."

"You're the leader of Arawn's house on earth. Your voice will be respected."

"Then listen to my voice when I tell you I won't wait."

The old woman spat in the dust. "Gladdic would wait."

Dante smiled strangely. "Then be glad I'm not like him."

She stared at him another moment, then shook her head and turned away. Giving up his claims of leadership felt as good as setting down a full knapsack at the end of a long day's hike. For once, he was nothing more than a soldier. It might be years before he felt so free again.

By the end of the morning, the six-part senate reached consensus. Over the rest of that day and the next, they would return to their towns and gather their armies. The day after that, they would march behind the hills just west of Collen. When the Mallish soldiers departed the city dressed as Colleners, the actual Colleners would emerge from behind the hill and cut the Mallish off.

As soon as Dante had a moment to himself, he looned Blays with the news.

"I was wrong," Dante said. "We're not going to war in three days. We'll be there in two."

"Good news. What's the plan?"

Dante laid out the gist. "The Colleners will be in charge of their own people. They should be more than a match for the

Mallish soldiers. But against the ethermancers or the Andrac, they'd be helpless."

"In other words, the role of fighting that which can't be fought by mortal men will fall to us."

"Exactly. That's the only thing we have to worry about."

"The only thing we have to worry about? Just like the only thing the beetle has to worry about is the sole of the boot?"

"There's no army to command," Dante said. "No territory to defend. We don't even have to worry about saving lives. Know why? Because if we don't kill Gladdic and the demons, there *is* no saving the Colleners."

"So our objective is to be as nasty as we please," Blays said. "No wonder you're so happy about this."

There was no explaining it. Olivander would have understood. Strange as it was to think, King Charles of Mallon and King Moddegan of Gask would have gotten it as well: the relief that came when, for the first time in years, you were freed to make a decision without having to consider how it would impact the thousands of lives that depended on you.

The townsfolk would attack in two days. Dante needed to be in the city by the time that happened, meaning he'd need to sneak in the night before: which was to say tomorrow night. He went about procuring supplies, most notably a mule for the Keeper. This proved somewhat difficult, as the army of Dog's Paw would need all the beasts of burden it could find. And since the Keeper had maintained her anonymity, to the senators, she was nothing but a ridiculously old woman. Dante didn't even try to come up with a lie for why he needed to bring her. Instead, he went to the stables with a story about how much magical bric-a-brac he'd need to carry with him in order to be able to fight the demons.

Naran found him at the stables arguing with the proprietor, who had insisted that pack animals were in short supply, but offered to provide Dante with two strong-backed men in lieu of a mule. Naran waited patiently until Dante fabricated a lie to the effect that the presence of other humans would disturb the alchemy he needed to conduct en route, finally convincing the stableman to hand over the gods damned mule.

As Dante walked out, Naran fell in beside him. "Were you intending to leave me here?"

"I didn't know you were intending to come along."

The captain quirked a brow. "I find myself unable to take your meaning."

"No offense, Naran. You're handy enough with a saber. But sabers aren't going to do much damage to the people we'll be up against. Especially the ones who *aren't* people."

"You're afraid I'll be of no use in the fighting."

"Aren't you?"

"This could be so," Naran said. "But if it is so, it seems there's a simple solution to keep me safe. All I have to do is get behind *you*."

Dante laughed. "We've made it through some ridiculous situations together, but don't mistake that for invincibility. I already gave up my shot at living forever."

"As I've pointed out before, I'm the one who got us into this mess. Whatever the outcome, if this is to be the battle that sends us to our ends, I should be there, too."

"After all that's happened, I'm not sure that any of us should be here."

"You don't truly believe that. You're not one to shut your eyes to the truth merely because you don't like what it's showing you. If you thought it better to leave, you would already be gone."

"Is that so?" Dante said. "Then what's keeping me here?"

"A man who spreads fear of a harmless god. Who burns the innocent." Naran nodded to their shadows stretching across the dirt. "And who uses demons to annihilate an entire people."

It was a small comfort. Yet with what lay before them, any comfort was welcome.

The sun cut from the west in yellow blades. They moved across the desert, Dante and Naran on foot, the Keeper on the back of the mule.

The butte clarified ahead. The sun sank, faded, and disappeared. Crickets chirped from the darkness. Mice moved through the patchy yellow grass. A half mile from the butte, they stopped and the Keeper dismounted. She smacked the mule on its flank. It gave her a look, then trotted back in the direction of Dog's Paw.

"We're almost there," Dante said into the loon. "How's it look?"

"Quiet," Blays replied. "For now."

"How thick are the patrols?"

"Not thick enough to see *me*. I'll meet you at the well."

Dante closed the connection and finished the trek to the side of the butte. With no desire to risk the Keeper's health, they took their time ascending, with Dante carving steps out of the rock whenever her stiff knees found the climb too painful. The smell of fresh water tumbled from the mouth of the tunnel Dante had excavated on his last visit. He ducked his head and climbed inside, advancing on hands and knees through the darkness until he exited into the cavern that held the pool.

He activated his torchstone. Naran and the Keeper crawled out from the tube and joined him at the pool. Cord and Blays had left a rope tied around a post at the water's edge, leading into the depths. The water felt colder than the last time they'd been through it.

On the other side, Dante burst from the surface, his gasp echoing from the close stone walls. A silhouette crouched at the edge of the water.

"There you are," Blays said. "Letting the Keeper bring up the rear again like the gentleman you are?"

Dante slogged from the pool, wringing water from his clothes. "She's fine. With the ether, she can stay down there longer than any of us."

Naran had already broken the surface. The Keeper followed a few seconds later. After they took a minute to squeeze as much water out of their clothing as they could, Blays took them up the steps of the massive well. The night breeze cut through Dante's damp doublet.

"They've got a curfew going," Blays said. "Give me a minute to scout the way ahead."

He disappeared into the darkness, leaving the three of them crouched at the top of the staircase down into the well. Blays was back within five minutes. He led them through the deserted streets to a closed-up cobbler's.

In the apartments upstairs, Cord rose from her vigil at the window. "You're here."

"Nothing could keep me away," the Keeper said. "This ends tomorrow."

"And we'll taste Gladdic's blood."

Blays and Cord had a change of clothes waiting for each of them. Once Dante was into dry clothes, he pulled Blays aside. "How's it been?"

Blays bugged his eyes and shook his head. "Most of them still don't know what's happening. If we'd told them, the city would be tumbling down around our ears."

"But they'll be ready to fight?"

"You know how some people claim they were born ready? I think these people tumbled out of the womb with wheels in hand."

"Then I feel great sorrow for their mothers."

Blays gazed across the room at Cord and the Keeper, who were engaged in conversation. "It's going to get ugly tomorrow. The Mallish aren't going to surrender. They found the bodies by the river."

"I should have buried them."

"Maybe it's for the best. If any of the bluecoats *were* to surrender, we'd witness another massacre."

Dante grimaced. "What happens if we knock Gladdic out early? The Mallish will know they don't stand a chance. If they try to give up, are we going to let the Colleners kill them?"

"Since when did you care about the bluecoats' lives?"

"Since their wanton slaughter might provoke King Charles into sending a second force in search of revenge."

"This is just a philosophical exercise, right? You can't stop the Colleners. I think you'd have more luck stopping a wave with a broom."

Dante made a thinking noise. "We could say we'll quit helping them."

"I thought we were doing that anyway."

"*They* don't know that."

Blays felt around for a chair, dabbing at his forehead. "You'll have to excuse me. Your display of moral grandeur is so dazzling I think I'm about to faint."

"It's for their own good. Killing a few hundred Mallish soldiers while they're trying to surrender will only bring more troubles to the basin."

"And yet threatening to cut off help we have no intention of giving them makes me feel like...you know. That mucky stuff that gathers at the edges of ponds."

"Scum?"

"Yes. It makes me feel like scum."

That night, Dante barely slept. The sun rose on a city that seemed to be standing in the doorway of a house it feared to leave. With the right paperwork, citizens were allowed to move through the streets during daylight hours, and throughout the morning, the cobbler's store received several visits from Cord's friends. According to them, the Mallish were gathering up the day's "refugees" just as they'd done for the last few days. There was no indication they were aware of the impending attack from the six outer towns.

Two hours before the refugees were to be led down the switchbacks, the five of them snuck through the streets, aided by Collenese lookouts, and relocated to the top floor of a row house overlooking the entry to the plateau. The minutes that followed were among the longest of Dante's life.

As afternoon advanced, male voices rose from the street. A hymn. Dante knew it well enough to hum along, but it was a minute before he recognized it as the Hymn of Good Travels. Gray-robed priests broke into the open, leading a large group of citizens toward the road down from the cliffs. The people carried bundles and packs. They looked anxious, but not particularly fearful.

Face after tan face passed beneath the row houses. After more than a hundred had gone by, with twice as many strung out behind them, Cord sank to the floor, arm braced over her knee, brow pressed to her forearm.

"I can't watch this any longer," she said. "Tie me down before I run from this room with my wheel in my hands."

"Is it that bad?" Dante gestured to the column of people.

"Aren't they minutes away from claiming their deathright?"

Cord lifted her head. "Are you mocking me?"

"I'm curious. I thought it was every Collener's dream to die at the hands of the Mallish. When I saved your friend from that fate, he challenged me to a duel. I'm always having to talk you guys out of getting yourselves killed. So why does this upset you?"

"My people shouldn't die like baby lambs. They should die fighting! If they were from Narashtovik, could you sit and watch them walk to a death they don't know is coming?"

Dante watched the last of the refugees being led away from the butte. "Do you know what happens to us when we die?"

She turned back to the window. "The Mallish say we stand before Taim to be measured. The just are brought to the Blue City. The unjust are banished to the Blasted Lands."

"The Mallish are as wrong about that as they are about everything else."

"I know what *your* people think. You join Arawn on the hill beneath the stars." She laughed darkly. "Not much to look forward to. Why have my people spent centuries dying for such a belief?"

"My people are wrong, too," Dante said. "Or maybe they're right, but only about a piece of the truth."

"I thought your people believed whatever you tell them to believe. So how can they be wrong?"

"Because I haven't seen them since I learned the truth."

Cord's eyes shifted to his. Her lower lip was thrust forth, the skin wrinkled on her heavy brow. "What's the truth?"

"When we die, the first thing we do is dream of ourselves. Alone, we sort through our wishes and fears. When we finally know ourselves as we really are, we wake up. We rejoin our people. Past and present. And we live as we did before the cracking of Arawn's Mill. No pain. No sickness. No fighting or death.

"This time, instead of finding ourselves, I think we're searching for peace. For some people, this only takes a few years. For others, it's the work of centuries. In time, though, we all find it. And we leave our selves behind to join everything that's ever been."

Outside, the Colleners were now gone from the plaza. A handful of blue-uniformed soldiers milled about.

"That sounds so good." Cord swallowed, blinking back what might have been a tear. Abruptly, her face clouded with suspicion. "*Too* good, I say. If it's true, why don't we all die right now? There's no peace in this world. Why shouldn't we leave it behind for this other place?"

Dante shrugged. "I don't know."

"What kind of priest doesn't know why we exist?"

"An honest one."

The woman laughed, shoulders bouncing. "I think the gods eat suffering. That's why they've put it everywhere you look: so anywhere they go, they'll always be fed."

They weren't the only ones watching from a window. How many of the other faces studding the row houses were biding their time until the coming fight? Since Dante had arrived the night before, Cord had claimed with complete certainty that somewhere between one and three thousand citizens would rise up and take arms. What if it was only five hundred? Or fifty?

He supposed that was the Colleners' problem. Whether they rallied forth or hid in their homes, he would put an end to Gladdic's lock on the city.

The butte's edge cut off sight of the town below. As a result, they couldn't see any comings and goings from the cavern where the "blessings" were taking place. About an hour after the citizens had disappeared down the switchbacks, the soldiers—now dressed in the clothes of the slain—appeared on the road west toward Mallon.

Dante shifted in the open window. "They're on the move. Be ready."

Blays joined him at the sill. "What happens if the townies don't show?"

"They'll come," Cord said. "Or they'll be damned."

Hundreds of feet below, the soldiers walked on, careful not to march in anything resembling a formation. A low hill loomed two miles ahead of them. Twenty minutes later, when they were within half a mile of its slopes, an irregular column of troops poured from around the north end of the hill.

Cord pounded Dante on the back. "I told you they'd come!"

Dante winced, rubbing his shoulder. "Blays was the doubter. Hit *him*."

The Colleners hurtled pell-mell toward the town abutting the butte. The Mallish soldiers halted. And hesitated. Maybe they were discussing whether to give up their ruse and flee back to the city, or to run west as if spooked, only to turn and pincer the Colleners after the rebels were engaged with the garrison remaining in the city.

Whatever the case, it took them almost three minutes before they turned to run back to the road to the cliffs. They'd barely backtracked a quarter of a mile before it was obvious they wouldn't get there before the Colleners cut them off. Realizing this, they halted again. As they contemplated their next move, a second force of Colleners surged over the hill to the west.

Dante jumped as horns blared from the square. Gladdic must have had more soldiers hidden among the buildings in case the residents caught on to the atrocity unfolding in the cavern: for within moments, bluecoats were rushing into the plaza. They streamed downhill to reinforce the soldiers in the basin, who were now moving south at a good clip, separating themselves from both of the Collenese forces.

Blays clapped his hands. "Gladdic will be right down there in the cavern. As soon as his troops are engaged on the plain, we can serve him up to the gods."

Dante's pulse picked up. "Are there any escape routes from the cavern?"

"None," Cord said. "It's right where he should die. Let his soul be surrounded by the hundreds he's killed."

The afternoon wasn't particularly warm, but sweat tickled down Dante's ribs. In the corner of the room, the Keeper stretched her legs and back. Dante kept expecting a Mallish force to seize the top of the road. That's what he'd do, had he committed most of his army below and was concerned about a revolt: archers behind the cover of wagons or hasty barricades, a few infantry to support them. Mix in a handful of priests, and they'd be positioned to annihilate any rebels who tried to take the road.

But by the time the bluecoat reinforcements descended to the prairie below, the plaza remained empty.

"He suspects something," Dante said. "He's keeping the demons in reserve."

Blays put his hand to his mouth. "Then the revolt's doomed. Unless someone had the foresight to enlist a crack team of sexy demon-slayers."

"There's no sense waiting any longer. Cord, where are your warriors?"

"Waiting to be called." Cord leaned out the window, stuck two fingers in her mouth, and blew three notes, two short and one long. Satisfied, she swung back inside and leaned against the wall.

The whistle repeated up and down the streets. Doors banged open. Men and women trotted outside, tying ribbons of twelve different hues around their elbows. Dante laughed in admiration. Either the Mallish patrols were as lazy and foolish as a drunken child, or the Colleners' coordination was without compare.

"Well?" Cord spread her arms wide. "I brought you an army. Are you going to wait for the Andrac to start eating it before you step outside?"

Dante stood from the window. "When the demons come, it's just as we practiced in the Bloodlake. Blays and I will handle any priests. If there are too many troops, we fall back and call in the Colleners. Otherwise, we get to Gladdic as fast as we can."

They tromped down the steps. Even the Keeper kept pace; if it hurt her, she didn't show it. In the plaza, dozens of Collenese soldiers gathered, bearing swords and wheels and slings. Some lay prone at the cliff's edge, watching the armies maneuvering below.

Cord was first to reach the trailhead. Dante sped up to catch her, skidding in the dirt. He wheeled his arms, crouching to stop himself from spilling off the side of the switchback.

When he straightened, an inky figure stood on the road below them.

Dante lifted his hands high. In one, he called the shadows. In the other, he called the light.

He smiled down at the demon. "It ends now."

27

Gaits smiled down at her. "Bad news, Raxa. Your glorious reign is at an end."

Seated in the soapy tub, Raxa gripped its rim. "What do you mean, you have my kids?"

"Those little projects of yours. Your orphans. I've taken them to a safe location. But if anything were to happen to me, rendering me unable to send a message at the appropriate time, that location would become tragically unsafe."

"You're a dead man."

"Afraid not. That's the entire point of these elaborate preparations. As well as the presence of my sorcerous friend." Gaits motioned to the gaunt and feverish man. "I may not be able to see where you go when you disappear. But he can."

Raxa's mind clicked like the tumblers of a lock. "When I saved you from the Crows outside the Marrigan. You were awake. You saw."

Gaits' tone was the definition of pedantic. "First off, you didn't *save* me. It was important for me to be seen being captured by the Crows. Once they'd taken me out of sight, I was to mount a daring escape that would only add to my legend."

"You've been protecting the real culprit all along. When Kerreven got too close to the truth, you had him killed. And now that I'm near, you're here for me."

"Oh, don't try to paint me to be such a villain. If I hadn't talked you into buying a house, everything you own would have been lost when the Crows burned the Marrigan. I used every trick I knew to throw you and Kerreven off the trail. Even then, we could have avoided this. If Gurles hadn't made such a pretty speech, leadership would have fallen into my hands. I would have prosecuted the war against the Little Knives. We would have won and I would have thrown an amazing party. A few weeks from now, everything would have returned to normal."

"There was no guarantee you'd get the crown. What if Anya had taken the vote?"

"Why, I imagine she would have been assassinated."

"Let me guess. Your investigation would have turned up links to the Little Knives."

He cocked his head. "How *do* you do what you do, anyway? Vanishing like that? Is it magic?"

"Yes," Raxa said. "Why did you do it?"

"We flew too high, Raxa. Dreamed too big. After the job we pulled on the Citadel, they came for me. A woman named Cee. Fancies herself the Black Star. She's more or less the Citadel's equivalent of us. She told me they were going to destroy the Order. She offered me a choice: I could help them do so, and survive. Or they'd kill me then and there and slaughter the Order anyway. What choice did I have?"

"To die without betraying your friends?"

He snorted, flecks of saliva flying from his lips. "Spare me. You'd have done the exact same. You've always been in this for yourself."

"Maybe so," she said. "But you're too smart to take the first offer. What else did you make them give you?"

"The only thing worth more than land, Raxa."

"A title."

Gaits looked immensely pleased with himself. "Just so. You're now looking at *Count* Gaits."

"You said we were going to build the Order as high as Ivars. As strong as the Citadel."

"I meant to. But they don't let people like us climb out of the gutter. If we try to stand tall, they chop off our heads." His expression fell. She could almost believe the sadness and regret in the darkness of his eyes. "I've given you more than enough answers. You can puzzle out the rest during your stay beneath the stars on Arawn's hill."

"All right," she said. "At least let me die on my feet."

Raxa took her hand from the tub's rim and lowered it into the sudsy water. With her other hand, she braced herself on the tub's lip and stood halfway, bent forward, water cascading down her bare skin. Gaits glanced down her body with no particular interest. The large man and the feverish one both locked on her chest. They had the same look in their eyes. Hungry. Calculating. Raxa gave them a moment to get lost in their imaginations.

Gaits' eyes left her figure and traveled to her right hand. His jaw dropped. "She's got a—"

She sprung from the tub. Water whisked from the blade of the bone sword as she swung it toward the feverish nethermancer. Shadows jumped to the man's hands. Before he had the chance to use them, the sword ripped through him, sending his two halves crashing to the stone floor in a storm of blood.

Raxa tensed, ready to swing a backhand through the big man, but he was already crashing into her side, driving her across the bathroom. His arm wrapped around hers, clamping the sword to her hip. She staggered sideways, fighting to keep her footing.

Wasn't going to happen. He outweighed her by eighty pounds and she was already on the brink of falling. Rather than fighting it, she dropped away from him, her sudsy skin slipping from his grasp. She hit the ground. He stumbled past. She popped to her feet, wheeled her sword, and slammed it through his back.

She whirled. Gaits was charging her, dagger in hand. Seeing the black sword between them, blood flowing down the curve of its blade, he stopped mid-stride.

Raxa rushed sideways to put herself between Gaits and the door. "Drop the knife."

His throat worked. He looked ready to retch. He opened his hand. The dagger fell to the floor with an off-key clang.

"Thought there was something funny about that sword." His voice was strained. "Where'd you pick that up? The Citadel?"

"It looked useful." Raxa's voice was as flat as the floor. "Where are the kids?"

"I'd like to tell you that. Really, I would. However, if I do so, I have the strangest suspicion you'll kill me."

"It'll be fast."

"What a generous offer! With such finely honed diplomatic abilities, it's no wonder the Order saw fit to crown you."

She shuffled half a step closer. "Tell me where they are."

Gaits laughed, crow-like. "Or what? You'll kill me? Do you see why this isn't much of a deal for me?"

"You want a deal? You tell me where they are. And I'll tell everyone that, in your last moments, you turned away from the monster you'd become."

"Yes, yes, you want me dead. Have I taught you nothing, Raxa? In negotiations, you always have to give up something. You don't get to hear where they are *and* kill me. We're going to have to strike a bargain."

She didn't move a muscle. "You've crossed over. Bargain with a demon, and you trade away your soul."

He sighed, ragged and exasperated. "So now you're the saint ready to judge the devils? How righteous were you when you were carving your way through the city for a pile of silver? And after you murder me—by the way, if any gods are watching, let me remind them I'm unarmed—are you going to walk away from this life? Renounce our years of fell deeds? Or are you going to return to lead a band of thugs, thieves, and killers against those who live within the law?"

"That one," Raxa said. "But first, I'm going to shut you up."

She cocked back her arm. The shadow of the sword swept over his face.

"Wait!" He cringed, barring his arms above his head. "I can take you there! I can get you inside!"

Her mouth twitched. "You forget, Gaits. I've already found a way inside the Citadel."

It was just a gambit, seizing on a potential slip. But the way his eyes went wide, she knew she'd found the truth. As her bare biceps tightened, a stark and childlike fear flooded Gaits' face.

Her stroke fell. So did his head. It rolled against the wall, expression frozen in place.

Her breathing rasped from the stone walls. She wiped her blade on Gaits' motionless chest, then ran to her room, not bothering to towel off before she tugged on her clothes. As soon as she had her boots on, she ran downstairs into the street.

Gaits had done her one favor. The house he'd talked her into buying was on the north end of the city, only a mile and a half from the cemetery on the hill. Ten minutes later, she entered the grassy field. A couple walked hand in hand along the path to the doorway carved into the hill's base. Their faces were shocked, bereft. As if they'd lost their only child.

Gaits had claimed that, if he didn't return in time, her kids would be put to death. Raxa didn't think he was bluffing. He'd known what she could do. The only way to keep her on a leash was to make her truly believe the kids' lives were on the line.

She blanked into the shadows and sprinted toward the cavern. She knew they were in the Citadel, but the Citadel was the size of a small town. How long did she have? Nightfall? Midnight? Surely no more than that.

She entered the hallways of the carneterium and split to the right. Distantly, someone was sobbing. Raxa came to the tunnel toward the Citadel. Inside it, she let herself fall from the netherworld, continuing forward in darkness until her outstretched fingers tapped into the tunnel's dead end.

There, she walked through the stone wall and into a dungeon cell. Empty. Rather than returning to reality, which would only have drunk up more of her juice, she crossed through the cell's wall into the hallway that ran down the middle of the dungeon.

Someone was crying from one of the other cells. Not that remarkable. It was a dungeon, after all. But the pitch of that crying was as high as a sparrow's cheeps.

"It's okay," a voice whispered, hardly any deeper than the one that had been crying. "She'll come for us. You'll see."

Raxa shut her eyes and breathed out in relief. Of course they were in the dungeon. Whoever was keeping them in the Citadel couldn't let their peers see them menacing a bunch of scared children.

She opened her eyes and dropped out of the shadows. "Fedd?"

"Raxa?" Fedd's voice bounced from the end of the hallway. A small, pale hand thrust through the bars of the window set in a cell door. "Is it really you?"

"You were right," she said. "I'm here."

She grabbed the lantern from the wall and jogged to the cell. Fedd drew his hand inside the window. The door was bolted from the outside. Raxa wrenched it open. Inside the cell, six pairs of big bright eyes stared up at her.

Her voice went hoarse. "Is everyone okay?"

Fedd raced toward her. She scooped him up in a hug. The others dashed over, clinging to her legs and hips. They smelled sweaty and fearful, but they looked intact.

She wanted to hold tight to them until her arms gave out. Instead, she gave them each a squeeze, then detached herself and stood. "I need you to follow me. We're going to go down a few tunnels. They'll be dark. They'll smell even worse than this place. But we'll be outside in a few minutes, okay? So no matter what happens, stay quiet and follow me. Got it?"

She looked to each of them in turn, making sure they all nodded their understanding. She stood, lantern in hand, and moved back into the hallway, meaning to return to the cell she'd entered the jail through.

A footstep scraped from the stairwell.

Raxa froze. She'd taken the only lantern in the dungeon. Its light barely reached the far end of the hall, silhouetting a woman whose build looked more than capable of handling the sword that hung from her hand.

Her voice was as clear as the glass in a prince's window. "You're Raxa, aren't you?"

"He told you about me?"

"Warned, more like."

"That must make you the Black Star." Raxa reached for her sword.

The woman twitched up the end of her blade. "Don't move another inch."

"If you think you can hurt me, he must not have told you much."

Cee laughed brightly. "Can I hurt you? Maybe not. But right

above our heads, there are four hundred elite soldiers. Sixty trained nethermancers. If I turn and run, do you think you can catch up to me before they catch up to us?"

"Let's find out." Raxa lurched forward. Quick as a minnow, Cee turned and raced up the steps, shoes echoing in the tight space. Raxa turned back to her kids. "Come on now. Don't stop for a second."

She led them into the cell she'd come in through. The wall was blank, solid rock.

"Stay back." She walked to the wall, raised her sword, and whispered a quick prayer to Carvahal. Just in case, she repeated it to Urt.

She smashed her sword into the wall.

Hitting the stone was the first time she'd felt the blade face real resistance. Even so, it cut cleanly, chips of stone spattering the ground. With one blow after another, she cut a doorway through to the other side. The faint smell of death wafted from the tunnel.

She sheathed the sword and hoisted the lantern. "Don't be afraid. I know the way."

She jogged forward. The six children followed her through the tunnel and into the passages of the carneterium. She didn't slow until they reached the foyer. There, an old man blinked at her and the procession of youngsters. Raxa nodded significantly. He cocked his head but let her pass without a word.

Outside, the sun waned. Summer was gone. Soon, the nights of the northern winter would stretch twice as long as the daylight.

Raxa didn't care for the cold, but she didn't mind the darkness. For people like her, the night was home.

28

Gladdic watched with keen annoyance as the ambush unfolded on the plain.

"Horstad," he said. "Bring me General Billings."

Horstad bobbed his head and hustled away. Gladdic bit his teeth together. It wasn't that he was especially surprised by the attack. He had expected to face difficulties keeping the purification process concealed from the outlying towns. If and when they began to piece together the rumors, he'd had no doubt they would mount an offensive on the city, no matter how desperate their chances. Due to this inevitability, he had, in fact, *planned* to let slip what was happening, both to control the timing of the attack, and to justify counterstrikes against the remainder of the basin.

But that was not supposed to have happened until the city's population had been significantly reduced. Today was quite possibly the worst possible timing.

Even so, having anticipated the event, he was merely annoyed rather than panicked or shocked. For one thing, he already knew exactly how to proceed.

Billings had been stationed in a cave a few switches up from the Cavern of Blessings and was thus able to arrive in less than two minutes. He was the fourth son of the king's brother Lionel, and knowing this, Gladdic had expected him to be surly and resentful of a lifetime of being assigned to tasks such as a (what should have been hopeless) invasion of the Collen Basin. But the man was the opposite. Dedicated to his duty, no matter how low-status it compared to the endeavors of his cousins and older brothers.

"General Billings," Gladdic said. "Our soldiers below are outnumbered. We will send the second garrison to aid them. The second garrison will be accompanied by four of my priests."

Billings, as usual, was far more direct with Gladdic than most dared. "Sir, that may be unwise. There's been heavy movement in the streets. We're expecting a revolt."

"And?"

The general's jaw bulged; he stared as if Gladdic had just ordered him to draw his sword and gut himself. "Am I missing the obvious, Ordon? If we send out the second garrison, most of our soldiers will be committed to the field. With that many priests with them, if the citizens revolt, we may lose Collen."

"The rebels below," Gladdic said. "I've seen no evidence of nethermancers. Have you?"

"I have not."

"Then with the aid of our priests, our army will surely be victorious."

The general nodded stiffly. "If Collen falls in the meantime?"

Gladdic was silent, allowing the man another moment to think this through.

Billings' face went carefully blank. "The demons."

Gladdic offered him a tight smile. "They can rebel, if they wish. But they will have no answer to the Andrac. As this unfolds, our forces below will defeat the Colleners with minimal loss to ourselves, then return to restore order. Move quickly now."

Billings saluted and turned on his heel. With admirable swiftness, he had the soldiers and their attachment of priests heading down the slopes. Gladdic withdrew painted bones from the satchel slung over his shoulder and arranged them on the road in a hexagon with a bent arm extending from one of its vertices.

The symbol was obscene. Like an old man with his pants down. Gladdic had spent the last nine years of his life searching for configurations of bones that would reach into the opposite realm—the ether—but he'd never felt the faintest trace of its presence. At times, his heart's core had feared he couldn't find it because it wasn't there. Because the netherworld was all that awaited the souls of the dead.

Yet this doubt was what Arawn wanted. The poisonousness of the black god's mind was why he'd been locked behind the starry vault. To give in to such doubt was to lay the path for the foul god to return to the world he'd been purged from.

Gladdic closed his eyes and plunged his mind into the abyss of shadows. The Andrac stood still, but he could feel its impatient strength, like the snows of a mountain waiting to tumble down and engulf everything beneath them.

Come, Gladdic told it.

Its eyes blazed with heatless, colorless fire. As if the ether itself burned within its eyes and throat. Gladdic opened his eyes. The demon crossed into the world of the living. Rather than emerging as if it were stepping through a doorway, in defiance of the gods' laws, it unfurled upward, banner-like. A thrill coursed up Gladdic's spine. It was an abomination, yes. But it was his to wield. If he spent it destroying other crimes against the Celeset, the gods could never fault him.

The demon loomed above him. Gladdic refused to step back. *Wait. Soon, my enemies will come—and you will consume them all.*

The violation gnashed its jaws. It held its place. Keeping one eye on the demon, Gladdic turned to watch the field beneath the butte, where the presence of Billings' reinforcements had forced the two rebel columns to stop their pursuit of Gladdic's disguised soldiers. As the rebels attempted to regroup into a single unit, Billings led a charge. Ether sparked from his front lines, visible even in the full light of day.

The two sides clashed. Shouts and the ring of steel on steel floated from below. With the ether blinking on and off like fireflies, the Colleners broke, retreating toward a nearby hill. The bodies they left behind were dark specks against the sun-faded gray of the plain. Gladdic kept watch for the arrival of a third column of rebels. Without further reinforcements, the Collenese rebellion would be smashed within the hour.

A soldier called from the top of the plateau. Gladdic swiveled his head. Five figures broke the heights above. Distant though they were, he knew their shape.

He met eyes with the demon, then returned his eyes to the heights and nodded once, slowly and deeply. *My enemies.*

The Andrac surged toward them, eschewing the switchbacks to bound straight up the hill, as if weightless. During the fighting below, Horstad had returned to stand almost but not quite at Gladdic's side. Watching the demon leap from rock to rock, the secretary did his best to hide his shudder.

Gladdic's mouth twitched. "Does it trouble you?"

Horstad folded his lip between his teeth. "It's not my place to question your methods, lord."

"That's not what I asked."

"I am troubled by its strength. And its...origins."

"Would it surprise you to hear that it troubles me as well?" Gladdic didn't bother to wait for Horstad to find the combination of words the secretary believed wouldn't offend him. "But there is satisfaction from crushing Galand with a weapon every bit as profane as himself. Do you know what troubles me far worse than the Andrac? The vision of remaining mired in an endless war with Collen while Narashtovik continues to corrupt one land after another, until the daylight is gone, and Bressel is no more than a lone fire in the night."

A frown crept over Horstad's face. Above, the Andrac neared the crown of the butte. Galand and Blays Buckler, his pet swordsman, stood in front of their three allies. Yet why were they standing at all? Had Gladdic's strategy in the basin rendered them that desperate? A beguiling thought. But the more beguiling a thought, the less it could be trusted.

Gladdic began to jog up the switchbacked road.

Horstad fell in behind him. Above, the swordsman bent his knees, preparing to meet the demon. Ether flared from the hands of an old woman. Light streamed to Buckler's weapons, shining upon the steel. Gladdic's chest tightened. Where had the ethermancer come from? The Andrac leaped onto the final leg of road and slowed to a confident walk, arms flexed from its sides, clawed fingers contracting and expanding.

Buckler spouted words. No doubt they were the height of wit.

Gladdic couldn't hear them above the crunch of gravel under his feet. The Andrac lunged toward the swordsman. Gleaming blades whirled forth, ripping into the demon's outstretched arms. The demon yanked back its limbs. Shadows sprayed from its wounds, dispersing into the air.

The Andrac swiped a second time. Again, the bright blade cleaved into its arm. This time, the demon dropped back several steps, head cocked in confusion. Untroubled, the swordsman skipped forward.

Gladdic's chest clasped on itself until it felt like his heart would squeeze through his ribs, but he refused to let his pace slacken. Buckler jabbed at the demon. It slipped the thrust and clawed at his face. Buckler reeled back with preternatural quickness, clipping the Andrac's arm with a backhand strike. As Gladdic ran on, man and demon exchanged a flurry of blows. Each time the Andrac was cut open, the shadows congealed on the wound, but pieces of its body were looking thinner. A white dart flew from Dante's hands and pierced the Andrac's chest, opening a hole straight to the other side.

Gladdic's mind split three ways. One mind was curious. The attacks and maneuvers of his foes appeared thoughtful and coordinated. Furthermore, they'd stood their ground as if expecting the confrontation to unfold in this manner. Where had they learned to battle the demons? This tactic of quenching the swordsman's weapons in ether—what tome had that come from? Had they discovered a method to somehow annihilate the Andrac altogether?

A second mind was relieved that the abomination of the demon was being stricken from the world. Though this was at odds with Gladdic's immediate goal, he was glad for the presence of this thought, for it proved he remained holy.

And his third mind was furious. To see the Andrac threatened, yes. But mostly, to see Galand profane the ether through its use.

Gladdic gathered a sphere of purity and sent it streaming toward Galand. As it neared, the nethermancer turned and thrust forth his hand, fingers splayed. Shadows swarmed to him from beneath the rocks of the trail—and, strangely, from the latest wound Buckler had slashed across the Andrac's thigh. The demon grasped at the nether escaping its body, but the shadows slipped through its claws like the water of a rushing stream.

Its body was becoming thinner yet; transparent patches let sunlight shine through. If the demon was dispatched to the netherworld, Gladdic could resummon it. But the bone portal had been spent; he'd need to arrange another. That would take time, which he suddenly had very little of. Of far greater importance, when the demons were banished and resummoned, they grew...unpredictable. No different than a trained bear which, while generally docile, grew furious if gored. Enough to turn on the very person who'd summoned them.

"Horstad." He maintained perfect flatness in his voice. "Bring the remaining priests. Along with all our soldiers who remain on the road."

His secretary nodded, jowls jerking, and rushed downhill.

Fall back, Gladdic sent. *Buy time.*

For a moment, the beleaguered Andrac continued to swipe at the harrying swordsman. Gladdic turned his back and retreated down the path. When next he glanced up, the demon was jumping down to the switchback below the swordsman. Bolts of ether flew after it, slamming into its back.

Gladdic descended one more level, then stopped and knelt. He spilled his bag of bones across the dust, hastening to arrange the hexagon. Finished, he stepped back and shut his eyes.

Come.

The second demon traipsed forward, eager to feed, angry that it had been left in waiting. Up on the slopes, the first creature stumbled. Its body was as thin as mist. Streamers of nether trailed from its shredded arms and trunk.

Its replacement unfurled before Gladdic. He met its dazzling eyes. *Stay back. Help my men hold this road.*

The Andrac stared down at him. *Feed.*

Gladdic shook his head. *First you must –*

FEED!

Gladdic pointed uphill. The wounded Andrac hauled itself from where it had fallen. From the old woman's hands, ether streamed through the air like lines of light drawn across the page of the sky. They hit the demon at five different points. Its silhouette flickered, fading until the rocks were visible behind it, then vanished.

It wished to feed as well, he sent. *Wait until the time is right, and thousands will be yours.*

The demon opened and shut its jaws. When Gladdic turned, it followed him downslope.

Horstad met him in the company of five men in the gray of Taim and thirty more in the blue of the king.

"Hold the road." Gladdic pointed down to a spot halfway between them and the enemy. "Allow them no further than that."

He hurried downhill. The silence behind him made him glance over his shoulder. His priests were watching him go, faces blanched. His blood heated—they were so faithless they thought he was abandoning them, running away to save himself. They deserved no reply.

But perhaps he deserved to make one. Most people, priests and common folk alike, held pride to be a sin. Yet wasn't Taim proud? And didn't he have the right to be?

"Do you think you are our last line of defense?" Gladdic let his laughter peal up the cliffs. "Retain your faith. I have powers of which they can't dream."

With a sweep of robes, he turned away and hurried on. By the time he reached the Cavern of Blessings, his priests were engaged with the enemy. Black and white sparks rained from above. Galand and his minions had halted, however.

Gladdic entered the cave. Despite the efforts of those who cleaned it, the room stank of blood and offal. He had almost grown used to it. Perhaps it wasn't entirely the fault of lazy servants. After all, bones were laid out along the base of the walls, ringing the entire room. The bones were quite fresh, as bones went, but the marrow inside them was starting to rot.

He closed his eyes and reached out. The stains of the dead ran together like drops of juice squeezed from an orange. As they joined, Gladdic gasped at what he wrought.

EDWARD W. ROBERTSON

29

The fight with the Andrac went off as smoothly as a stroll down the king's road.

Coated in ether, Blays' swords ripped into the darkness of its body one lash after another. Dante and the Keeper stood ready to harry it with bolts of light, but once it became clear Blays was as apt at dueling the full-sized demon as he had been with the miniature one they'd practiced on, the two sorcerers hung back, conserving their strength.

Only when Blays faltered did they hammer it with more light — and then again at the end, when the demon began to grow faint. As Dante and the Keeper pelted it with ether, a scintillating bolt winged up from down the road. Gladdic. Dante smiled grimly and reached for the nether. Shadows streamed from the packed dirt and broken rocks of the trail. Others flowed from around the fraying demon, where the air was fuzzy with loose nether. The demon jerked back, as if stung, but Dante couldn't see the source of its troubles: the Keeper hadn't struck it, and Blays stood back from it, regaining his footing after the last encounter.

The incoming bolt was only a blink away. Dante batted it aside in a spray of twinkling motes. Below them, Gladdic said something to his portly assistant, who trotted away. Blays and the demon clashed again and the Andrac came away leaking nether from three fresh wounds. Gladdic turned and hurried down the trail. The Andrac jumped from the road onto the slope below. The Keeper hurled ethereal darts into its back, stumbling it long enough to allow Blays to catch up. Downhill, Gladdic stopped and dumped out a bag of slender white objects—bones.

Naran moved beside Dante, saber in hand. "Is he fleeing? We must stop him!"

"I'd say he's calling another demon," Dante said. "So unless you want to be close enough that, when it arrives, you can reach out and shake its claws on a good job being summoned, I suggest you stay put. Cord!"

She moved forward with a grin, wheel tucked under her right arm. "About time I got the chance to sweep this foulness from my city."

"And you'll be accomplishing that task by going to get the city's rebels."

"Who are you to give me orders?"

Downhill, Blays' shining blades sliced at the fading Andrac, knocking it from its feet.

"In a moment, we'll kick that thing back into the nether," Dante said. "And we'll do the same to the next one Gladdic throws at us. After that, we'll have him—if we have the manpower to go forward."

She tipped back her head. "I'll see that we do."

Cord turned and dashed up the road. Ether flew from the Keeper's hand, separating into five tendrils. When they tore into the Andrac, it vanished into the netherworld.

Further down the hill, however, a second shadow stood beside Gladdic.

"I wish these things had faces," Blays called from a level below. "I would have loved to see the look on the demon's face when it got beaten by a human."

Gladdic turned and the demon followed. Dante motioned the others downhill. A body of troops emerged from one of the shops carved into the cliff walls, rushing up to meet Gladdic. Most were common infantry, but a handful of gray-robed ethermancers moved among them.

"Priests," Dante muttered. "Blays, you handle the Andrac. The Keeper and I will keep the sorcerers off you. Naran, eyes sharp for Cord's return or any surprises."

The first surprise came moments later when Gladdic continued to retreat rather than face them, leaving his demon alongside the reinforcements. A few bolts of ether flew up from below, probing strikes which Dante turned aside with minimal expenditure of nether. Blays stood with swords ready, but the new Andrac stayed close to the Mallish, gazing up with its silvery eyes.

The two sides came to a halt some fifty vertical feet away. Dante continued to swat down the testing spears of ether, firing back just enough counterattacks to keep the priests honest. Below, Gladdic disappeared inside a cavern. Did he have a secret passage to the basin floor? Then again, if he wanted to escape, all he had to do was continue down the road; his soldiers had battled off the army of the six towns, driving them to regroup in the hills to the west.

Dante moved into the nether in the cliffs above the priests, looking to bring the rocks crashing down on their heads, but the men were wary for such things and knocked his focus loose from the stone. His second effort fared no better.

For several minutes, the fighting on the switchbacks slowed. With both sides conserving strength, it was less like a pitched battle for the city and more like a lawn game played with paddles, a net, and pairs of lords too drunk to keep score.

"Cord!" Naran shouted. "She returns!"

At the top of the road, silhouettes stood against the sky. Cord thrust up her wheel and bellowed. Dozens of soldiers spilled onto the road, ribbons of all colors fluttering from their elbows. Others bore no markers of shrines—common citizens rallied to the cause.

Blays punched his fist into the air and whooped. Dante turned back to the priests, but they'd already begun to move down the road. The Andrac lingered at the rear of the column, watching Blays.

"What's our next move?" Blays said. "I say we clear the road, stick Gladdic's head on the largest spike we can find, and then go drink the largest beer we can find."

Dante brought the nether to his palms. "That was the deal. Once Gladdic and the demons are gone, the rest is up to the Colleners."

He started downhill, slowly enough to let Cord's warriors catch up, but fast enough to stay relatively close to the Mallish withdrawal. As the enemy passed the stretch of road where Gladdic had disappeared, Dante rocked to a stop.

A black river gushed from the mouth of a cavern. At first, Dante thought Gladdic had unleashed the pools within the butte to wash out the road and cover their retreat. Then the river bent to the right and flowed uphill. Within moments, it was thirty feet long and eight across. A thinner black rivulet stretched up the rutted trail.

A huge round glob swiveled from the front of the flow. Silver eyes the size of melons opened and fixed on Dante.

Even then, he didn't understand what he was seeing until the Andrac opened its mouth and revealed the star burning within its mouth.

Among the Collenese soldiers, a grown man screamed. Dante's own throat was too dry to do so. Downhill from the cavern, the Mallish priests broke into a dead run, opening space between them and the gigantic demon.

"Oh," Blays said. "*Shit.*"

"Get back!" Dante yelled to Cord. "Back up the hill!"

Cord couldn't tear her eyes away from the Andrac, but her mouth moved of its own accord, relaying orders to the city's soldiers. Dante ran uphill, accompanied by Blays and Naran. The Keeper, who'd been lagging at the rear, stood transfixed as the Andrac finished flowing out of the cavern. Now fifty feet long, it got to its knees and stretched its arms above its head. Its claws were as long as a man's arm from elbow to fingertip.

Dante grabbed the Keeper's bony shoulder. She lurched forward, moving upward with a speed he didn't know she was capable of.

"Run, Galand!" Gladdic's voice thundered from below, amplified through some trick of the ether. "Yet I'll find you wherever you go. The darkness of your soul is a beacon stronger than the sun."

Be that as it may, Dante ran as fast as he could. Outside the cavern, the Andrac dug its claws into the cliff and pulled itself to its full height of fifty feet. It took a step uphill, then wobbled, leaning against the cliffs for support.

"It's like a newborn," Dante said.

Blays goggled between him and the demon. "I would offer condolences to the father for the explosion of the mother, but by the look of that thing, the father must be an angry god."

"I thought he was summoning them. But he's creating them. He must have used the traces of all the people he's slaughtered."

"Please tell me this revelation has come with a plan to kill it."

"Sure. I figured we'd throw you at it same as the last one."

They ran on. The demon shook out its legs and stamped its feet, blasting vast waves of dust from the road. Cord's troops spilled onto the top of the butte.

The light on Blays' swords was starting to fade. "Really though, what *is* the plan?"

"I think," Dante said, "we lose."

"There has to be a way out of this."

"Maybe if my sorcerers were here. But I don't see how we fight that thing. The Keeper and I don't even have the power to banish a person-sized Andrac."

"Right. But I do."

"Wonderful," Dante snapped. "How is that going to help us do away with the tower-sized Andrac? Do you really think you can fight it alone?"

Blays fell silent, words lost in favor of the rasp of their breath, the thump of their feet, and the rattle of scabbards and armor.

"No," Blays said. "But I don't have to be alone. You and the Keeper can coat Cord's wheel in ether, too. And the weapons of all of her friends."

"None of these people have ever fought a Star-Eater."

"What's there to know? It's just like fighting a person. Who takes dozens of blows to kill and only one to kill you. And in this case is also a giant."

Reflexively, Dante had pegged it as a terrible idea. As he ran on, however, it seemed less absurd. Cord and Naran had dueled the tiny Andrac, hadn't they? Why couldn't the Colleners stand and fight now?

He spared a glance downhill. The massive demon took a hesitant step upward. "Think they'll go for it?"

"If it helped to defeat the Mallish, these people would swallow a live rooster. Anyway, if it wasn't so easy to talk soldiers into hopeless causes, there would be no kingdoms at all."

Dante went to the Keeper and told her the plan. She looked even graver than usual. "Many will die. But this is the only answer I see."

The top of the road hung above them, a single turn of the road away. Below, the Andrac neared the bend of a switchback and climbed up to the next one as if it was a step. Dante scrambled to the top of the plateau. There, a few Colleners were fleeing headlong into the city, but most remained in a tight bunch. Dante found Cord and hastily explained the idea.

Dante motioned to the top of the road. "When it steps forth, do you think they'll lose their nerve?"

"Only a fool wouldn't fear the demon," Cord said. "But you know what I fear worse? Losing my lands to the man who made that monster."

She moved to her soldiers, who now numbered over two hundred, with more entering the plaza by the second. The Keeper went from person to person, bathing their swords and the tips of their wheels with light. Dante spent most of his remaining ether recoating Blays' swords and Naran's saber, then unsheathed his blade and treated it, too. So far, the Keeper had emblazoned twenty blades and was still going.

"It's coming!" a woman yelled from the edge of the road. "The demon nears!"

Dante's heart thumped in his ears. His palm sweated on the hilt of his sword. Far from the first time, he wished he'd brought the sword of Barden with him to Gallador. There had been no need to have it during the peaceful work on the tunnel he'd been building for the merchants—he'd been concerned about it being lost or stolen—but he should have learned long ago that, for him, there was no such thing as peace.

A black sun rose from the edge of the cliffs. Sandals rasped on gravel as dozens of Cord's warriors stepped back. The Andrac's eyes crested the ridge, followed by the searing light within its throat, which silhouetted fangs as long as a man's hand. It planted its hand in the dirt, fingers spread wide enough to snatch a horse. Two-foot claws scraped stone and sank into the earth.

Blays grimaced. "I don't suppose it will listen to reason?"

As it stepped onto the surface of the butte, steel clanged. A score of Collenese soldiers had dropped their weapons to run away with all their speed. Two of the fallen arms shined with ether. A pair of soldiers flung aside their mundane blades and picked up the treated weapons, staring up at the towering Andrac. Swords wobbled in shaky hands. The point of Dante's blade twitched, too, but watching the wonder of the soldiers standing their ground against the black titan, a coolness entered his veins.

With a boom, the Andrac stepped forward.

The Keeper was still painting other blades with shimmering white. Dante's mind raced, searching for a strategy of attack. To his right, Cord shouted orders, obviating his need to find an idea. Six soldiers edged forward, blades glowing. They kept themselves well separated from each other. The demon stopped. With no pupils in its eyes, it was difficult to tell where it was looking, but it seemed to be focused on their weapons.

Cord trotted forward, wheel held in two hands. The Andrac swung its leg forward, closing on her in a single stride. It dipped its hips and raked its claws toward her. She fell on her back, its claws whisking over her, and swung up her wheel, gashing through the demon's palm as it passed by.

Shadows gushed from the wound. The demon yanked back its hand and opened its jaws wide, roaring with a sound like wind over crackling logs.

Cord sprung to her feet, pointing her wheel at its palm. "It bleeds. Whatever bleeds can die!"

With a cry, her six soldiers ran toward the monster's legs. White weapons jabbed and slashed its shins, spilling shadows. Dozens of other Colleners yelled and charged. More than half of them bore weapons of plain metal.

Naran gripped his saber. "Gentlemen. Shall we?"

Blays looked ready to offer a rejoinder, then his face blanked, too focused on the task for words. He ran forward. Feeling insane, Dante followed.

Soldiers hacked at the demon's legs like they were trying to chop down a pitch black tree. Claws swooshed through the air. A soldier fell prone, attempting to mimic Cord's maneuver, but the Star-Eater caught on, ripping its claws along the dirt. They shredded into the man's torso. Blackening hunks of meat spun through the air.

The demon was now "bleeding" from dozens of wounds, nether swirling about it in a dark fog. But its steps didn't appear hampered in the slightest. And the first cuts it had suffered were already knitting shut. As Dante neared, the Andrac crouched and swept its claw in an arc around its legs. Its claws sliced a woman in half. Its palm crashed into another man. His legs snapped like timbers, but in small consolation, no part of his body went dark.

The Andrac's foot came down ten feet from Dante. He ran forward, wheeling his sword and slamming it into the demon's foot. Nether burst free like silent steam. Typically, the shadows were odorless, but these carried the tang of worms crushed beneath clean iron.

Claws whisked over the field, sending bodies flying. Soldiers jumped to hack at the demon's fingers. It lifted its foot and stomped on a soldier, paving stones cracking under its heel. Dante cut through the back of its ankle, but any hope of crippling the creature faded as it stepped again, trampling another man flat.

Dante glanced at Blays to ask if they had any chance. The stretched, pained look on Blays' face was answer enough. Claws hissed downward. Dante was thrust into their shadow. He tossed himself to the stones, the wind of the claws passing over his back.

He pushed himself to his feet. Already, twenty bodies scattered the grounds, half blackened with the taint of the demon's claws, the others merely crushed. Soldiers darted between legs and ducked beneath claws, chopping at anything they could reach. The Andrac scooped up the closest man, tipped back its head, and bit the soldier in half. It tossed the hips and legs aside like the green sprig of a carrot.

The Colleners with un-ethered weapons had started to flee.

Several with glowing swords were standing back, sweaty hair plastered to their temples as they examined the Andrac for signs of damage.

Cord stepped back, too. Her face was sheened with sweat and the blood of a cut on her left eyebrow. "Despair defeats more men than steel. It bleeds—and it *will* die!"

She leveled her wheel and dashed toward the demon. Spying her, it swung its foot forward like the ram of a siege engine. Cord juked to the side, but the Andrac moved with terrible speed, the outer edge of its foot clipping her ribs. With an audible snap of bone, Cord flew fifteen feet back and to the side, landing in a motionless heap.

A woman raced to her side, skidding in the dust. A man gawked at her. "She's dead. And what did she expect? Fighting a *demon?*"

Without another word, the man broke into a dead run toward the buildings across the square. As if that were their cue, the survivors disengaged, following in the man's wake. The Star-Eater tipped back its head and gave its crackling, windy scream. In moments, Dante, Blays, and Naran were the only ones within thirty feet of the beast, with the Keeper standing back.

"Ah," Blays said. "Run?"

Before Dante could agree, the Andrac lumbered forward. Dante prepared to open the ground beneath himself, but the monster's eyes were locked on the scores of soldiers who were still retreating into the city beyond. It bounded past.

Dante swerved toward Cord, kneeling beside her. Blood leaked from scrapes on her face and hands. Her eyes were closed. Dante put his fingers to her neck. A pulse beat softly.

"She's alive." Dante drew on the shadows and sank them into Cord's skin, sending them to her broken ribs and gouged organs. Beneath the layers of blood and dust, the damage melted away.

She groaned, hand spasming. Her eyes fluttered open. "Did we win?"

"Not exactly." Across the square, the Andrac hammered its fist into the corner of a building, spraying bricks into the street. Dante reached out a hand. "Are you strong enough to stand?"

Cord snorted and pushed herself to her feet. No sooner was

she standing than she swayed, clamping Dante's shoulder for support. "What..?"

"We weren't enough. Come on." Before any new threats could climb up from the switchbacks, Dante led her and the others to the buildings to the east.

Screams carried from the north. Often, the Andrac's chest and head were visible above the rooftops. More than once, a body tumbled through the air before disappearing into the row houses.

"Keeper," Dante said. "How much ether do you have left to command?"

"Little," she croaked.

"Same here." They drew alongside a row of shuttered shops. As the buildings' shadows crossed over them, a heaviness settled on Dante's shoulders. "Cord, we can't beat this thing. What do you want to do?"

"To do." Cord blinked slowly; he guessed her mind was still fuzzed. "If we try to fight, we'll be slaughtered. But if we flee to one of the towns, it's only a matter of time before Gladdic comes for us there. What *can* we do?"

Blays examined the sword in his right hand. "At the risk of offending your pride with a pragmatic idea, you could leave the basin."

The Keeper widened her stance. "And if we depart our homes for now, will Narashtovik help us retake them?"

"I can't promise that," Dante said.

"Then we can't leave. Without Collen, what are the Colleners?"

"Alive," Cord said. Teeth bared in anguish, she pressed her fist against her brow. "Where will we go?"

Dante gestured north. "There's plenty of empty land around Narashtovik. We still have housing in the city, too. There's no need to die here."

The Keeper shot him a poisonous glance, then turned on Cord. "You can't contemplate this. We have *never* left our homeland. Leaving means turning our backs on what our ancestors have spent a thousand years fighting for."

"I thought the fight itself was what mattered," Cord murmured. "The noblest act of all. But I've never had to look out for anyone but myself. Now that I speak for so many people, I wonder how noble it is to commit them to die."

"Nobler than to let the Mallish take our home as their own!"

In the distance, the Andrac gave another gusty, crackling bellow. Cord pointed in the sound's direction. "Do you know how to kill that thing?"

The Keeper went silent.

"Then if we stay, it kills *us*. And our culture with us. But if we leave?" Cord grinned. It wasn't happy, nor wry, but the grin of a warrior who'd battled through a night she thought would never end and now looks out on the dawn. "We take our culture with us. And we, and it, live on." She gave Dante a nod. "We evacuate the city."

"We'll buy you as much time as we can," he said. "But that's going to be a lot less time than you'd like."

"Then I'd better quit wasting it." She grinned again and took off at a jog.

Dante sighed through his nose, searching the rooftops for the Andrac. "I can't believe I've signed us up to fight that thing again."

"I made no such vow," the Keeper said. "Nor to leave. The only vow I'm bound to is the one to keep my people's history safe. I will return to the Reborn Shrine." She turned and tottered down the road to the east.

Dante laughed humorlessly. "When the Mallish make this city theirs, who's going to send food down to you? If you stay in the shrine, a month from now, you'll be dead. And your lore will die with you."

The Keeper turned halfway, her washed-out blue eye as cold as chips of ice. "What other choice do I have?"

"Escape today. And come back here with me tomorrow night. I'll open a tunnel to your library. We'll get out as many books as we can. Your apprentices, too."

"Why would you do this? Because you care for Collen that much?"

"No," he said. "Because I care for history. And knowledge. With access to the struggles of those who came before us, we can stride beyond where they had to stop. Their wisdom is more valuable than a mountain of gold. When we lose our past, our future gets that much further away."

The old woman's shoulders sagged. "You make it sound so easy to break my vows. But that doesn't make them any less broken."

Men barked orders near the cliff's edge. Dante thought he heard Gladdic's voice. "All they'll think they have to do is hold onto the road while the Andrac does its work. Let's slow it down long enough for Cord to evacuate as many people as she can."

The Keeper closed her eyes and nodded. He led them north. Often, the buildings were packed too tight to see the demon, but the sound of shattering masonry was a dead giveaway for its location. The screams were another. Garbage and waste strewed the streets. Most of the refuse looked at least a week old, the product of an occupation that cared nothing for the city. A few stray cats poked through the leavings, scampering from sight as soon as they saw Dante.

Within a few blocks, fresh rubble lay heavy in the streets. Bodies studded the broken bricks. Most of the dead were unremarkably crushed, but many showed the blackened wounds of the Andrac. Holes gaped in the faces of buildings, which dribbled pebbles into the road, threatening to collapse. Dante moved as fast as he could across the uneven sprawl.

The demon roared again, the sound unnatural and ghastly. Three blocks north, its head and shoulders stood above the rooftops. Dante took them to the east, stopping at the corner of a pottery shop.

Two blocks away, the Andrac smashed its fist through the roof of a building, sending chunks of gray bricks racketing through the street. Like a bear scooping out a honeycomb, it reached inside the exposed room and grabbed two men. They wailed as the creature lifted them to its mouth and chewed, letting the pieces tumble carelessly to the road forty feet below its churning jaws. For all the damage Cord's soldiers had inflicted on it during the initial battle, it appeared completely unscathed.

Hand on the corner of the potter's shop, Dante stared dumbly at the demon. "How did we think we were going to do this again?"

"Oh, did we have a plan?" Blays whispered. "I assumed we'd made yet another promise we couldn't possibly keep."

With the demon's back turned, a young woman crept from a doorway and jogged toward the corner to the west. She moved in almost perfect silence, but the demon whirled, closed on her, and clenched her in its fist. It lifted its arm and bashed her head and torso through a roof, smearing blood across the broken tiles.

"Well," Naran said stonily. "I don't recommend we fight it."

The Andrac dropped the remains of the woman's body and moved on. Dante swore softly. When things got rough, his first instinct was always to hurl as much nether at the problem as he could safely summon. Usually, that was enough.

At other times, though, the best magic was the subtlest.

He called to the nether, feeding it with a cut on his right elbow he'd suffered in their first encounter, and directed it into the least-destroyed bodies he could see. Four corpses hauled themselves to their feet like bloody marionettes. He sent them running in opposite directions as fast as their mangled legs could manage. At a clatter of stone, the Andrac spun. It leaped on the first of the zombies, tearing it in half.

Dante ordered its legs to dash away while the torso clawed its way through the debris. The Andrac pounced on the legs, gnawed them to pieces, and did the same to the torso. Running down and slaughtering the remaining three zombies wasted a good minute of the demon's time.

When the street was motionless again, the titan threw back its head and bellowed in triumph. It stalked up to the next block. Dante followed. There, it tore open several buildings, laying waste to those who tried to hide. Unable to help them, Dante consoled himself with the thought that their deaths would grant time for others to escape.

Again, he lifted the bodies up into undeath. The Andrac spent little time dispatching them. But when it turned around to advance up the street, it found itself facing a solid brick wall—an image Dante had summoned while the demon was distracted. The Andrac cocked its head, then glanced down the street, considering an alternate route. Rejecting the idea of detouring, it waded into the side of one of the row houses it had already torn into and smashed its way clear to the other side.

"Not all that bright, is it?" Dante murmured.

Blays shrugged. "When you're that big, you don't *have* to be smart."

Dante advanced northward, keeping even with the demon. His control of the nether remained tight, but at his current pace, he'd exhaust himself in less than an hour. Cord would need more time than that. As the Andrac ripped its claws into another building, Dante sent the nether to the middle of the street and shaped it into the figure of a young man.

He hadn't been practicing his illusions in some time and the work was far from his best. The figure was recognizably humanoid, however—two legs, two arms, a head, some smudges that more or less resembled a face—and this was enough to send the Andrac running toward it. As the demon neared, Dante sent the figure dashing right through the creature's towering legs.

The Andrac spun to give chase. Dante moved the young man inside a doorway, obligating the demon to tear into the facade. Dust billowed in choking clouds as it clawed enormous handfuls of bricks across the street. When the building was nothing but rubble, Dante sent the illusion skipping away to the west.

The demon lashed at it. Dante made the image fling itself prone, but from his vantage, the claws clearly passed through the young man's back. Oblivious, the Andrac chased on. The illusion swerved inside another three-story home. Dutifully, the demon began to clobber this one to shards as well.

"A neat trick," Naran said. "How many times do you suppose the beast will continue to fall for it?"

"This Star-Eater seems more foolish than the others." Dante shifted against the wall of the tavern they were hiding behind. "Probably because it's so young. But they're capable of learning. We've bought Cord half an hour, but if we want to give her the chance to clear the city, we're going to need to come up with a lot more ideas."

Down the street, the demon completed the demolition of the house. This time, it anticipated the young man's sprint for new cover, grabbing him up. Only the illusion squirted free and ran on.

The Andrac straightened, regarding the retreating figure. The demon's limbs stilled. After a long moment, it turned its head and looked directly at the corner Dante peeked from behind.

Dante jerked from sight. "It knows."

Its footsteps thundered down the road, shattering the paving setts.

"Spread out and run!" Dante brought the nether to his hands. "Regroup at Cord's well."

Before any of them could argue, he ran into the street. Already, the demon was within a stride and a half. Dante thrust his right hand forward. A flock of shadows swarmed the demon's head, condensing around it into a shadowsphere. The creature gave one of its crackling shouts, but this one was higher-pitched — confusion and outrage.

It ran on, wheeling its arms for balance. Dante took a quick look behind him. He couldn't see where Blays had gone. Having given the Keeper his arm, Naran was cutting to the east, long legs churning. Blinded, the Andrac tripped past Dante, colliding into the four-story tenement across the street. The demon tumbled to the ground in an avalanche of bricks. The building came down with it, spilling over Naran and the Keeper.

Dante's wordless shout was drowned out by the clamor of the tenement's collapse. Half-buried, the Andrac writhed, clawing for purchase. Dante took off at a dead run to the north. His mind was numb, but he kept the ball of darkness locked firmly around the demon's head.

At the next intersection, he swung east, skidding on the flat, rectangular stones. He was halfway to the next block when he heard the Andrac thump to its feet and unleash an airy bellow.

After another block, he veered back to the north. The demon's feet boomed behind him. Closer with each step. It was still blind; could it hear him? Detect him through some unknown sense? Yet it hadn't seemed to be able to sense that his illusions weren't flesh — or to detect him until it had learned the figure *was* an illusion. Then it had come straight for him. As if following a path.

Or the tendril of nether connecting him to his illusion.

He dropped the shadowsphere. The demon's steps halted.

Dante ran on, zagging between the north and the east. After a few moments, claws scraped on stone. Brick crashed to the street. At an intersection, he glimpsed the demon laying waste to another row house.

Five minutes later, with his lungs burning, Dante drifted to a stop. The streets around him were as silent as fresh snow. To the south, the Andrac was still pounding away on the cityscape, drawing screams from everyone it exposed, but it was at least half a mile away.

He leaned against a shuttered woodworker's shop. Fear and despair threatened to drown his heart. Had Blays made it out? Or had he fallen, too? Dante didn't think so—Blays had more tricks than a brothel—but it had happened so fast.

The only thing to do was to head to the well and wait. While he was still catching his breath, footsteps approached at a jog. Dante took the nether in hand, shaping it into a killing blade.

Blays rounded the corner, noting him at once. Breathing hard, the blond man gave a short nod. "Shadowalked out. Followed you."

"Naran and the Keeper," Dante said. "The building fell on them."

"A better death than the Colleners are getting."

Dante glanced up at the sky. The sun was still climbing, warming the morning. "It's been less than an hour since Cord left. She can't have had time to save more than a fraction of the city."

"Do you want to go back? Run the Andrac around some more?"

"Won't work. It figured out what I was doing. If I try again, it'll trace the nether right back to me."

"I could try this time," Blays said. "Maybe things will be different in the netherworld."

"How so? Are you planning to grow ten times as tall? Or bring your sword to life, teach it to fight on its own, and grow *it* ten times as tall? We had a small army against the Andrac and we still failed. If we try to fight or distract it again, we'll die. And I'm not dying today. Not for these people."

"What's that look for? I don't want to go back there any more than you do."

"Is that so? Sometimes I think you'd sacrifice yourself for an elderly milk cow if it looked at you sadly enough."

Blays ran his hand down his face. Dust stuck to the sweat and blood dewing his skin. "I would have died for the norren. I might have for the Kandeans. But this place..."

"I know. It's different."

They gazed at each other. The words didn't need to be spoken. Dante didn't know if he *could* speak them. Led by Gladdic, the Mallish were attempting to commit a heinous crime. There was no forgiving it, no justifying it; everyone with the glimmer of a soul would condemn it out of hand, recognize it at once as blasphemy against life.

Dante had been happy to help the Colleners resist this fate. But there were limits to his commitment. Limits which ran deeper than the desire to protect his own life, or the fact that the Colleners, while sympathetic, weren't his people. Centuries of fighting had warped them. Turned them into people who would slaughter disarmed Mallish soldiers as readily as the Mallish would slaughter them.

Dante couldn't blame them. Yet he couldn't die for them, either. All that remained was to walk away.

"We'll head for the well," Dante said. "Try to find Cord. And get out as many people as we can before the Mallish catch on or the Andrac comes for us."

He struck northeast toward the well. Blays roved beside him, eyes darting to the movement of every pigeon and mouse. Thoughts of Naran and the Keeper hovered above Dante like a cloud of mosquitos, but the reality of their loss couldn't sink into his mind any more than oil could sink beneath water. Twice, they heard the furor of fighting on nearby streets, but they did nothing to get involved.

As they neared the well, a handful of bedraggled people appeared on the road before them. The citizens turned fearfully, shrinking into the cover of buildings as Dante and Blays jogged past. The well's carved arches and pillars stood in the mid-morning sunshine like rugged bones exposed from a dune of sand. Frightened voices carried from the depths, echoing in the shimmery way of words in the presence of standing water.

Dante moved down the steps. Scores of people were packed into the chamber with the pool, faces lit by the flutter of torches. The air smelled of stagnant water and stale sweat. Some of those in the chamber were soldiers, but many were young children or white-haired elders with crooked backs. Dante passed among them, asking after Cord.

"She's gone to Trapp Square," said a man with a gold elbow-ribbon. "Many people hid there when the Mallish raised the alarm of war."

"You need to start getting people through to the other side," Dante said. "There's no stopping the demon. It could arrive at any moment."

The soldier nodded uncertainly. Dante secured directions to Trapp Square, which was located a half mile to the east. He jogged into the daylight, orienting himself to the dome of the Reborn Shrine, and headed for the square.

"How many people do you suppose were down there?" Blays' voice was as colorless as an old rag. "Three hundred?"

"Thereabouts."

"Out of a city of thirty thousand. We barely made the swim to the other side. All those kids, old people—how many of them do you think will make it?"

"More than none."

Blays laughed strangely. "For all our efforts, we'll save a few dozen lives. I can't wait to have children so I can tell them the story of how I heroically let tens of thousands of Colleners die."

Dante's boots slapped the street as he ran. He was used to being the one who questioned the point. The one who wondered whether it would have been better not to have tried at all. Seeing Blays this way, he was taken by the gut-deep fear of a responsibility he wasn't sure he could discharge.

"We came to the basin with three people," Dante said. "They had an army. Fronted by monsters no one's ever defeated before. This might not feel like victory, but we're lucky to be leaving with our own lives, let alone some of the citizens."

Blays ran beside him in silence.

"What more could we have done?" The words spilled from

Dante. "We've saved these people from starvation. Spent weeks learning to fight the demons. Rallied the towns to come here and seize the opportunity to throw the Mallish off their backs. I hate this just as much as you do. But when I look back on this day, once the regret and anger have faded, I know what I'll feel: pride. The kind that only comes from knowing you did everything you could. From having fought so hard that even when your enemies tell the story, all those who listen will bow their heads and wish they'd known you."

Blays remained silent. The flatness of his expression shifted, growing thoughtful. His eyes lit up. "Look."

Dante followed his gaze. Hundreds of yards to the south, the black head of the Andrac bobbed on a path nearly parallel to theirs. The creature moved with deceptive speed, striding between the buildings like a grown man walked among children. Watching it—its bulk, its power, the empty blackness of its form and the painful whiteness of its eyes—Dante grew dizzy. Within moments, its long strides carried it past them.

Blays grunted. "It's heading for the shrine."

Dante kept one eye out for Cord and another on the progress of the Andrac. As Blays predicted, it neared the shrine, one of the few buildings in the city taller than it was. The demon stopped. A voice carried from the east. Furious. Defiant. Dante couldn't make out the words, but there was no mistaking the deep bleat of the voice.

Dante's jaw dropped. "That's the Keeper."

"She survived!" The excitement in Blays' eyes cooled like a just-forged sword quenched in water. "She can't stand against that thing by herself."

"But we may be able to get her away from it."

Still running eastward, they exchanged a long look. As it had been when they'd decided to abandon the fight and go to the well, their conversation was wordless. Minutes ago, Dante had been ready to leave. Perhaps it was the speech he'd just given. Or perhaps it was the roar of hope he heard in the Keeper's booming voice.

"One last stand," he said. "Just long enough to grab the Keeper. Then our job is done."

They broke into an all-out sprint. The shrine was only a quarter of a mile away, but every second dragged like a sledge through dry sand. The Andrac stooped from sight. When it reappeared, three bodies soared into the air, limbs twirling. The Keeper's shouts held strong. The demon lifted a young woman to its eight-inch teeth and chewed. Even as the warrior died, she jabbed her shining wheel at the Andrac's eye.

Light flashed brighter than the sun. The Andrac swayed back, crunching into the side of one of the shrine's lesser towers. Impossible hope flared in Dante's chest. Then the beast righted itself, screamed its crackling scream, and swept its claws toward the ground.

Dante burst into the grounds around the shrine. There, bluecoats skirmished with wheel-wielding Colleners. Whenever the Andrac stomped their way, soldiers on both sides scattered like baitfish. The shrine's roof was pocked with holes. The carefully tended shrubs and flowers were trampled flat, littered with bodies and dismembered limbs.

"There she is." Blays pointed his sword, but Dante's eyes had already been drawn to the white sparks forming in the Keeper's hands. She stood outside the doors of the shrine, yelling to her dwindling soldiers. Her tan cloak was torn, bright with blood.

Dante wasn't the only one drawn by the light. The Andrac launched across the plaza toward the Keeper. Light sizzled from her hands, striking it in the face. It didn't so much as slow down.

Nether coiled in Dante's hand. He hurled it at the demon, wrapping its head in a ball of darkness. The Andrac staggered and stopped.

"Keeper!" Dante yelled. "Get out while—!"

The demon spun and charged him, its course unerring despite the shadows locked around its head—it had learned to let go of its sight and follow the nethereal connection instead. Dante dashed to the side. A silver spear pierced the Star-Eater's back, but it didn't seem to notice. It was already upon him, swinging its claws down toward his head. He flung himself to his right, rolling as he struck the setts. He popped to his feet, but the Andrac was already slashing toward him again, its claws scraping over the pavement.

Dante reached into the earth and commanded the stone to rise. It shot eight feet upward, walling him off from the incoming blow. The beast's claws slammed into the rock. Chunks of basalt pounded into Dante's turned back, knocking him from his feet.

With a groan, the rest of the wall gave way, pinning him to the ground.

30

It was a perfect afternoon. The sun glowed overhead with the soft warmth of fall, welcome after the morning's cold dew. That same dew hinted at the hardness of the winter on its way, but that only made the warmth all the sweeter.

A shadow fell over Dante's face. To all sides, men shrieked in fear and pain. His back and ribs hurt, but he knew that, like that touch of dew, the ache was the smallest taste of the cold to come.

He twisted his neck. Above him, two-foot claws jutted from stubby fingers and a palm big enough to lift a rain barrel like a cup. Andrac. Star-Eater. Dante tried to push himself to his feet, but something was holding him down. A rock. The one he'd summoned. It had stopped the demon's strike, saving his life.

And then it had fallen on him. Breaking his bones. Leaving him helpless to the Andrac's next blow.

The demon towered above him. The monsters were almost expressionless, but it appeared to be confused—likely because Dante's injuries had caused him to drop the shadowsphere from its eyes. This bought him a few seconds as the Andrac shook its head, reorienting itself. Small consolation. Or maybe one last piece of misfortune: it gave him that many more seconds of pain to live out.

A smear arced from the tower to his left, falling swiftly toward the demon. A trick of his eye as his body gave out? The smear cohered into the outline of a man. One carrying a blazing sword in each hand.

Blays landed on the demon's side with a thump, stabbing his swords into its chest. The Star-Eater squealed, straightening. Blays removed one blade from the Andrac and inserted it an arm's length above the other, hauling himself up the monster's body.

Dante's head buzzed like a ball of bees, but an instinct older and deeper than words told him what to do next. He reached into the rock, melting it into mud. It flowed away from him. He inhaled hard, pain knifing into him as his ribs expanded. Broken. He was bleeding from a dozen blunt gashes, too.

But the presence of his blood meant the nether was already there. Dante reached for it with both hands, sending it flowing into his veins and marrow. The flames within his chest dampened to coals. The Andrac staggered toward him, slapping at Blays, who'd pulled himself between the creature's shoulder blades. Dante got to his knees and faltered. He reached for more nether. Some drew from the ground. Other scraps flitted from the bodies of the dead.

But most gushed from the gashes Blays had carved in the Andrac's side.

Dante's heart thundered. At the time, he'd been too preoccupied to understand, but he'd seen the same thing fighting the human-sized demon on the road down the cliffs. He cleared his mind and spread his arms wide, calling to the nether. It swirled madly from the Andrac's side. Dante poured it into himself, erasing the pain remaining in his chest, then turned it to the sprain in his knee and the fracture in his shin.

"Keep hurting it!" he yelled up to Blays. "Keep stabbing!"

"What do you think I'm *trying* to do?" Blays heaved himself up the Star-Eater's shoulders, finding purchase on its neck.

Dante sucked more and more shadows from the giant. Usually, the nether was cool enough for him to hold it until he was ready to put it to use, but this kind—perhaps because it was from the traces of the dead—stung him like nettles, insisting he use it at once. Everything he drew, he shaped into lances and slung at the nearby Mallish soldiers, who were on the brink of breaking the threadbare Collenese defenders.

Blays wrapped his arms around the Star-Eater's throat, set his blades against the demon's black skin, and yanked them back. Shadows spewed forth. When Dante lifted his hand, nether flowed from the demon's neck as if Blays had slit its jugular. A gray-robed man ran from one of the shrine's outbuildings, a globe of ether gathering in his hands. Dante fired the stinging nether into the priest's chest, blasting him back through the doorway he'd exited.

The Andrac slapped at the back of its neck. Blays tried to drop down, but the demon's palm crashed into him, knocking him loose. With a cry, he slammed to the earth, skidded toward the shrine, and lay still.

Dante stepped toward the demon. "You may be made of nether. But I'm its master."

A stream of shadows flew from the Andrac's throat. The monster drained as readily as a tapped keg, but Dante could feel resistance within its body. A lesser nethermancer would be able to draw no more than a trickle. For him, it was a raging cataract—yet the demon's body was as deep as an ocean.

The Star-Eater strode toward him. When it planted its foot, its leg gave out beneath it, dropping it to one knee. Its head lolled. Patches of its neck and chest grew translucent. Shuddering, it lifted its head and glared down at him, fangs bared. Then it too reached for the nether, holding tight to its dark fluids.

Tendrils of shadows flowed across the gash in its neck, thickening into ropes. Dante drew harder yet. The Andrac reeled backward toward the shrine. Dante stalked after it, flinging bolts of nether at any bluecoat that caught the corner of his eye.

As slowly as if it bore the world on its shoulders, the demon strained to its feet. Dante siphoned more nether from its neck, but the wound had already knit halfway shut and was shrinking by the second. The Star-Eater flexed its claws and grasped the shadows. For a moment, the two of them neared stasis. The former river of nether flowing from the demon's throat had stanched to a weak stream.

The Andrac's snarl twisted to a grin. Black threads knitted across its wounds, pulling them tighter. The shadows slowed to erratic droplets. Panic rising in his chest, Dante battered the monster with its own nether, but this dissipated into dark motes, useless against the vessel that had contained it. The demon took a lumbering step forward. Dante reached for its nether, but all that came was that which lay in the rock and dirt. The Andrac was closed to him.

He fell back a step. As the demon stood over him, its face grew as sober and focused as a child's. It bent its knees and raised a clawed hand high into the sky. Dante's mind became a blank.

Light flared to his right. The Keeper lumbered forward, limping heavily, a cube of ether clutched in her gnarled hands. "You are made of our people. Our own deaths turned against us. I release them!"

The demon didn't bother to glance her way. But when the spear of light flew from her hands, it flinched, sidestepping toward the western wing of the shrine. The ether ripped into its chest, knocking it back onto the tile roof.

Shadows leaked from the wound, which stretched diagonally from its left hip to its right shoulder. Dante thrust his mind into the cut. Nether geysered like water from a breached dam. The Andrac struggled to slow the tide, but its focus was weakened by its prior injuries. Shadows spun around Dante in a whirlpool, as thick as the clouds on a mountain's head. Each drop stung him. Their weight pressed as greatly as the slab of basalt he'd freed himself from, threatening to rip from his grasp. And tear him apart with them.

The Star-Eater was graying from head to toe. Dante drew out its shadows until he was surrounded by stormheads of nether, reducing the world to shapes and suggestions. Mentally, the demon struggled against him, pushing him to the brink—then fell back, exhausted.

Dante seized on its weakness, ripping into it with everything he had. The swirling nether threatened to black out the world. His entire body felt pricked by needles. The nether surged, pushing everything else from his mind. When at last it ebbed, leaving him able to think again, he knew the next pulse would be bigger than he could contain.

"Run!" he yelled to the Keeper. "As fast as you can!"

She took off in a loping limp. The Andrac leaned heavily against the shrine, clawing like a drunk man trying to keep himself from falling off the world. Patches of its body were as transparent as shadowcut glass. Shadows spilled forth, coating Dante's skin as if they wanted to burrow inside him.

The tide of nether swelled again. In another moment, it would burst from Dante's control. There was nothing he could do to stop the coming devastation. The only thing he could do was try to control its shape.

Blays remained motionless on the ground behind him. Dante tore into the shadows beneath the unconscious man. The ground dropped six feet, taking Blays from sight. Dante yanked a shelf of rock across the hole, sealing him against whatever was to come. If Dante died, Blays could shadowalk out when he woke up.

Assuming he woke before he ran out of air.

The Keeper was now sixty feet away. The dozens of soldiers on each side had cleared out as well, leaving Dante alone with the Star-Eater. Like a tooth ready to pop loose from the socket, the creature was on the brink of giving. Dante drew forth every drop of nether he could touch. As the tide threatened to overwhelm him, he unleashed the nether, centering it on the Andrac's chest—and raising a wall of rock before himself.

A hollow boom thundered through the plaza. The demon vanished in an expanding sphere of black motes. Dante flung himself flat behind the seamless wall of basalt. With a deafening crackle, the nether tore through the Andrac and into the shrine. Stone exploded in all directions, slamming into Dante's wall.

Something cracked into his head. The world flashed white, then went as black as the trace left by death.

"Awaken." The voice was like that of a stone door. Dante wanted to stay in the darkness—there was no pain there, no strife—but the voice bore an authority he couldn't deny.

His eyes fell open. The gentle warmth of an autumn day touched his face. The air smelled of cracked rock. Blood, too. Given the dampness of his clothes, it was probably his own.

The Keeper kneeled over him, face creased with concern.

"You live on."

"So do you," Dante said thickly. "How?"

"When the building fell, I used the ether to keep a piece of it in its original shape. It formed a pocket around us."

"What about Naran?"

"He was hurt. But he lives. My people have taken him to safety."

Dante stretched his limbs and learned they all worked. "The Andrac. Is it banished?"

"More than banished." She grinned, fox-like. "It is eradicated. Nothing remains but its stain."

Dante pushed himself up on his elbows. Flakes of basalt clattered from the folds of his clothes. Around him, the ground was a talus field. The sky felt wider. In part, this was because the gigantic demon was now gone.

But so was the Reborn Shrine.

Its west wing was utterly flattened. Its central dome had collapsed, taking its front wall with it. The back wall remained upright, but it was little more than a shell. Tapestries lay twisted and shredded. Pages spewed across the ruins. Glazed shards of pottery shined in the sunlight.

"The shrine," he said dully. "I'm so sorry."

The Keeper smiled. "The shrine has been rebuilt before. It will be again."

Dante's body ached and his clothes were sodden with blood, but his flesh was smooth and clean. The Keeper had mended him while he was unconscious. He got to his feet, troubled by the idea that there was something he needed to do. To retrieve. It felt fairly important, but the details eluded him. Something he needed to do before...

He spun in a circle, trying to locate the smooth spot of ground he'd buried Blays beneath. Everything was coated in gravel and stone dust. Near the edge of the shrine's footprint, soldiers dragged themselves out of the rubble, inspecting each other for injury and whacking grit from their trousers, but the Keeper was the only other person within a hundred feet of him.

"Blays," Dante said. "I sank him into the ground. Do you know where that was?"

The Keeper frowned. Before she could answer, Dante plunged his thoughts into the earth, questing about until he found a hollow space. He pulled back the rocky lid covering it. Blays lay at its bottom. His eyes were closed and his clothes were blood-soaked, but his chest rose and fell.

The Keeper shuffled beside him, ether shining in her hands. She sent it streaming down to Blays.

Blays inhaled suddenly, sitting upright. He gaped at the walls hanging above him. "What's this? A grave?"

"It was a way to keep you from needing one." Dante extended a hand. Blays picked up and sheathed his swords, grabbed Dante's hand, and swung himself over the lip of the hole.

He blinked at the blasted surroundings, turning in a circle. "Question. Where'd the shrine go?"

"We're standing on it," Dante said. "Parts of it, anyway. All that nether in the Andrac had to go somewhere."

"So you chose to slam it into Collen's holiest temple?"

"I chose to crash it into the Andrac. Which happened to be leaning on Collen's holiest temple." Gazing about the rubble, his pride dimmed—and was replaced by elation. "The demon's dead, Blays. Cord and her people are free to fight back!"

"Our soldiers have already gone to find her," the Keeper said. "They'll seize the road from below, then cleanse the city."

"Then we have to find Gladdic before he learns the tide's turned."

"He was seen coming here. When the Andrac died, he fled southwest."

Blays caught Dante's eye. "Toward the road. Sounds like we'd better hurry."

With the need for as much speed as they could muster, they left the Keeper behind. The city streets were clogged with debris and skirmishes, so they drifted south toward the open ground that ringed the butte, sprinting across the paving stones. Dante felt remarkably good. It wasn't just the triumph of having destroyed the Andrac. The Keeper was a skilled healer.

Shouts carried from the interior of the city. Before, they'd been scared. Now, they were defiant. As Dante ran, he caught glimpses of mixed groups of soldiers and citizens jogging down the street, weapons in hand.

"They're going to retake the city," Blays said. "When they do, suppose they're going to reprise the slaughter at the river?"

"If they've got a brain between them, they'll keep the prisoners as leverage. But it doesn't matter. As soon as we finish Gladdic, we're going to find Naran and put this place behind us for good."

Hearing the shouts of their fellow citizens, people had begun to open their shutters. As Dante and Blays ran on, Blays called questions to the residents, asking if they'd seen Gladdic pass. Three confirmed having seen a tall, cadaverous man in plain gray robes. As Dante and Blays neared the south side of the city, however, a woman in a window told them that rather than going to the road, Gladdic had continued past it to the west.

Blays glanced to all sides. "The road's the only way down from here. Why would he go back into the depths of the city?"

Dante shook his head. "Maybe some of his people were trapped by the Colleners. Or he's going back for a relic of some kind."

"Or maybe it's a trap."

They headed west. Within three blocks, heavy footfalls sounded ahead. Gladdic bobbed down the street at a fast walk. He glanced over his shoulder, double-taking as he spotted them, then broke into his best effort at a sprint.

Dante and Blays caught up easily, spreading apart as they neared. Blays held his swords in hand, Dante the nether. Breathing heavily, Gladdic turned. His face was sweaty, red, and contorted with fear.

"I know how this looks," the priest said. "But there's been a mistake."

Sick to his stomach, Dante laughed. "It was an *accident* that you tried to murder everyone in this city?"

"You don't understand. That wasn't me! I'm not—"

Dante clenched his teeth. "You put thousands of innocent citizens to their deaths. Now, you answer for that."

Nether slashed through the air in a black blizzard. Dante hurled it at Gladdic. The priest shrieked and flung his hands over his face. Droplets of ether shimmered in Gladdic's grasp, but they were torn aside by the storm of shadows.

Blood squirted into the priest's robes. With an airy gasp, he flopped to the dirt. Gladdic lifted his hands, a marble-sized ball of ether shining in each palm. Dante gathered more shadows. Hands shaking, Gladdic turned the ether on himself.

His body contracted, shortening and plumpening. His gaunt cheeks filled out. His gray hair darkened; his face went round, wrinkles smoothing under a boyish layer of fat. He was no longer a tall, ropy man in late middle age, but a short, rotund youth.

Bleeding into his robes, the young man gave them a tired, baleful look, like that of an old bloodhound. As if to say "I told you so." He collapsed on his back, hands plopping to the ground, eyes staring vacantly into the warm autumn day.

"A second ago, wasn't he all gangly?" Blays said. "What did you hit him with? A plate of bacon?"

"This was a decoy." Dante spat in the dirt. "An illusion. To cover his tracks while he escaped down the cliffs."

"If you're smart enough to have figured that out, then what are you doing standing around while Gladdic escapes?"

It felt like Dante had spent the entire day running. Even after the Keeper's ministrations, he barely had the strength to jog back to the road down from the butte. Collenese soldiers had taken the top of the road and were digging in, leery of a counterattack from the small Mallish army that remained on the plain. The Colleners reported that a plump young man in gray robes had been seen descending the switchbacks fifteen minutes ago, but peering down the road, Dante saw no sign of Gladdic there or in the fields below.

"He's been operating out of one of the caves, hasn't he?" Blays motioned downslope. "Think he might be hiding out there?"

"Why would he do that?"

"Because worms feel most at home in dank, dark places?"

With no other ideas, Dante headed downhill to the cavern where Gladdic had brought forth the gigantic Star-Eater. The doors remained open. Dante blew on his torchstone, lighting it. The cavern beyond was big enough to hold hundreds of people. Clean bones lined the walls. The smell of recent incense couldn't quite cover the lingering odor of blood.

"This was where he was killing them," Dante murmured. "Careful. Earlier, he had a second Andrac guarding the slopes. I haven't seen it since."

Other than the bones and a small platform near the back, the chamber was empty. A passage at the rear curved into a second room as large as the first.

Dante stopped in his tracks. Hundreds of bodies lay on the floor, packed shoulder to shoulder, three to five layers deep. Most showed blackened, withered wounds. The predominant smell was that of skin; beneath it were notes of urine and feces, but there was no rot whatsoever.

Thousands of them. Dante had seen more dead in one place on the battlefields of Gask, but those men had died fighting. They'd been armed, uniformed, equipped. These people had been fed to a demon and then stripped to their smallclothes.

Blays nosed the air. "This wasn't all from today, was it? How can they be so well-preserved?"

"Ether. It's holding them in their ideal state. Unable to decay."

"Why would he preserve them? Part of another ritual?"

"I don't think he could dispose of them without tipping off the city as to what he was doing. He preserved them so they wouldn't smell. Once everyone was dead, I'm sure the bonfire would have been visible from Dog's Paw." Dante tried to make a quick count of the bodies. "How do you think the others will react to this?"

"By making the local vendors of torches and pitchforks very rich."

"And the hatred the Colleners hold for Mallon will only burn hotter. It's already beyond control. I wonder if it wouldn't be better to bury the dead before the survivors find them."

"They already know what Gladdic was doing." Blays sheathed his swords. "Anyway, I thought we were done meddling with this place."

They headed to the town below the butte, but it was completely vacant. If Gladdic had come through it, there were no witnesses. Even if there had been people there to see, most likely, Gladdic had left in disguise. They spotted a handful of people hastening west through the desert, but even if, by luck alone, they chose the one that was Gladdic, they wouldn't know it until and unless he revealed himself—which, if it happened, would most likely occur as he was attempting to slay them.

"He'll go back to Bressel," Dante said. "We'll find him there."

"That worked so well for us before."

"Things are different now. We've destroyed his source of shaden. Learned to defeat the Andrac. He doesn't have any more weapons left to use against us."

"But this time, he'll know we're coming."

Dante smiled thinly. "Do you think that will matter?"

"No," Blays said. "I don't."

They trudged back up the road. At the top, four hundred Colleners had gathered to defend the chokepoint into the city. Many had blood on their weapons and clothes.

Cord jogged from their ranks. "Ah, there you are. We've retaken the city!"

"That was fast," Blays said. "Though I suppose everything goes a little faster when you don't have monsters trying to bite you in half."

Dante motioned downhill. "We think Gladdic's fled the city. Have any of your people seen him?"

She queried her defenders. A couple of them confirmed having seen Gladdic heading west past the road, but that meant they were referring to the dead young man who'd been disguised as the older priest. They were still interviewing the soldiers when a runner approached Cord, sweating heavily.

She spoke to him briefly, then made her way to Dante. "The Keeper's at the Reborn Shrine. She insists we join her."

"Insists?" Dante looked to the east, but after the devastation of the shrine, no part of it rose above the rest of the city. "What's this about?"

"She said nothing more. But she's the Keeper. Her request is enough."

Cord let her lieutenants know she was stepping out, then walked to the east at a good clip. Dante and Blays fell in beside her. People were singing in the streets. Others had started cook fires, aided and surrounded by men and women who'd gone gaunt during the occupation. Seeing their celebrations and relief, Dante's heart soared with pride.

The shrine lay in its own ruins. Hundreds of people had been drawn to the spectacle of its shattered walls and tumbled dome. They stood in silent disbelief, glancing from the wreckage to the new arrivals.

The Keeper stood in front of the bronze front doors, which had fallen, dented and half-buried. Before her, she had assembled a gut-high cairn, each of its rocks seemingly made of a different type of stone. The woman's pale blue eyes flitted to Dante, then drifted over the heads of the crowd.

"Time after time," she said, voice booming like the northern surf, "the Mallish have torn this shrine to the ground. No matter how many times they've forced us to rebuild it, we have never despaired. For the prophecy has always told us that, after the twelfth time the Mallish razed the shrine, we would rebuild it yet again. And on that day, Arawn himself would appear to lead us to lasting victory."

She gazed up at the ragged back wall of the Reborn Shrine. "History tells us that, before today, the shrine had been razed and rebuilt ten times. That was a lie. One meant to lull the Mallish into complacency. In truth, they have destroyed it eleven times. And eleven times it's been reborn."

Placing one hand on her back for support, she stooped and picked up a jagged slab of basalt. Arms quaking, she stood. "Today, our foes tore down our shrine for the twelfth time. Now let it be reborn."

She placed the stone atop the cairn. As soon as it was in place, a squiggly line of light sprung from either side of it, converging in front of the monument. Dante recognized it at once. Duset. The two rivers.

Symbol of Arawn.

The crowd thrust up their fists and cheered as if the god himself had arisen behind the Keeper. In disbelief, Dante wandered closer. The Mallish hadn't blown up the temple. During his research into the Andrac, hadn't he read an account from her archives confirming the shrine had been destroyed and rebuilt *ten* times?

He drew within twenty feet of her and stopped. Around him, the audience quieted, watching.

"I don't understand, Keeper," he said. "Your prophecy said the Mallish had to destroy the shrine." He gestured to the broken stone. "They didn't do this. I did."

The Keeper laughed wisely. "But you *are* Mallish." She uplifted her hands to the sky. "Behold! The man who freed his people from the empire of Gask. The man who exposed Mallon's lies about our past and brought us the truth: that the ruining of our land wasn't our fault. Behold the man who slew the demons that threatened to kill every last one of us. The man who commands the nether as the gods themselves."

The Keeper lowered her arm and pointed at Dante. "My people! The avatar of Arawn appears among us—and he will lead us to victory in Mallon."

Every eye in the square locked on him. Before, the crowd's shouts had been furious. Now, they were frenzied. The manic, euphoric cries of losing your mind to a belief far grander than yourself.

The Keeper kneeled to him, bowing her head. Hundreds of Colleners did the same. Dante stood alone, like an idol before the masses. Ones convinced that he'd been sent by the gods to put an end to a war that had burned for nine hundred years.

Once, many years ago, an old man had used him as an unwitting weapon against a mighty kingdom. As the people began to chant his name, and the old woman grinned at the ground, he understood.

The cycle had repeated.

AUTHOR'S NOTE

If you're getting a kick out of these characters, you can read about their younger exploits in *The Cycle of Arawn* trilogy.

ABOUT THE AUTHOR

Along with *The Cycle of Arawn*, Ed is the author of the post-apocalyptic *Breakers* series. Born in the deserts of Eastern Washington, he's since lived in New York, Idaho, L.A., and Maui, all of which have been thoroughly destroyed in *Breakers*.

He lives with his fiancée and spends most of his time writing on the couch and overseeing the uneasy truce between two dogs and two cats.

He blogs at http://www.edwardwrobertson.com

Made in United States
Troutdale, OR
06/12/2024